THE REAL RILEY MAYES

RACHEL ELLIOTT

BALZER + BRAY
Imprints of HarperCollins*Publishers*
HARPER alley

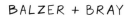

Balzer + Bray is an imprint of HarperCollins Publishers.
HarperAlley is an imprint of HarperCollins Publishers.

The Real Riley Mayes
www.harperalley.com

Library of Congress Control Number: 2021948580
ISBN 978-0-06-299574-2 (pbk.) — ISBN 978-0-06-299575-9

The artist used brush pens, markers, and Bristol paper to create the illustrations for this book.
Typography by Dana Fritts. Hand-lettered by Rachel Elliott.
22 23 24 25 26   GPS   10 9 8 7 6 5 4 3 2 1
❖
First Edition

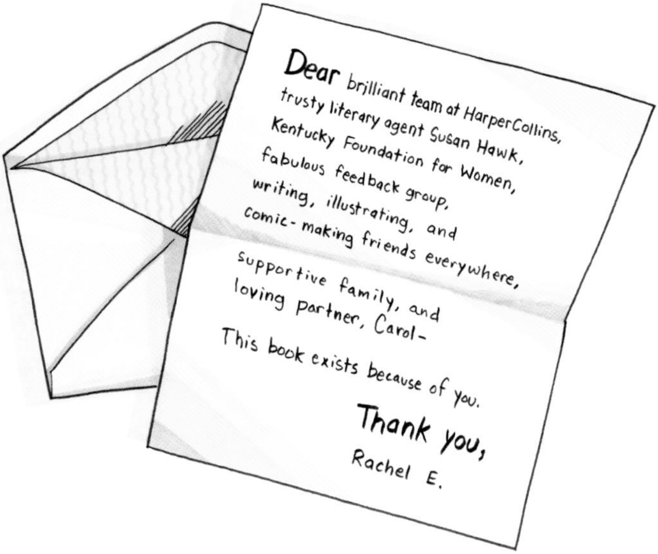
Dear brilliant team at HarperCollins,
trusty literary agent Susan Hawk,
Kentucky Foundation for Women,
fabulous feedback group,
writing, illustrating, and
comic-making friends everywhere,
supportive family, and
loving partner, Carol-
This book exists because of you.
Thank you,
Rachel E.

CHAPTER 1

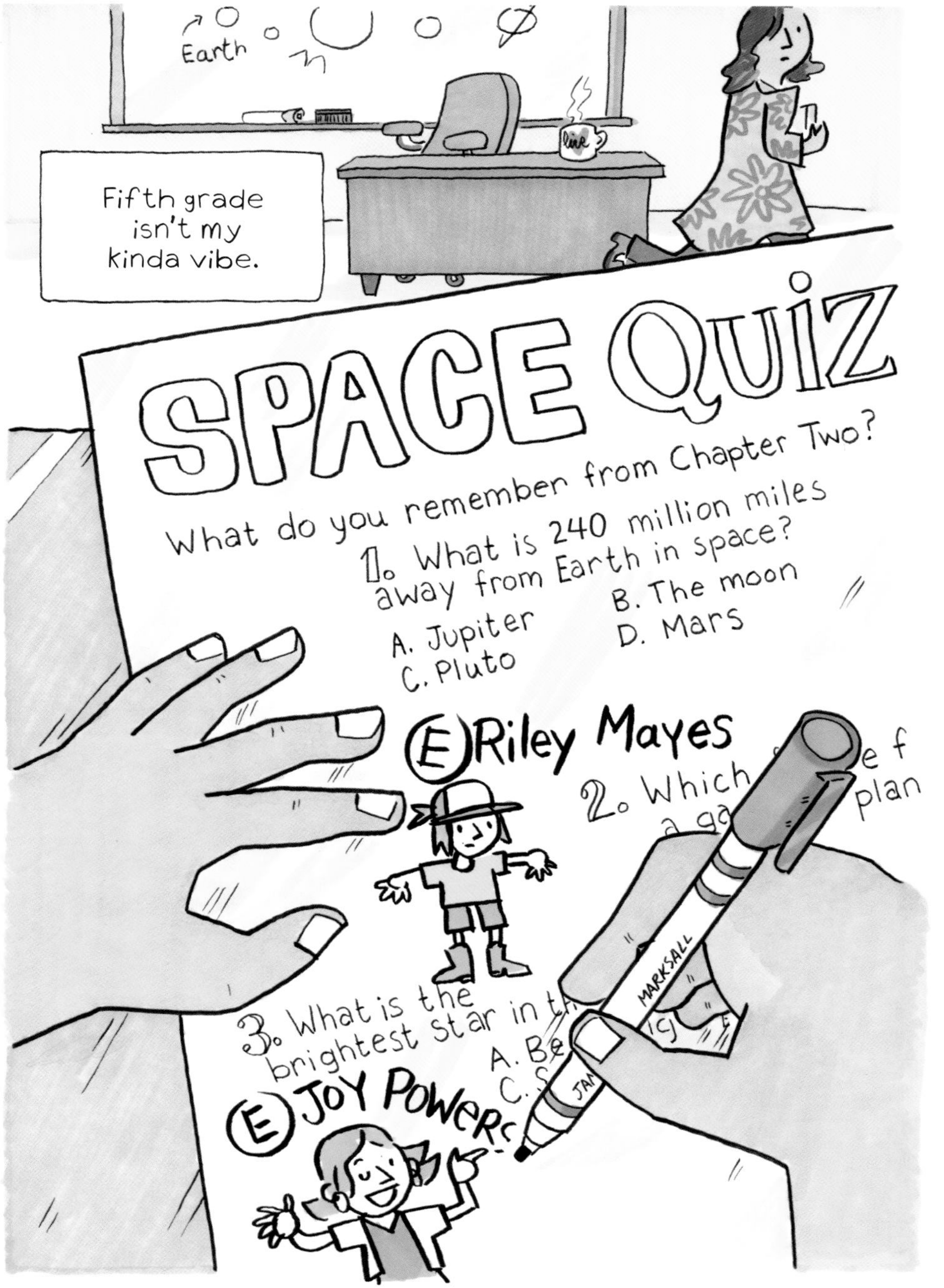
Earth
Fifth grade isn't my kinda vibe.
SPACE QUIZ
What do you remember from Chapter Two?
1. What is 240 million miles away from Earth in space?
A. Jupiter
B. The moon
C. Pluto
D. Mars
(E) Riley Mayes
2. Which
3. What is the brightest star in
(E) JOY POWERS
MARKSALL

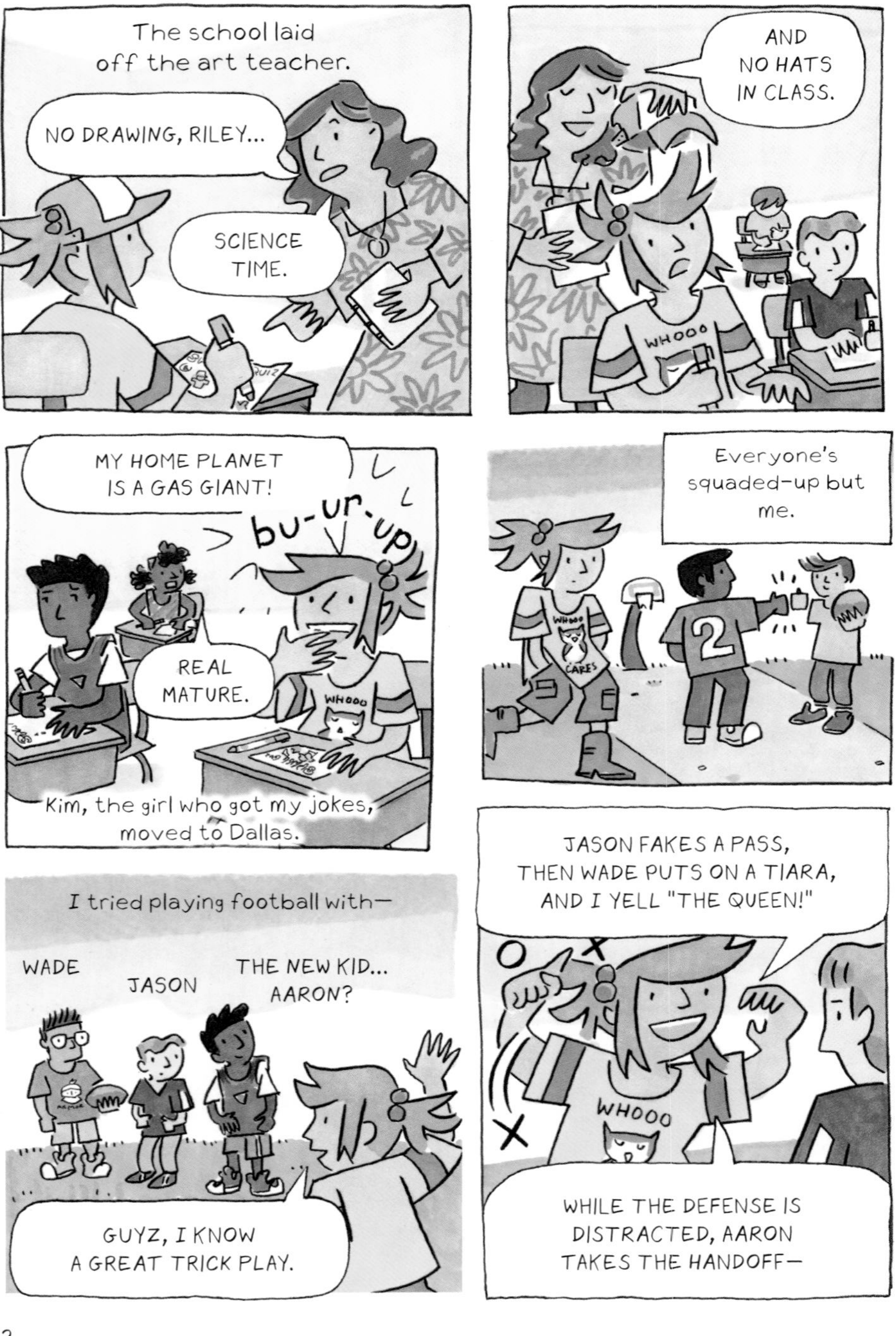

The school laid off the art teacher.
NO DRAWING, RILEY...
SCIENCE TIME.
AND NO HATS IN CLASS.
WHOOO
MY HOME PLANET IS A GAS GIANT!
bu-ur-up
REAL MATURE.
WHOOO
Kim, the girl who got my jokes, moved to Dallas.
Everyone's squaded-up but me.
WHOOO CARES
2
I tried playing football with—
WADE
JASON
THE NEW KID... AARON?
GUYZ, I KNOW A GREAT TRICK PLAY.
JASON FAKES A PASS, THEN WADE PUTS ON A TIARA, AND I YELL "THE QUEEN!"
WHOOO
WHILE THE DEFENSE IS DISTRACTED, AARON TAKES THE HANDOFF—

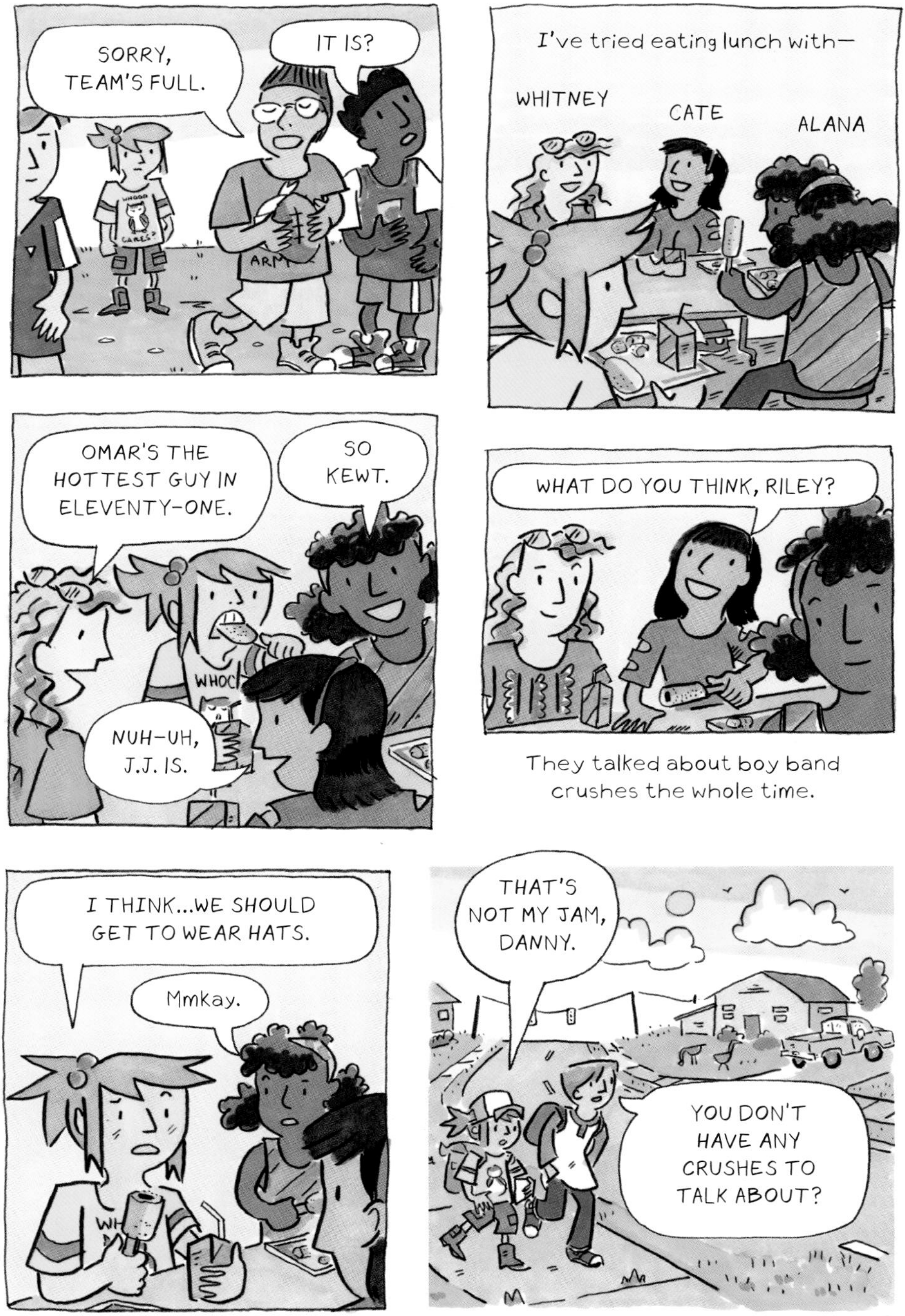
SORRY, TEAM'S FULL.
IT IS?
I've tried eating lunch with—
WHITNEY
CATE
ALANA
OMAR'S THE HOTTEST GUY IN ELEVENTY-ONE.
SO KEWT.
NUH-UH, J.J. IS.
WHAT DO YOU THINK, RILEY?
They talked about boy band crushes the whole time.
I THINK...WE SHOULD GET TO WEAR HATS.
Mmkay.
THAT'S NOT MY JAM, DANNY.
YOU DON'T HAVE ANY CRUSHES TO TALK ABOUT?

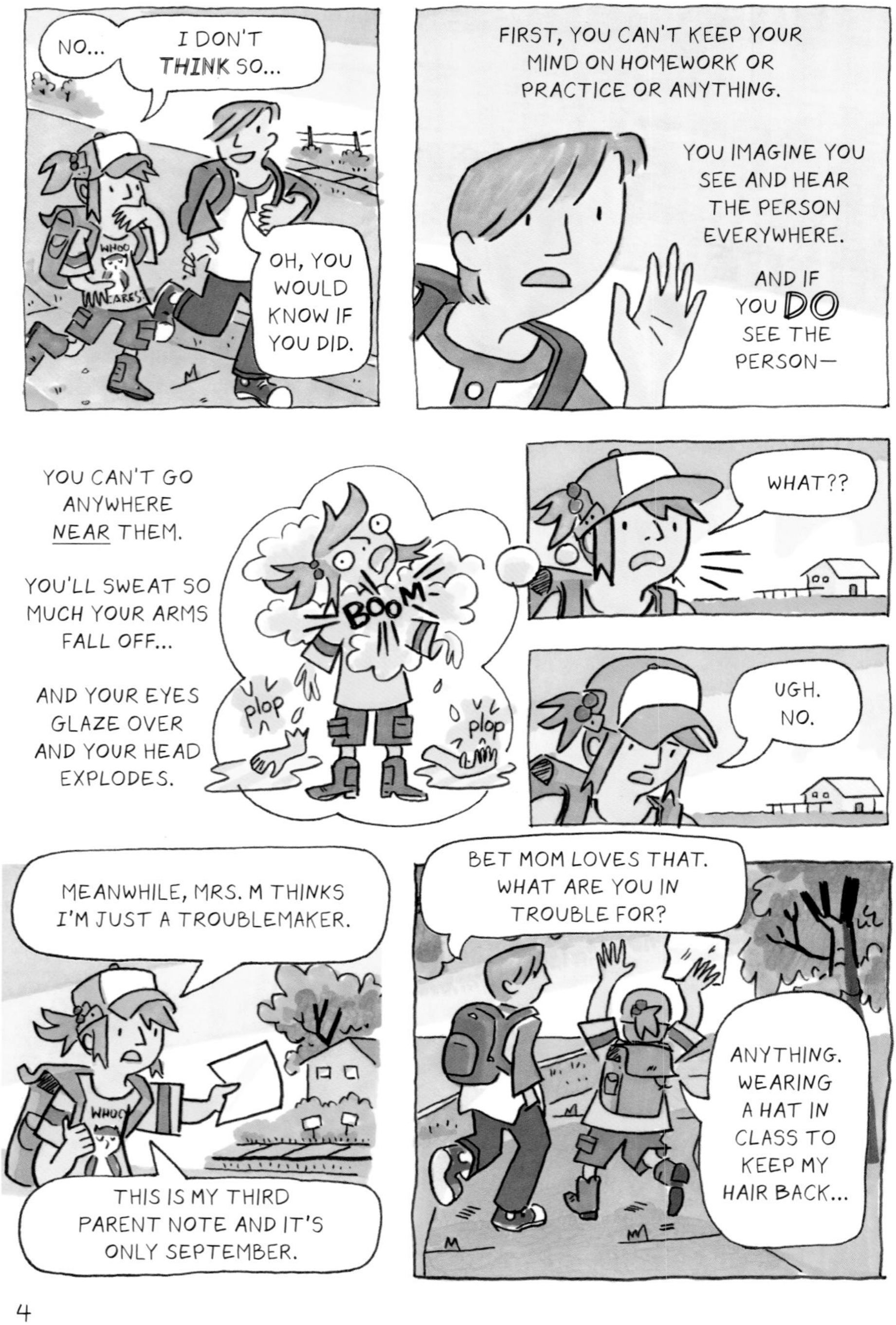
NO...
I DON'T THINK SO...
OH, YOU WOULD KNOW IF YOU DID.
FIRST, YOU CAN'T KEEP YOUR MIND ON HOMEWORK OR PRACTICE OR ANYTHING.
YOU IMAGINE YOU SEE AND HEAR THE PERSON EVERYWHERE.
AND IF YOU DO SEE THE PERSON—
YOU CAN'T GO ANYWHERE NEAR THEM.
YOU'LL SWEAT SO MUCH YOUR ARMS FALL OFF...
AND YOUR EYES GLAZE OVER AND YOUR HEAD EXPLODES.
BOOM
plop
plop
WHAT??
UGH. NO.
MEANWHILE, MRS. M THINKS I'M JUST A TROUBLEMAKER.
THIS IS MY THIRD PARENT NOTE AND IT'S ONLY SEPTEMBER.
BET MOM LOVES THAT. WHAT ARE YOU IN TROUBLE FOR?
ANYTHING. WEARING A HAT IN CLASS TO KEEP MY HAIR BACK...

DOODLING JOY POWERS ON MY WORKSHEETS.

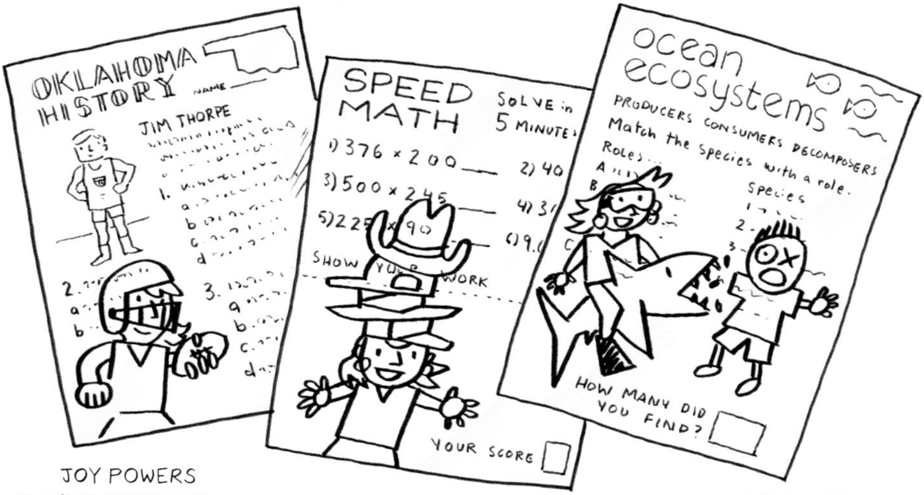

OKLAHOMA HISTORY
NAME
JIM THORPE
SPEED MATH
SOLVE in
1) 376 × 200
3) 500 × 245
YOUR SCORE
ocean ecosystems
PRODUCERS CONSUMERS DECOMPOSERS
Match the species with a role.
Roles...
Species
HOW MANY DID YOU FIND?

JOY POWERS PLAYING FOOTBALL...

JOY POWERS WEARING FOUR HATS...

JOY POWERS RIDING A SHARK THAT EATS WADE.

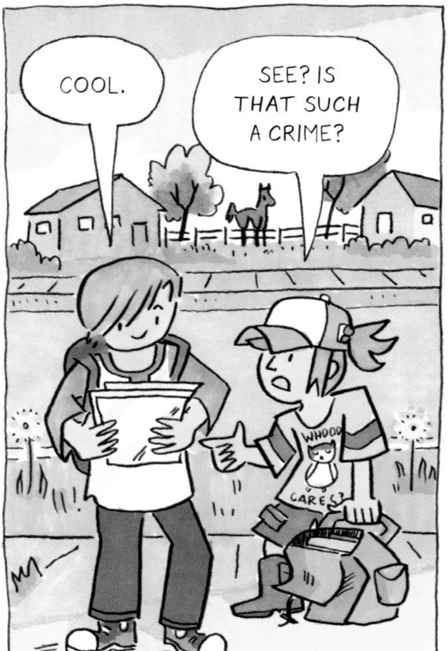

COOL.
SEE? IS THAT SUCH A CRIME?
WHOOO CARES?

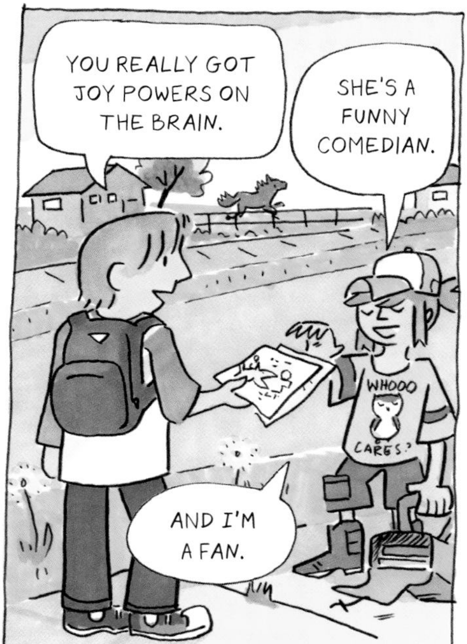

YOU REALLY GOT JOY POWERS ON THE BRAIN.
SHE'S A FUNNY COMEDIAN.
AND I'M A FAN.
WHOOO CARES?

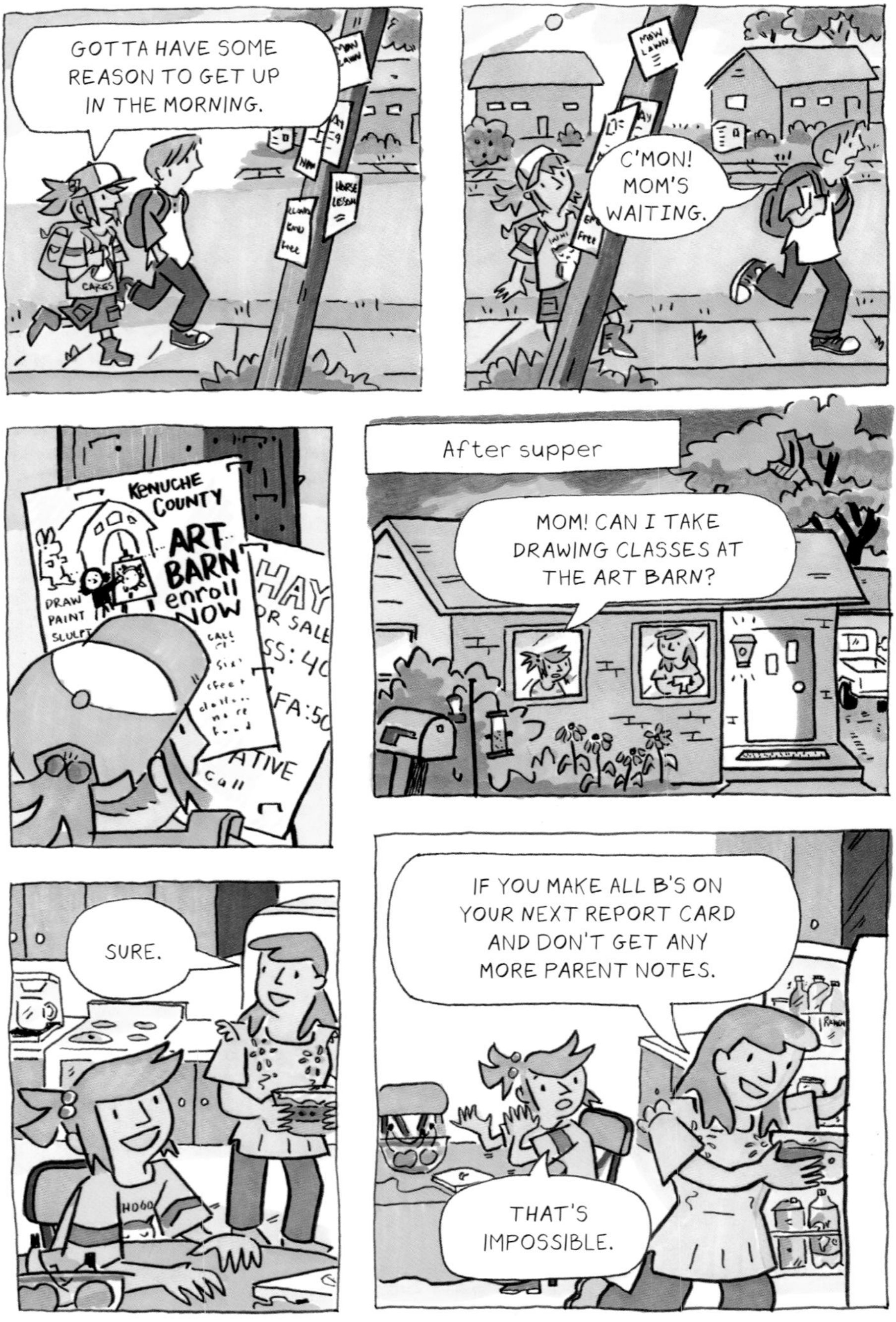
GOTTA HAVE SOME REASON TO GET UP IN THE MORNING.
C'MON! MOM'S WAITING.
KENUCHE COUNTY
ART BARN enroll NOW
DRAW
PAINT
HAY
After supper
MOM! CAN I TAKE DRAWING CLASSES AT THE ART BARN?
SURE.
IF YOU MAKE ALL B'S ON YOUR NEXT REPORT CARD AND DON'T GET ANY MORE PARENT NOTES.
THAT'S IMPOSSIBLE.

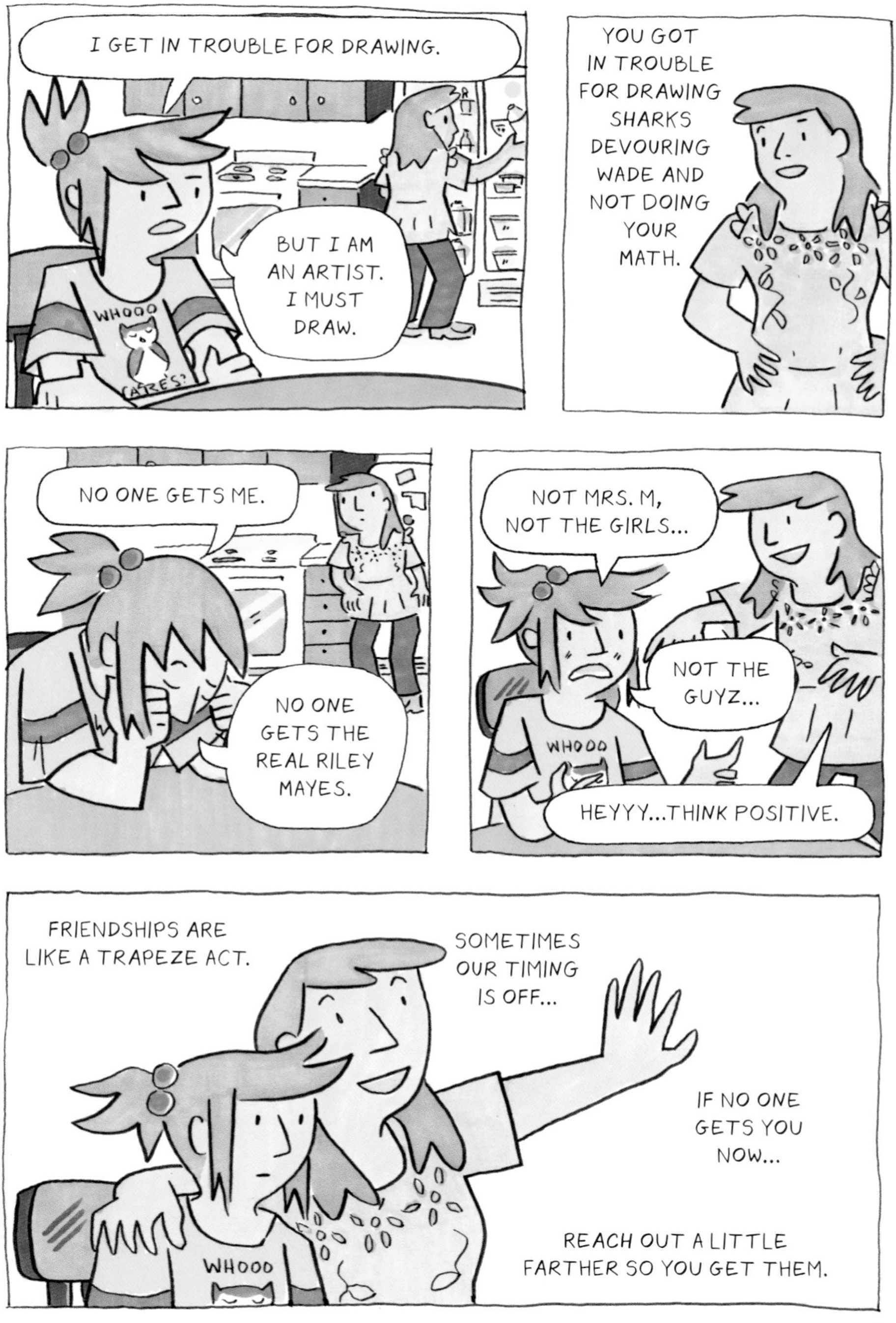
I GET IN TROUBLE FOR DRAWING.
BUT I AM AN ARTIST. I MUST DRAW.
WHOOO CARES?
YOU GOT IN TROUBLE FOR DRAWING SHARKS DEVOURING WADE AND NOT DOING YOUR MATH.
NO ONE GETS ME.
NO ONE GETS THE REAL RILEY MAYES.
NOT MRS. M, NOT THE GIRLS...
NOT THE GUYZ...
WHOOO
HEYYY...THINK POSITIVE.
FRIENDSHIPS ARE LIKE A TRAPEZE ACT.
SOMETIMES OUR TIMING IS OFF...
IF NO ONE GETS YOU NOW...
REACH OUT A LITTLE FARTHER SO YOU GET THEM.
WHOOO

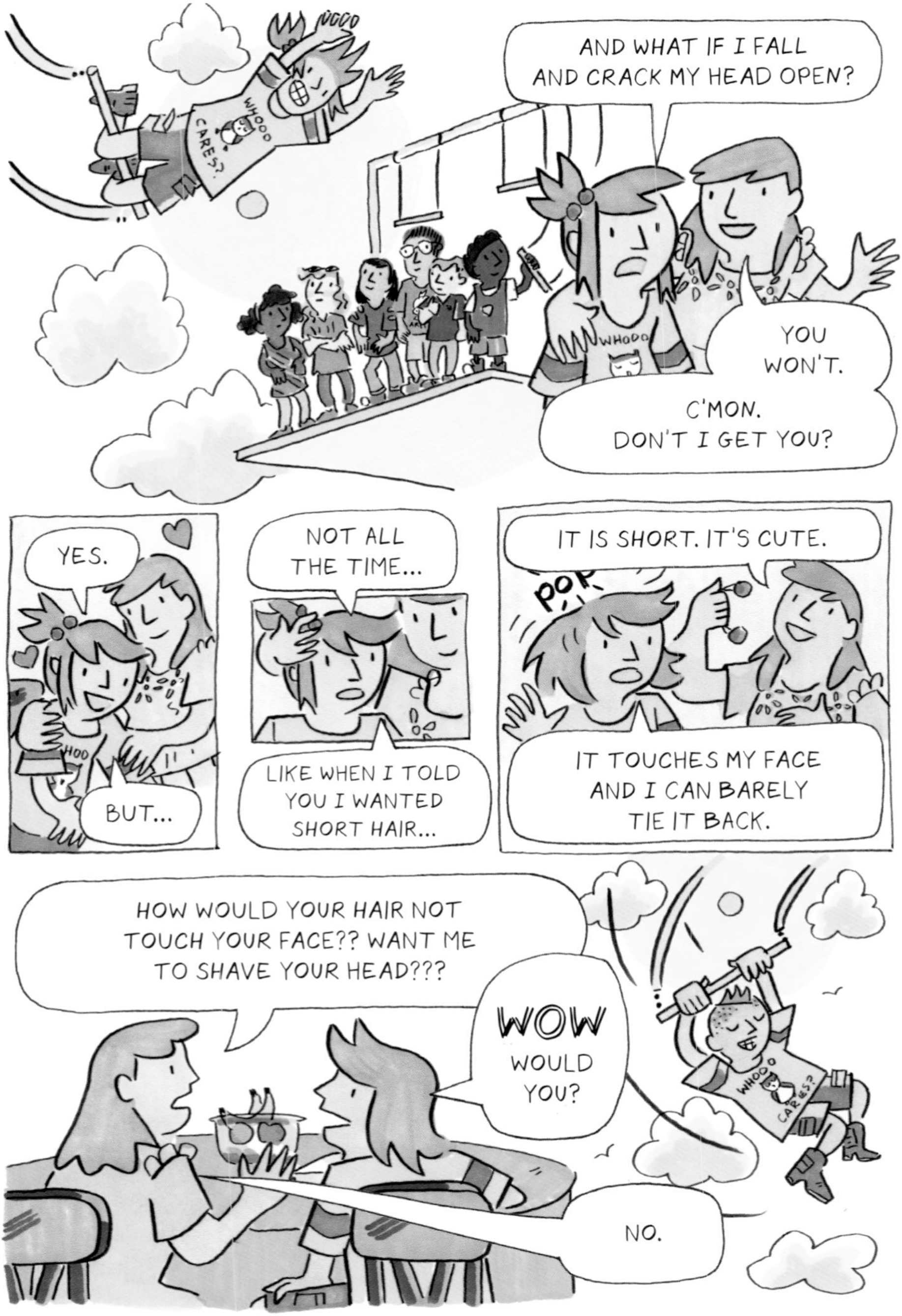
WHOOO CARES?
AND WHAT IF I FALL AND CRACK MY HEAD OPEN?
WHOOO
YOU WON'T.
C'MON. DON'T I GET YOU?
YES.
BUT...
NOT ALL THE TIME...
LIKE WHEN I TOLD YOU I WANTED SHORT HAIR...
IT IS SHORT. IT'S CUTE.
POP
IT TOUCHES MY FACE AND I CAN BARELY TIE IT BACK.
HOW WOULD YOUR HAIR NOT TOUCH YOUR FACE?? WANT ME TO SHAVE YOUR HEAD???
WOW
WOULD YOU?
WHOOO CARES?
NO.

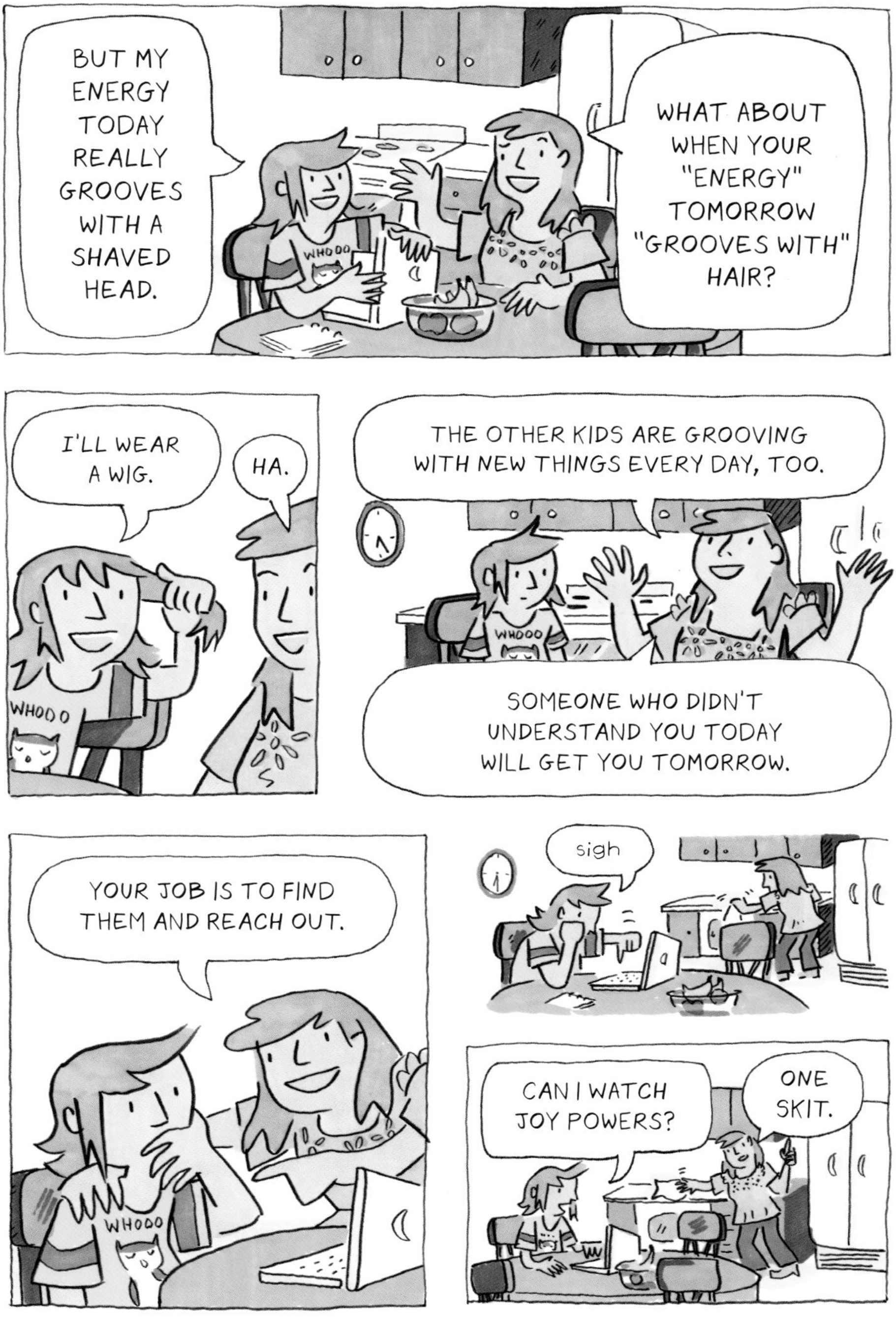
BUT MY ENERGY TODAY REALLY GROOVES WITH A SHAVED HEAD.
WHAT ABOUT WHEN YOUR "ENERGY" TOMORROW "GROOVES WITH" HAIR?
WHOOO
I'LL WEAR A WIG.
HA.
WHOOO
THE OTHER KIDS ARE GROOVING WITH NEW THINGS EVERY DAY, TOO.
WHOOO
SOMEONE WHO DIDN'T UNDERSTAND YOU TODAY WILL GET YOU TOMORROW.
YOUR JOB IS TO FIND THEM AND REACH OUT.
WHOOO
sigh
CAN I WATCH JOY POWERS?
ONE SKIT.

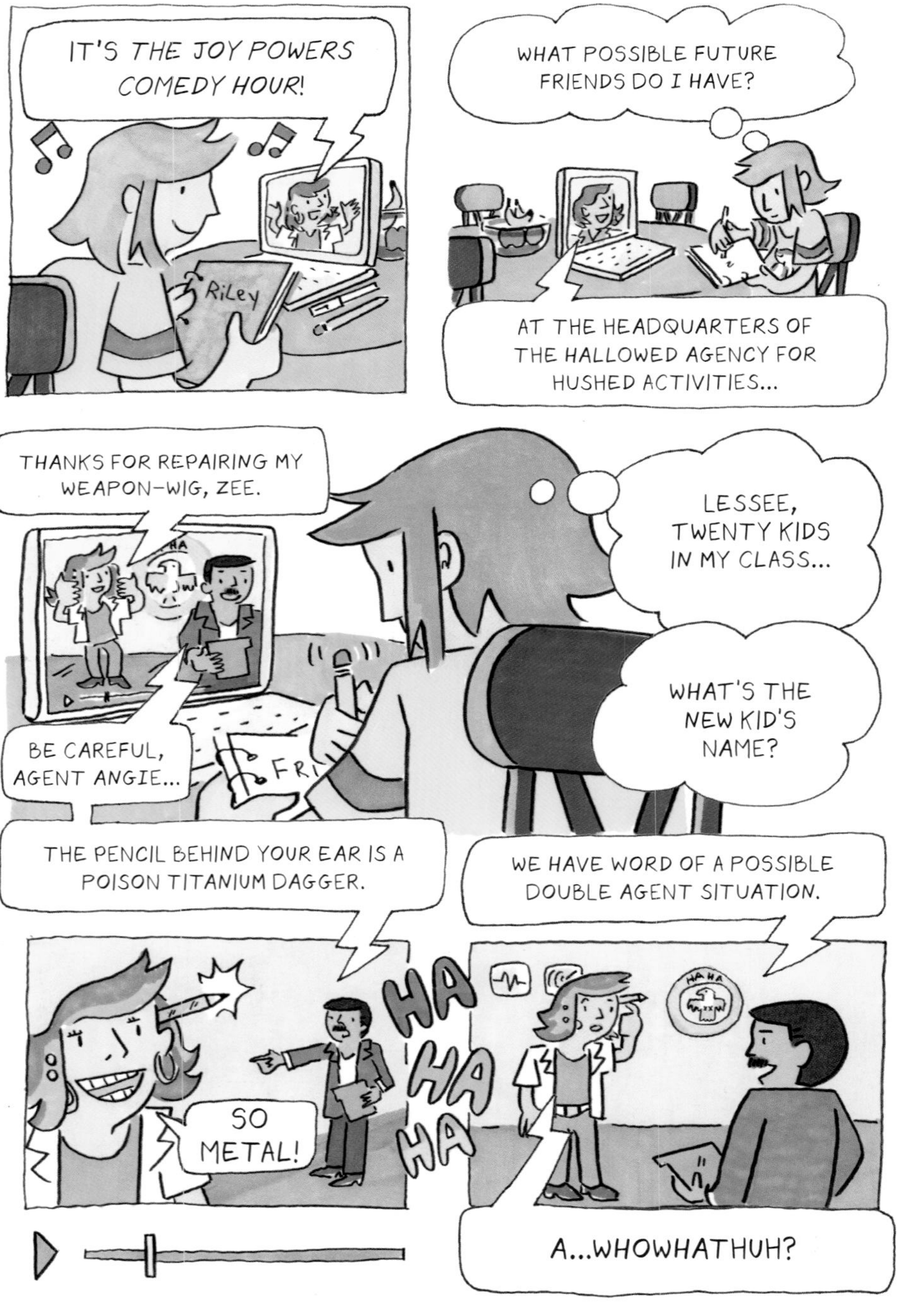
IT'S THE JOY POWERS COMEDY HOUR!
RiLey
WHAT POSSIBLE FUTURE FRIENDS DO I HAVE?
AT THE HEADQUARTERS OF THE HALLOWED AGENCY FOR HUSHED ACTIVITIES...
THANKS FOR REPAIRING MY WEAPON-WIG, ZEE.
LESSEE, TWENTY KIDS IN MY CLASS...
WHAT'S THE NEW KID'S NAME?
BE CAREFUL, AGENT ANGIE...
FRi
THE PENCIL BEHIND YOUR EAR IS A POISON TITANIUM DAGGER.
WE HAVE WORD OF A POSSIBLE DOUBLE AGENT SITUATION.
SO METAL!
HA HA HA
A...WHOWHATHUH?

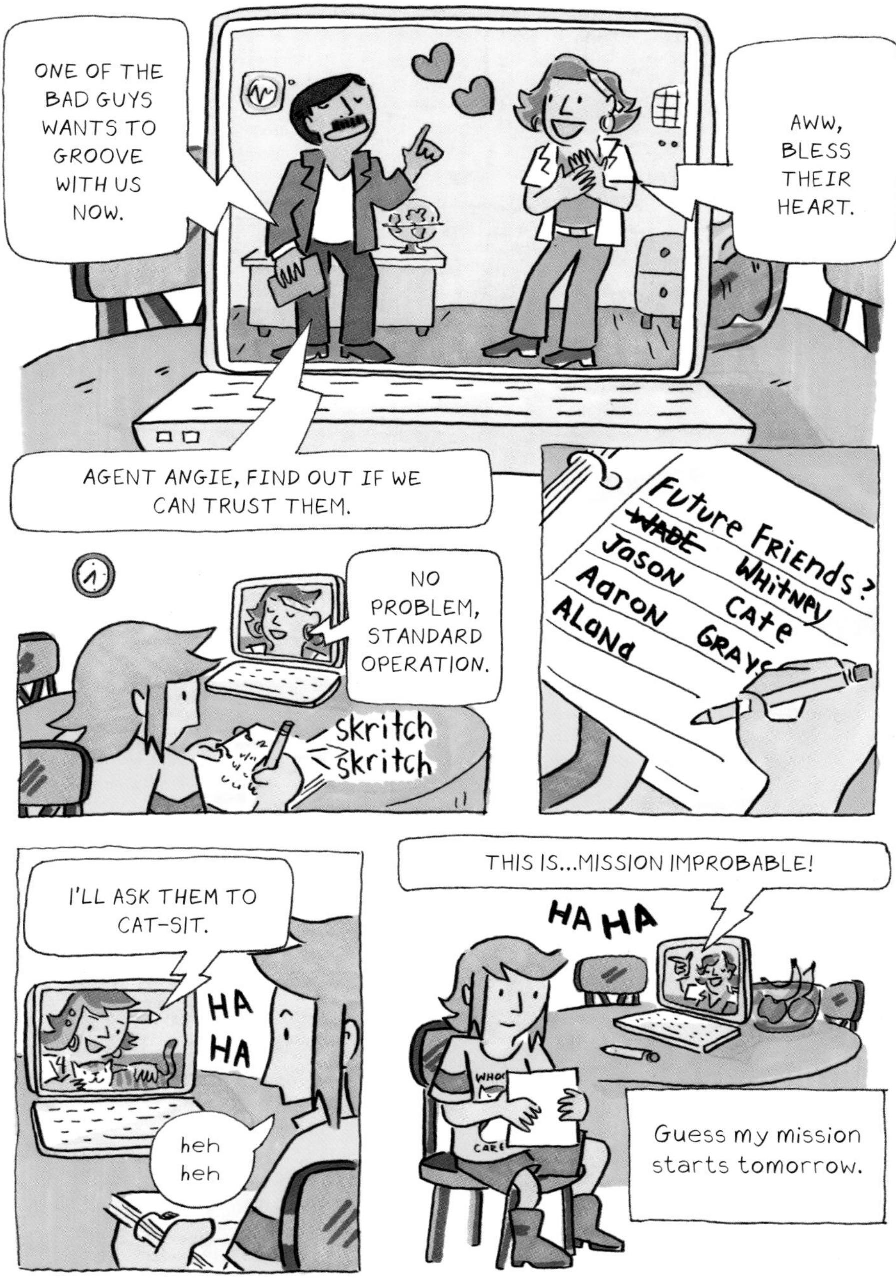
ONE OF THE BAD GUYS WANTS TO GROOVE WITH US NOW.
AWW, BLESS THEIR HEART.
AGENT ANGIE, FIND OUT IF WE CAN TRUST THEM.
NO PROBLEM, STANDARD OPERATION.
skritch skritch
Future Friends?
WADE Whitney
Jason Cate
Aaron Grays
Alana
I'LL ASK THEM TO CAT-SIT.
HA HA
heh heh
THIS IS...MISSION IMPROBABLE!
HA HA
Guess my mission starts tomorrow.

CHAPTER 2

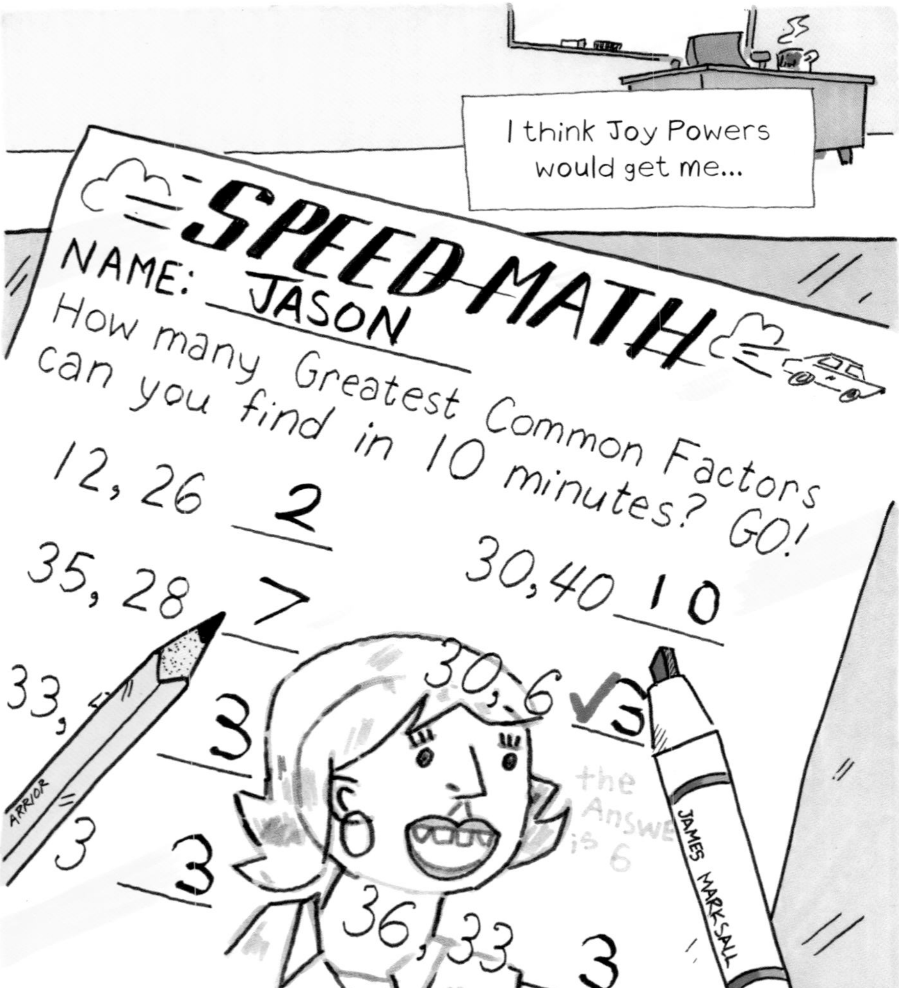

I think Joy Powers would get me...
SPEED MATH
NAME: JASON
How many Greatest Common Factors can you find in 10 minutes? GO!
12, 26 2
35, 28 7
30,40 10
30, 6 3
the Answer is 6
36, 33 3
Total Correct
JAMES MARKSALL
Too bad she isn't in fifth grade. She'd be at the top of my potential future friend list.

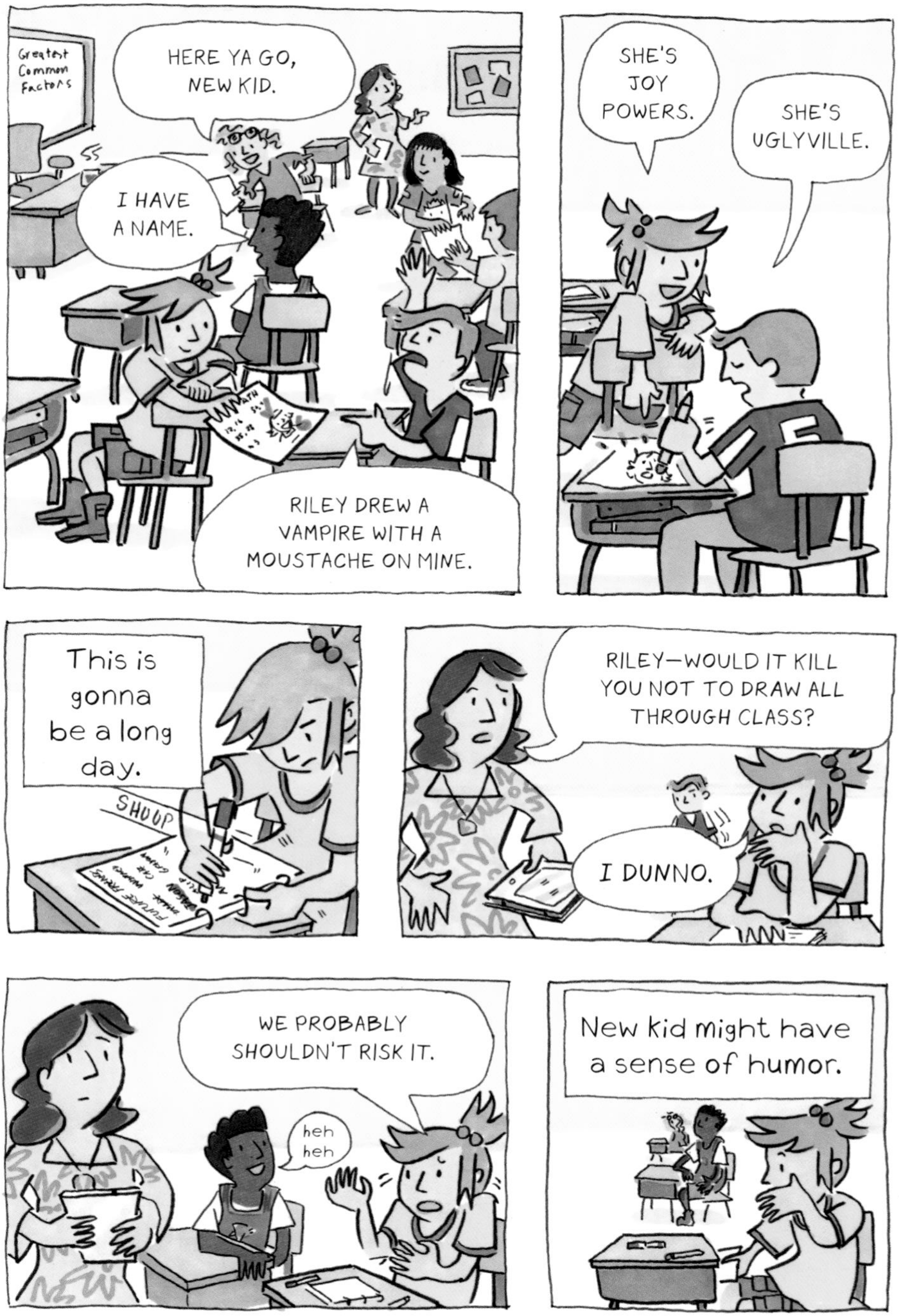
Greatest Common Factors
HERE YA GO, NEW KID.
I HAVE A NAME.
RILEY DREW A VAMPIRE WITH A MOUSTACHE ON MINE.
SHE'S JOY POWERS.
SHE'S UGLYVILLE.
This is gonna be a long day.
SHOOP
RILEY—WOULD IT KILL YOU NOT TO DRAW ALL THROUGH CLASS?
I DUNNO.
WE PROBABLY SHOULDN'T RISK IT.
heh heh
New kid might have a sense of humor.

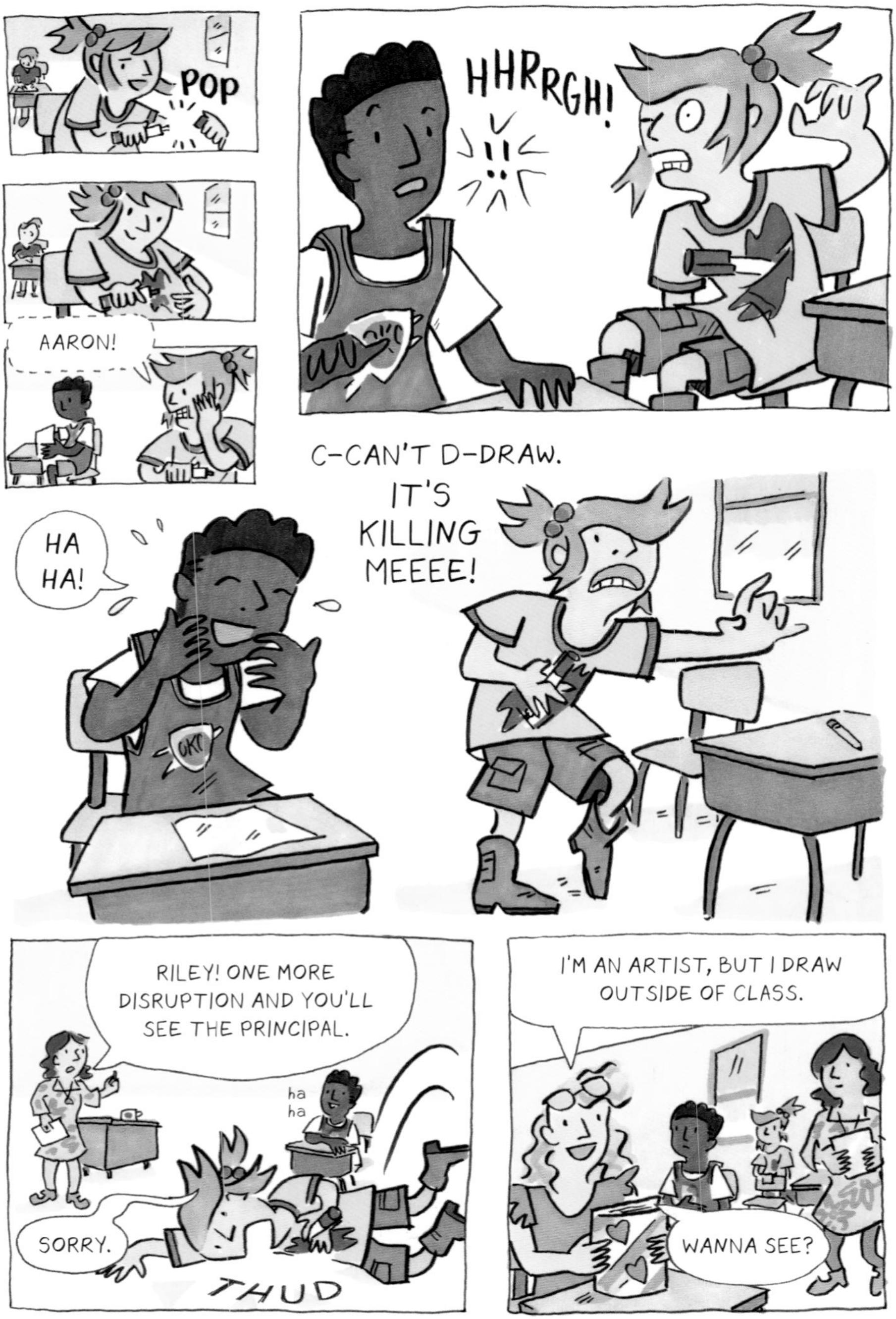
POP
AARON!
HHRRGH!
C-CAN'T D-DRAW. IT'S KILLING MEEEE!
HA HA!
RILEY! ONE MORE DISRUPTION AND YOU'LL SEE THE PRINCIPAL.
ha ha
SORRY.
THUD
I'M AN ARTIST, BUT I DRAW OUTSIDE OF CLASS.
WANNA SEE?

NICE, WHITNEY!

IT'S TOO BAD WE DON'T HAVE A BUDGET FOR ART TIME.

PSH. IT'S AN EMOJI WITH STICK LEGS.

BUT WE CAN BE CREATIVE WITH OUR WRITING PROJECT...

Writing Project

LETTERS!

OOH.

HUH?

FIRST, YOU'LL CHOOSE A WELL-KNOWN PERSON.

Writing Project LETTERS

WHAT DOES THIS PERSON DO THAT INSPIRES YOU?

TELL THEM IN A LETTER.

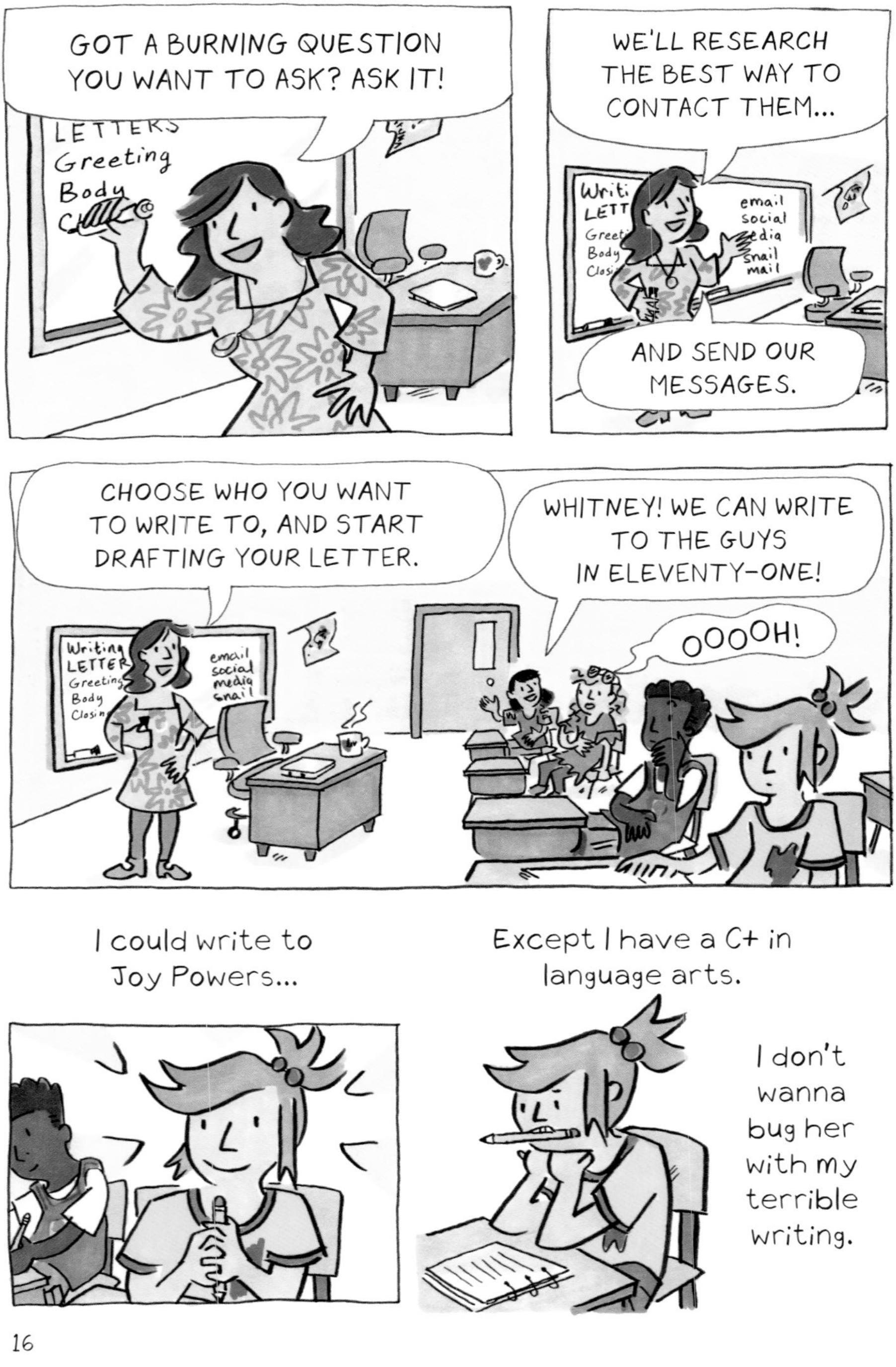
GOT A BURNING QUESTION YOU WANT TO ASK? ASK IT!
LETTERS
Greeting
Body
WE'LL RESEARCH THE BEST WAY TO CONTACT THEM...
email
social
media
snail
mail
AND SEND OUR MESSAGES.
CHOOSE WHO YOU WANT TO WRITE TO, AND START DRAFTING YOUR LETTER.
Writing
LETTER
Greeting
Body
Closing
email
social
media
snail
WHITNEY! WE CAN WRITE TO THE GUYS IN ELEVENTY-ONE!
OOOOH!
I could write to Joy Powers...
Except I have a C+ in language arts.
I don't wanna bug her with my terrible writing.

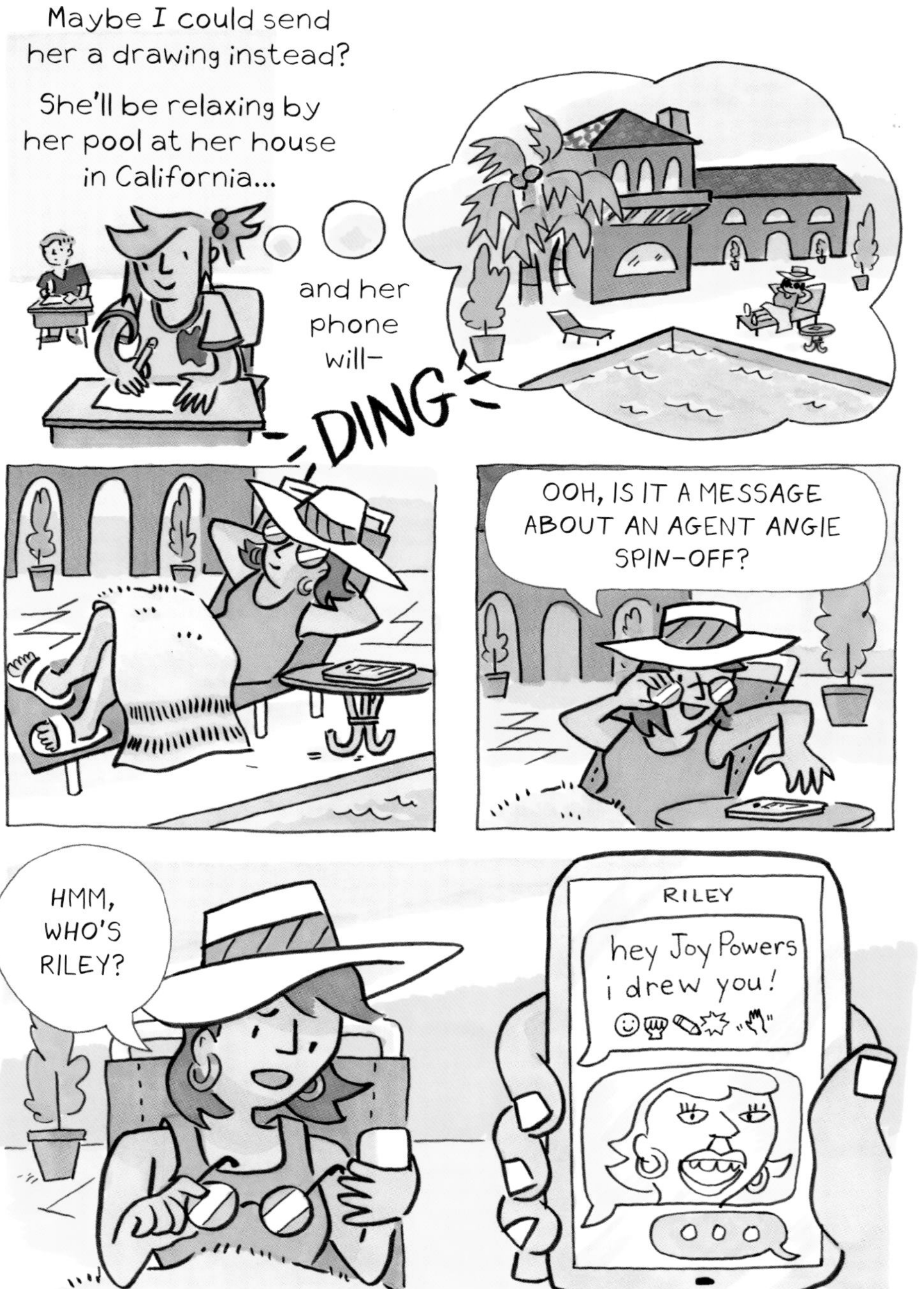
Maybe I could send her a drawing instead?
She'll be relaxing by her pool at her house in California...
and her phone will-
DING
OOH, IS IT A MESSAGE ABOUT AN AGENT ANGIE SPIN-OFF?
HMM, WHO'S RILEY?
RILEY
hey Joy Powers i drew you!

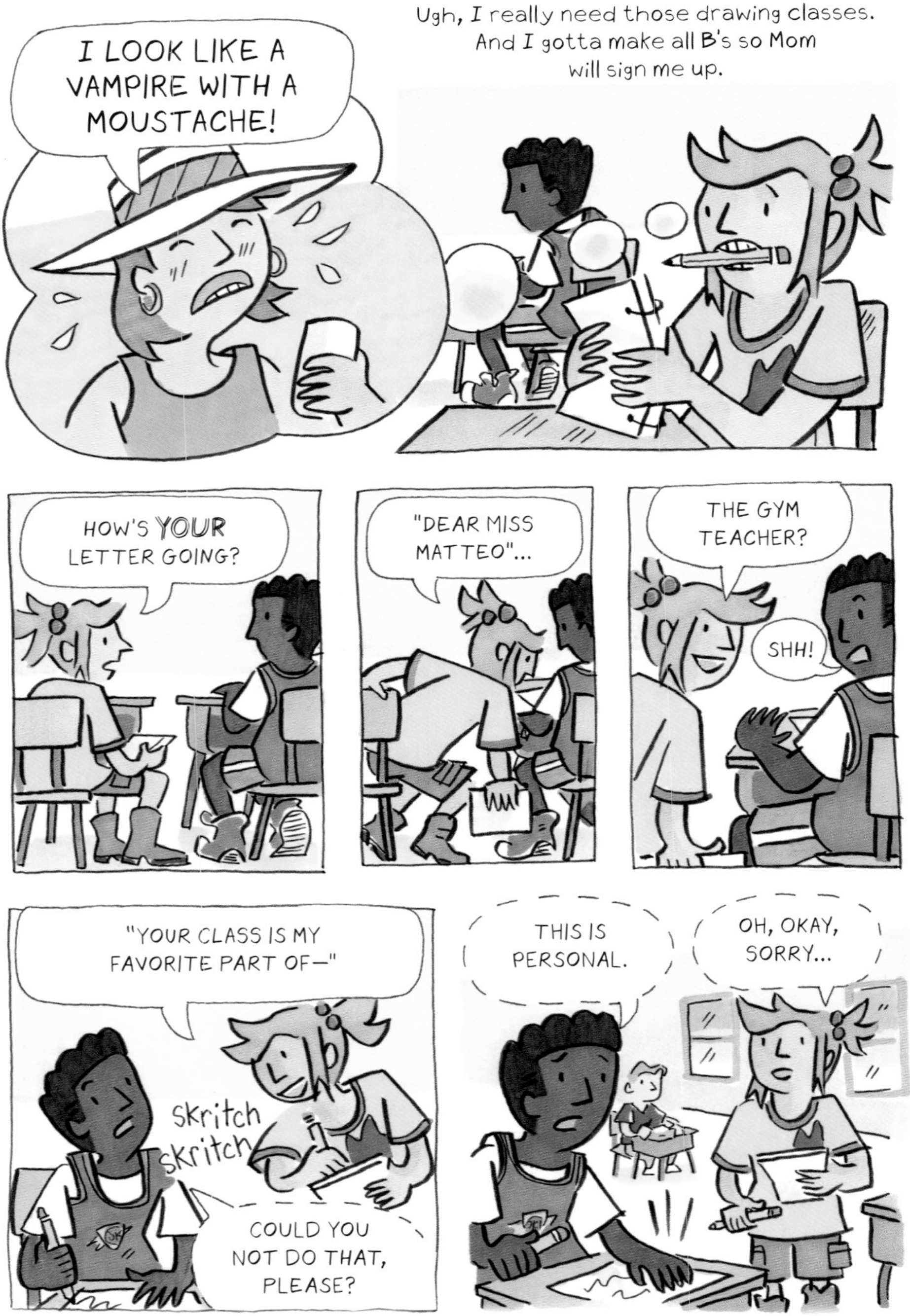
I LOOK LIKE A VAMPIRE WITH A MOUSTACHE!
Ugh, I really need those drawing classes. And I gotta make all B's so Mom will sign me up.
HOW'S YOUR LETTER GOING?
"DEAR MISS MATTEO"...
THE GYM TEACHER?
SHH!
"YOUR CLASS IS MY FAVORITE PART OF—"
Skritch skritch
COULD YOU NOT DO THAT, PLEASE?
THIS IS PERSONAL.
OH, OKAY, SORRY...

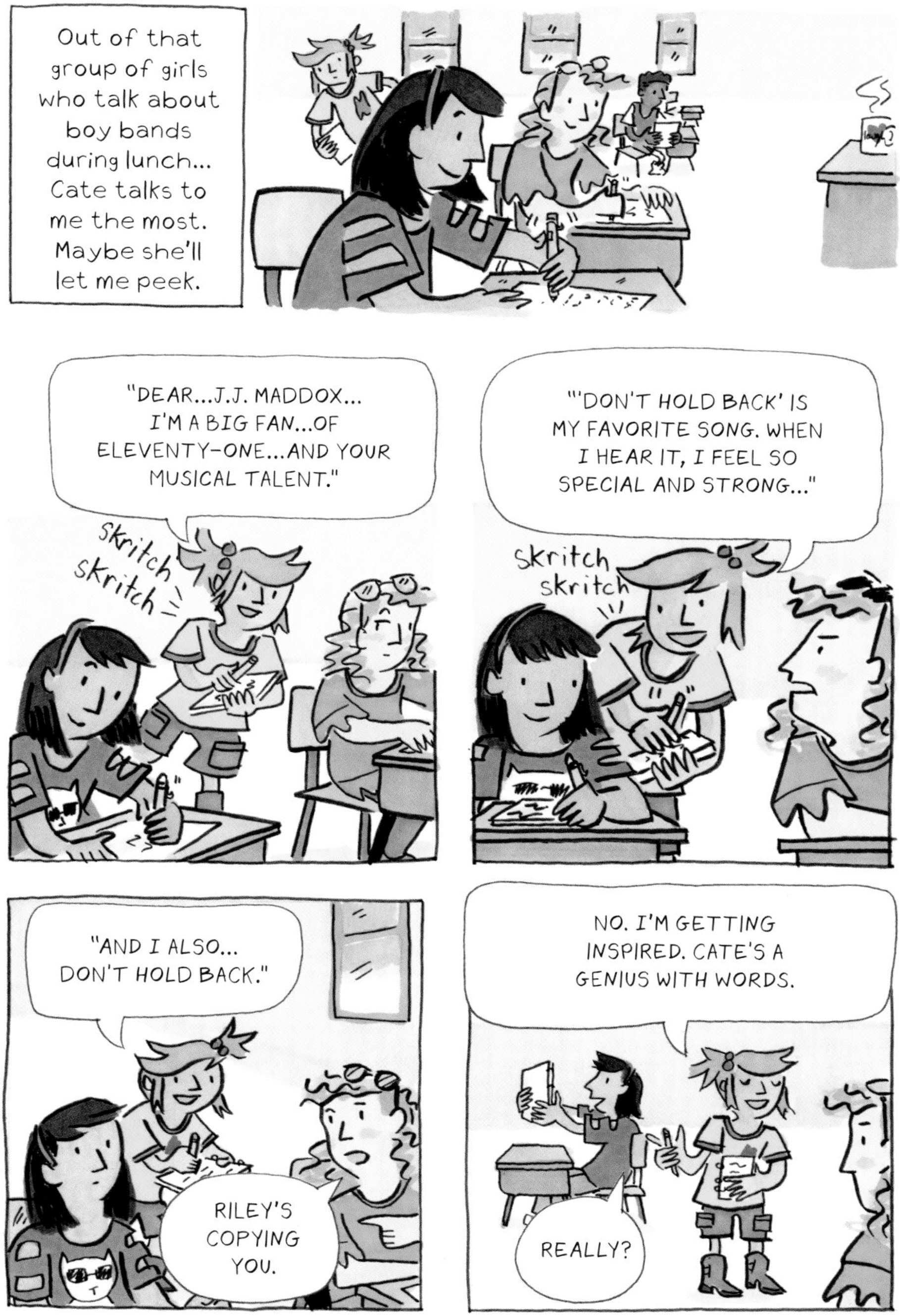

Out of that group of girls who talk about boy bands during lunch... Cate talks to me the most. Maybe she'll let me peek.
"DEAR...J.J. MADDOX... I'M A BIG FAN...OF ELEVENTY-ONE...AND YOUR MUSICAL TALENT."
SKRITCH SKRITCH
"'DON'T HOLD BACK' IS MY FAVORITE SONG. WHEN I HEAR IT, I FEEL SO SPECIAL AND STRONG..."
SKRITCH SKRITCH
"AND I ALSO... DON'T HOLD BACK."
RILEY'S ALSO COPYING YOU.
NO. I'M GETTING INSPIRED. CATE'S A GENIUS WITH WORDS.
REALLY?

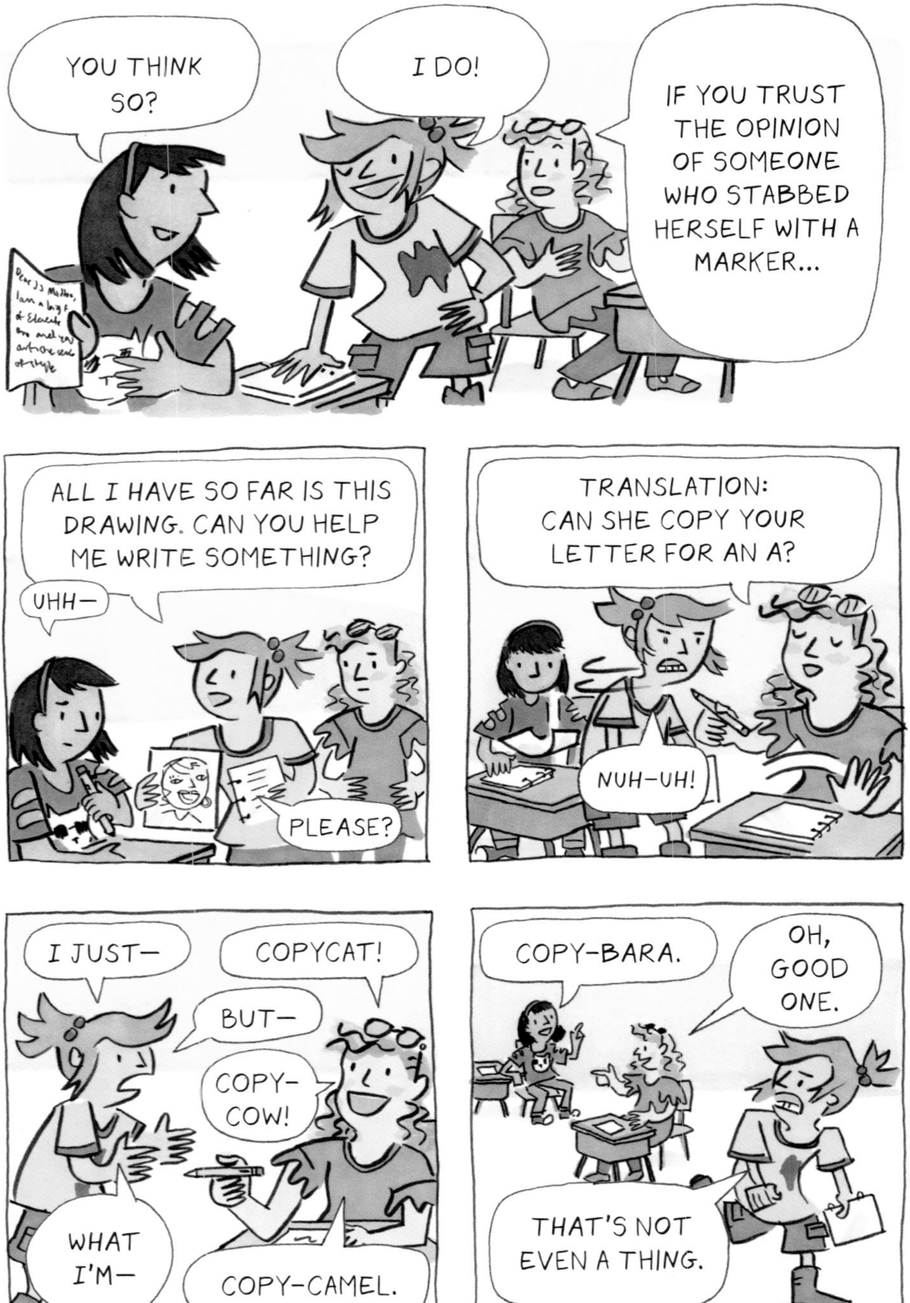
YOU THINK SO?
I DO!
IF YOU TRUST THE OPINION OF SOMEONE WHO STABBED HERSELF WITH A MARKER...
ALL I HAVE SO FAR IS THIS DRAWING. CAN YOU HELP ME WRITE SOMETHING?
UHH—
PLEASE?
TRANSLATION: CAN SHE COPY YOUR LETTER FOR AN A?
NUH–UH!
I JUST—
COPYCAT!
BUT—
COPY-COW!
WHAT I'M—
COPY–CAMEL.
COPY–BARA.
OH, GOOD ONE.
THAT'S NOT EVEN A THING.

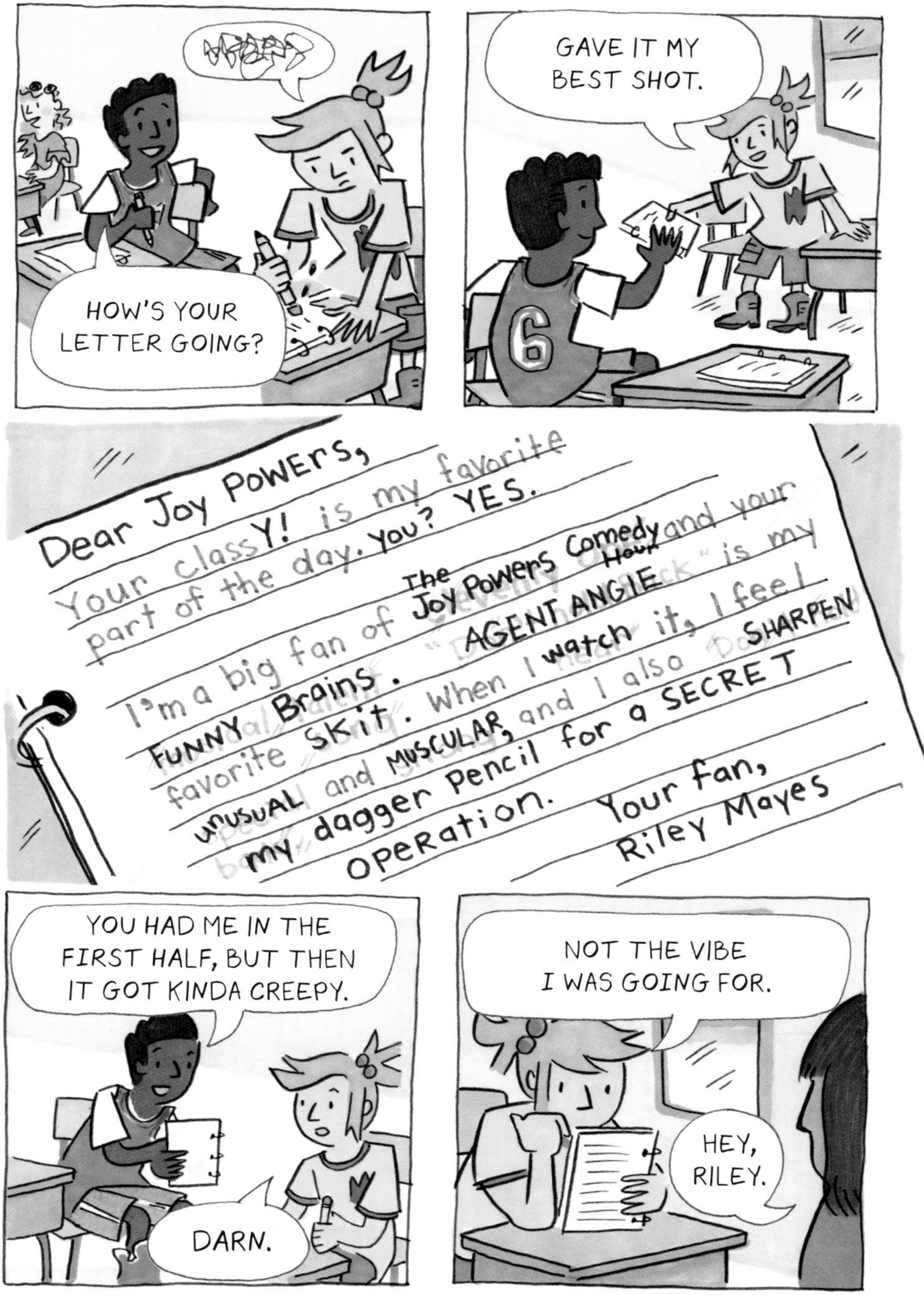
HOW'S YOUR LETTER GOING?
GAVE IT MY BEST SHOT.
Dear Joy Powers,
Your classY! is my favorite
part of the day. You? YES.
I'm a big fan of The Joy Powers Comedy Hour and your
AGENT ANGIE is my
favorite SKit. When I watch it, I feel
FUNNY Brains.
unusual and MUSCULAR, and I also SHARPEN
my dagger pencil for a SECRET
OPERATION.
Your fan,
Riley Mayes
YOU HAD ME IN THE FIRST HALF, BUT THEN IT GOT KINDA CREEPY.
DARN.
NOT THE VIBE I WAS GOING FOR.
HEY, RILEY.

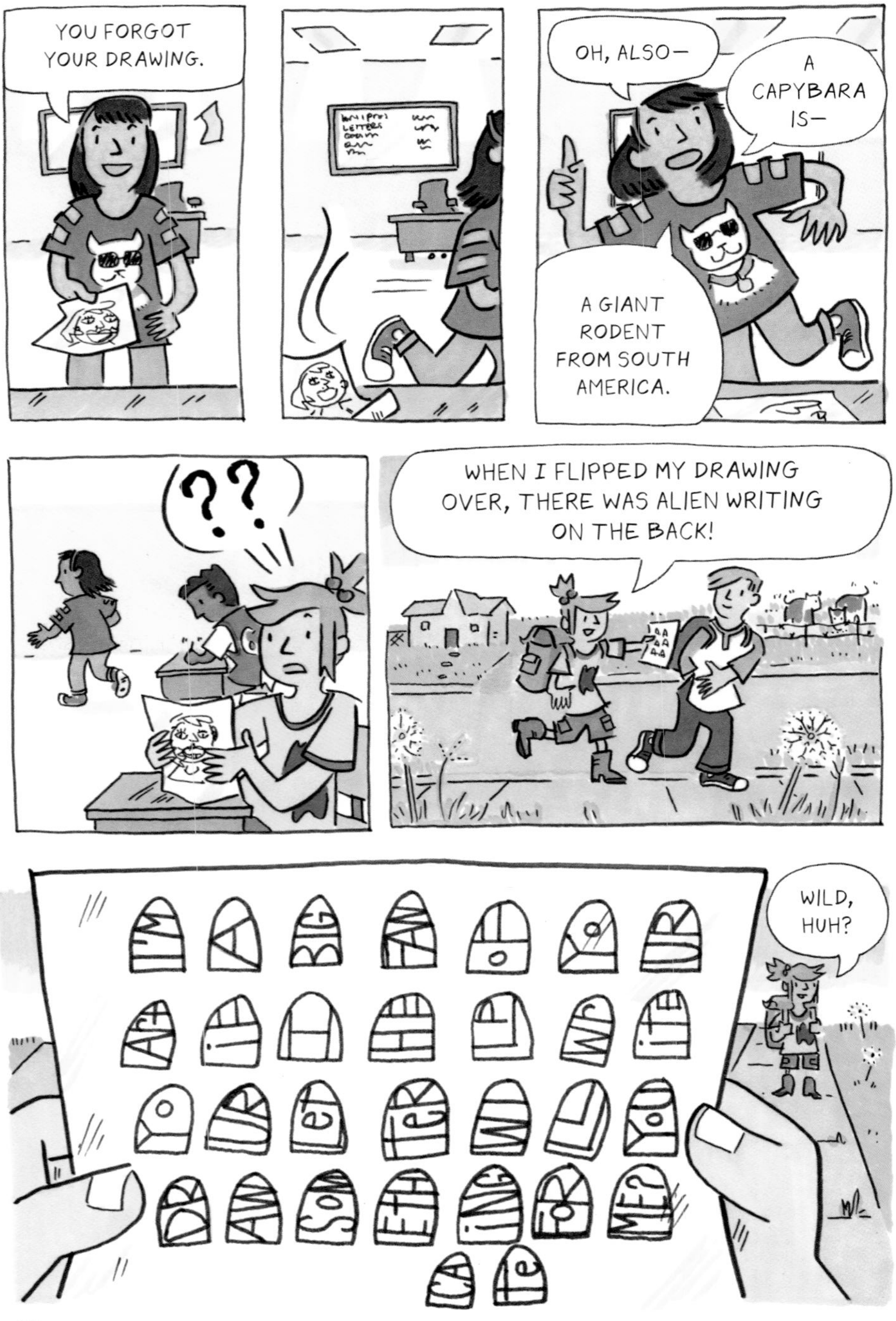
YOU FORGOT YOUR DRAWING.
OH, ALSO—
A CAPYBARA IS—
A GIANT RODENT FROM SOUTH AMERICA.
??
WHEN I FLIPPED MY DRAWING OVER, THERE WAS ALIEN WRITING ON THE BACK!
WILD, HUH?

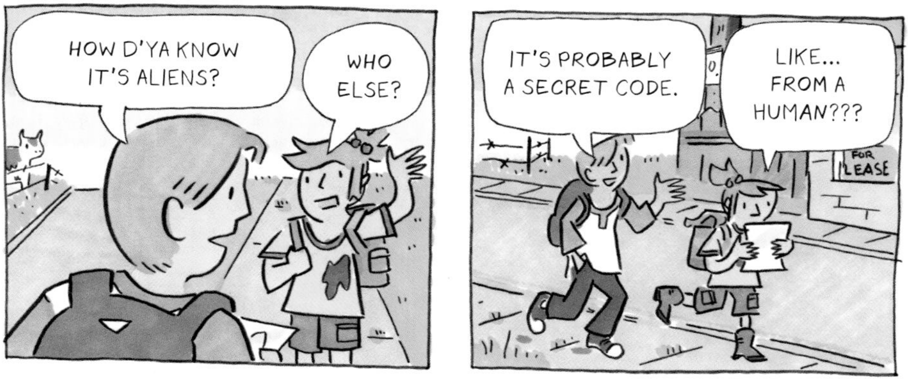
HOW D'YA KNOW IT'S ALIENS?
WHO ELSE?
IT'S PROBABLY A SECRET CODE.
LIKE... FROM A HUMAN???
FOR LEASE

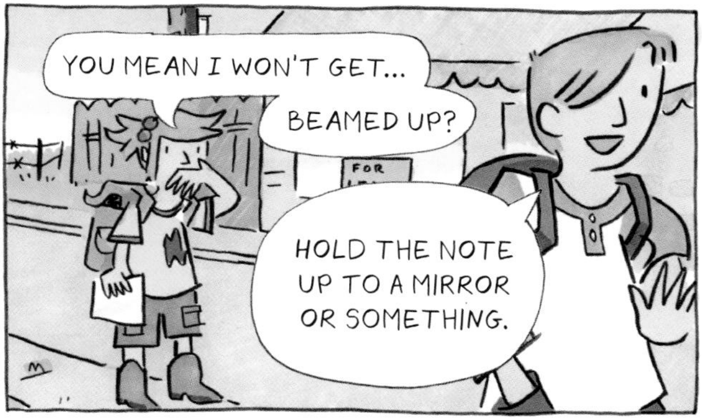
YOU MEAN I WON'T GET...
BEAMED UP?
HOLD THE NOTE UP TO A MIRROR OR SOMETHING.

Who had the time to write a code on my drawing?

What if it says something mean?

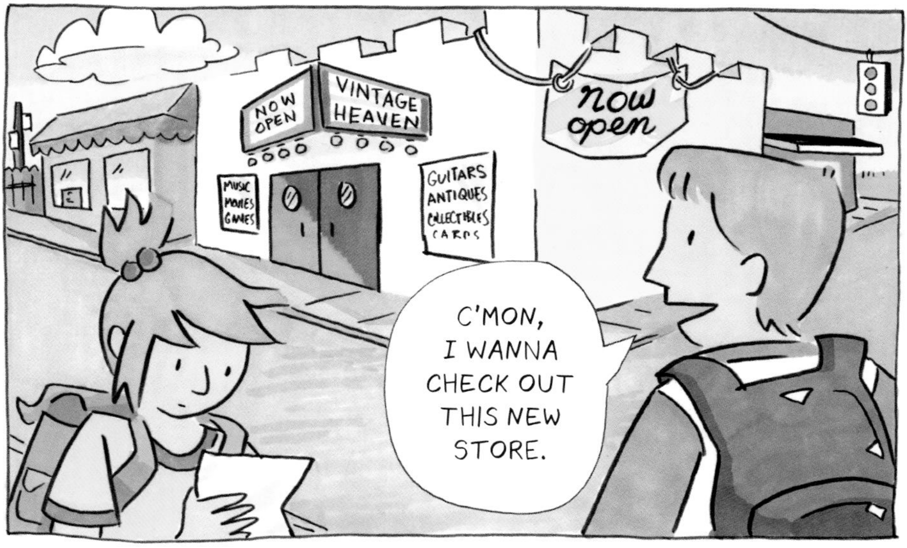
NOW OPEN
VINTAGE HEAVEN
now open
MUSIC MOVIES GAMES
GUITARS ANTIQUES COLLECTIBLES CARDS
C'MON, I WANNA CHECK OUT THIS NEW STORE.

CHAPTER 3

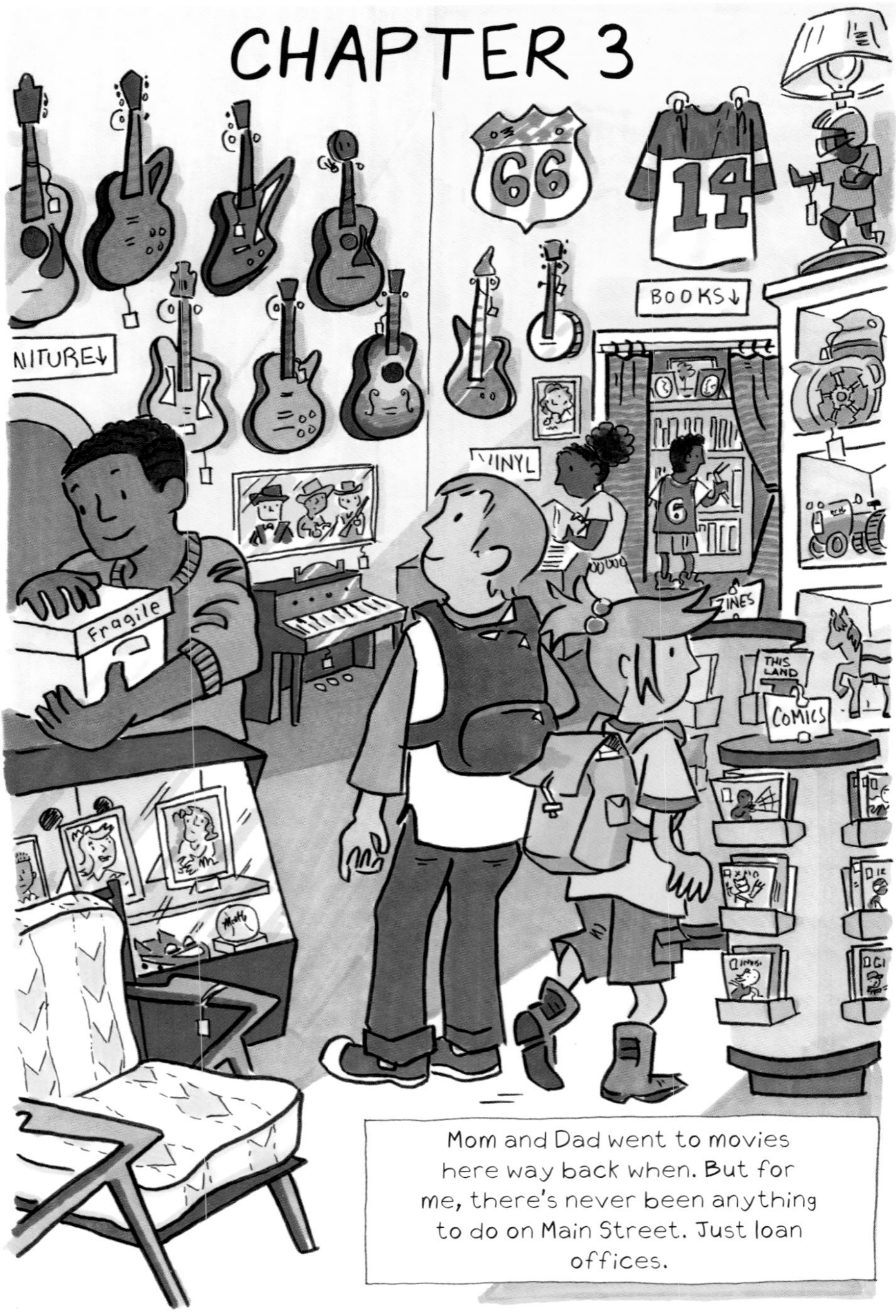
66
14
BOOKS↓
NITURE↓
VINYL
Fragile
ZINES
THIS LAND
COMICS
Mom and Dad went to movies here way back when. But for me, there's never been anything to do on Main Street. Just loan offices.

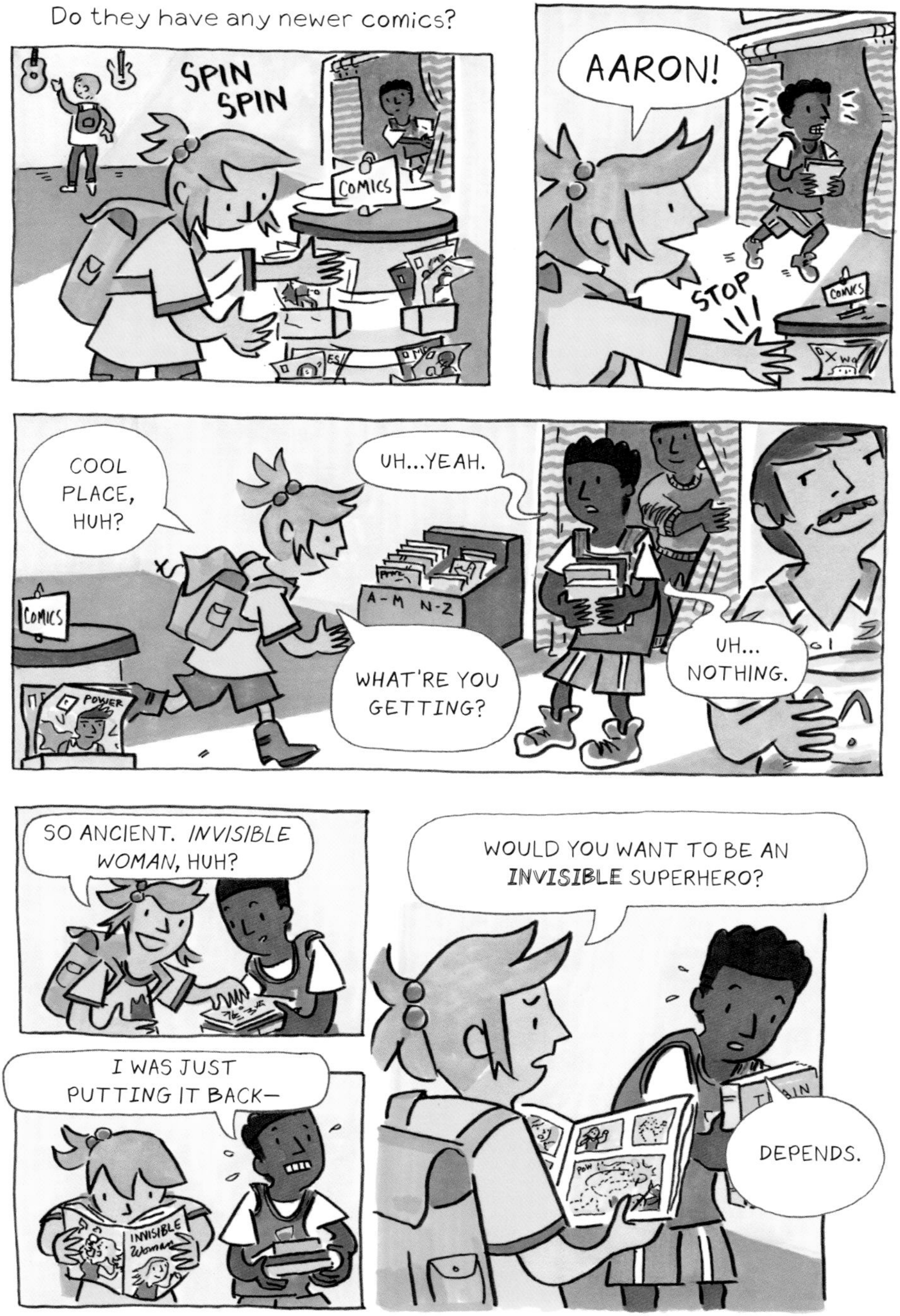
Do they have any newer comics?
SPIN SPIN
COMICS
AARON!
STOP
COMICS
COOL PLACE, HUH?
UH...YEAH.
COMICS
A-M N-Z
WHAT'RE YOU GETTING?
UH... NOTHING.
SO ANCIENT. *INVISIBLE WOMAN*, HUH?
I WAS JUST PUTTING IT BACK—
INVISIBLE Woman
WOULD YOU WANT TO BE AN INVISIBLE SUPERHERO?
DEPENDS.

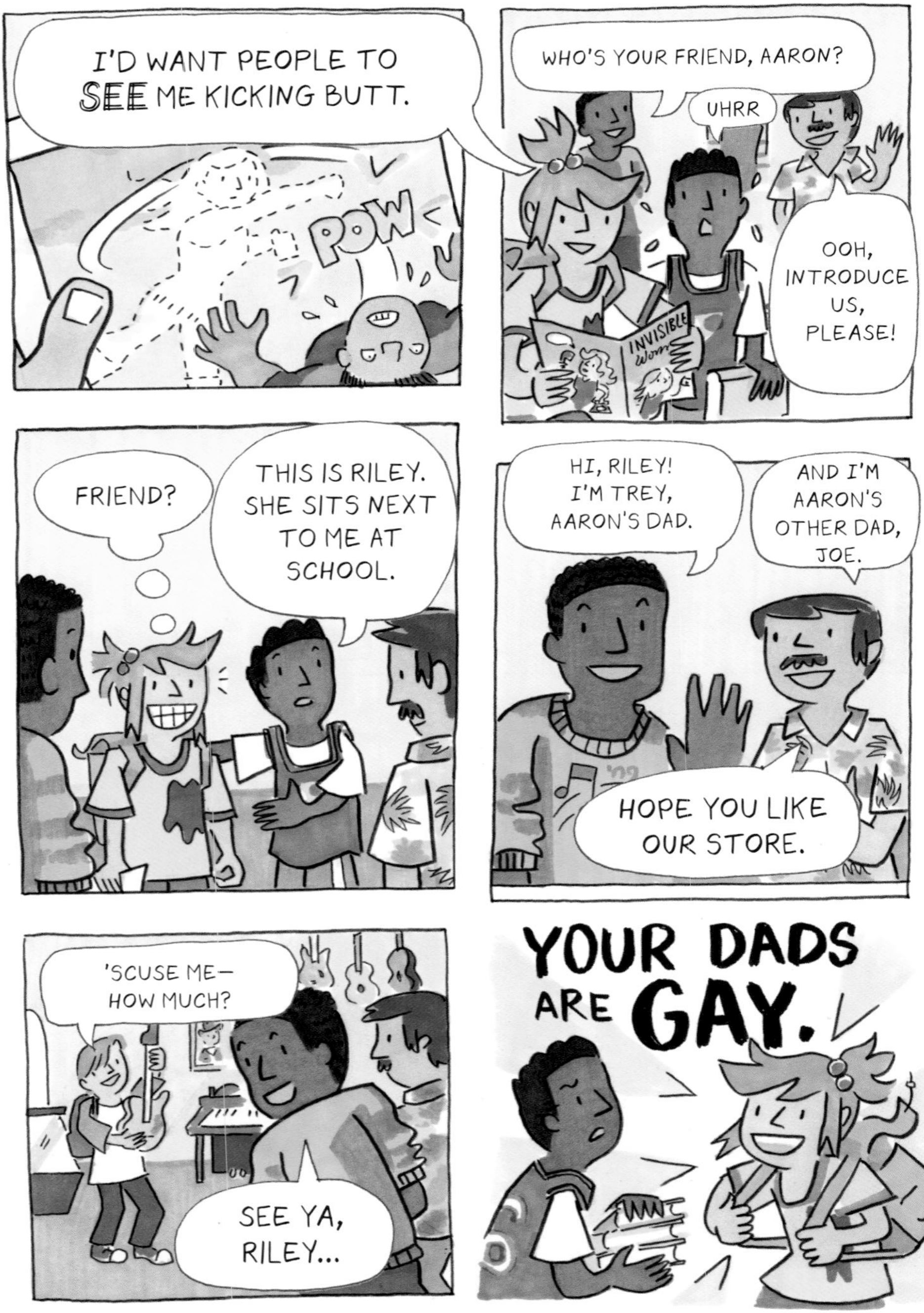
I'D WANT PEOPLE TO SEE ME KICKING BUTT.
POW
WHO'S YOUR FRIEND, AARON?
UHRR
OOH, INTRODUCE US, PLEASE!
INVISIBLE
FRIEND?
THIS IS RILEY. SHE SITS NEXT TO ME AT SCHOOL.
HI, RILEY! I'M TREY, AARON'S DAD.
AND I'M AARON'S OTHER DAD, JOE.
HOPE YOU LIKE OUR STORE.
'SCUSE ME— HOW MUCH?
SEE YA, RILEY...
YOUR DADS ARE GAY.

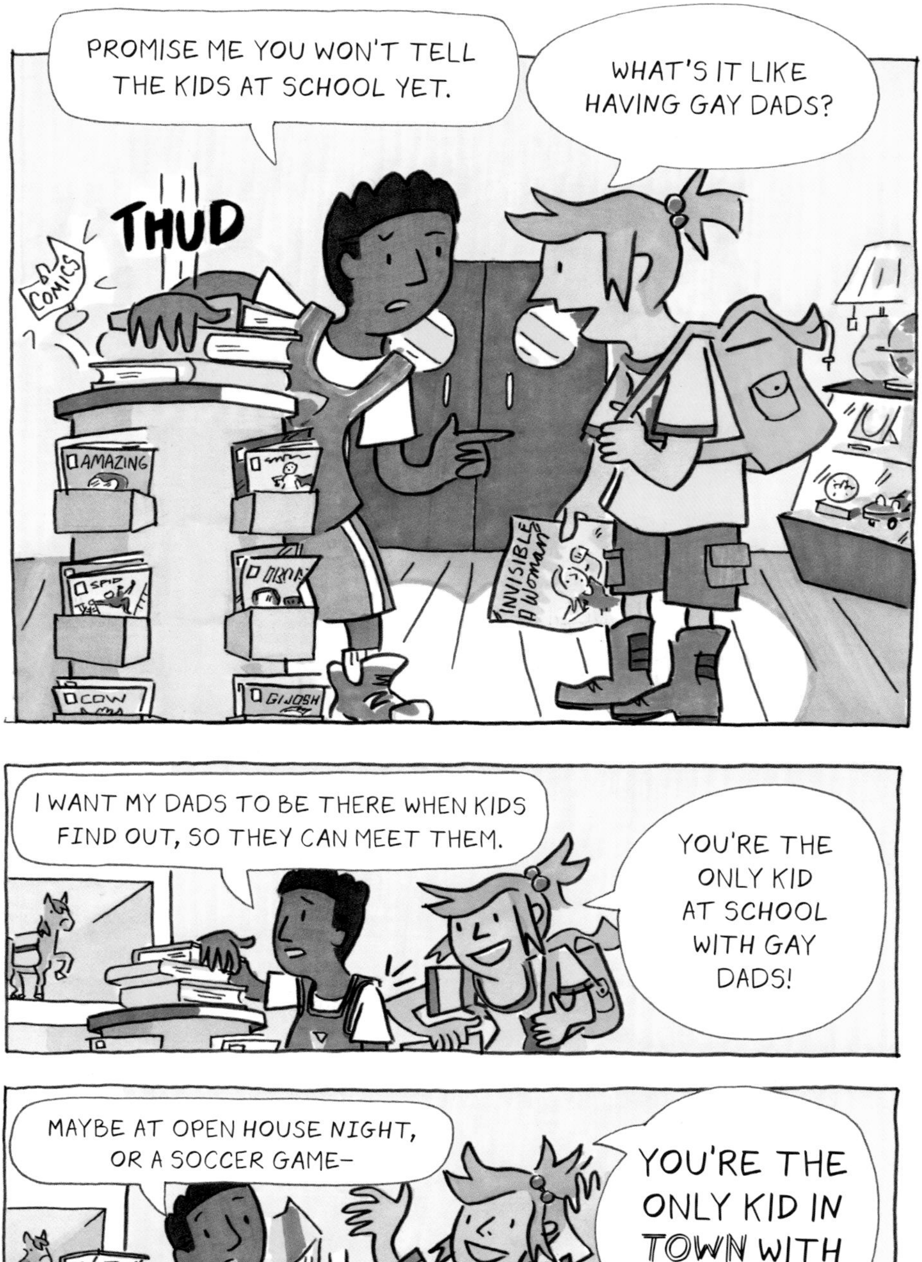
PROMISE ME YOU WON'T TELL THE KIDS AT SCHOOL YET.
WHAT'S IT LIKE HAVING GAY DADS?
THUD
COMICS
AMAZING
INVISIBLE WOMAN
COW
GI JOSH
I WANT MY DADS TO BE THERE WHEN KIDS FIND OUT, SO THEY CAN MEET THEM.
YOU'RE THE ONLY KID AT SCHOOL WITH GAY DADS!
MAYBE AT OPEN HOUSE NIGHT, OR A SOCCER GAME-
YOU'RE THE ONLY KID IN TOWN WITH GAY DADS!

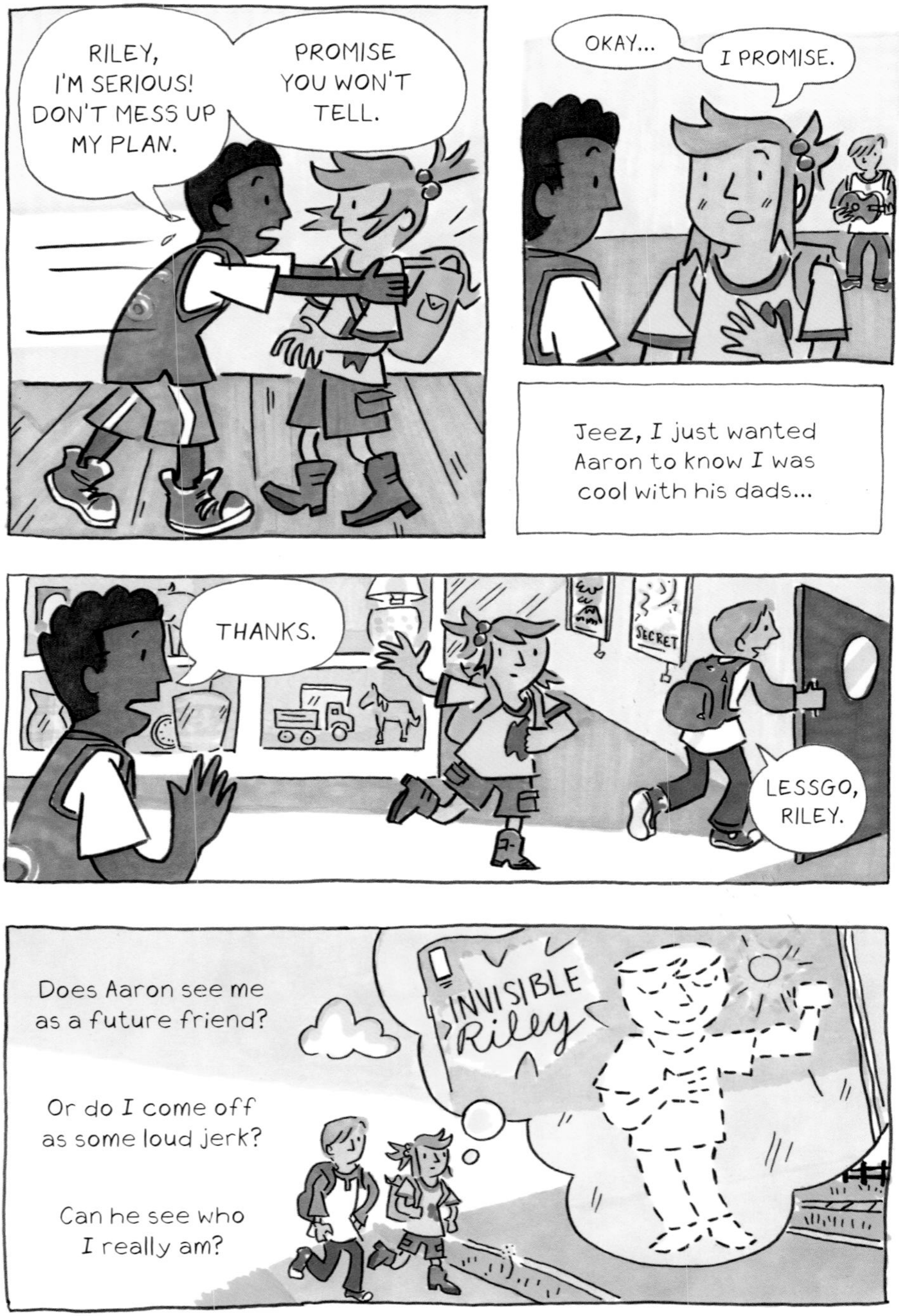
RILEY, I'M SERIOUS! DON'T MESS UP MY PLAN.
PROMISE YOU WON'T TELL.
OKAY...
I PROMISE.
Jeez, I just wanted Aaron to know I was cool with his dads...
THANKS.
SECRET
LESSGO, RILEY.
Does Aaron see me as a future friend?
Or do I come off as some loud jerk?
Can he see who I really am?
INVISIBLE Riley

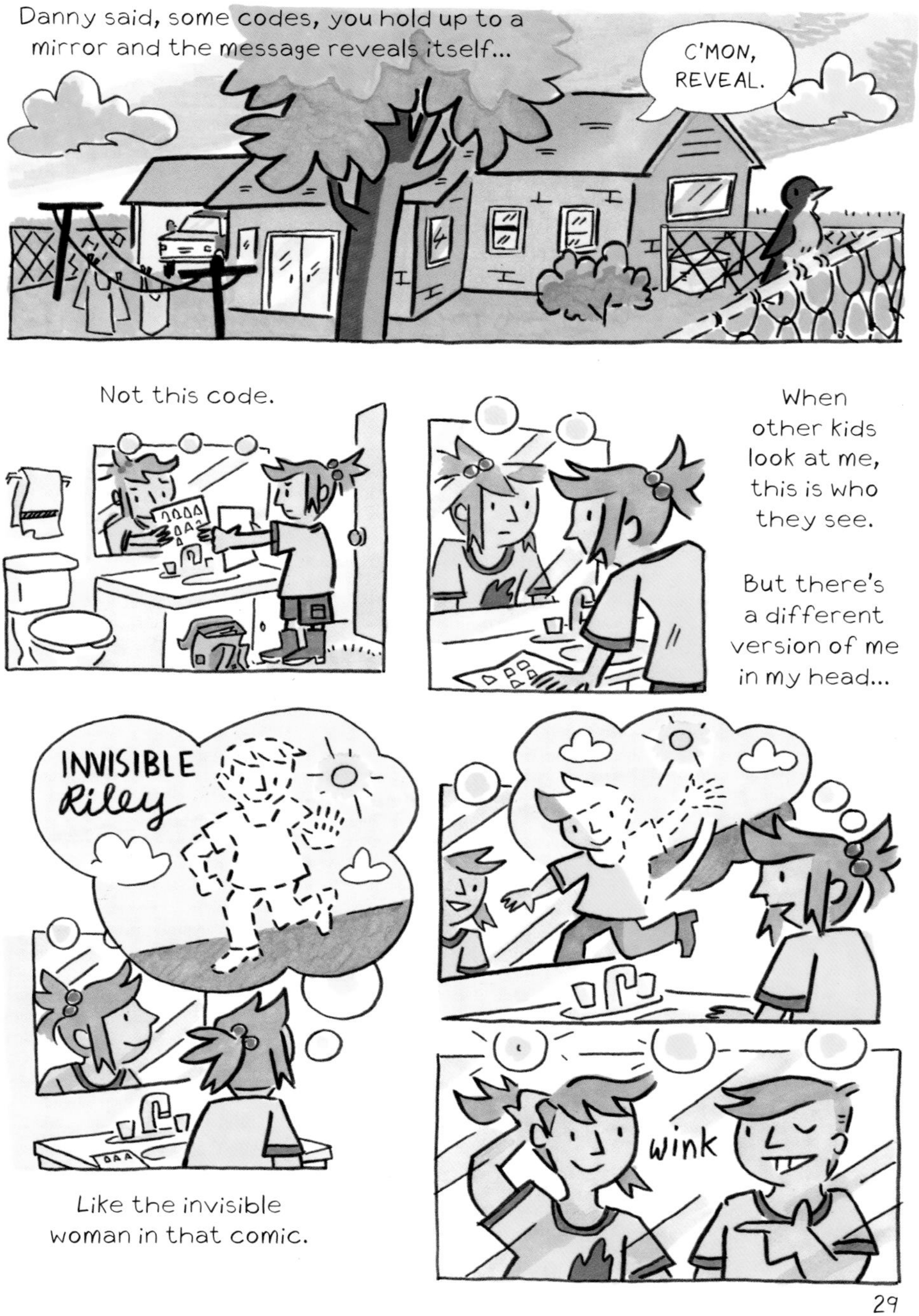
Danny said, some codes, you hold up to a mirror and the message reveals itself...
C'MON, REVEAL.
Not this code.
When other kids look at me, this is who they see.
But there's a different version of me in my head...
INVISIBLE Riley
Like the invisible woman in that comic.
wink

I see her all day, but no one else does.

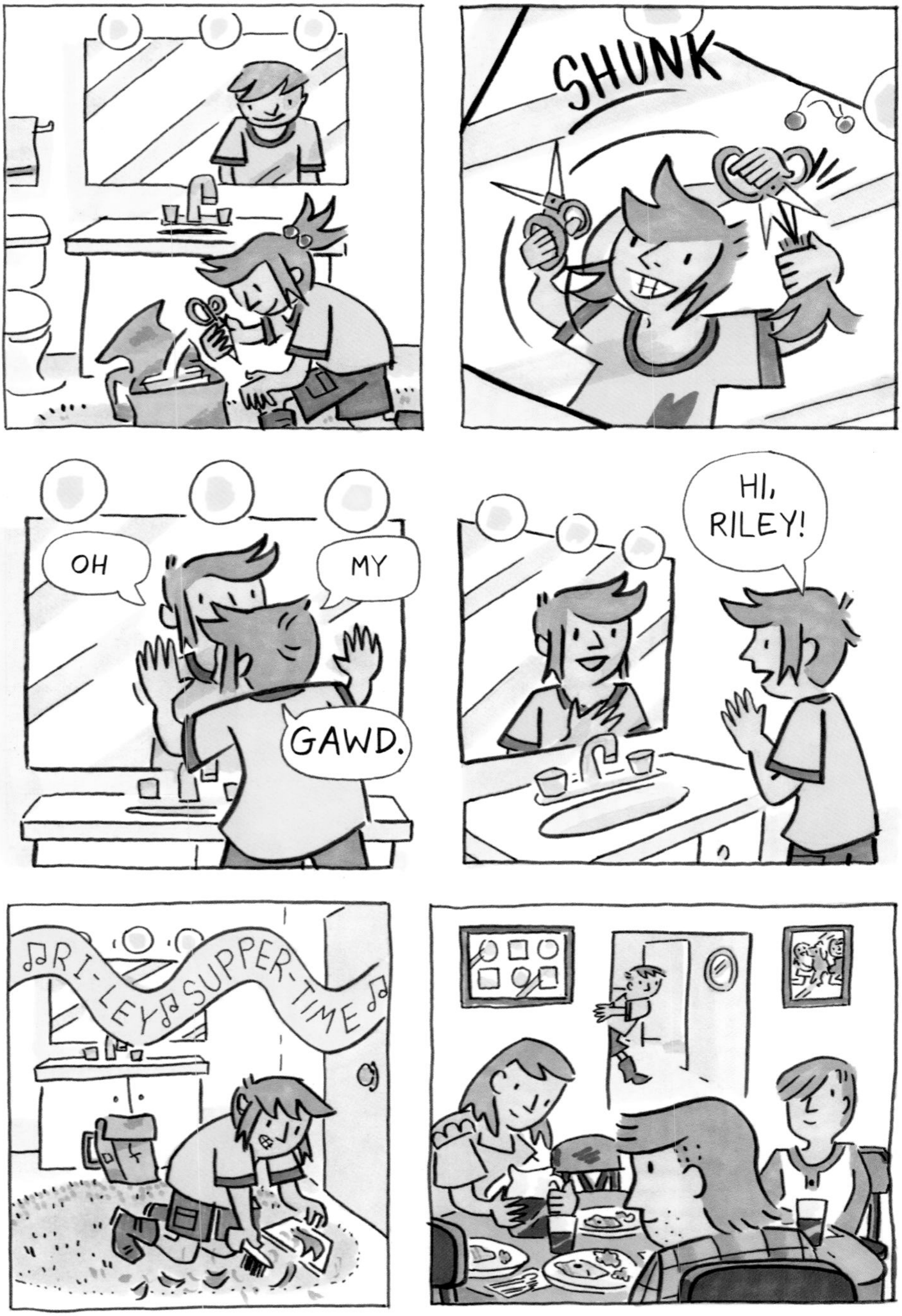
SHUNK
OH
MY
GAWD.
HI, RILEY!
♫RI-LEY♫SUPPER-TIME♫

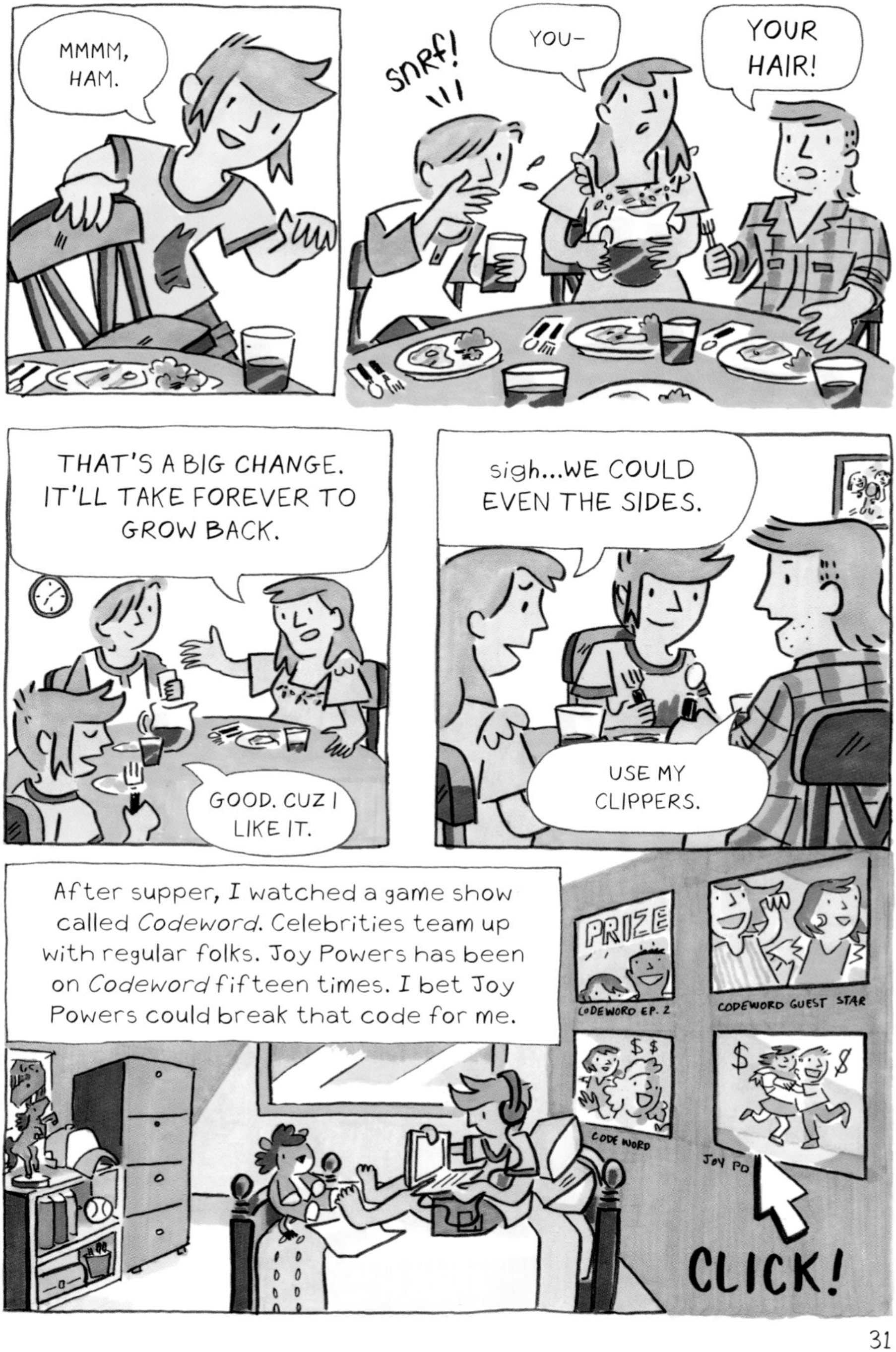
MMMM, HAM.
SNRF!
YOU-
YOUR HAIR!
THAT'S A BIG CHANGE. IT'LL TAKE FOREVER TO GROW BACK.
GOOD. CUZ I LIKE IT.
sigh...WE COULD EVEN THE SIDES.
USE MY CLIPPERS.
After supper, I watched a game show called *Codeword*. Celebrities team up with regular folks. Joy Powers has been on *Codeword* fifteen times. I bet Joy Powers could break that code for me.
PRIZE
CODEWORD EP. 2
CODEWORD GUEST STAR
$ $
CODE WORD
$ $
JOY PO
CLICK!

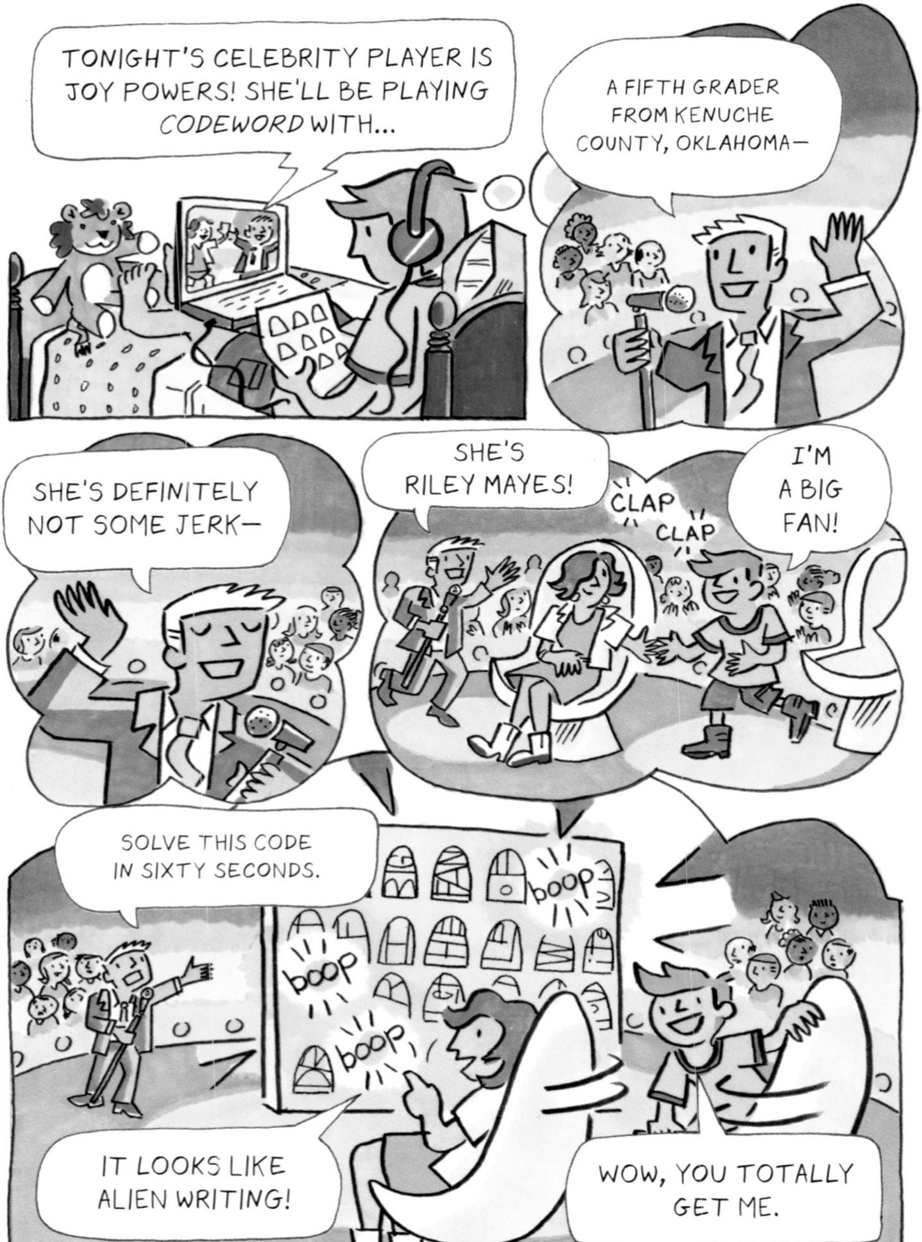
TONIGHT'S CELEBRITY PLAYER IS JOY POWERS! SHE'LL BE PLAYING *CODEWORD* WITH...
A FIFTH GRADER FROM KENUCHE COUNTY, OKLAHOMA—
SHE'S DEFINITELY NOT SOME JERK—
SHE'S RILEY MAYES!
CLAP CLAP
I'M A BIG FAN!
SOLVE THIS CODE IN SIXTY SECONDS.
boop
boop
boop
IT LOOKS LIKE ALIEN WRITING!
WOW, YOU TOTALLY GET ME.

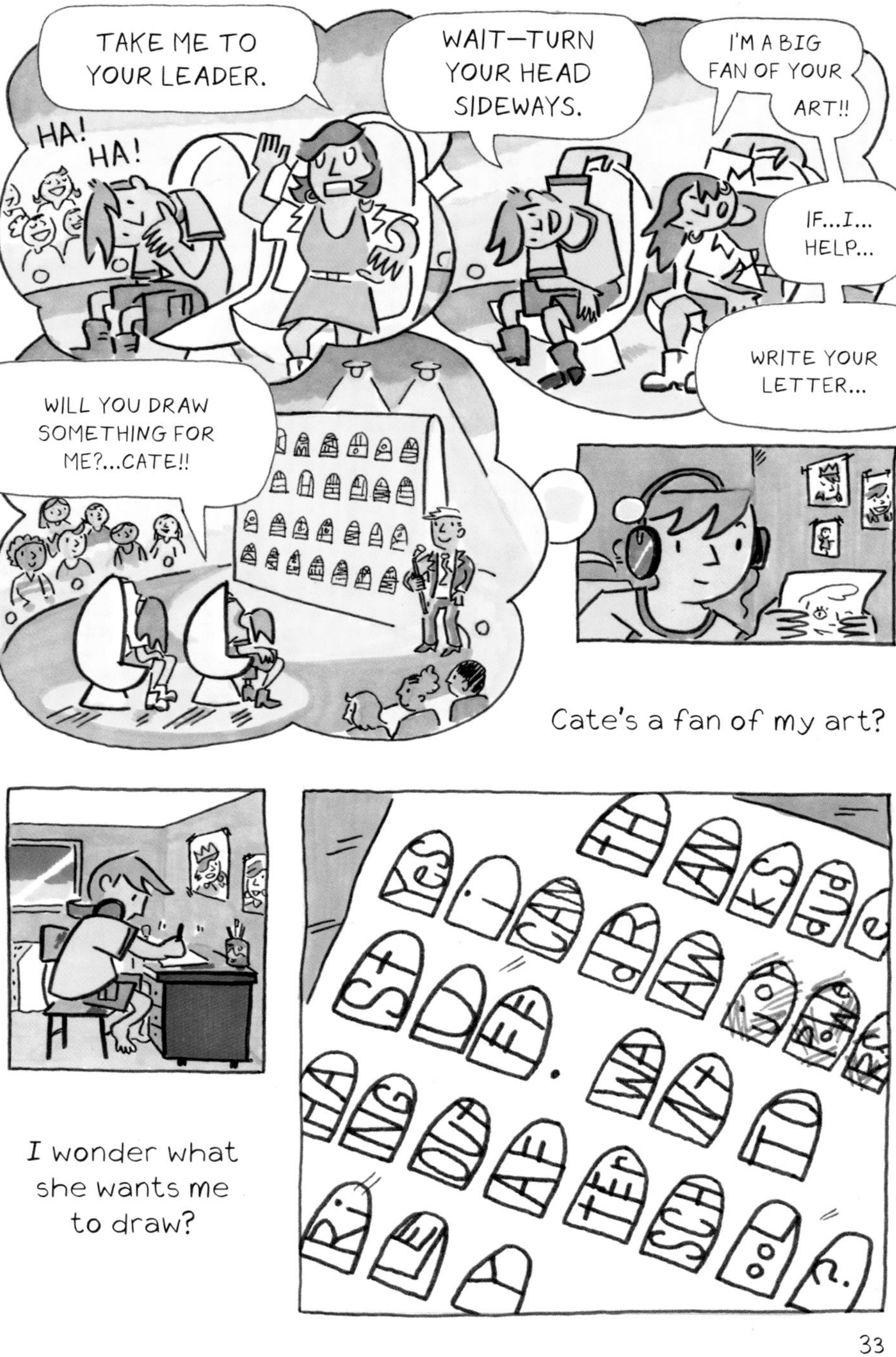
TAKE ME TO YOUR LEADER.
HA! HA!
WAIT—TURN YOUR HEAD SIDEWAYS.
I'M A BIG FAN OF YOUR ART!!
IF...I... HELP...
WRITE YOUR LETTER...
WILL YOU DRAW SOMETHING FOR ME?...CATE!!
Cate's a fan of my art?
I wonder what she wants me to draw?

CHAPTER 4

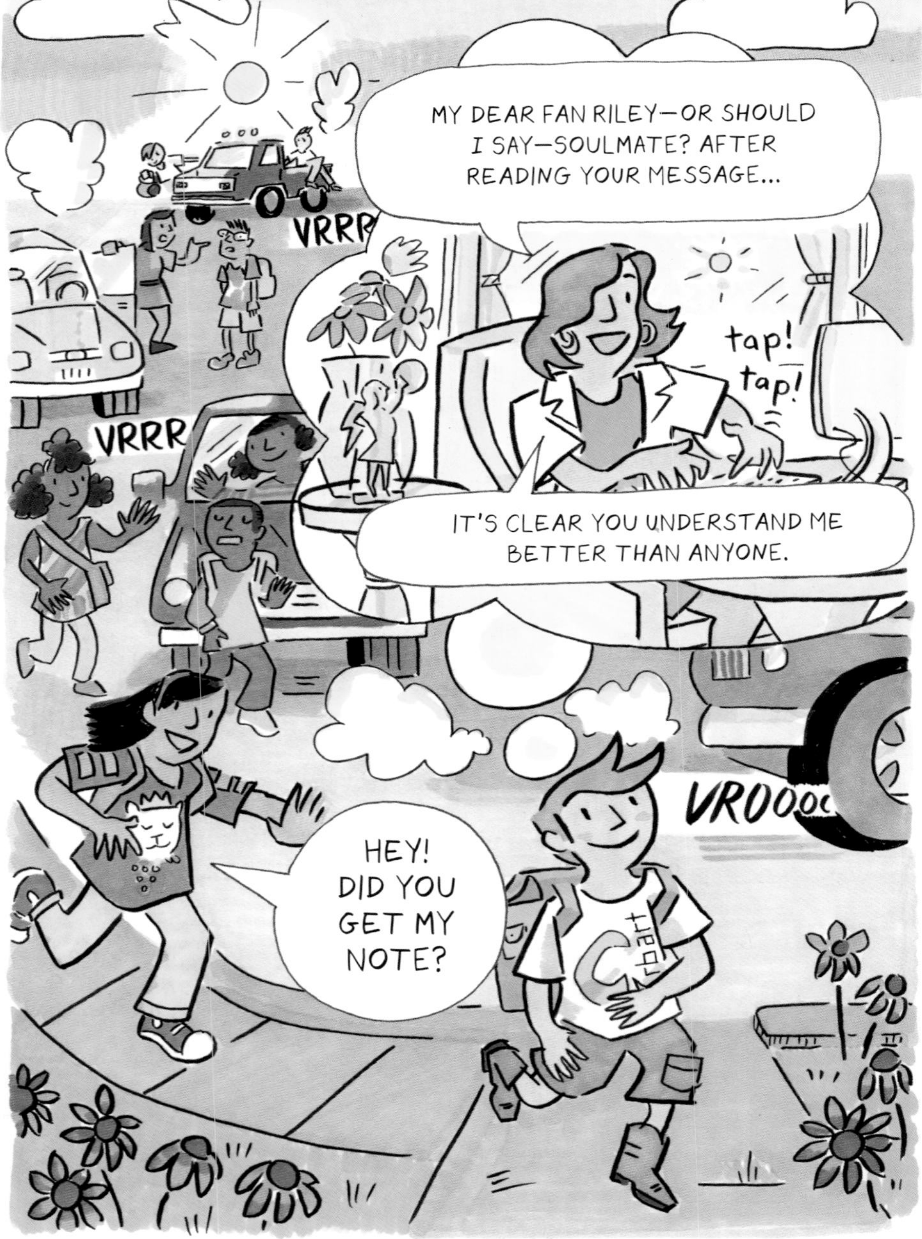
VRRR
MY DEAR FAN RILEY—OR SHOULD I SAY—SOULMATE? AFTER READING YOUR MESSAGE...
tap! tap!
VRRR
IT'S CLEAR YOU UNDERSTAND ME BETTER THAN ANYONE.
VROOO
HEY! DID YOU GET MY NOTE?

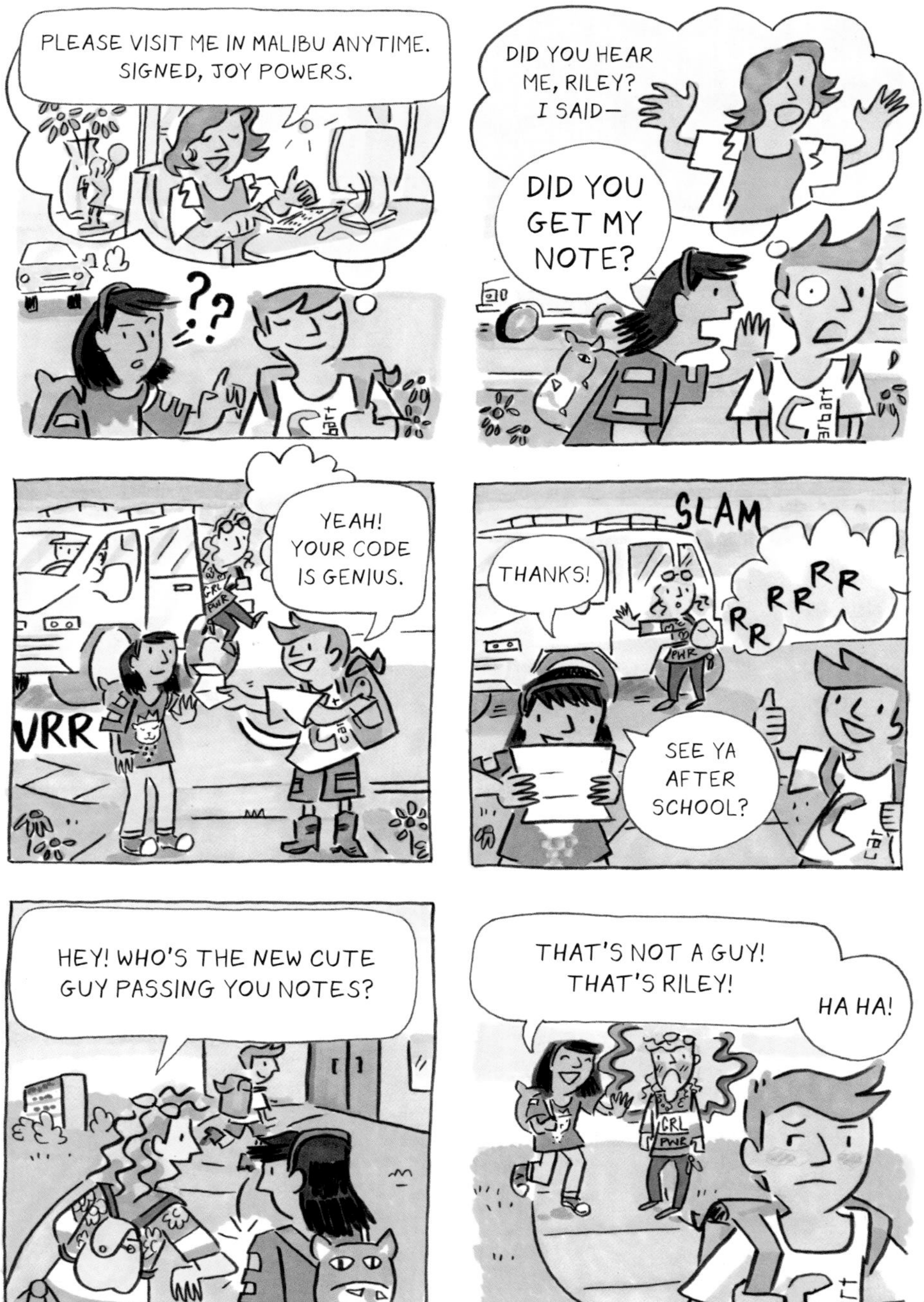
PLEASE VISIT ME IN MALIBU ANYTIME. SIGNED, JOY POWERS.
??
DID YOU HEAR ME, RILEY? I SAID—
DID YOU GET MY NOTE?
YEAH! YOUR CODE IS GENIUS.
VRR
SLAM
THANKS!
RRRRR
SEE YA AFTER SCHOOL?
HEY! WHO'S THE NEW CUTE GUY PASSING YOU NOTES?
THAT'S NOT A GUY! THAT'S RILEY!
HA HA!

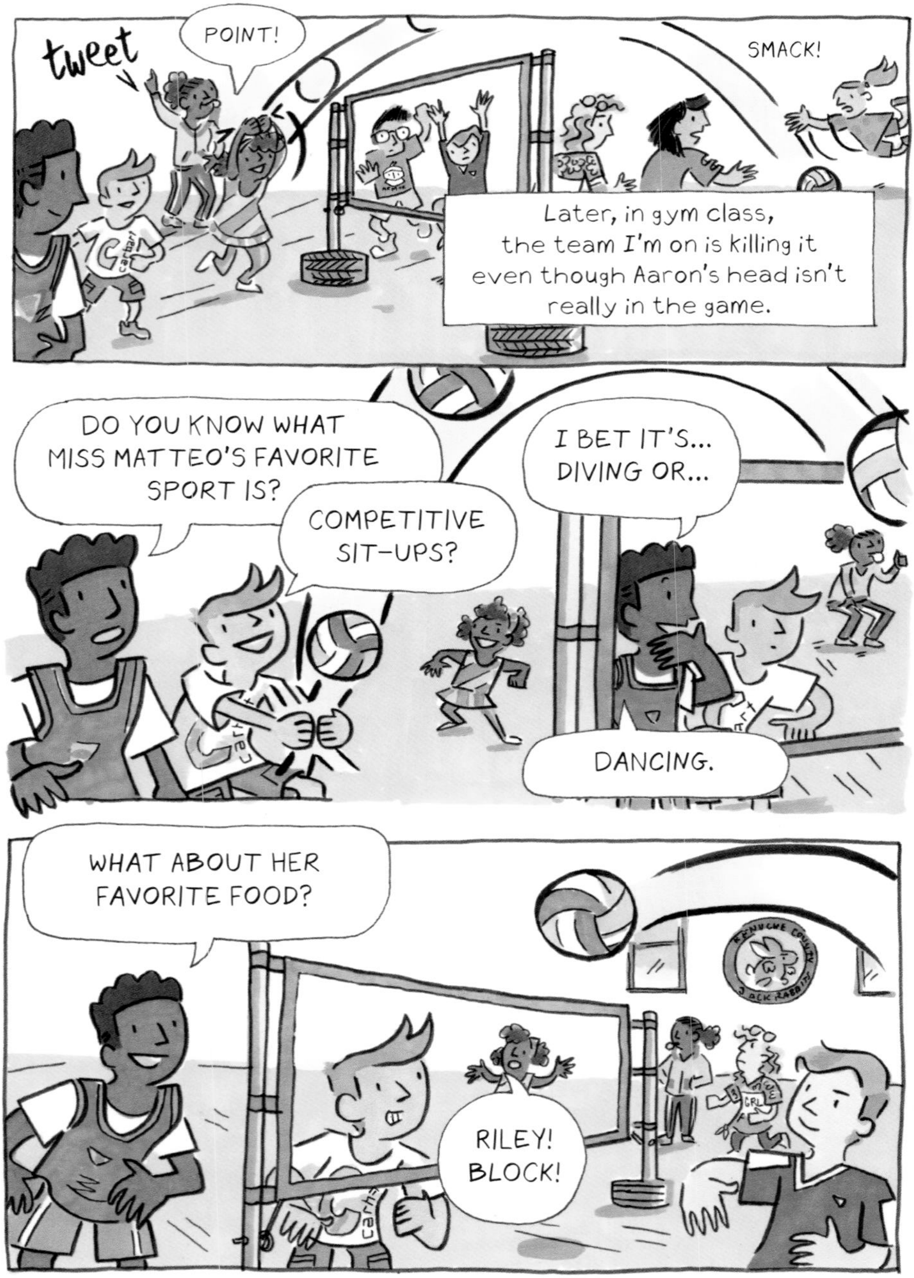
tweet
POINT!
SMACK!
Later, in gym class, the team *I'm* on is killing it even though Aaron's head isn't really in the game.
DO YOU KNOW WHAT MISS MATTEO'S FAVORITE SPORT IS?
COMPETITIVE SIT-UPS?
I BET IT'S... DIVING OR...
DANCING.
WHAT ABOUT HER FAVORITE FOOD?
RILEY! BLOCK!

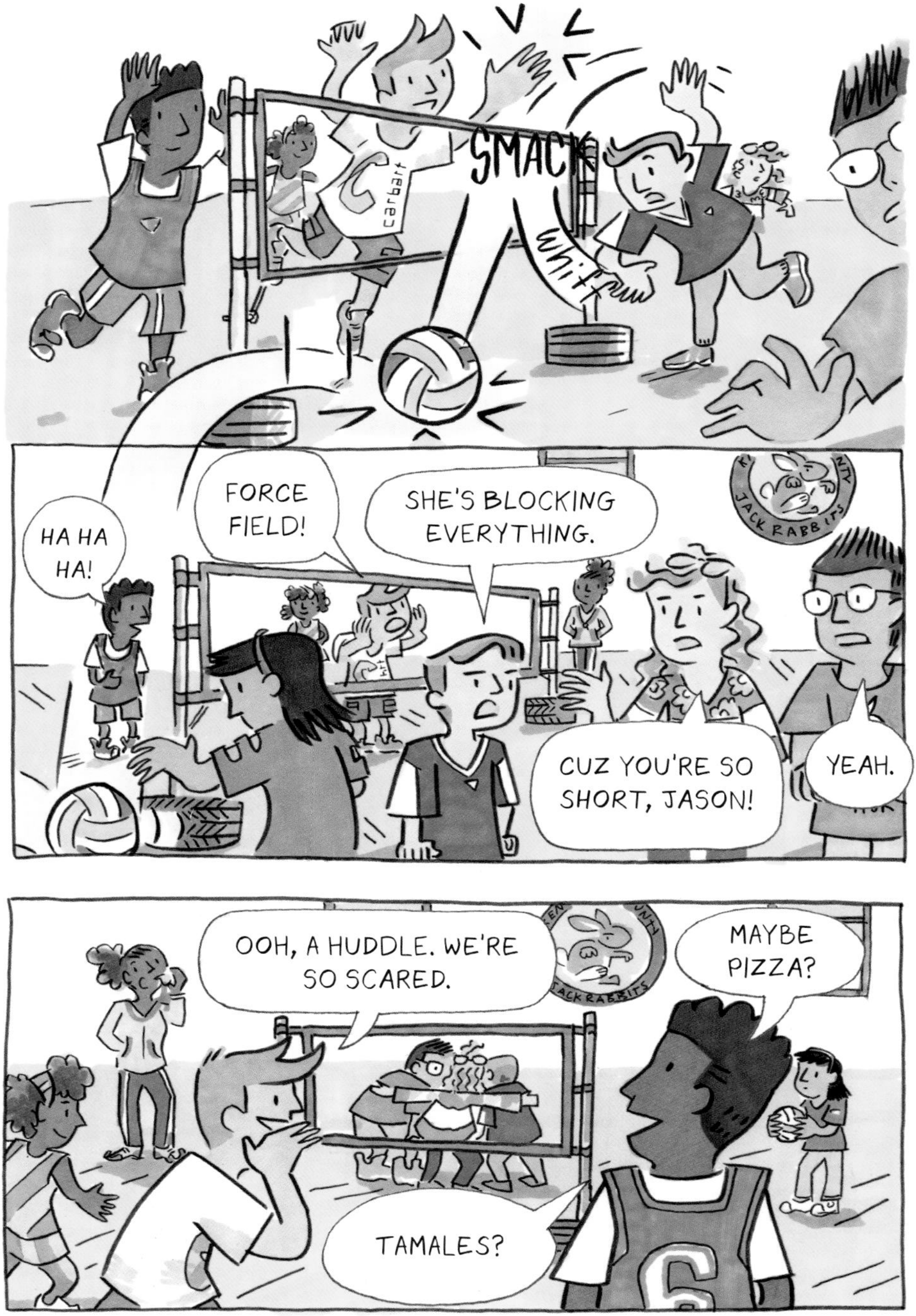
SMACK
whiff
HA HA HA!
FORCE FIELD!
SHE'S BLOCKING EVERYTHING.
JACK RABBITS
CUZ YOU'RE SO SHORT, JASON!
YEAH.
OOH, A HUDDLE. WE'RE SO SCARED.
MAYBE PIZZA?
TAMALES?

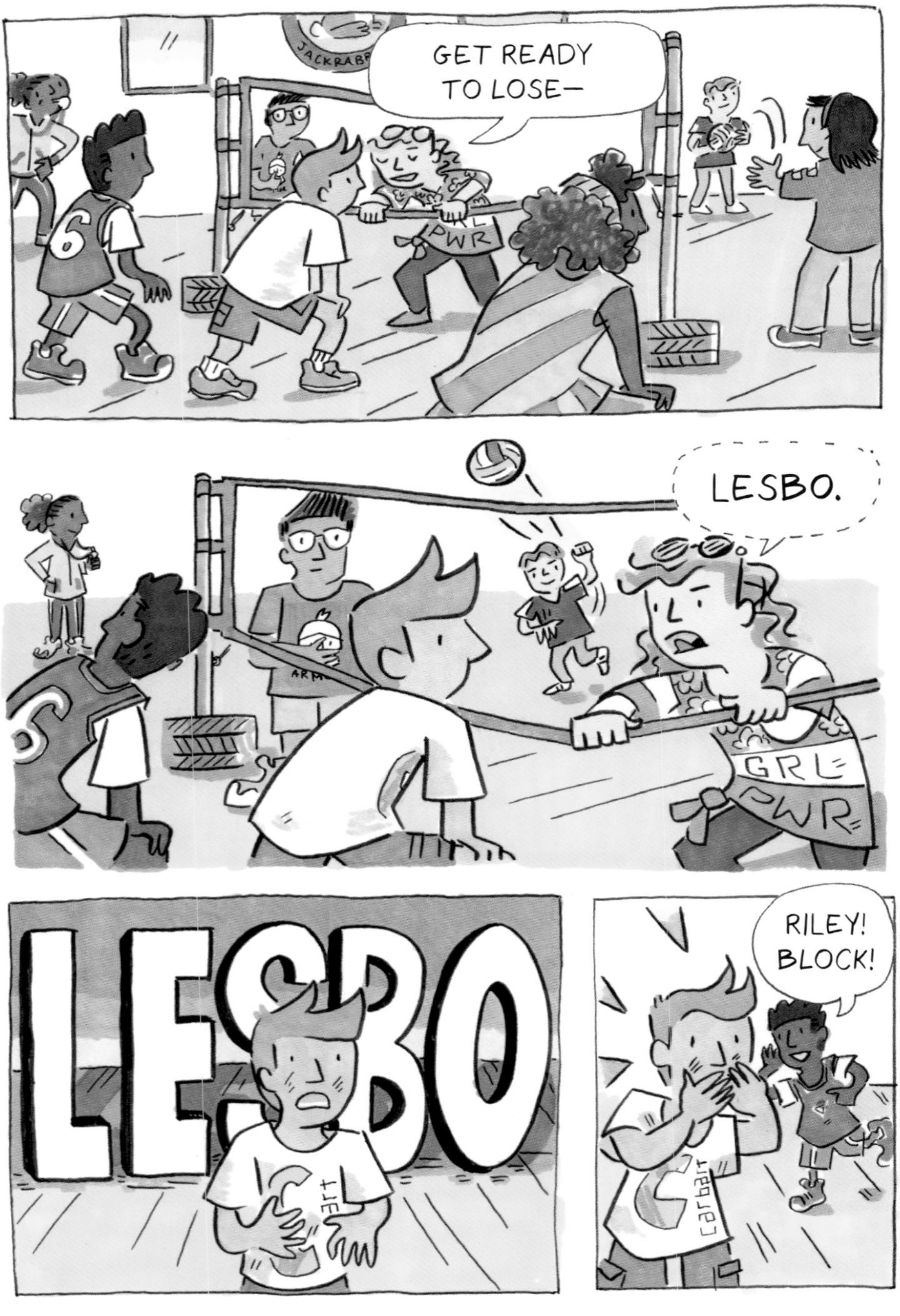
GET READY TO LOSE—
GRL PWR
LESBO.
GRL PWR
LESBO
RILEY! BLOCK!

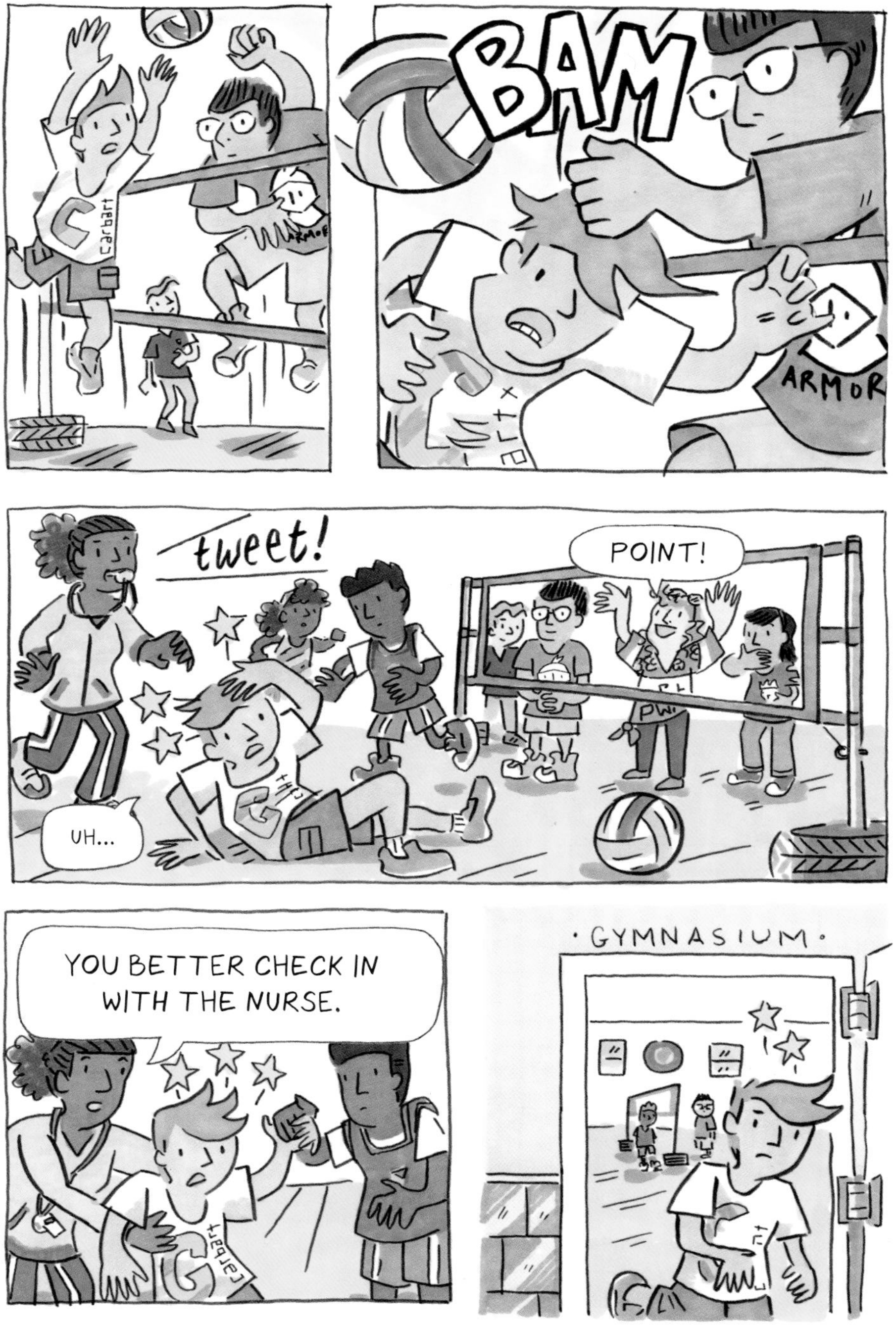
Carbart
ARMOR
BAM
ARMOR
tweet!
POINT!
UH...
YOU BETTER CHECK IN WITH THE NURSE.
Carbart
· GYMNASIUM ·

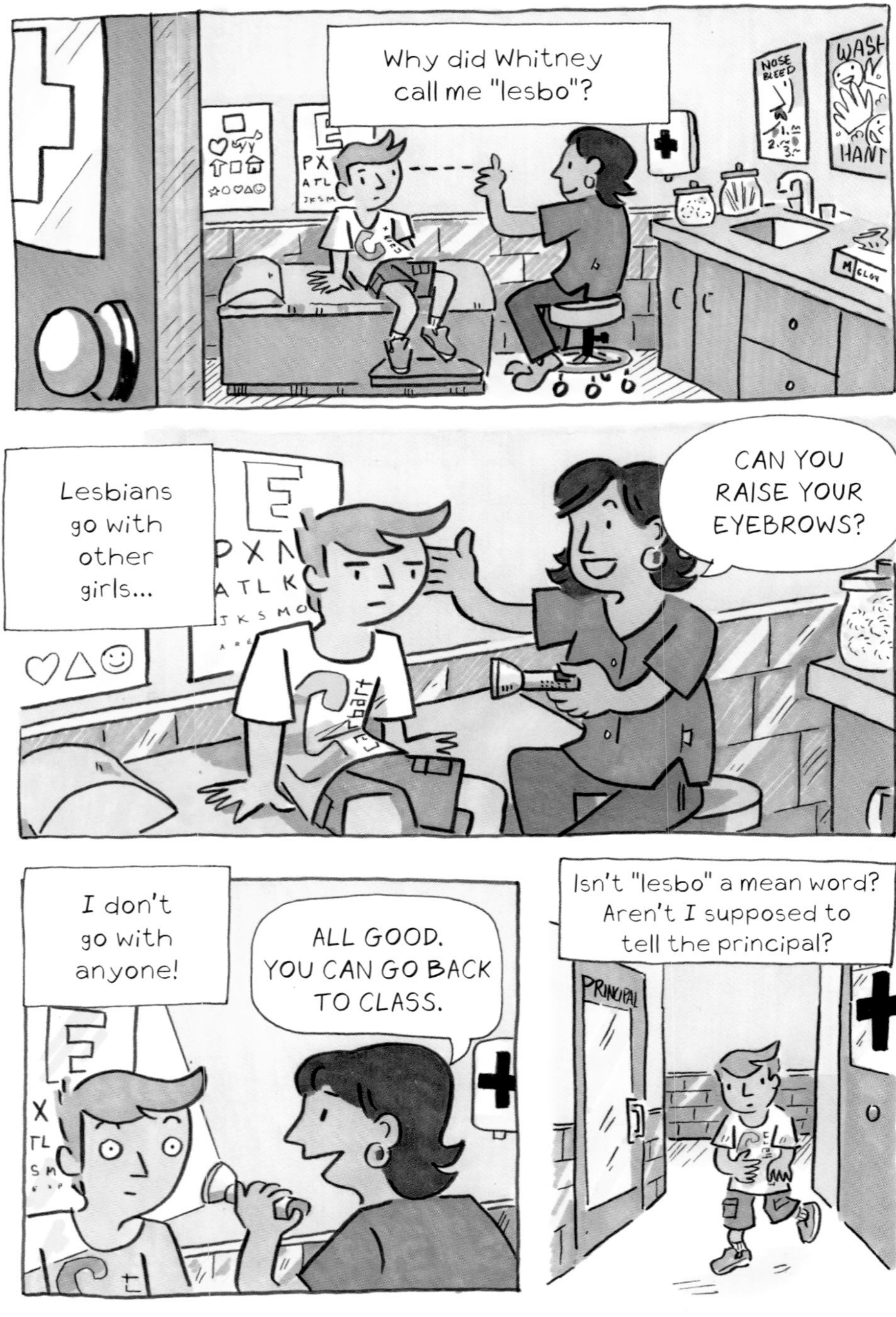
Why did Whitney call me "lesbo"?
NOSE BLEED
WASH
Lesbians go with other girls...
CAN YOU RAISE YOUR EYEBROWS?
I don't go with anyone!
ALL GOOD. YOU CAN GO BACK TO CLASS.
Isn't "lesbo" a mean word? Aren't I supposed to tell the principal?
PRINCIPAL

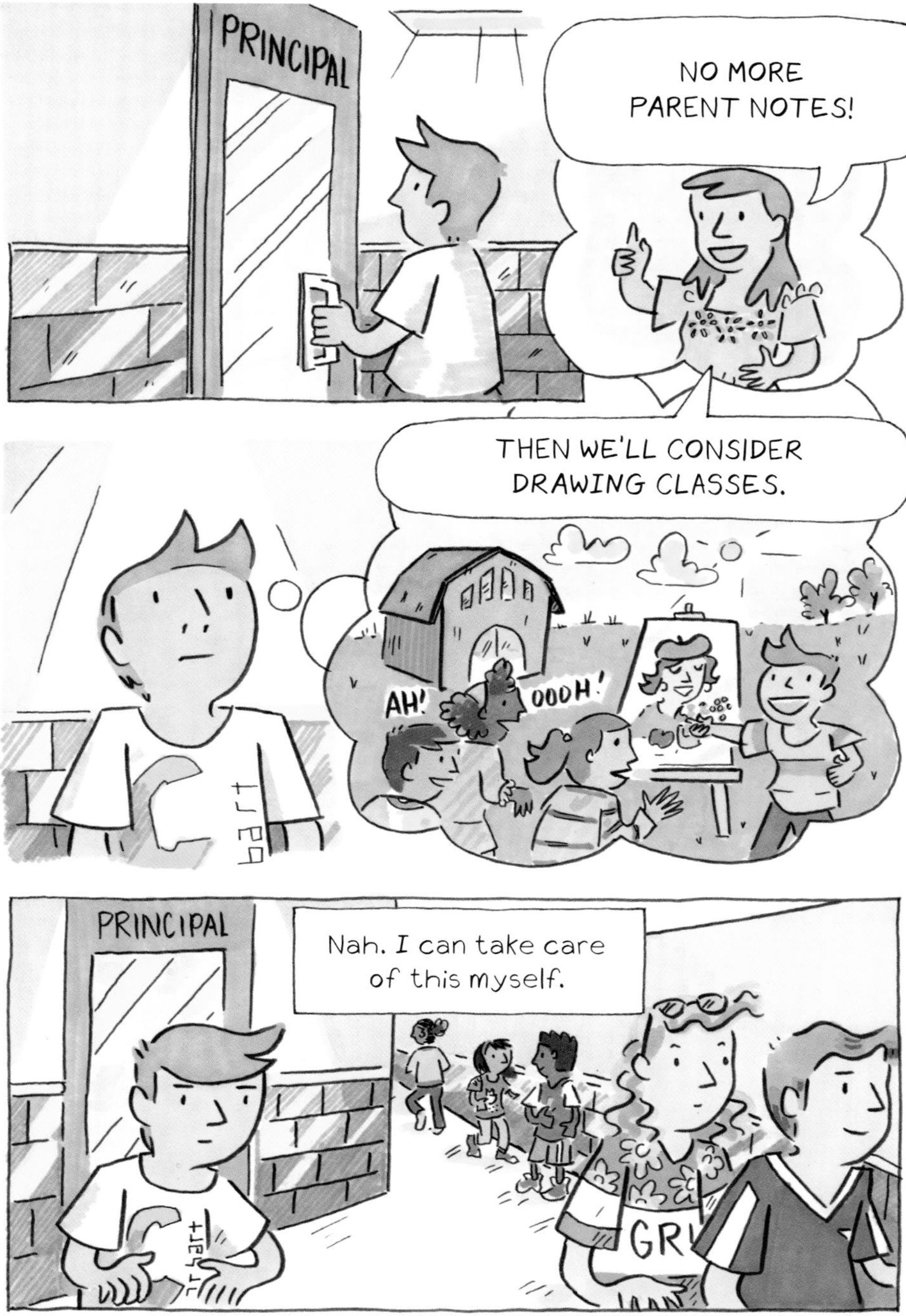
PRINCIPAL
NO MORE PARENT NOTES!
THEN WE'LL CONSIDER DRAWING CLASSES.
AH!
OOOH!
PRINCIPAL
Nah. I can take care of this myself.
GR

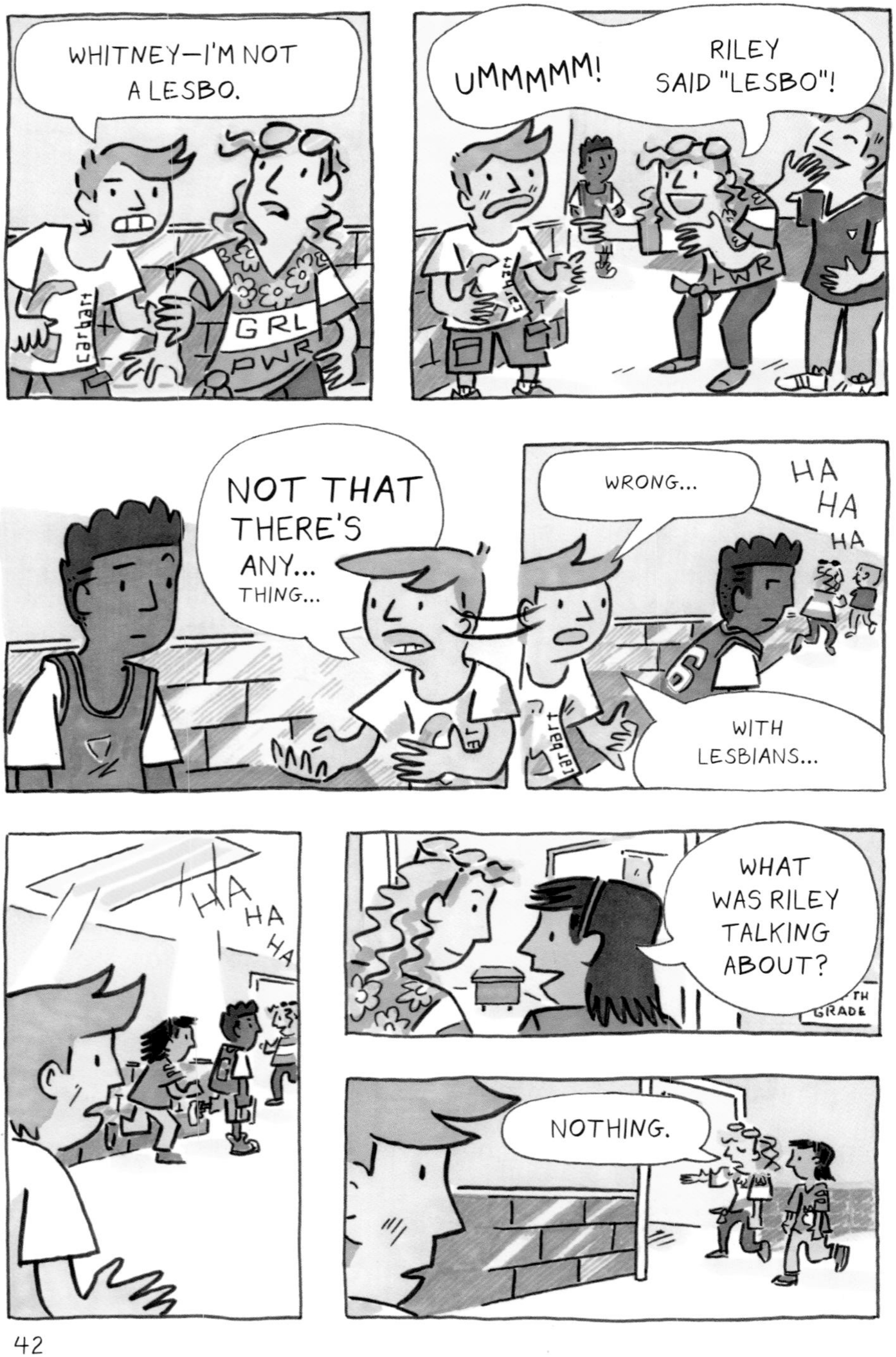
WHITNEY—I'M NOT A LESBO.
UMMMMM!
RILEY SAID "LESBO"!
GRL PWR
NOT THAT THERE'S ANY... THING...
WRONG...
HA HA HA
WITH LESBIANS...
HA HA HA
WHAT WAS RILEY TALKING ABOUT?
NOTHING.

CHAPTER 5

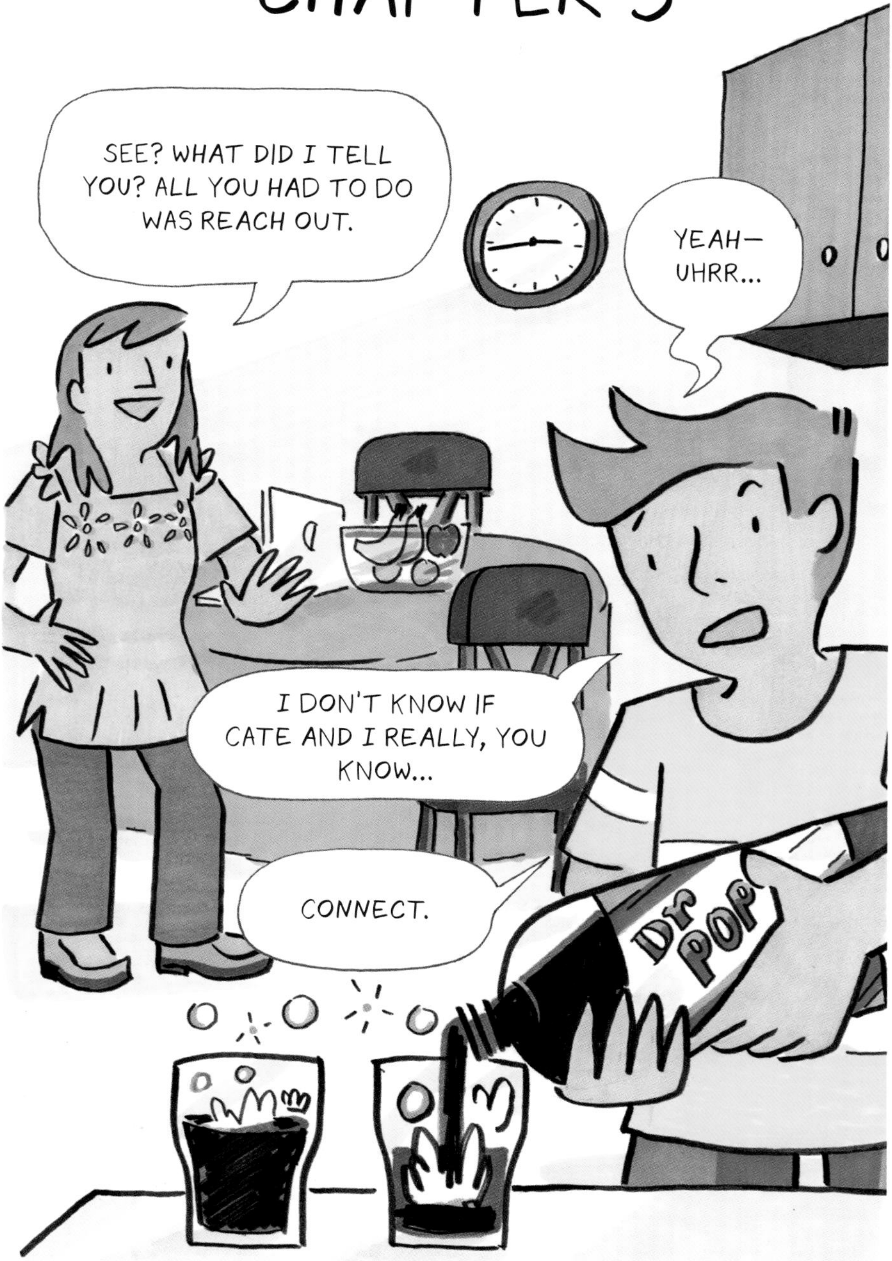
SEE? WHAT DID I TELL YOU? ALL YOU HAD TO DO WAS REACH OUT.
YEAH— UHRR...
I DON'T KNOW IF CATE AND I REALLY, YOU KNOW...
CONNECT.
Dr POP

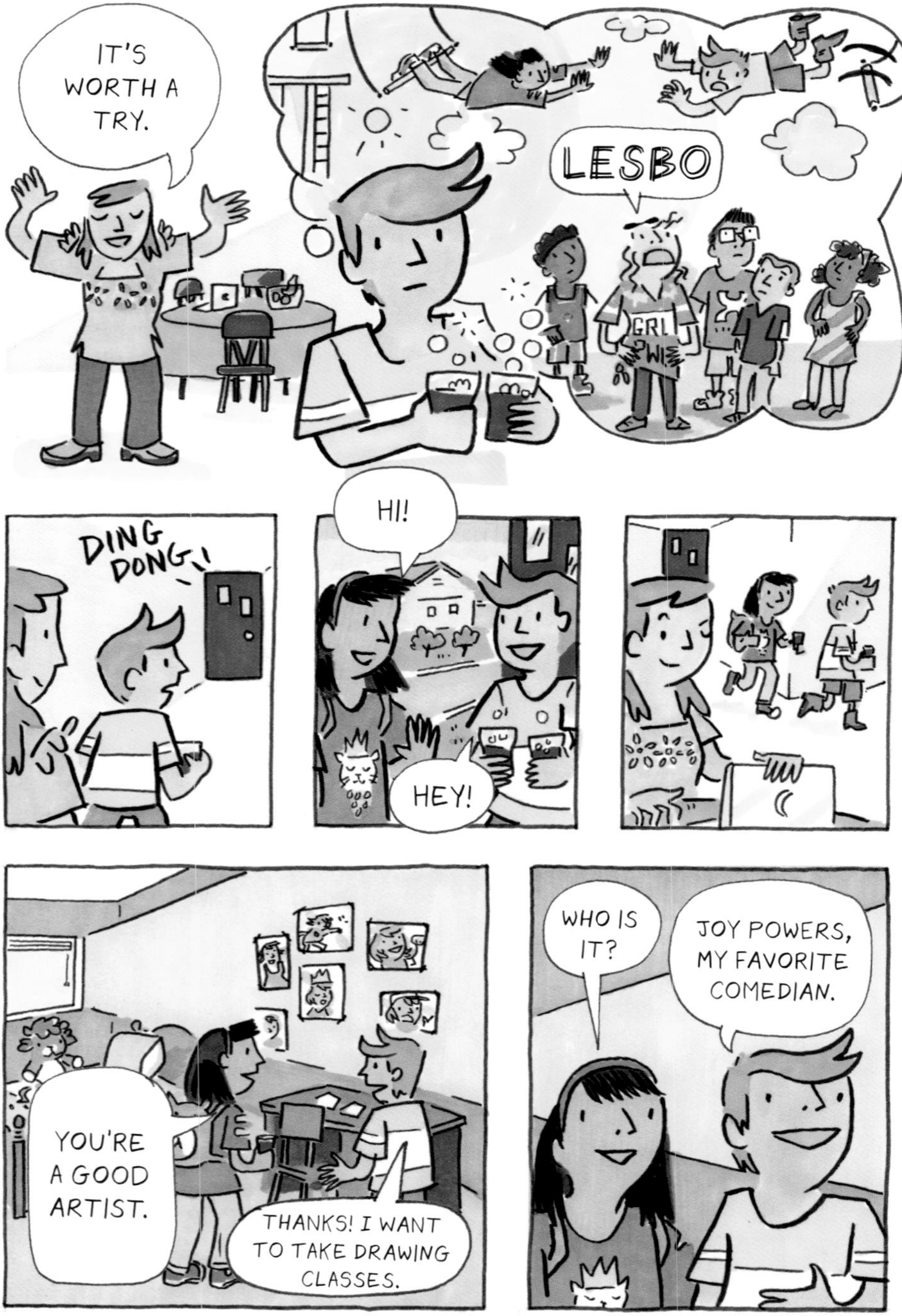
IT'S WORTH A TRY.
LESBO
GRL
DING DONG
HI!
HEY!
YOU'RE A GOOD ARTIST.
THANKS! I WANT TO TAKE DRAWING CLASSES.
WHO IS IT?
JOY POWERS, MY FAVORITE COMEDIAN.

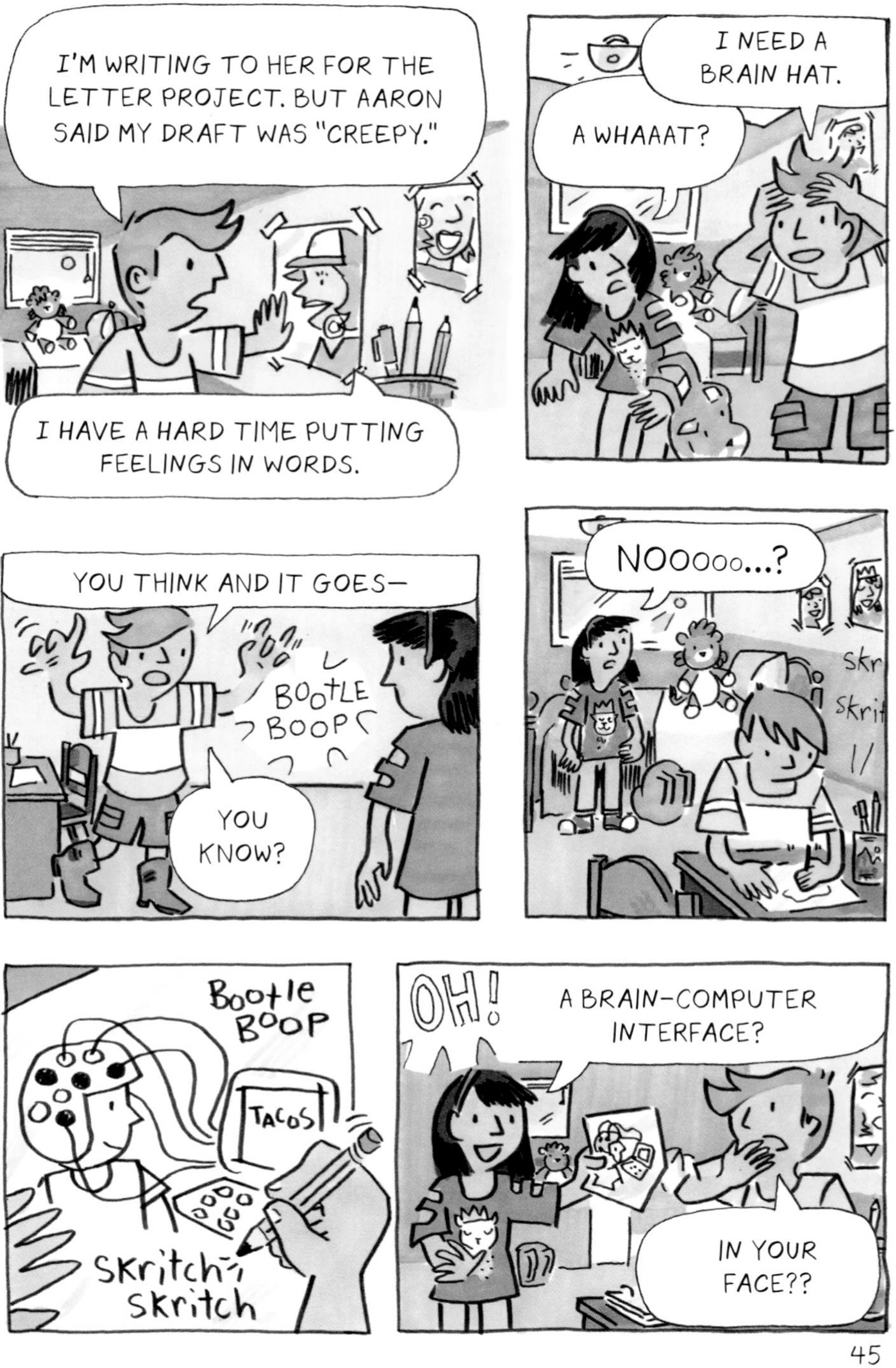
I'M WRITING TO HER FOR THE LETTER PROJECT. BUT AARON SAID MY DRAFT WAS "CREEPY."
I HAVE A HARD TIME PUTTING FEELINGS IN WORDS.
I NEED A BRAIN HAT.
A WHAAAT?
YOU THINK AND IT GOES—
BOOTLE BOOP
YOU KNOW?
NOOooo...?
Bootle BOOP
TACOS
Skritch Skritch
OH!
A BRAIN-COMPUTER INTERFACE?
IN YOUR FACE??

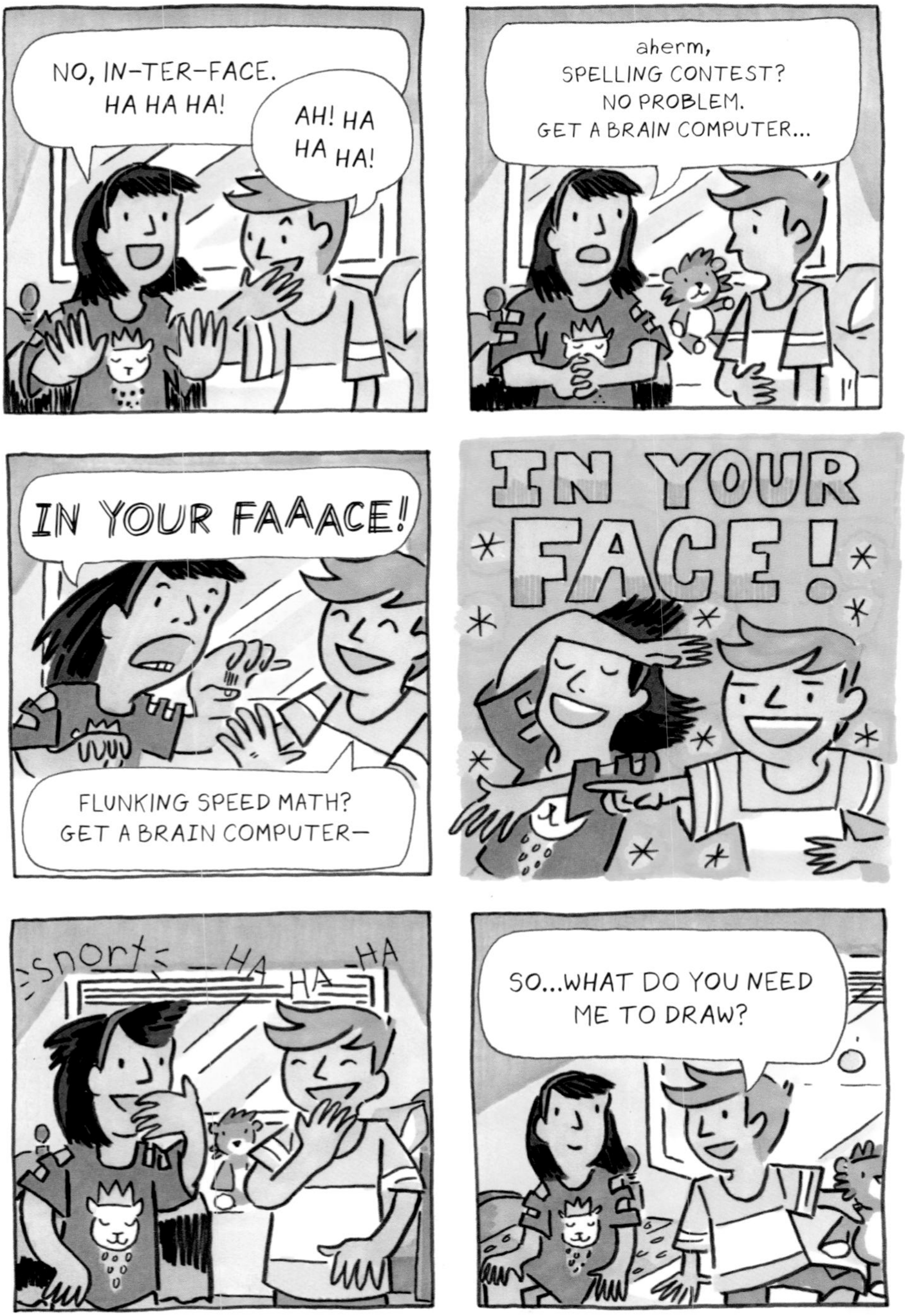
NO, IN-TER-FACE. HA HA HA!
AH! HA HA HA!
aherm, SPELLING CONTEST? NO PROBLEM. GET A BRAIN COMPUTER...
IN YOUR FAAACE!
FLUNKING SPEED MATH? GET A BRAIN COMPUTER—
IN YOUR FACE!
snort
HA HA HA
SO...WHAT DO YOU NEED ME TO DRAW?

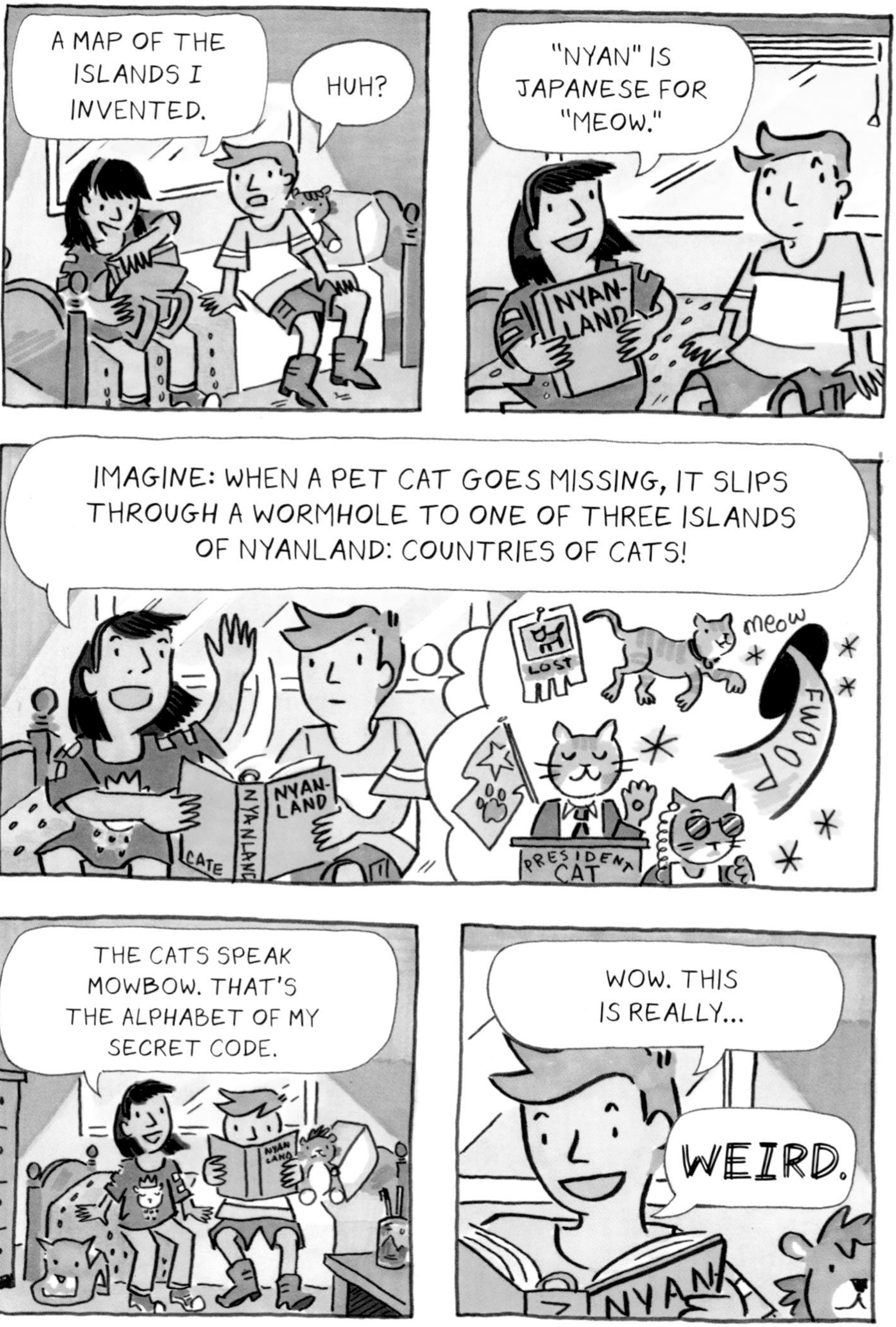

A MAP OF THE ISLANDS I INVENTED.
HUH?
"NYAN" IS JAPANESE FOR "MEOW."
NYAN-LAND
IMAGINE: WHEN A PET CAT GOES MISSING, IT SLIPS THROUGH A WORMHOLE TO ONE OF THREE ISLANDS OF NYANLAND: COUNTRIES OF CATS!
LOST
meow
FWOOP
NYAN-LAND
NYANLAND
CATE
PRESIDENT CAT
THE CATS SPEAK MOWBOW. THAT'S THE ALPHABET OF MY SECRET CODE.
WOW. THIS IS REALLY...
WEIRD.

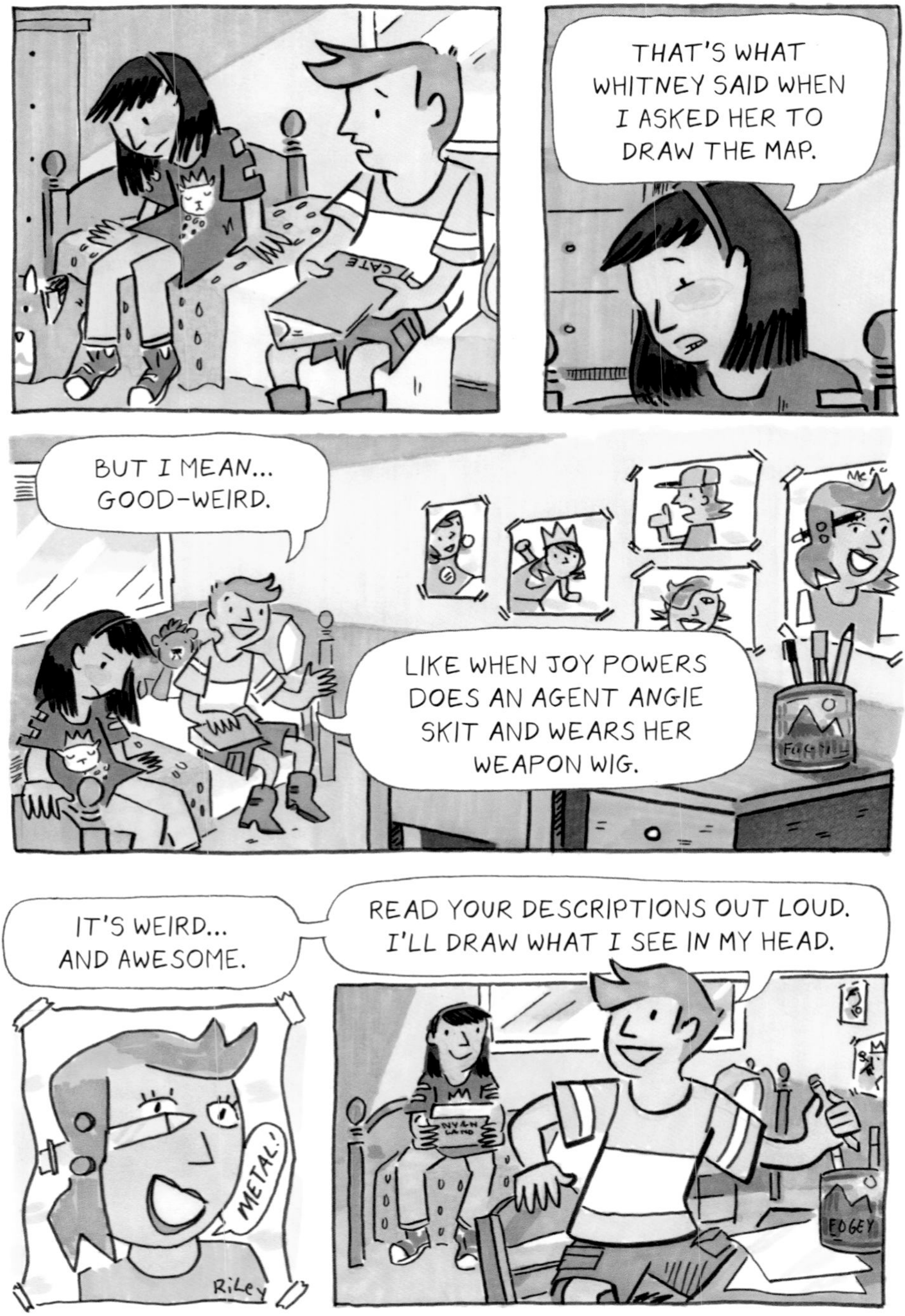
CATE
THAT'S WHAT WHITNEY SAID WHEN I ASKED HER TO DRAW THE MAP.
BUT I MEAN... GOOD-WEIRD.
LIKE WHEN JOY POWERS DOES AN AGENT ANGIE SKIT AND WEARS HER WEAPON WIG.
IT'S WEIRD... AND AWESOME.
READ YOUR DESCRIPTIONS OUT LOUD. I'LL DRAW WHAT I SEE IN MY HEAD.
METAL!
RiLey
FOGEY

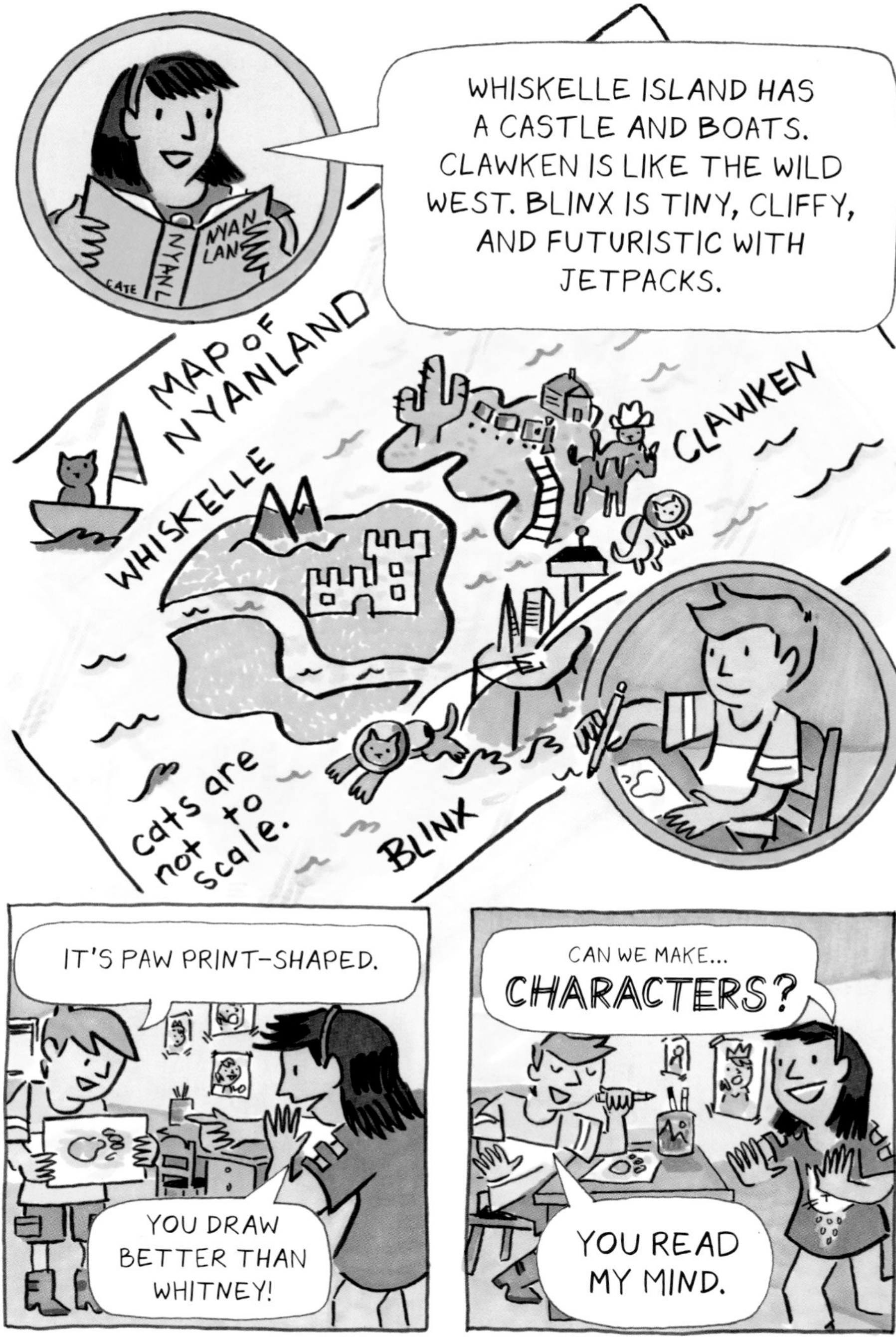
WHISKELLE ISLAND HAS A CASTLE AND BOATS. CLAWKEN IS LIKE THE WILD WEST. BLINX IS TINY, CLIFFY, AND FUTURISTIC WITH JETPACKS.
NYANLAND
NYAN LAND
CATE
MAP OF NYANLAND
WHISKELLE
CLAWKEN
BLINX
cats are not to scale.
IT'S PAW PRINT–SHAPED.
YOU DRAW BETTER THAN WHITNEY!
CAN WE MAKE... CHARACTERS?
YOU READ MY MIND.

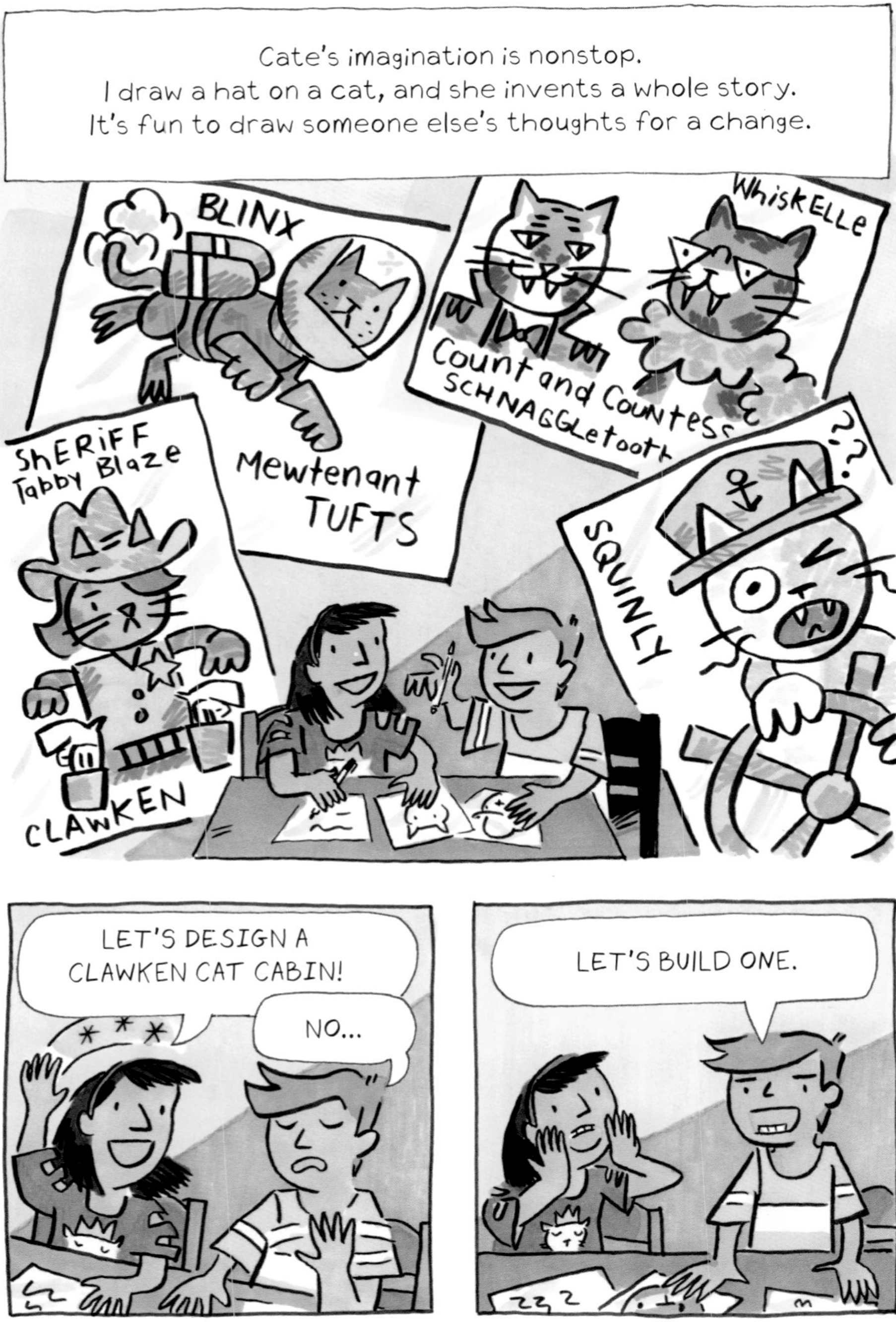
Cate's imagination is nonstop.
I draw a hat on a cat, and she invents a whole story.
It's fun to draw someone else's thoughts for a change.
BLINX
Count and Countess SCHNAGGLetooth
WhiskELLe
ShERiFF Tabby Blaze
Mewtenant TUFTS
SQUINLY
??
CLAWKEN
LET'S DESIGN A CLAWKEN CAT CABIN!
NO...
LET'S BUILD ONE.

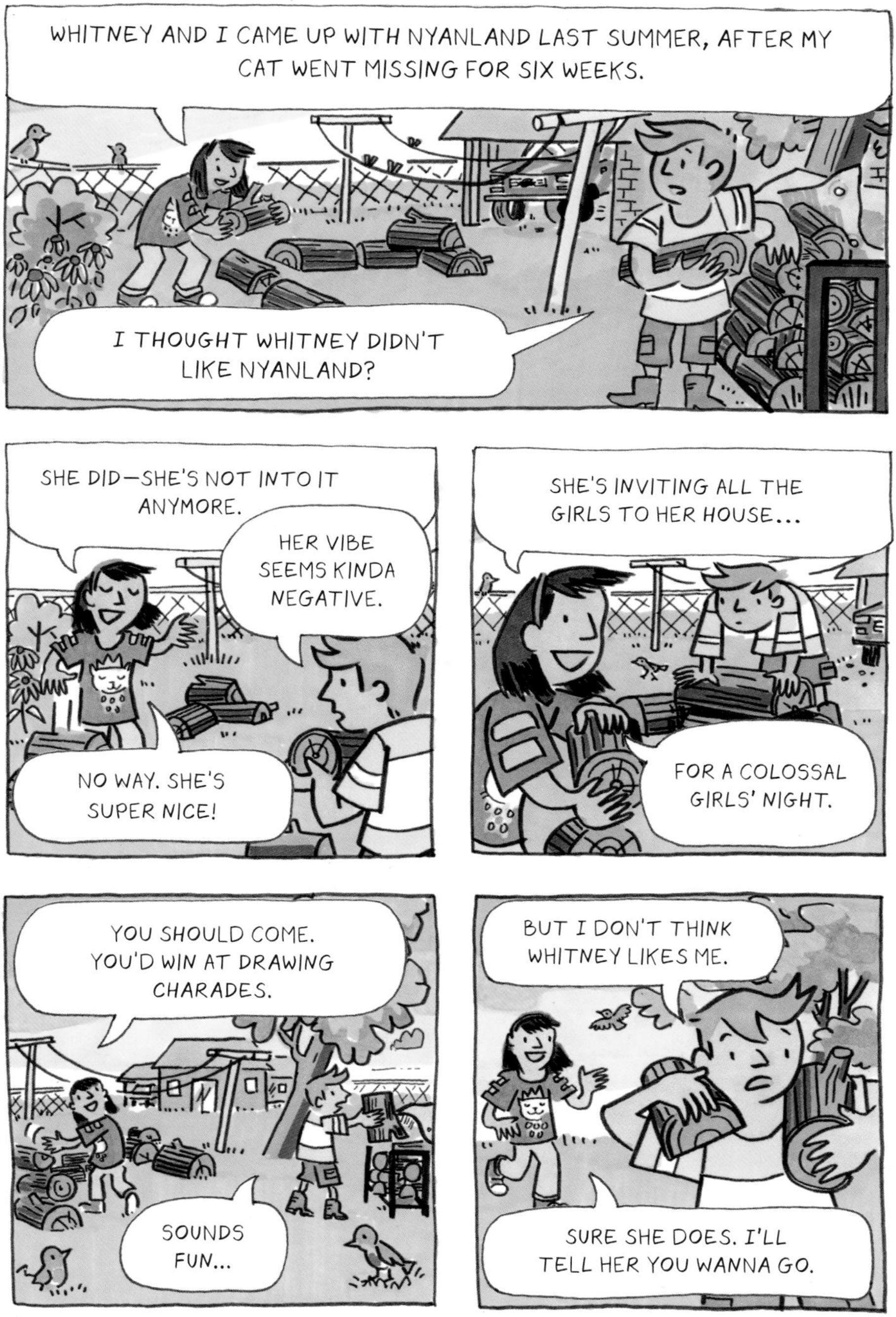
WHITNEY AND I CAME UP WITH NYANLAND LAST SUMMER, AFTER MY CAT WENT MISSING FOR SIX WEEKS.
I THOUGHT WHITNEY DIDN'T LIKE NYANLAND?
SHE DID—SHE'S NOT INTO IT ANYMORE.
HER VIBE SEEMS KINDA NEGATIVE.
NO WAY. SHE'S SUPER NICE!
SHE'S INVITING ALL THE GIRLS TO HER HOUSE...
FOR A COLOSSAL GIRLS' NIGHT.
YOU SHOULD COME. YOU'D WIN AT DRAWING CHARADES.
SOUNDS FUN...
BUT I DON'T THINK WHITNEY LIKES ME.
SURE SHE DOES. I'LL TELL HER YOU WANNA GO.

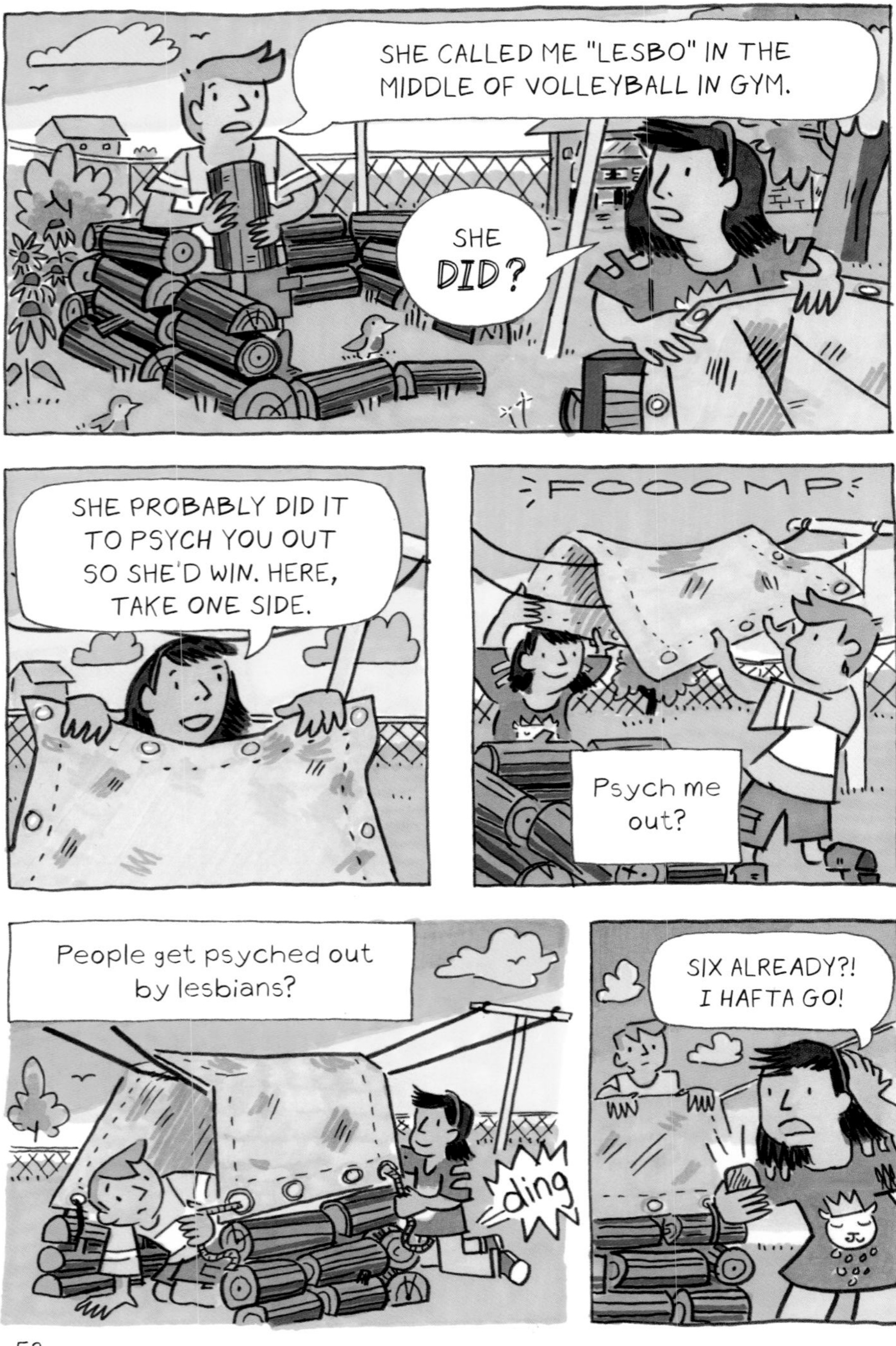

SHE CALLED ME "LESBO" IN THE MIDDLE OF VOLLEYBALL IN GYM.
SHE DID?
SHE PROBABLY DID IT TO PSYCH YOU OUT SO SHE'D WIN. HERE, TAKE ONE SIDE.
FOOOOMP
Psych me out?
People get psyched out by lesbians?
ding
SIX ALREADY?! I HAFTA GO!

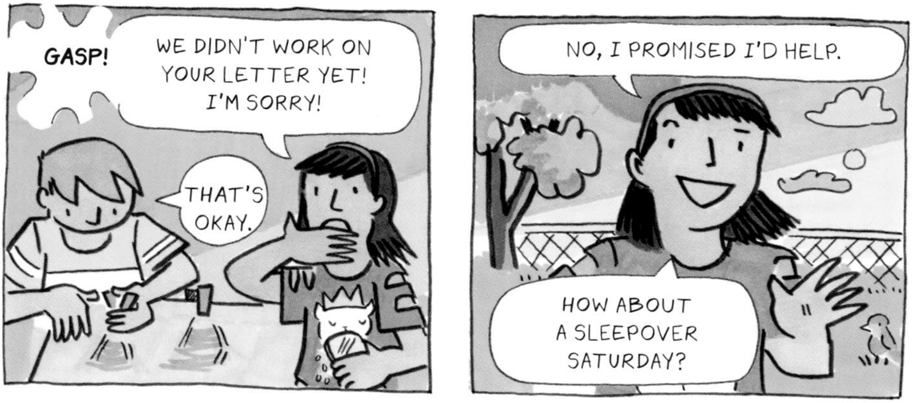
GASP!
WE DIDN'T WORK ON YOUR LETTER YET! I'M SORRY!
THAT'S OKAY.
NO, I PROMISED I'D HELP.
HOW ABOUT A SLEEPOVER SATURDAY?

If Mom is right and friendship is like a trapeze act—

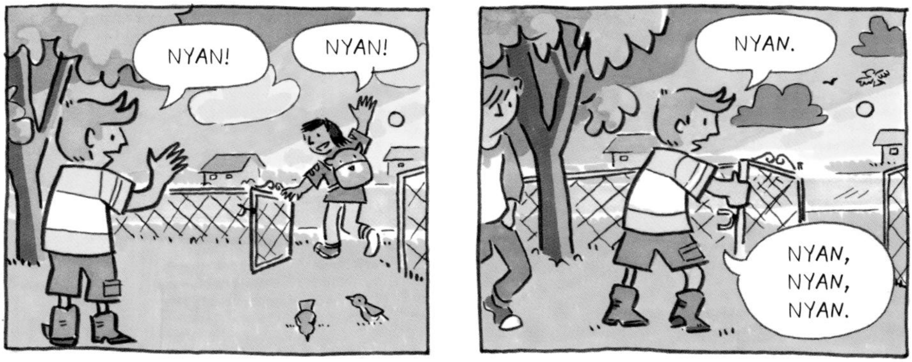
NYAN!
NYAN!
NYAN.
NYAN, NYAN, NYAN.

I'm starting to think Cate gets me.

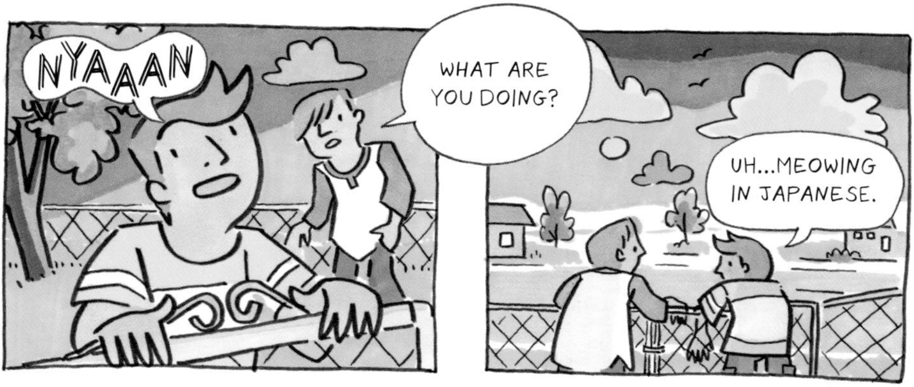
NYAAAN
WHAT ARE YOU DOING?
UH...MEOWING IN JAPANESE.

But I also kinda wish I had a safety net.

CHAPTER 6

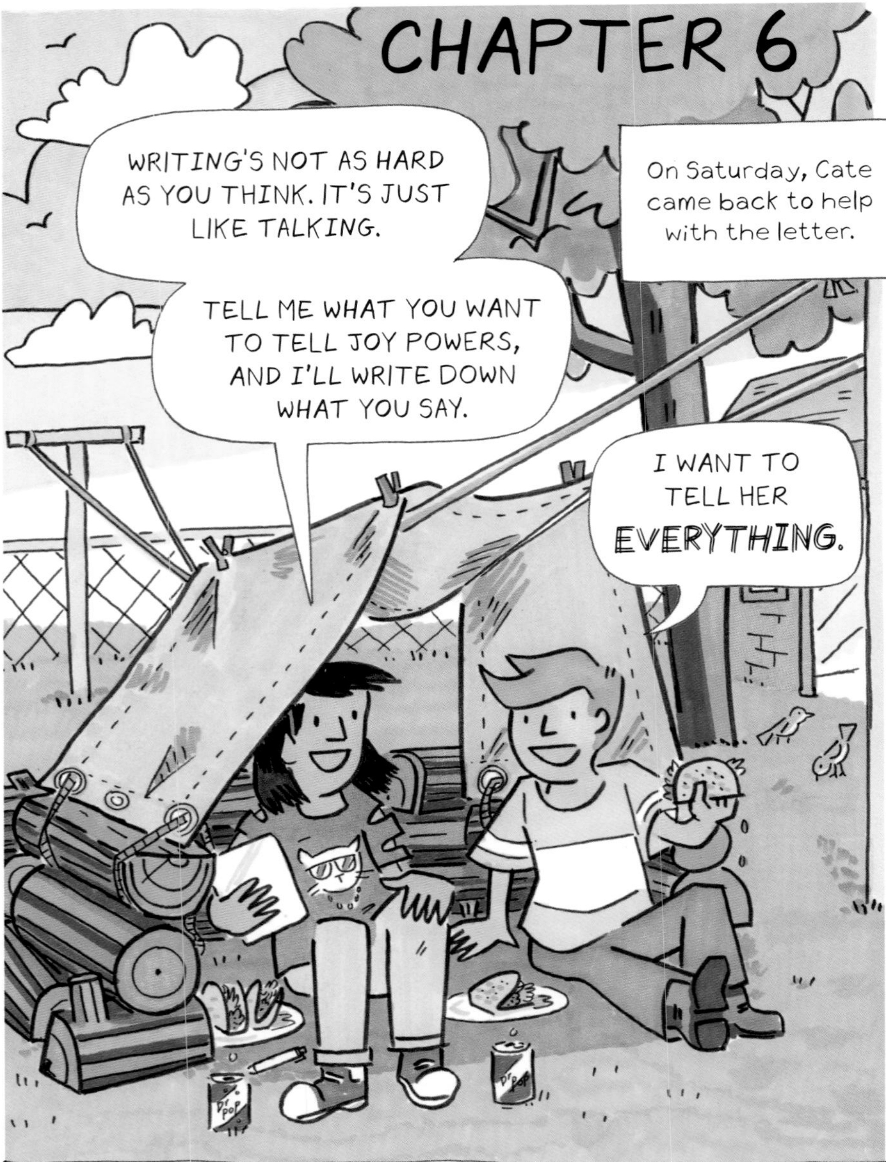

On Saturday, Cate came back to help with the letter.
WRITING'S NOT AS HARD AS YOU THINK. IT'S JUST LIKE TALKING.
TELL ME WHAT YOU WANT TO TELL JOY POWERS, AND I'LL WRITE DOWN WHAT YOU SAY.
I WANT TO TELL HER EVERYTHING.
Dr POP
Dr POP

Most kids in class don't listen when I start talking about Joy Powers, but Cate is different.

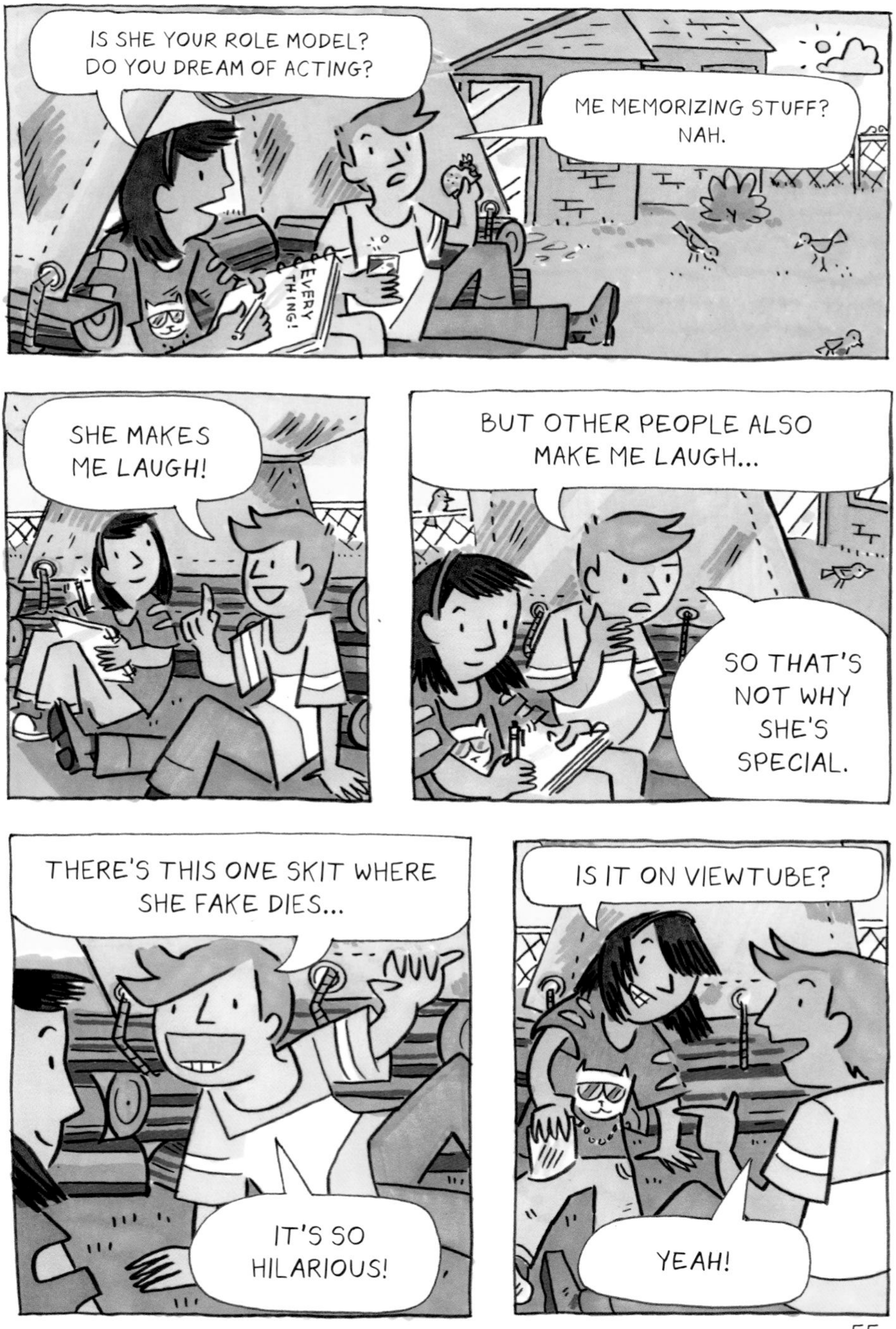
IS SHE YOUR ROLE MODEL? DO YOU DREAM OF ACTING?
ME MEMORIZING STUFF? NAH.
EVERYTHING!
SHE MAKES ME LAUGH!
BUT OTHER PEOPLE ALSO MAKE ME LAUGH...
SO THAT'S NOT WHY SHE'S SPECIAL.
THERE'S THIS ONE SKIT WHERE SHE FAKE DIES...
IT'S SO HILARIOUS!
IS IT ON VIEWTUBE?
YEAH!

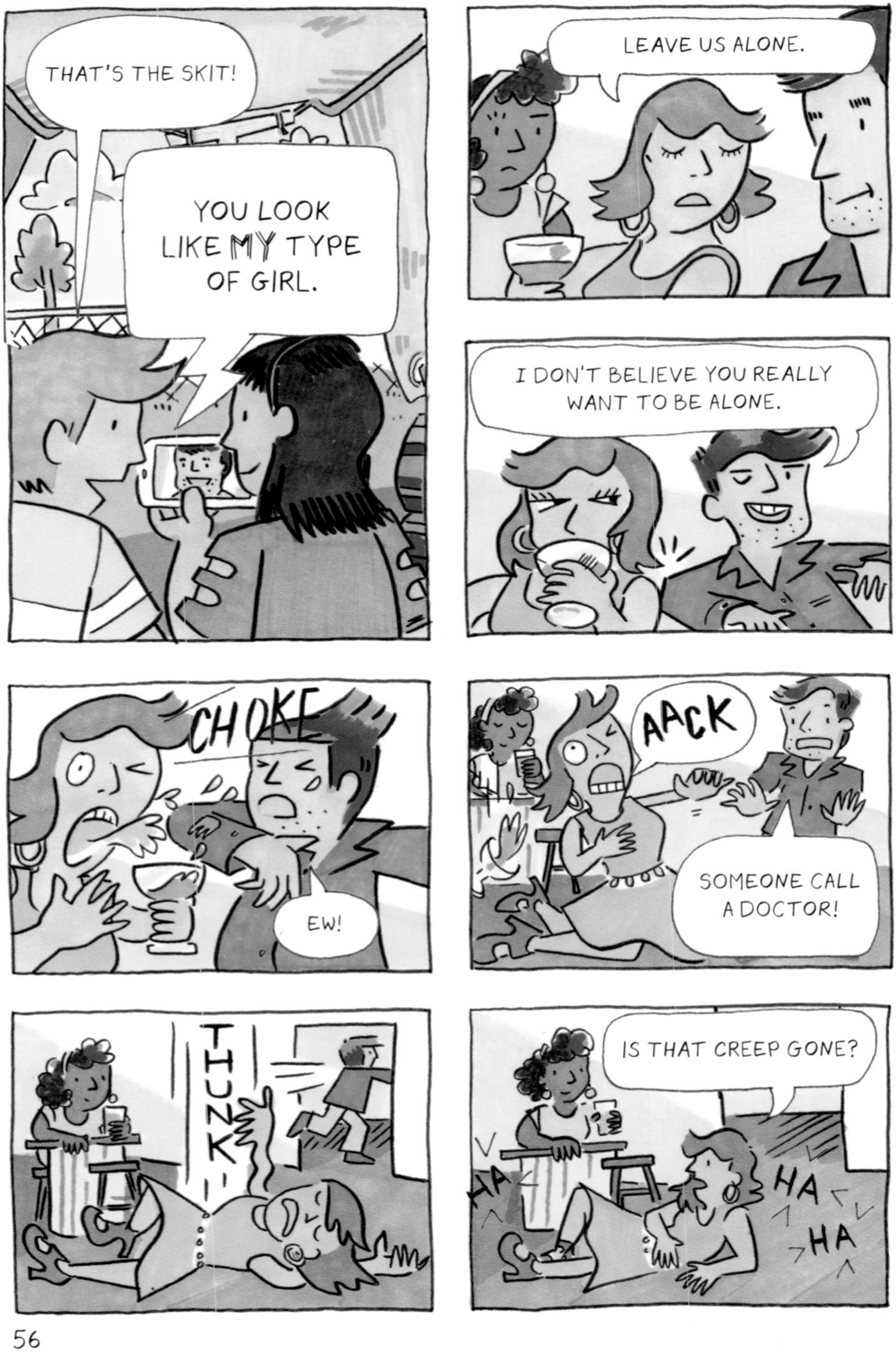
THAT'S THE SKIT!
YOU LOOK LIKE MY TYPE OF GIRL.
LEAVE US ALONE.
I DON'T BELIEVE YOU REALLY WANT TO BE ALONE.
CHOKE
EW!
AACK
SOMEONE CALL A DOCTOR!
THUNK
IS THAT CREEP GONE?
HA
HA
HA

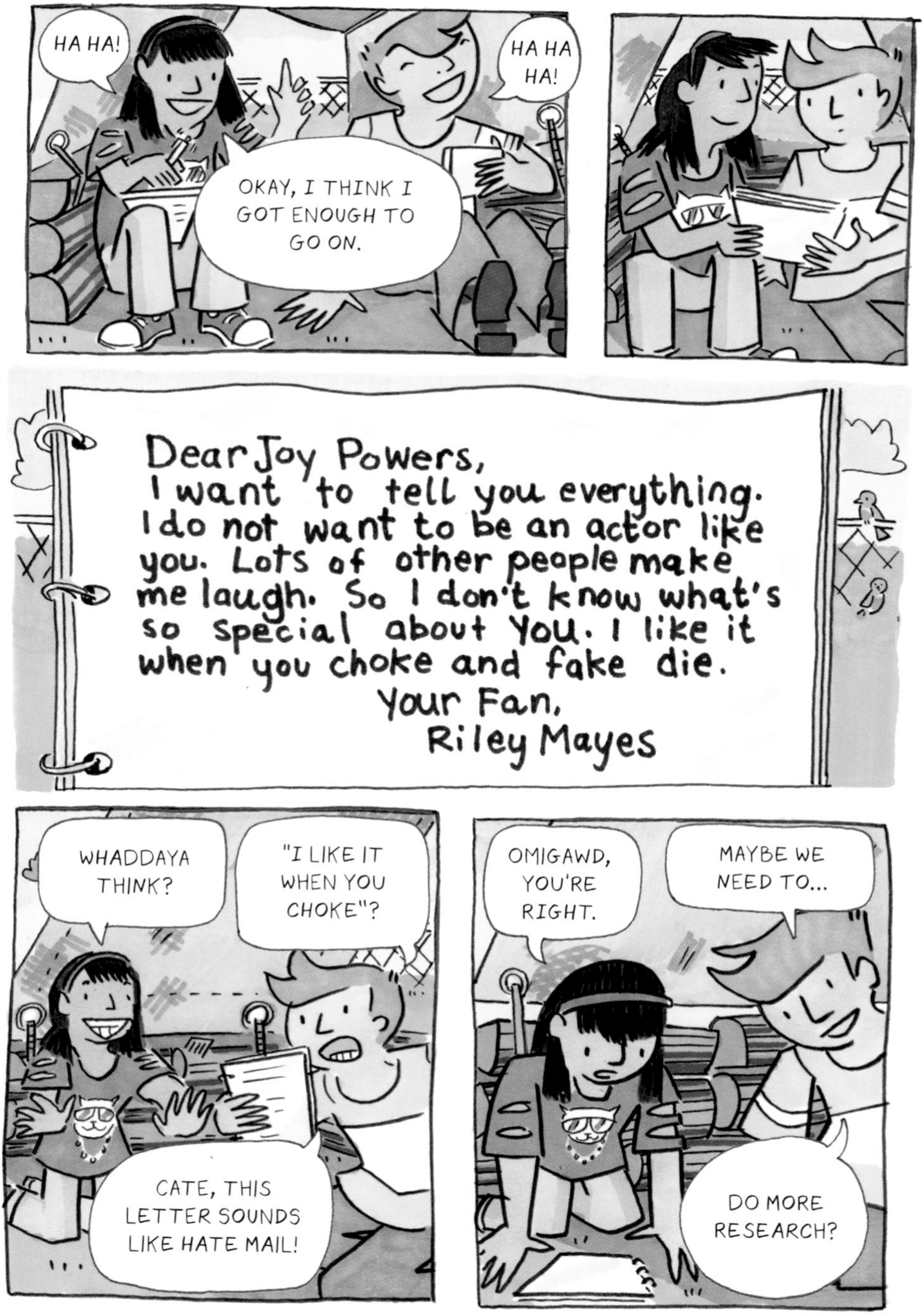
HA HA!
HA HA HA!
OKAY, I THINK I GOT ENOUGH TO GO ON.
Dear Joy Powers,
I want to tell you everything. I do not want to be an actor like you. Lots of other people make me laugh. So I don't know what's so special about You. I like it when you choke and fake die.
Your Fan,
Riley Mayes
WHADDAYA THINK?
"I LIKE IT WHEN YOU CHOKE"?
CATE, THIS LETTER SOUNDS LIKE HATE MAIL!
OMIGAWD, YOU'RE RIGHT.
MAYBE WE NEED TO...
DO MORE RESEARCH?

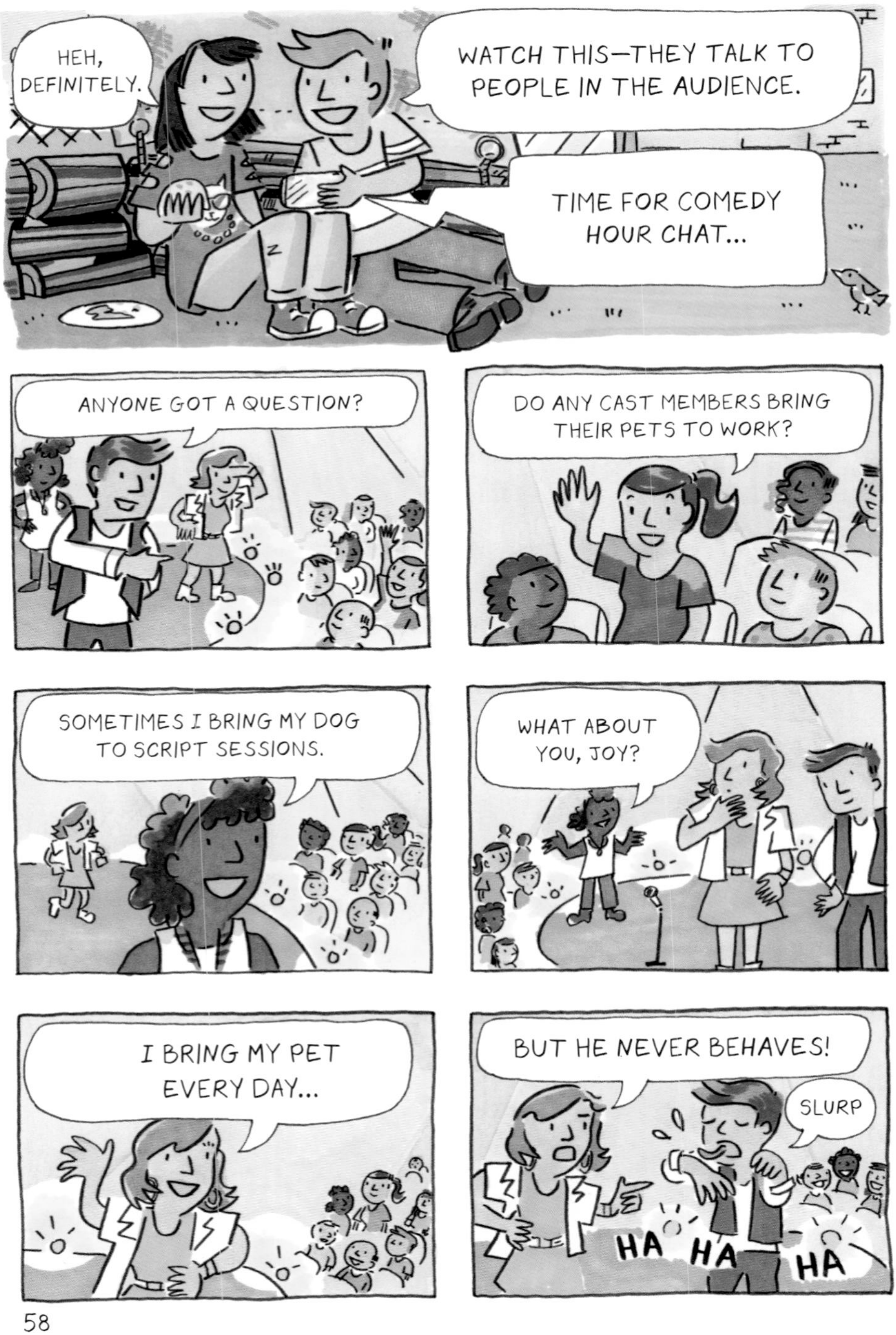
HEH, DEFINITELY.
WATCH THIS—THEY TALK TO PEOPLE IN THE AUDIENCE.
TIME FOR COMEDY HOUR CHAT...
ANYONE GOT A QUESTION?
DO ANY CAST MEMBERS BRING THEIR PETS TO WORK?
SOMETIMES I BRING MY DOG TO SCRIPT SESSIONS.
WHAT ABOUT YOU, JOY?
I BRING MY PET EVERY DAY...
BUT HE NEVER BEHAVES!
SLURP
HA HA HA

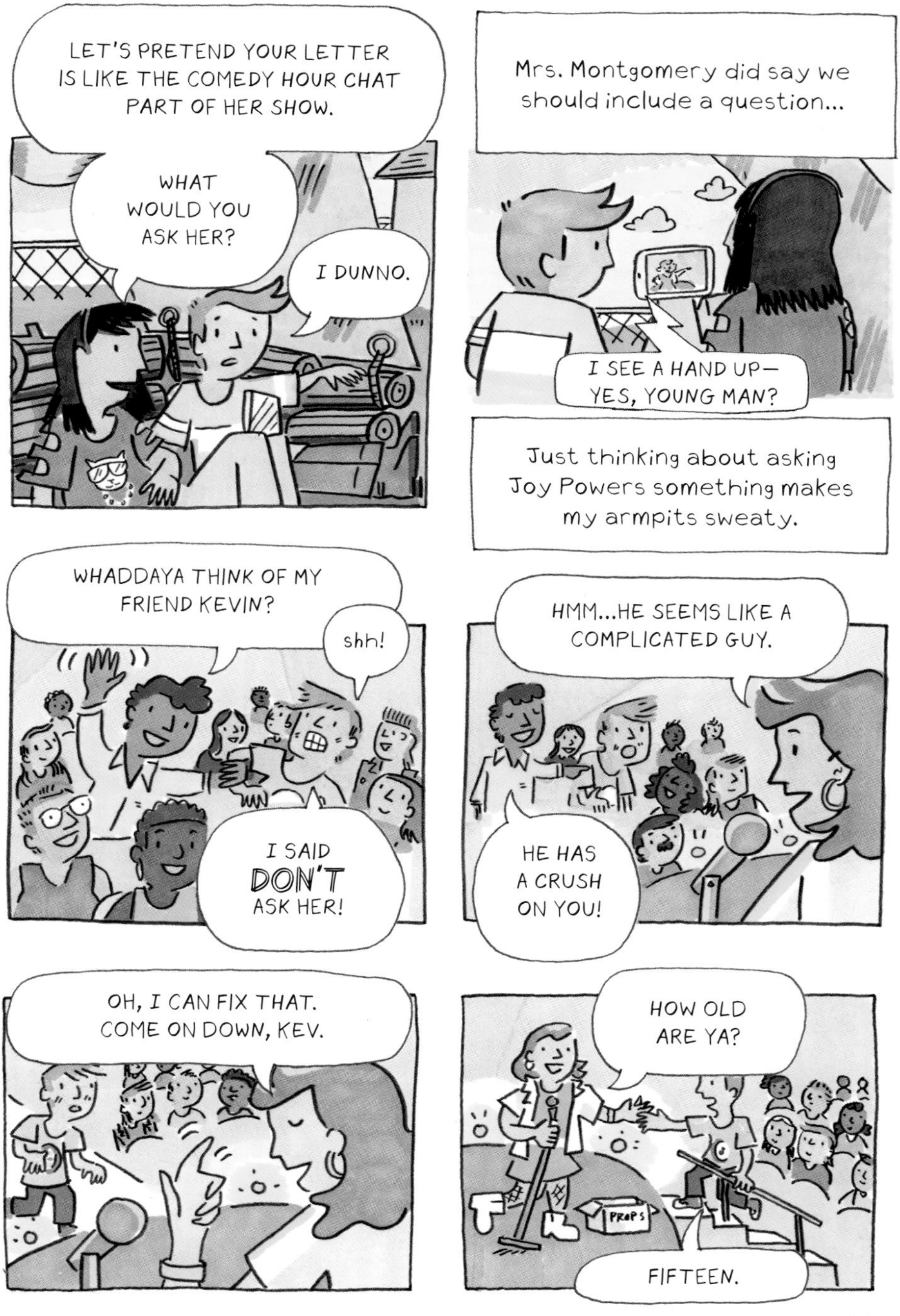
LET'S PRETEND YOUR LETTER IS LIKE THE COMEDY HOUR CHAT PART OF HER SHOW.
WHAT WOULD YOU ASK HER?
I DUNNO.
Mrs. Montgomery did say we should include a question...
I SEE A HAND UP— YES, YOUNG MAN?
Just thinking about asking Joy Powers something makes my armpits sweaty.
WHADDAYA THINK OF MY FRIEND KEVIN?
shh!
I SAID **DON'T** ASK HER!
HMM...HE SEEMS LIKE A COMPLICATED GUY.
HE HAS A CRUSH ON YOU!
OH, I CAN FIX THAT. COME ON DOWN, KEV.
HOW OLD ARE YA?
PROPS
FIFTEEN.

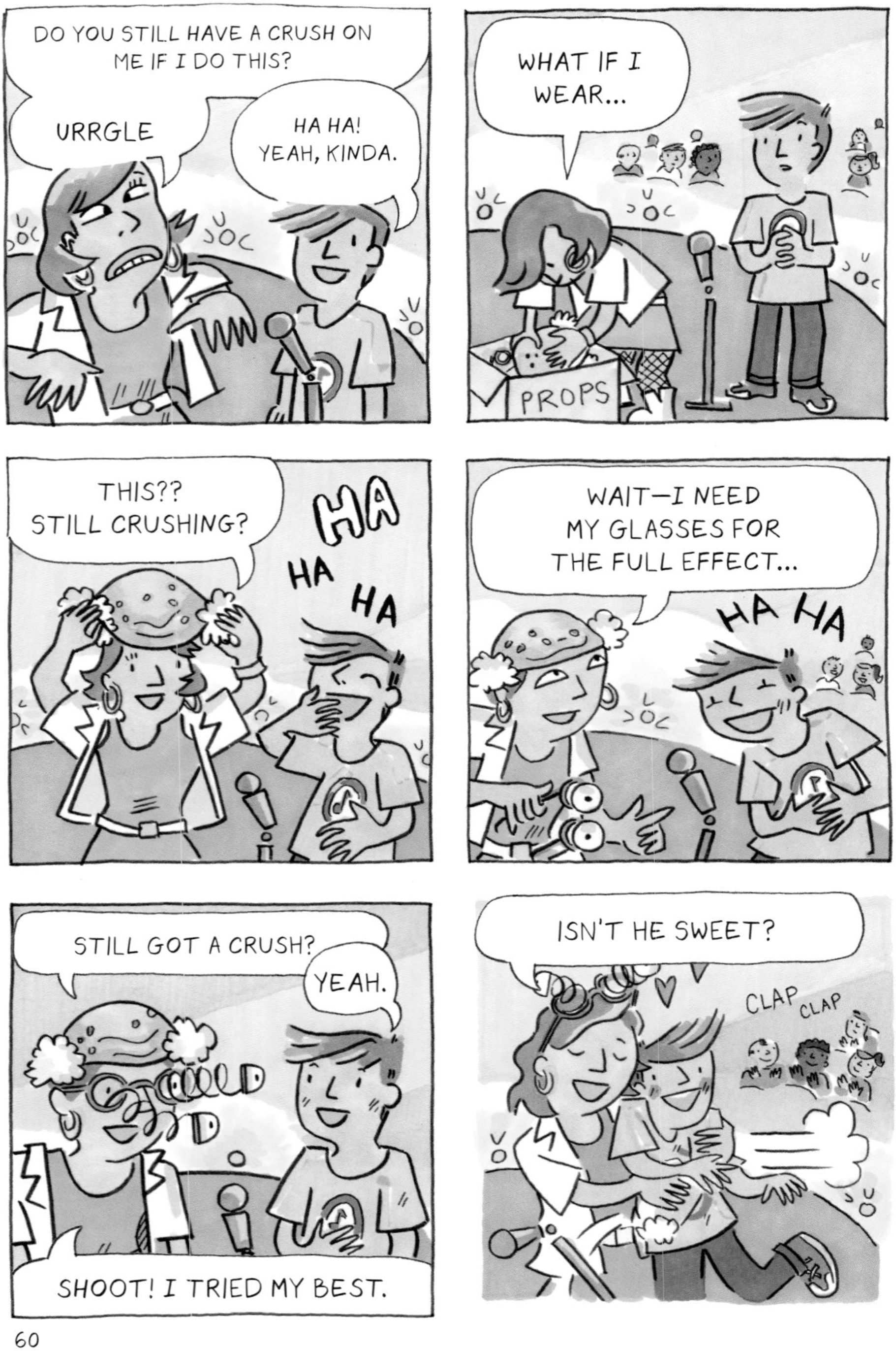
DO YOU STILL HAVE A CRUSH ON ME IF I DO THIS?
URRGLE
HA HA! YEAH, KINDA.
WHAT IF I WEAR...
PROPS
THIS?? STILL CRUSHING?
HA
HA
HA
WAIT—I NEED MY GLASSES FOR THE FULL EFFECT...
HA HA
STILL GOT A CRUSH?
YEAH.
SHOOT! I TRIED MY BEST.
ISN'T HE SWEET?
CLAP
CLAP

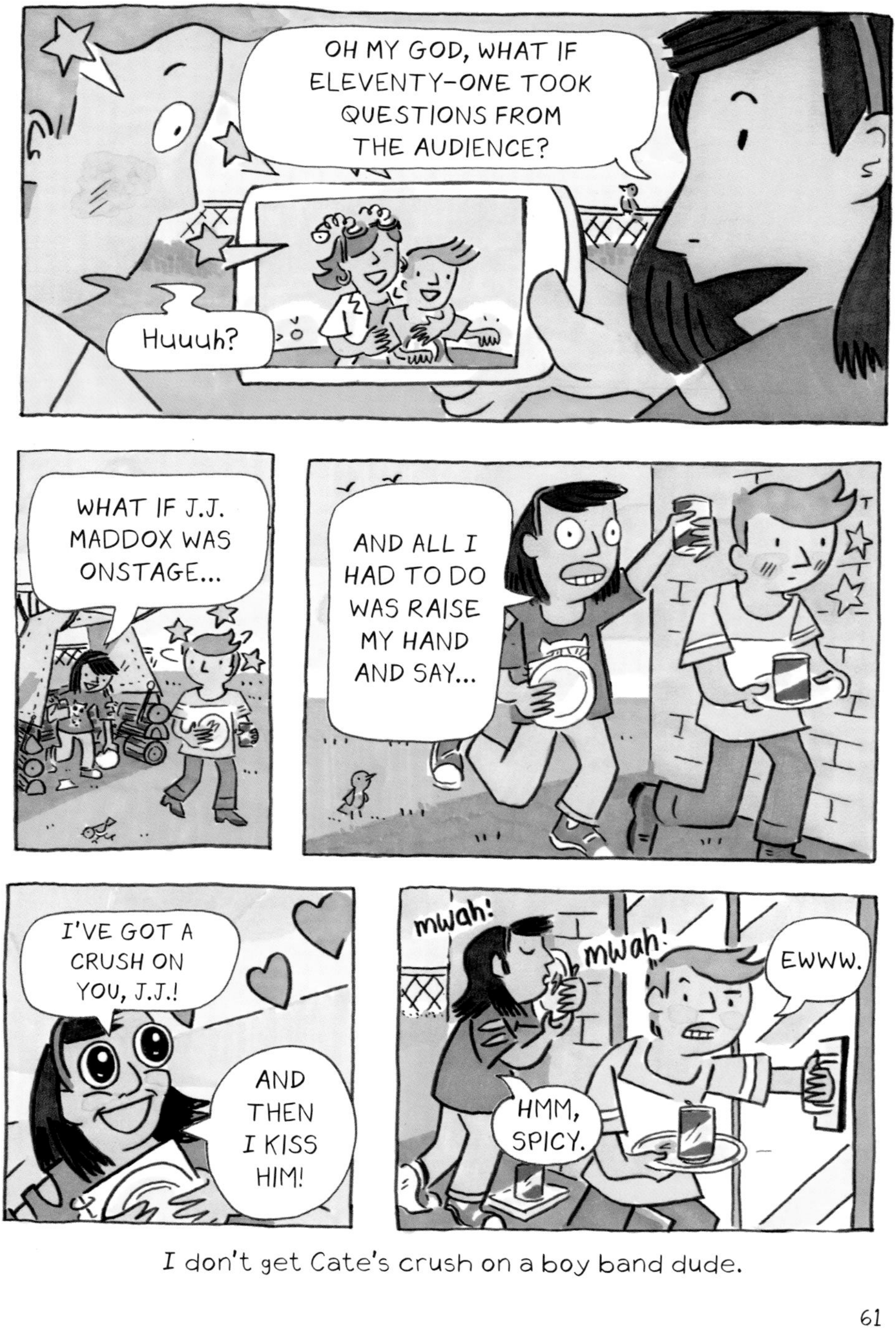
OH MY GOD, WHAT IF ELEVENTY-ONE TOOK QUESTIONS FROM THE AUDIENCE?
Huuuh?
WHAT IF J.J. MADDOX WAS ONSTAGE...
AND ALL I HAD TO DO WAS RAISE MY HAND AND SAY...
I'VE GOT A CRUSH ON YOU, J.J.!
AND THEN I KISS HIM!
mwah!
mwah!
EWWW.
HMM, SPICY.

I don't get Cate's crush on a boy band dude.

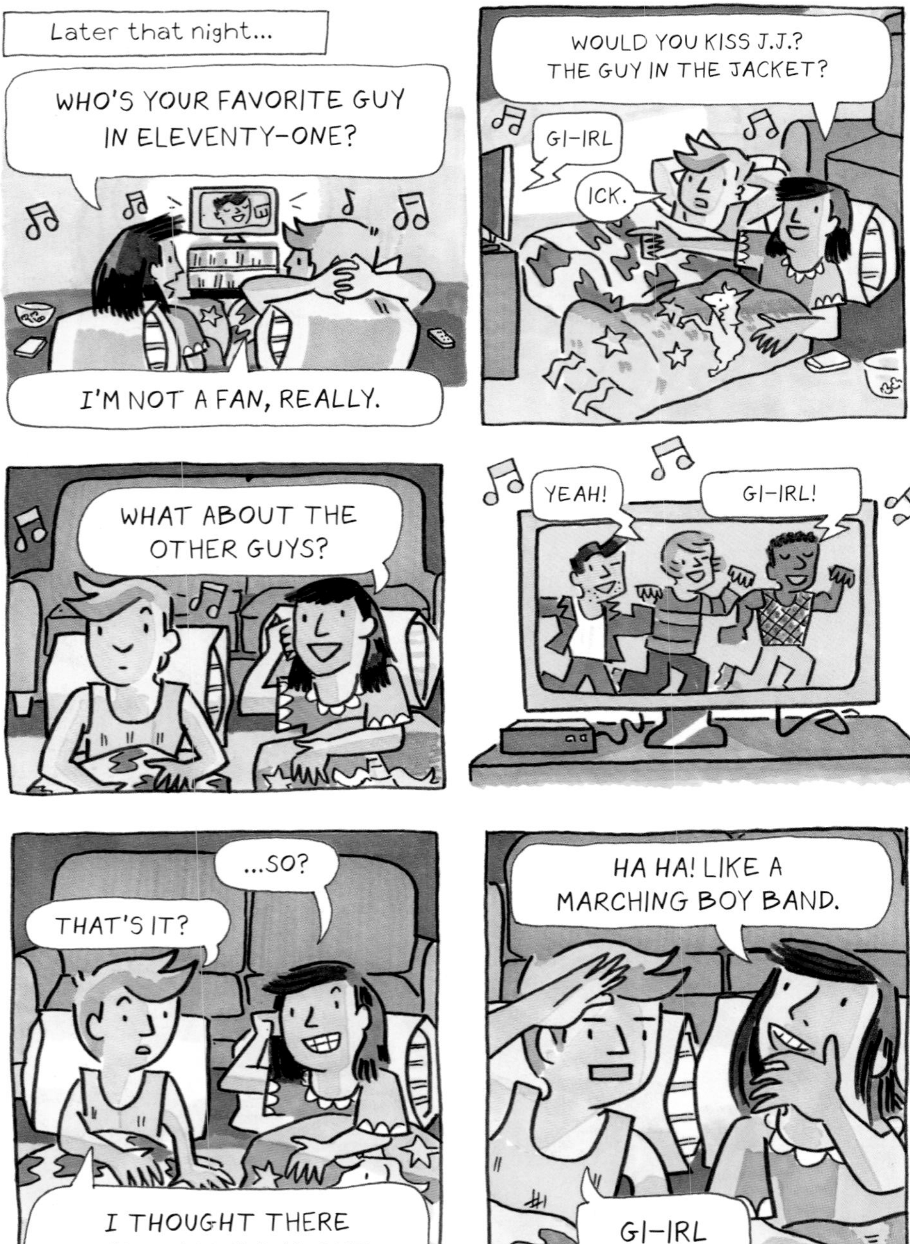
Later that night...
WHO'S YOUR FAVORITE GUY IN ELEVENTY-ONE?
I'M NOT A FAN, REALLY.
WOULD YOU KISS J.J.? THE GUY IN THE JACKET?
GI-IRL
ICK.
WHAT ABOUT THE OTHER GUYS?
YEAH!
GI-IRL!
...SO?
THAT'S IT?
I THOUGHT THERE WERE ELEVENTY-ONE OF THEM.
HA HA! LIKE A MARCHING BOY BAND.
GI-IRL YE-AH

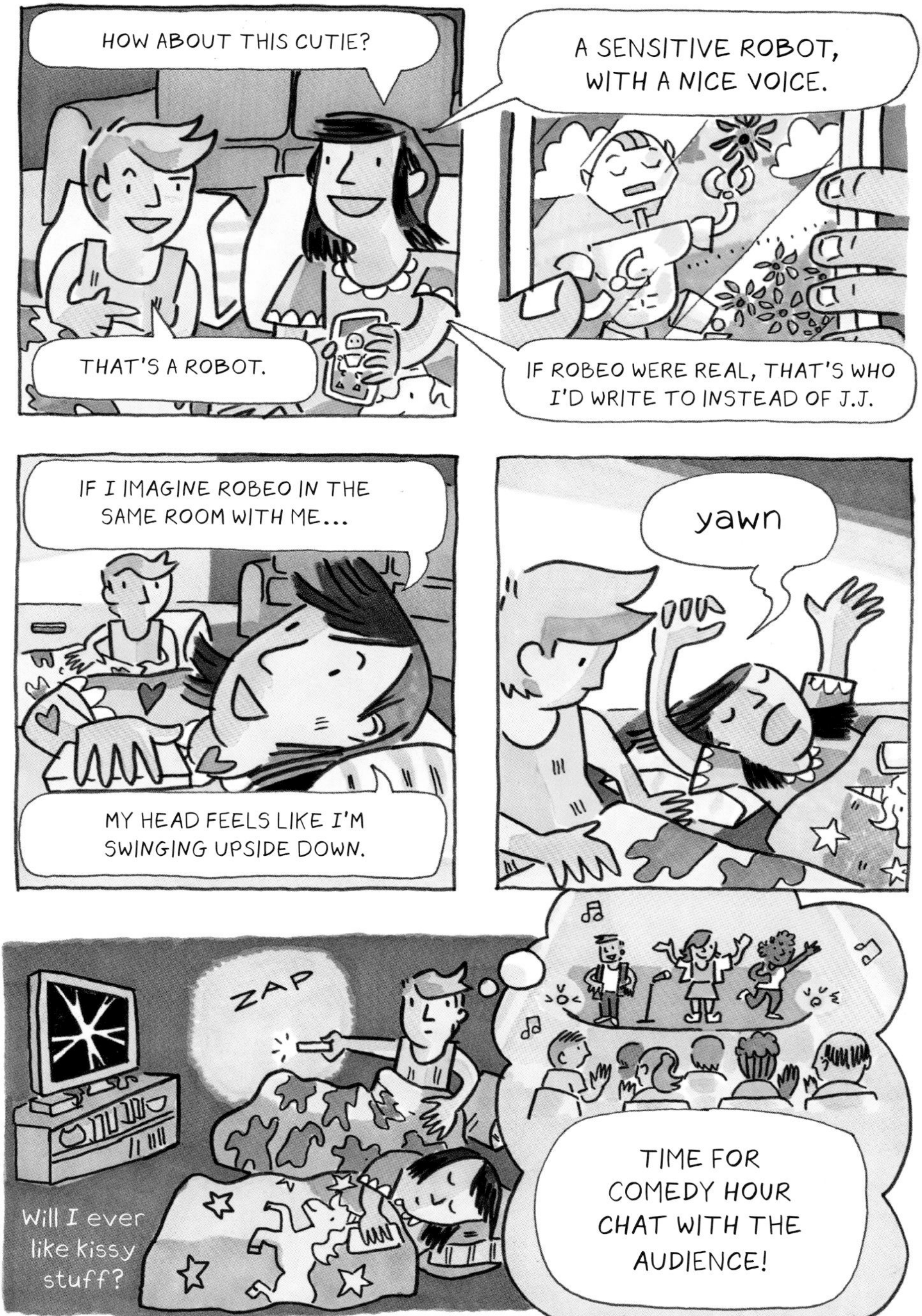

HOW ABOUT THIS CUTIE?
THAT'S A ROBOT.
A SENSITIVE ROBOT, WITH A NICE VOICE.
IF ROBEO WERE REAL, THAT'S WHO I'D WRITE TO INSTEAD OF J.J.
IF I IMAGINE ROBEO IN THE SAME ROOM WITH ME...
MY HEAD FEELS LIKE I'M SWINGING UPSIDE DOWN.
yawn
ZAP
Will I ever like kissy stuff?
TIME FOR COMEDY HOUR CHAT WITH THE AUDIENCE!

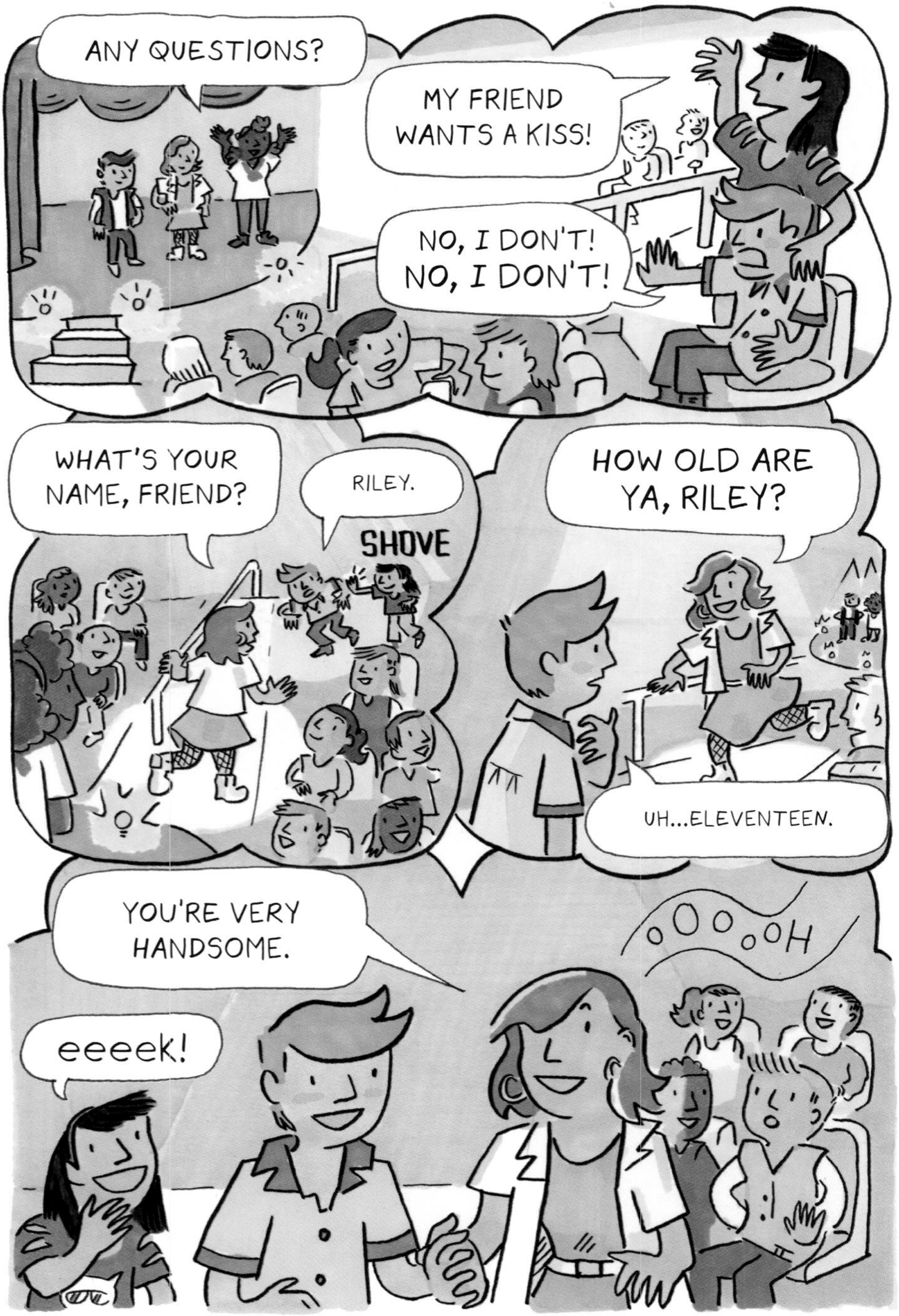
ANY QUESTIONS?
MY FRIEND WANTS A KISS!
NO, I DON'T! NO, I DON'T!
WHAT'S YOUR NAME, FRIEND?
RILEY.
SHOVE
HOW OLD ARE YA, RILEY?
UH...ELEVENTEEN.
YOU'RE VERY HANDSOME.
oOOooH
eeeek!

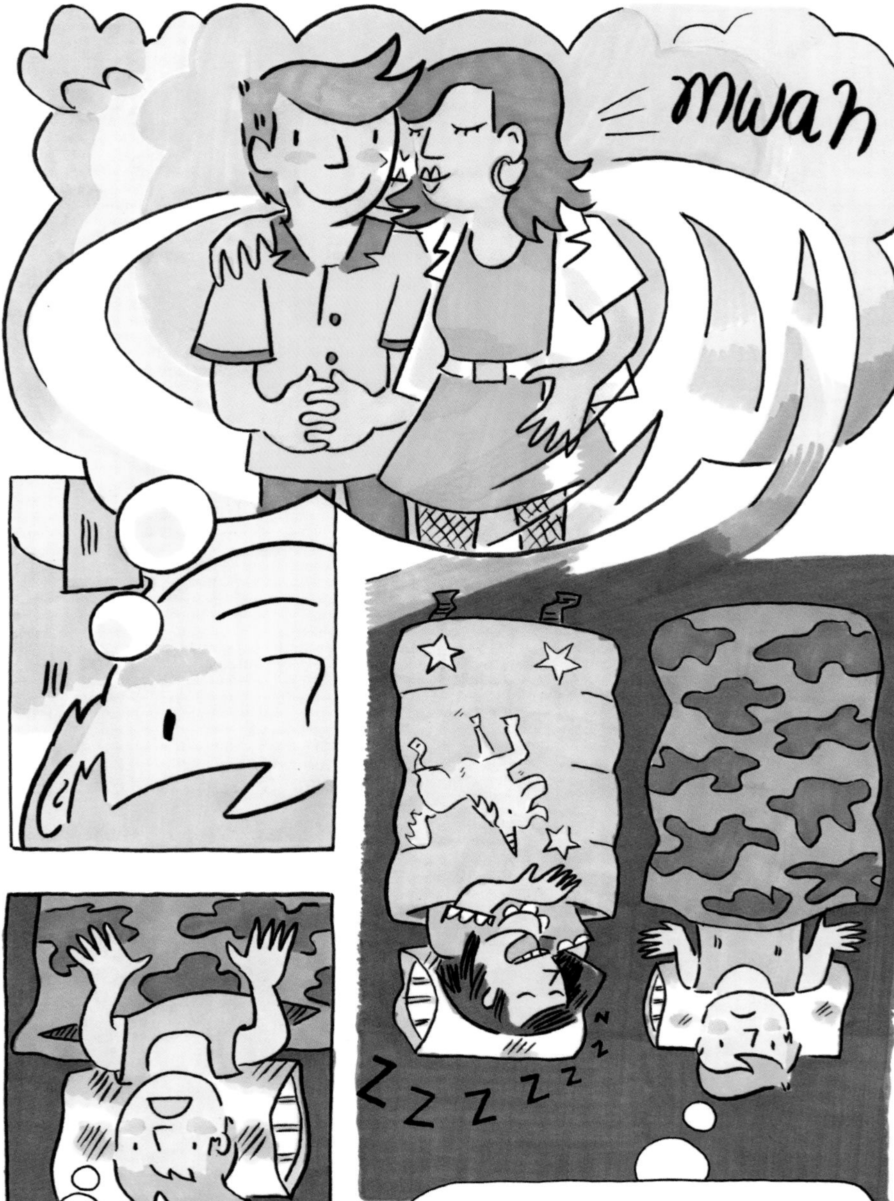
MWAH
ZZZZZZ
UH-OH.
I HAVE A CRUSH ON JOY POWERS!

CHAPTER 7

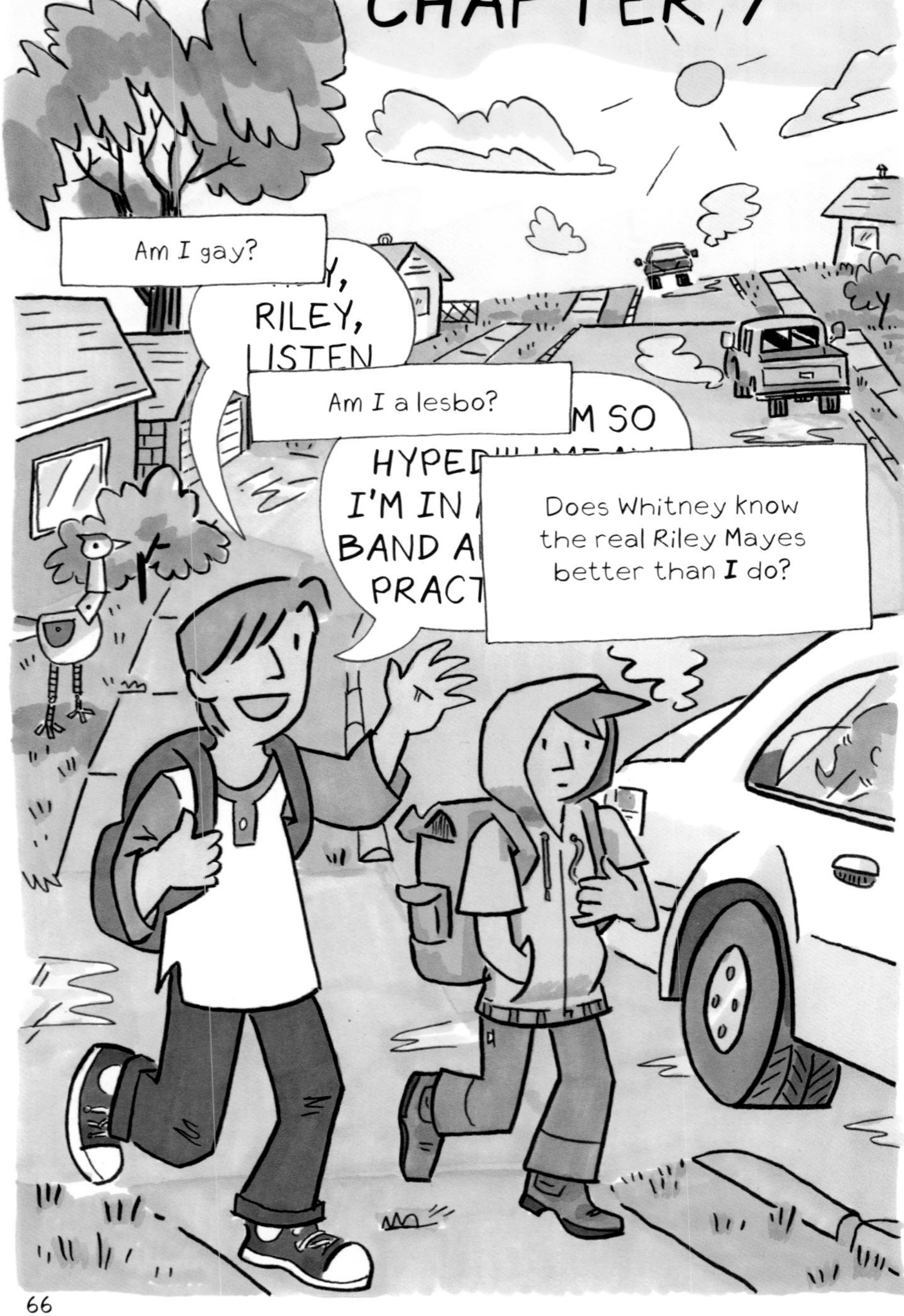
Am I gay?
RILEY, LISTEN
Am I a lesbo?
M SO HYPED I'M IN BAND A PRACT
Does Whitney know the real Riley Mayes better than **I** do?

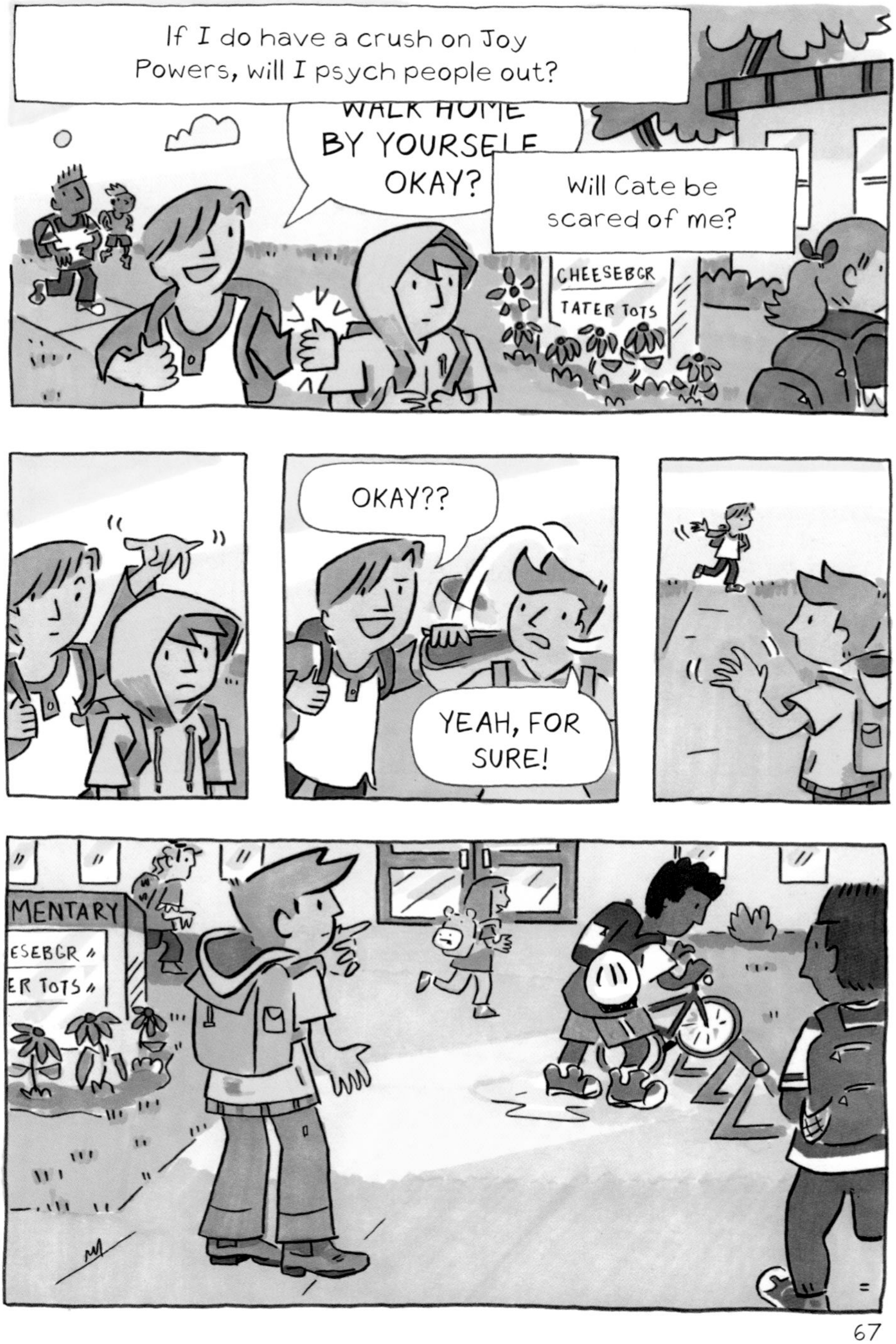
If I do have a crush on Joy Powers, will I psych people out?
WALK HOME BY YOURSELF OKAY?
Will Cate be scared of me?
CHEESEBGR
TATER TOTS
OKAY??
YEAH, FOR SURE!
MENTARY
ESEBGR
ER TOTS

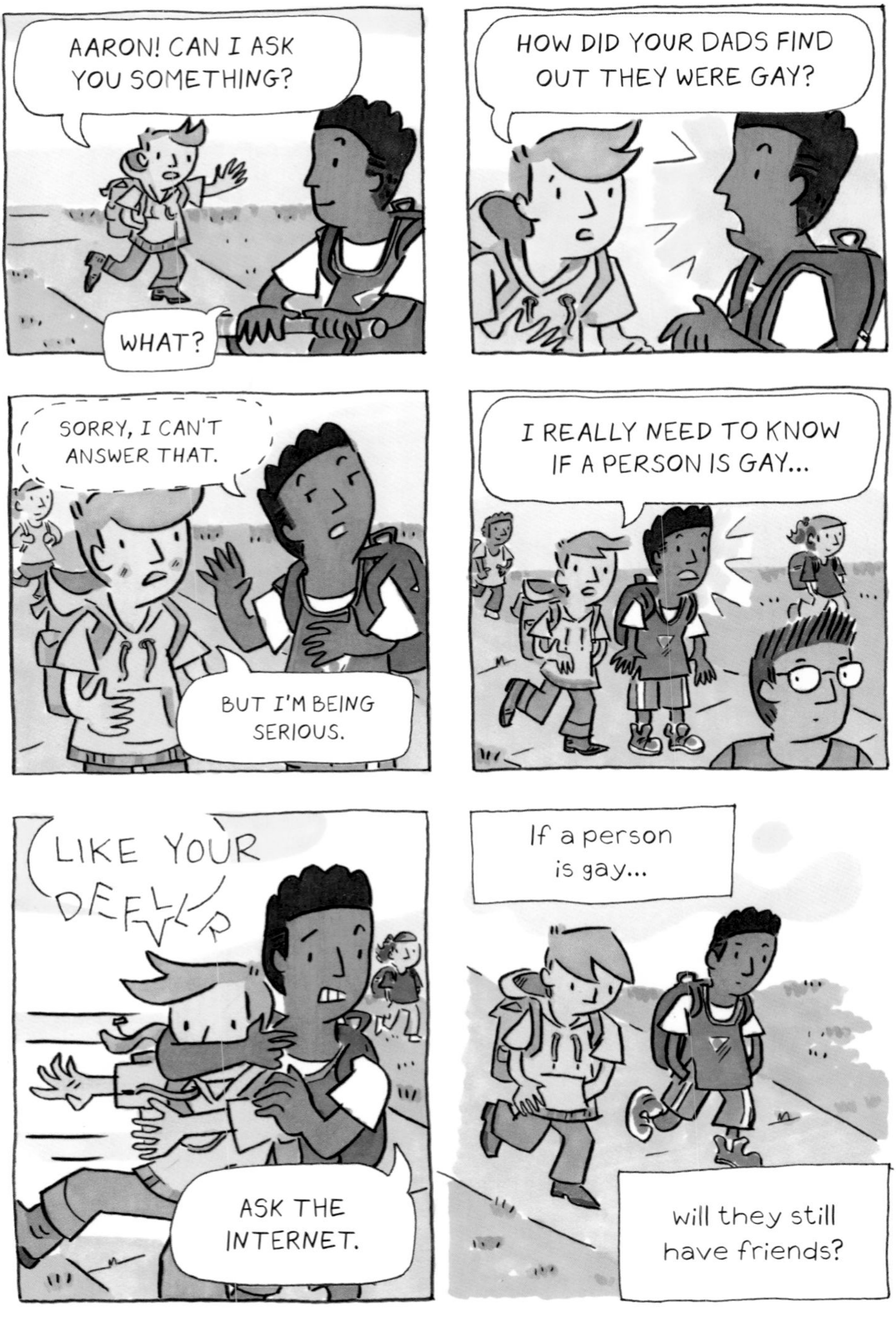
AARON! CAN I ASK YOU SOMETHING?
WHAT?
HOW DID YOUR DADS FIND OUT THEY WERE GAY?
SORRY, I CAN'T ANSWER THAT.
BUT I'M BEING SERIOUS.
I REALLY NEED TO KNOW IF A PERSON IS GAY...
LIKE YOUR
ASK THE INTERNET.
If a person is gay...
will they still have friends?

Mrs. M sent the whole class to the library.
I'm supposed to find a way to contact Joy Powers.

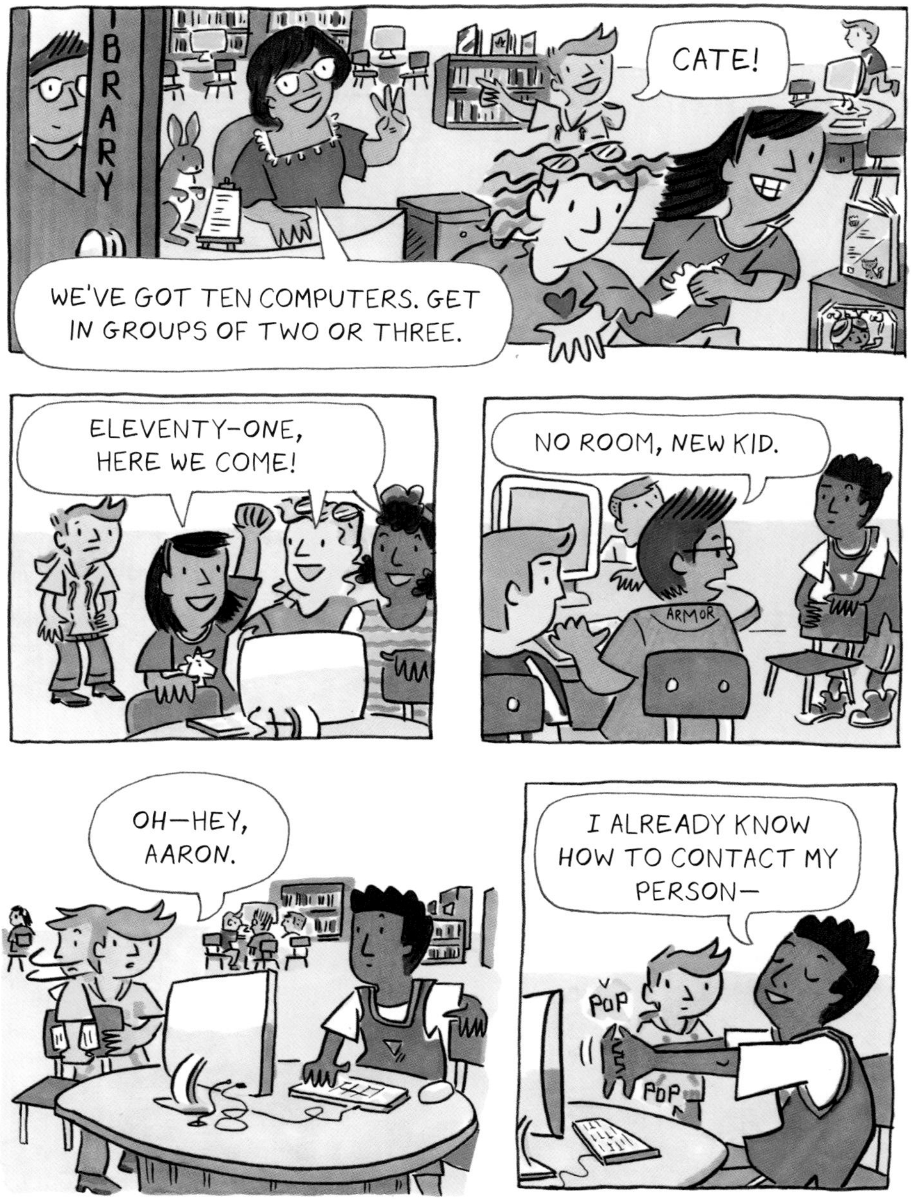
LIBRARY
CATE!
WE'VE GOT TEN COMPUTERS. GET IN GROUPS OF TWO OR THREE.
ELEVENTY-ONE, HERE WE COME!
NO ROOM, NEW KID.
ARMOR
OH—HEY, AARON.
I ALREADY KNOW HOW TO CONTACT MY PERSON—
POP
POP

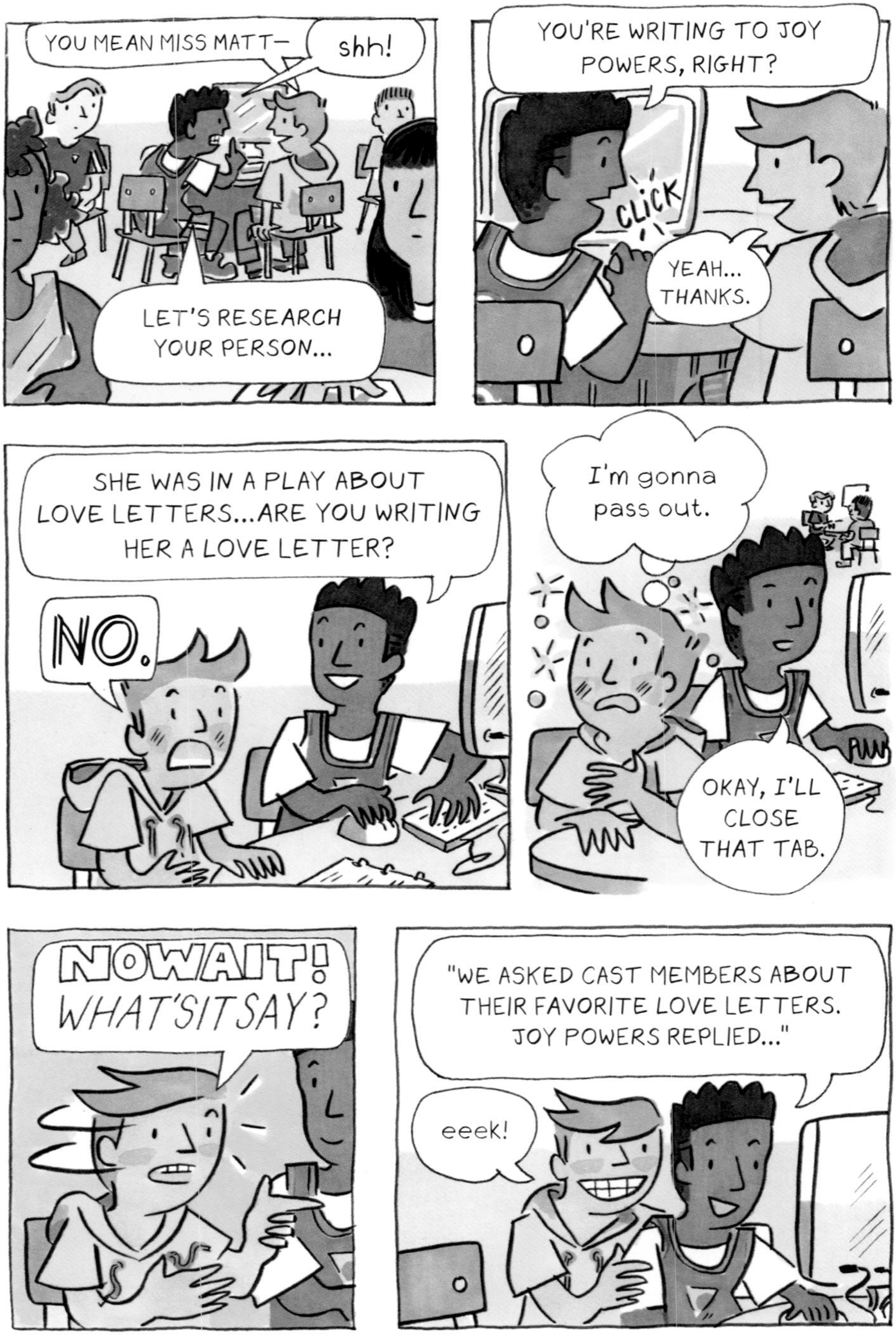
YOU MEAN MISS MATT—
shh!
LET'S RESEARCH YOUR PERSON...
YOU'RE WRITING TO JOY POWERS, RIGHT?
CLICK
YEAH... THANKS.
SHE WAS IN A PLAY ABOUT LOVE LETTERS...ARE YOU WRITING HER A LOVE LETTER?
NO.
I'm gonna pass out.
OKAY, I'LL CLOSE THAT TAB.
NO WAIT!
WHAT'S IT SAY?
"WE ASKED CAST MEMBERS ABOUT THEIR FAVORITE LOVE LETTERS. JOY POWERS REPLIED..."
eeek!

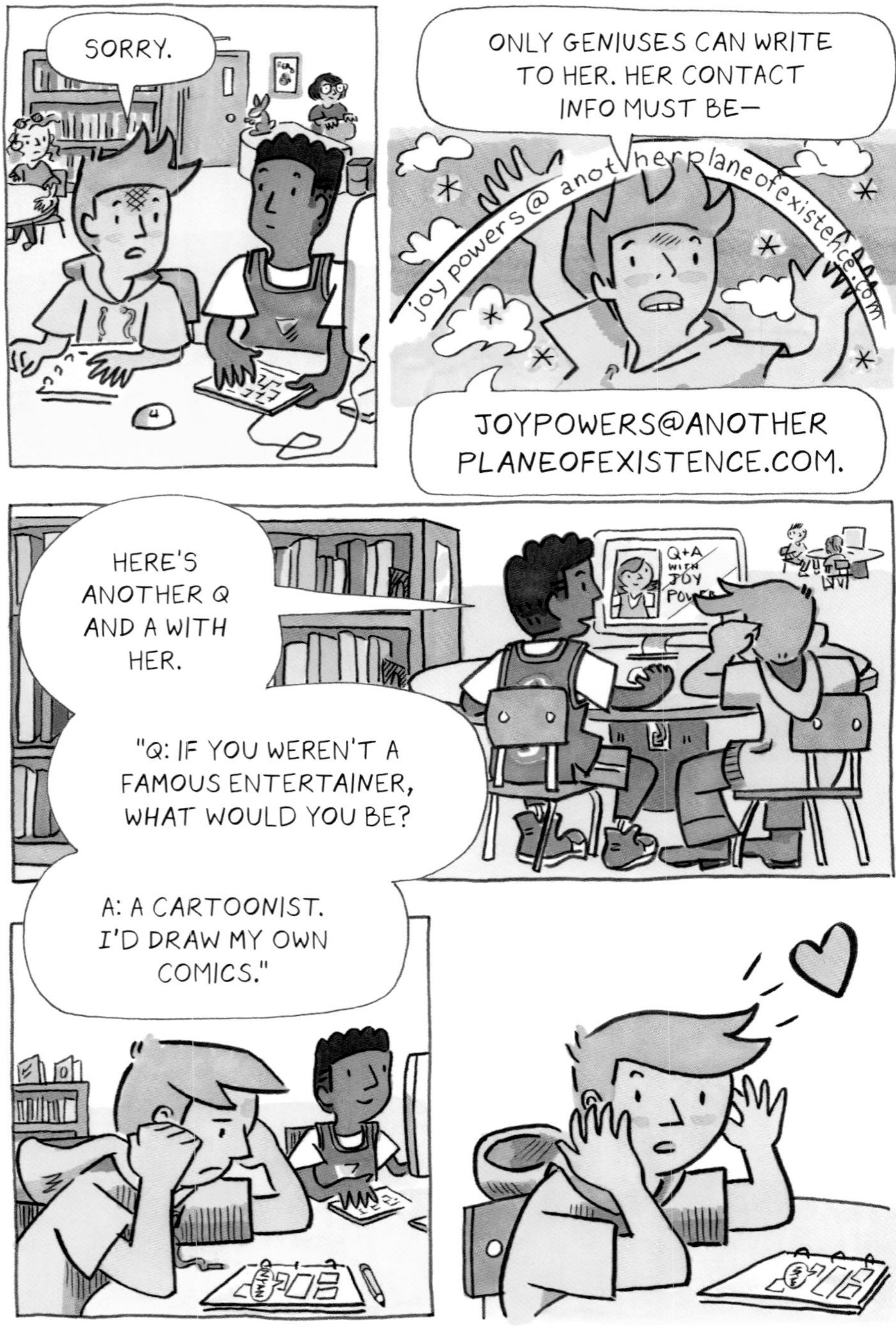
SORRY.
ONLY GENIUSES CAN WRITE TO HER. HER CONTACT INFO MUST BE—
joy powers@anotherplaneofexistence.com
JOYPOWERS@ANOTHER PLANEOFEXISTENCE.COM.
HERE'S ANOTHER Q AND A WITH HER.
Q+A WITH JOY POWER
"Q: IF YOU WEREN'T A FAMOUS ENTERTAINER, WHAT WOULD YOU BE?
A: A CARTOONIST. I'D DRAW MY OWN COMICS."

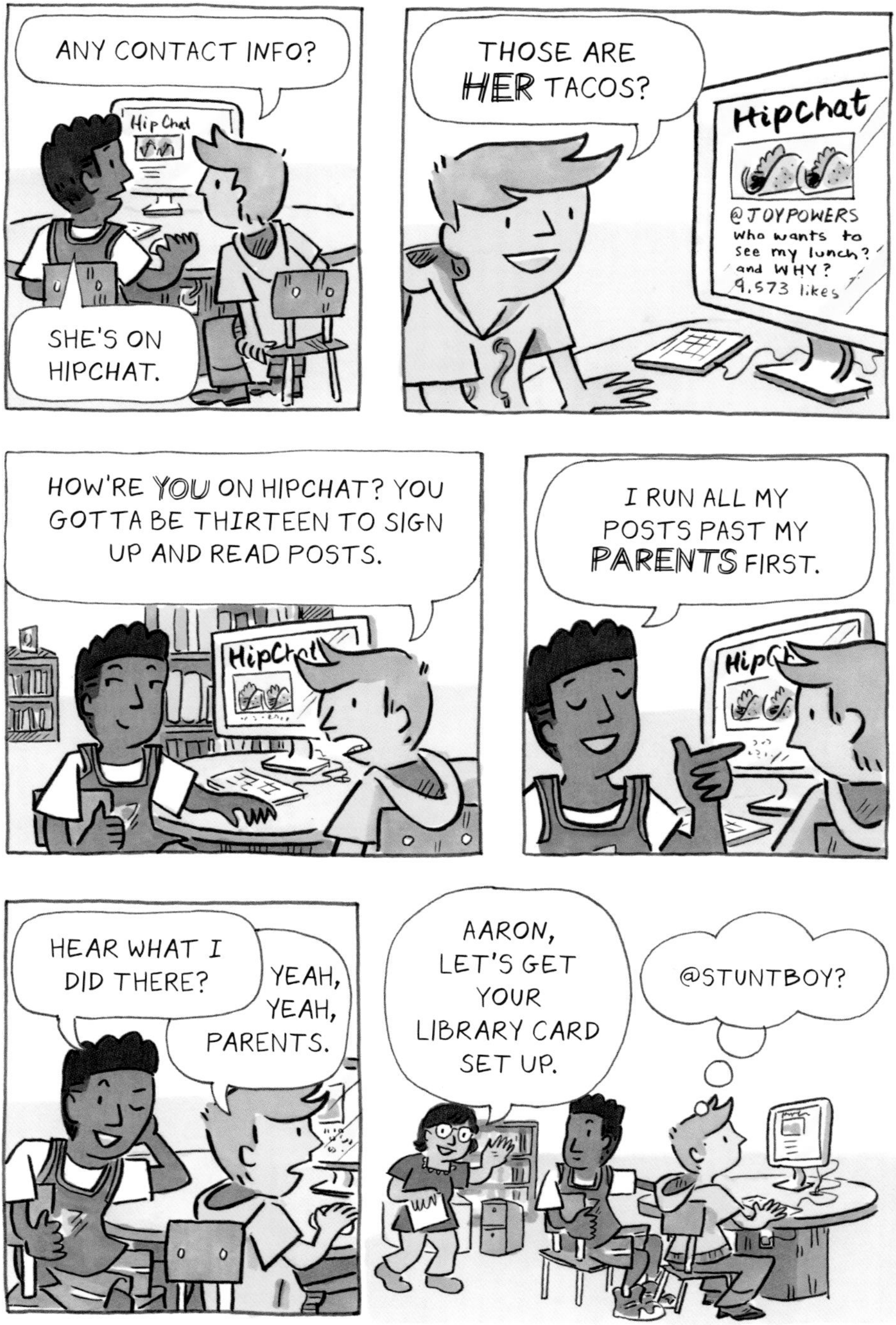
ANY CONTACT INFO?
Hip Chat
SHE'S ON HIPCHAT.
THOSE ARE HER TACOS?
Hipchat
@JOYPOWERS
Who wants to see my lunch? and WHY?
9,573 likes
HOW'RE YOU ON HIPCHAT? YOU GOTTA BE THIRTEEN TO SIGN UP AND READ POSTS.
HipChat
I RUN ALL MY POSTS PAST MY PARENTS FIRST.
HEAR WHAT I DID THERE?
YEAH, YEAH, PARENTS.
AARON, LET'S GET YOUR LIBRARY CARD SET UP.
@STUNTBOY?

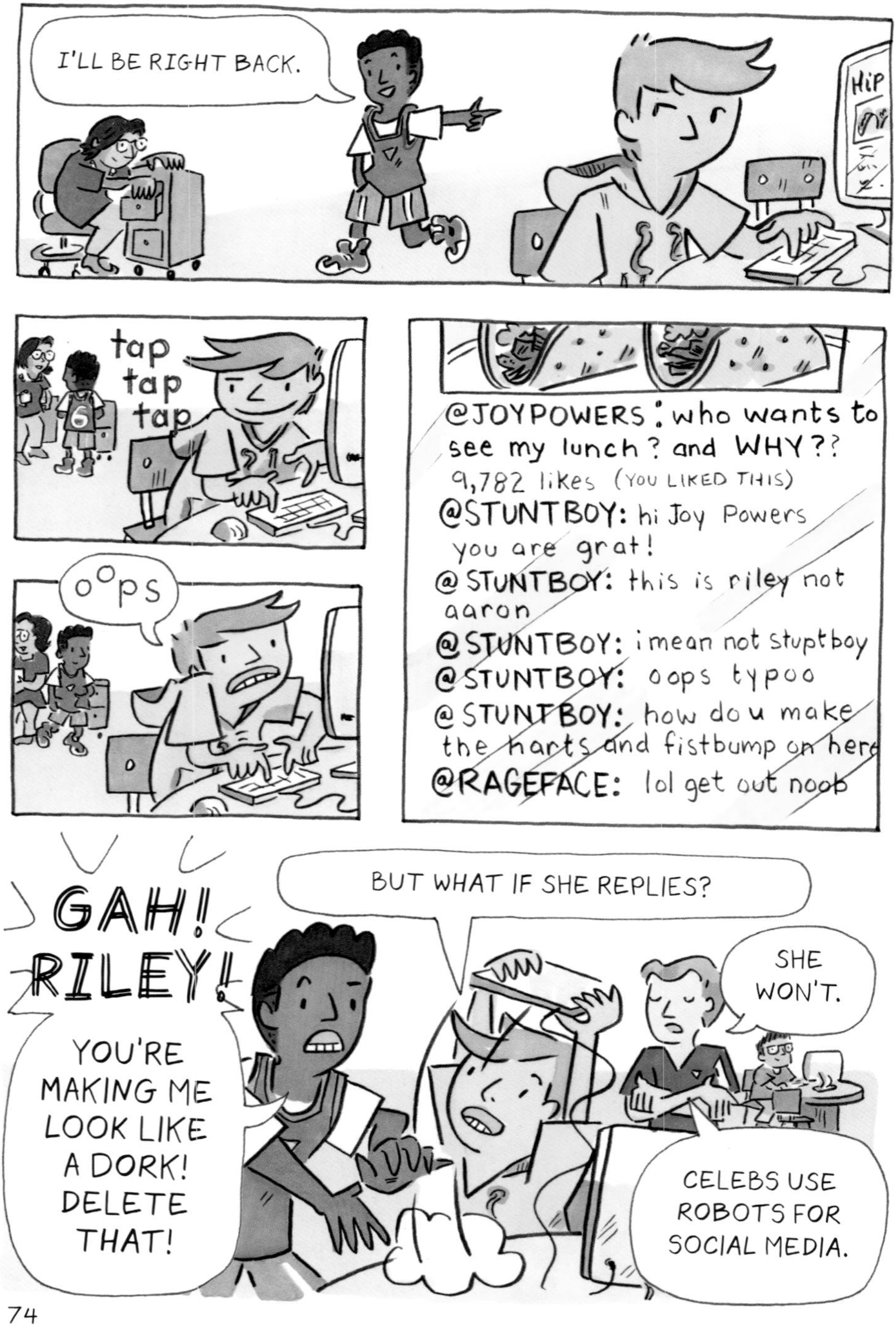
I'LL BE RIGHT BACK.
Hip
tap tap tap
@JOYPOWERS: who wants to see my lunch? and WHY??
9,782 likes (YOU LIKED THIS)
@STUNTBOY: hi Joy Powers you are grat!
@STUNTBOY: this is riley not aaron
@STUNTBOY: i mean not stuptboy
@STUNTBOY: oops typoo
@STUNTBOY: how do u make the harts and fistbump on here
@RAGEFACE: lol get out noob
oops
GAH! RILEY!
YOU'RE MAKING ME LOOK LIKE A DORK! DELETE THAT!
BUT WHAT IF SHE REPLIES?
SHE WON'T.
CELEBS USE ROBOTS FOR SOCIAL MEDIA.

CHAPTER 8

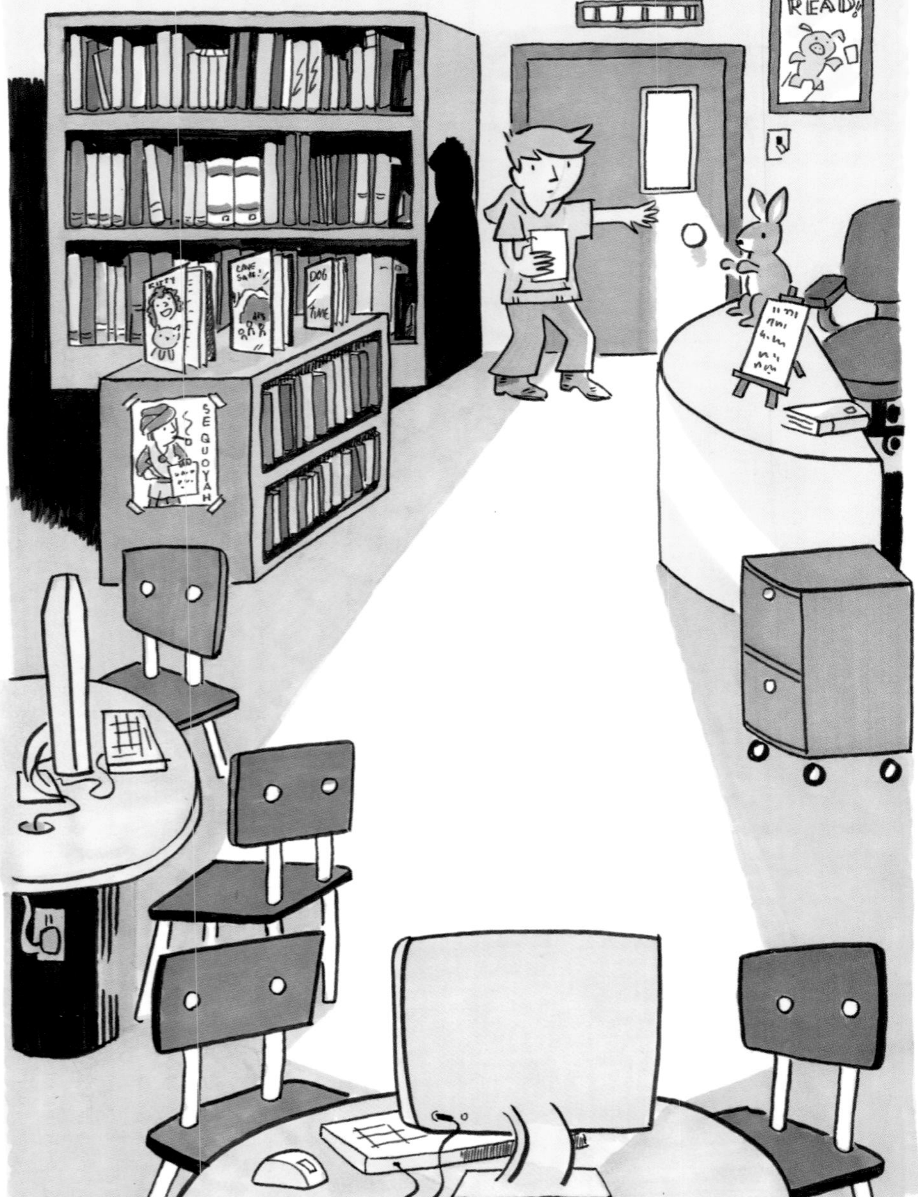
READ!
KITTY
CAVE SAFE!
DOG TIME
SEQUOYAH

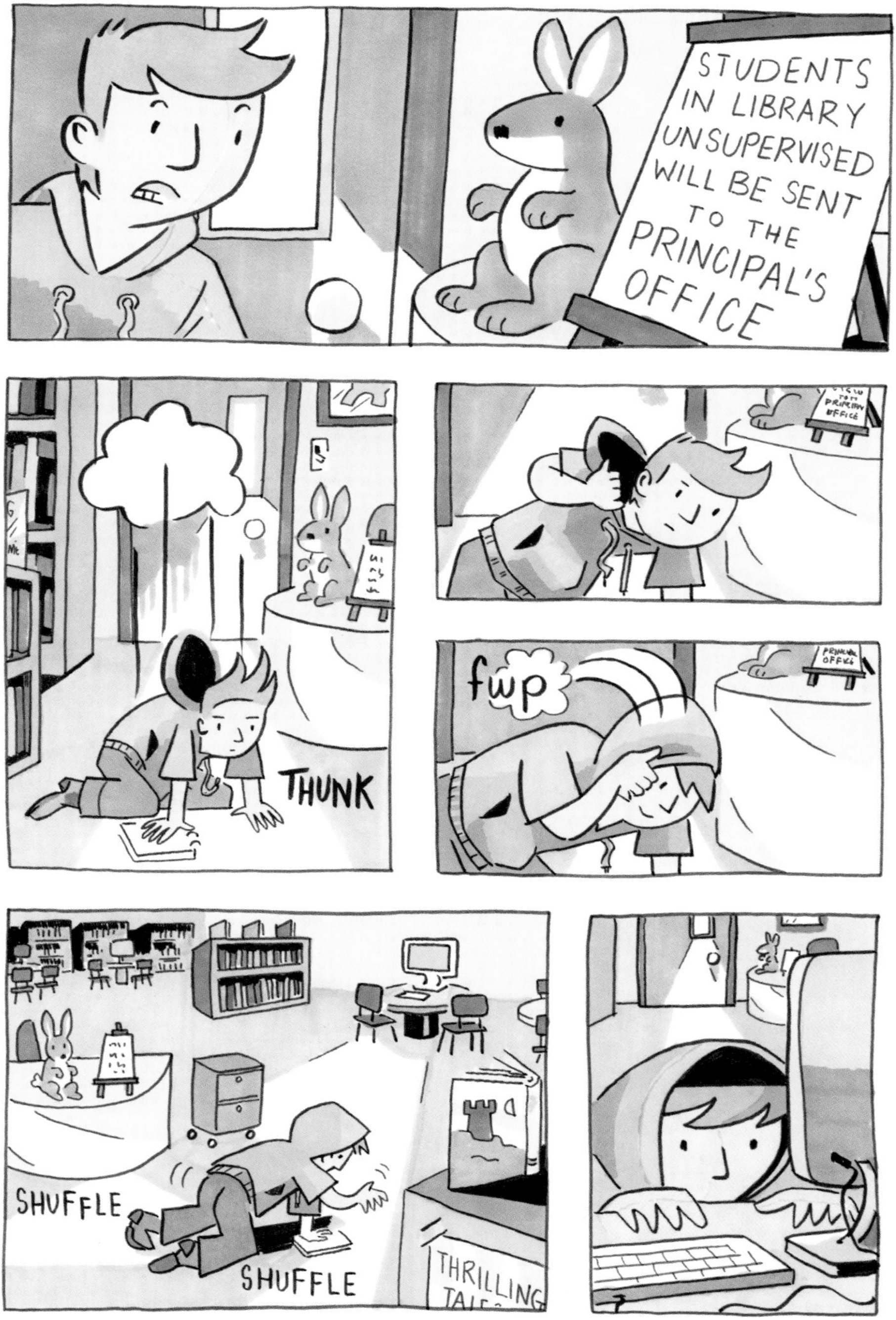
STUDENTS IN LIBRARY UNSUPERVISED WILL BE SENT TO THE PRINCIPAL'S OFFICE
THUNK
fwp
SHUFFLE
SHUFFLE
THRILLING

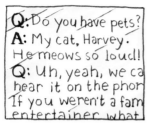

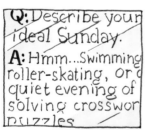

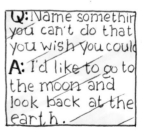

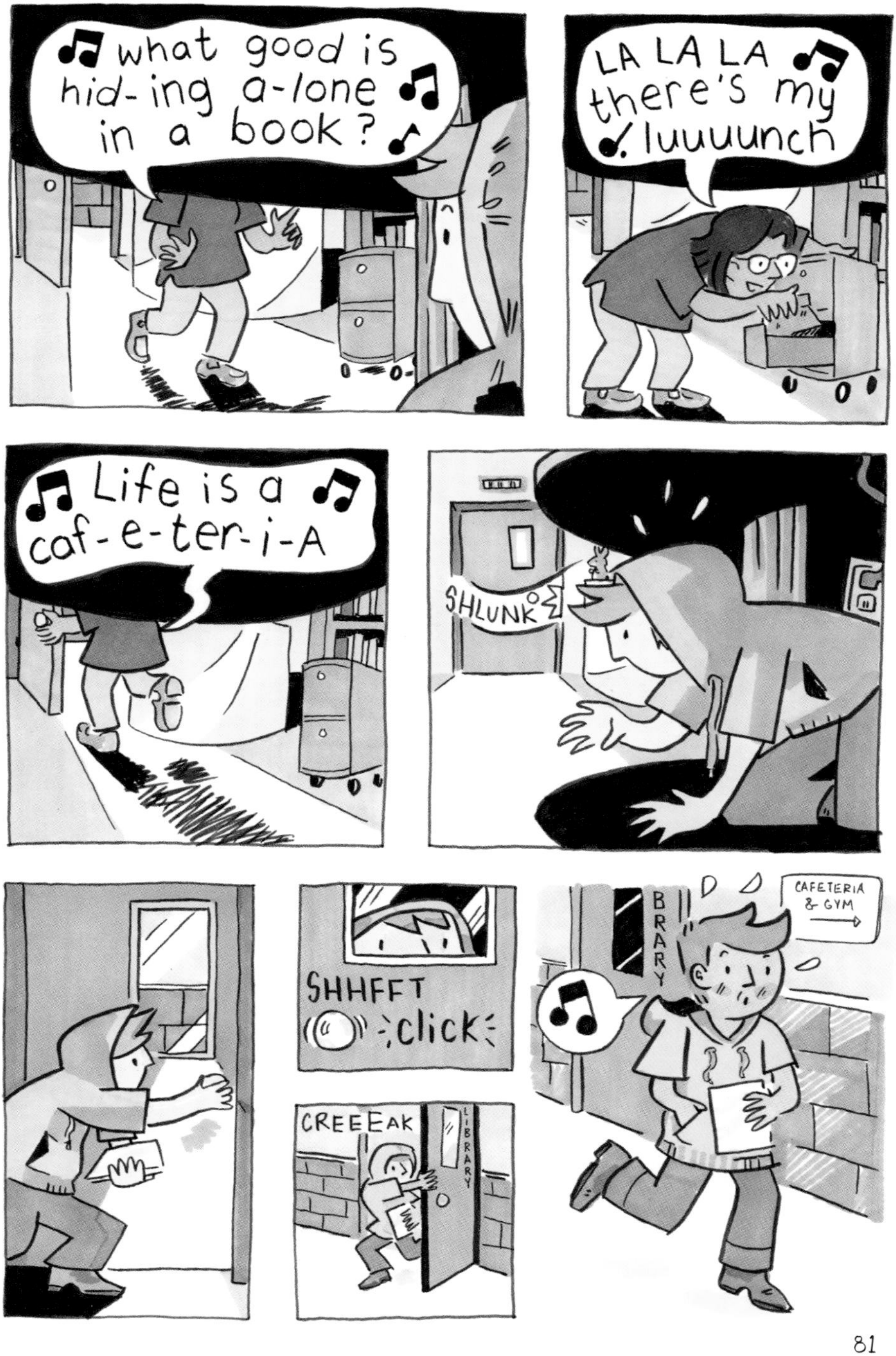
what good is hid-ing a-lone in a book?
LA LA LA there's my luuuunch
Life is a caf-e-ter-i-A
SHLUNK
SHHFFT
click
CREEEAK
LIBRARY
BRARY
CAFETERIA & GYM

CHAPTER 9

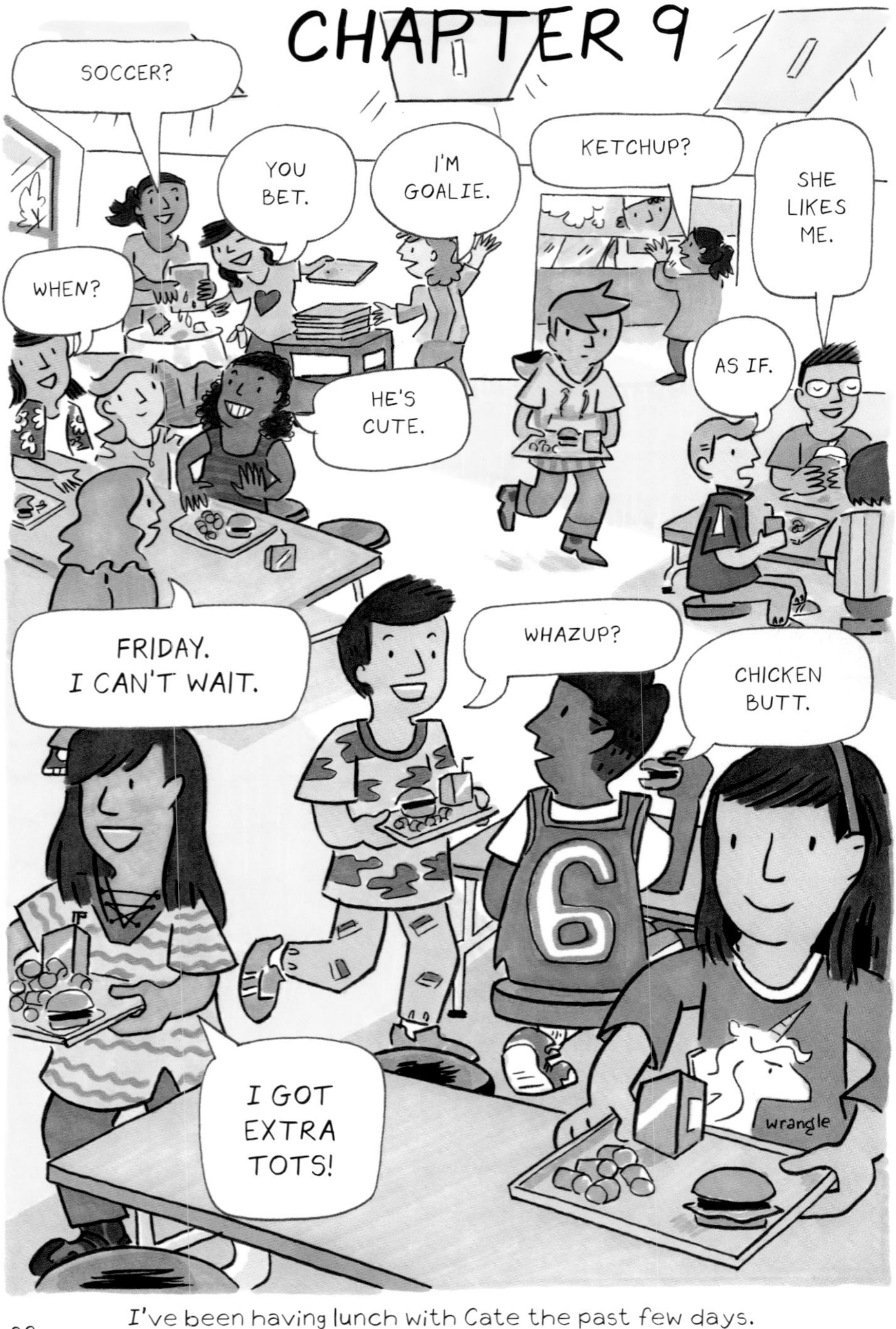
SOCCER?
YOU BET.
I'M GOALIE.
KETCHUP?
SHE LIKES ME.
WHEN?
HE'S CUTE.
AS IF.
FRIDAY. I CAN'T WAIT.
WHAZUP?
CHICKEN BUTT.
I GOT EXTRA TOTS!
wrangle

I've been having lunch with Cate the past few days.

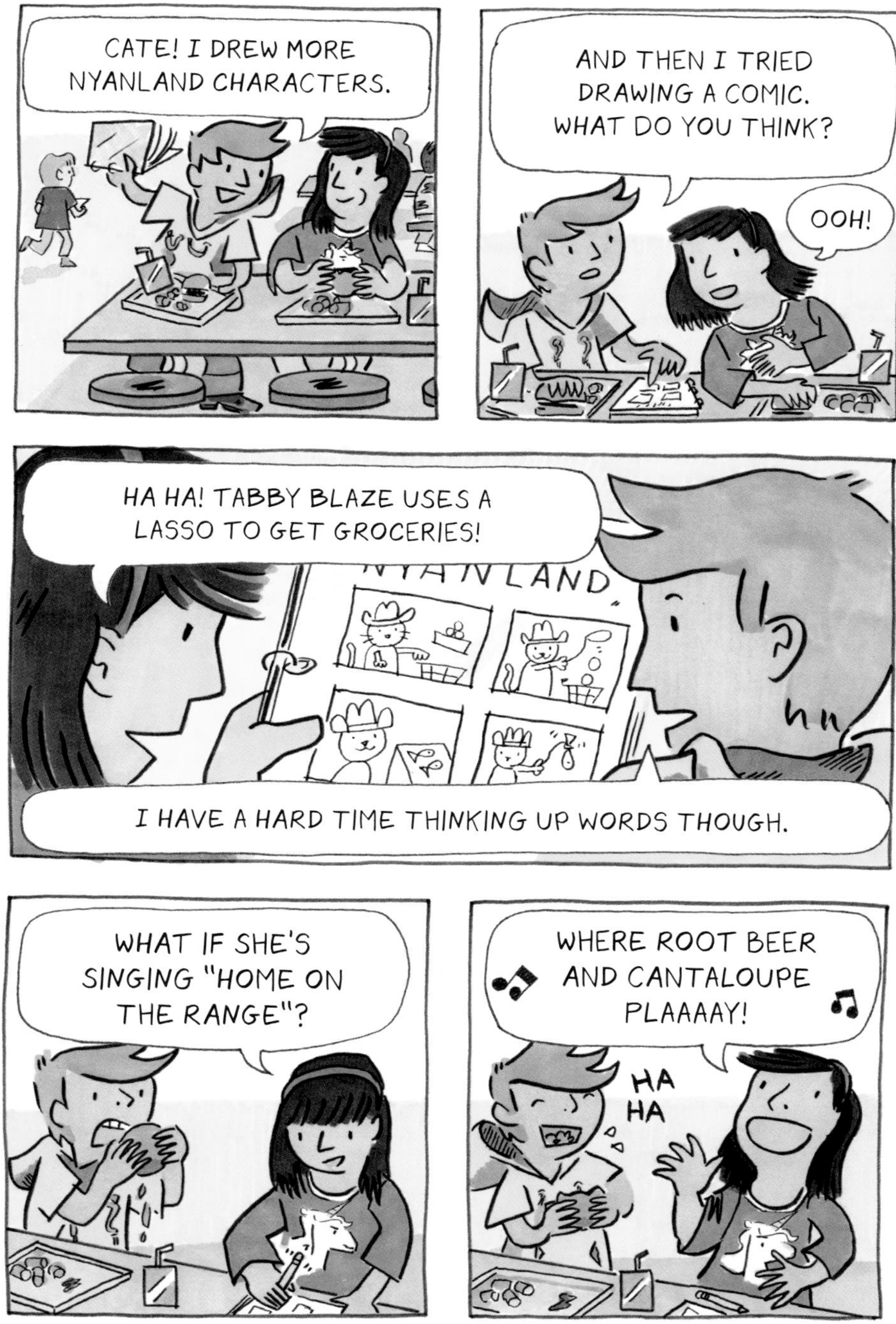
CATE! I DREW MORE NYANLAND CHARACTERS.
AND THEN I TRIED DRAWING A COMIC. WHAT DO YOU THINK?
OOH!
HA HA! TABBY BLAZE USES A LASSO TO GET GROCERIES!
NYANLAND
I HAVE A HARD TIME THINKING UP WORDS THOUGH.
WHAT IF SHE'S SINGING "HOME ON THE RANGE"?
WHERE ROOT BEER AND CANTALOUPE PLAAAAY!
HA HA

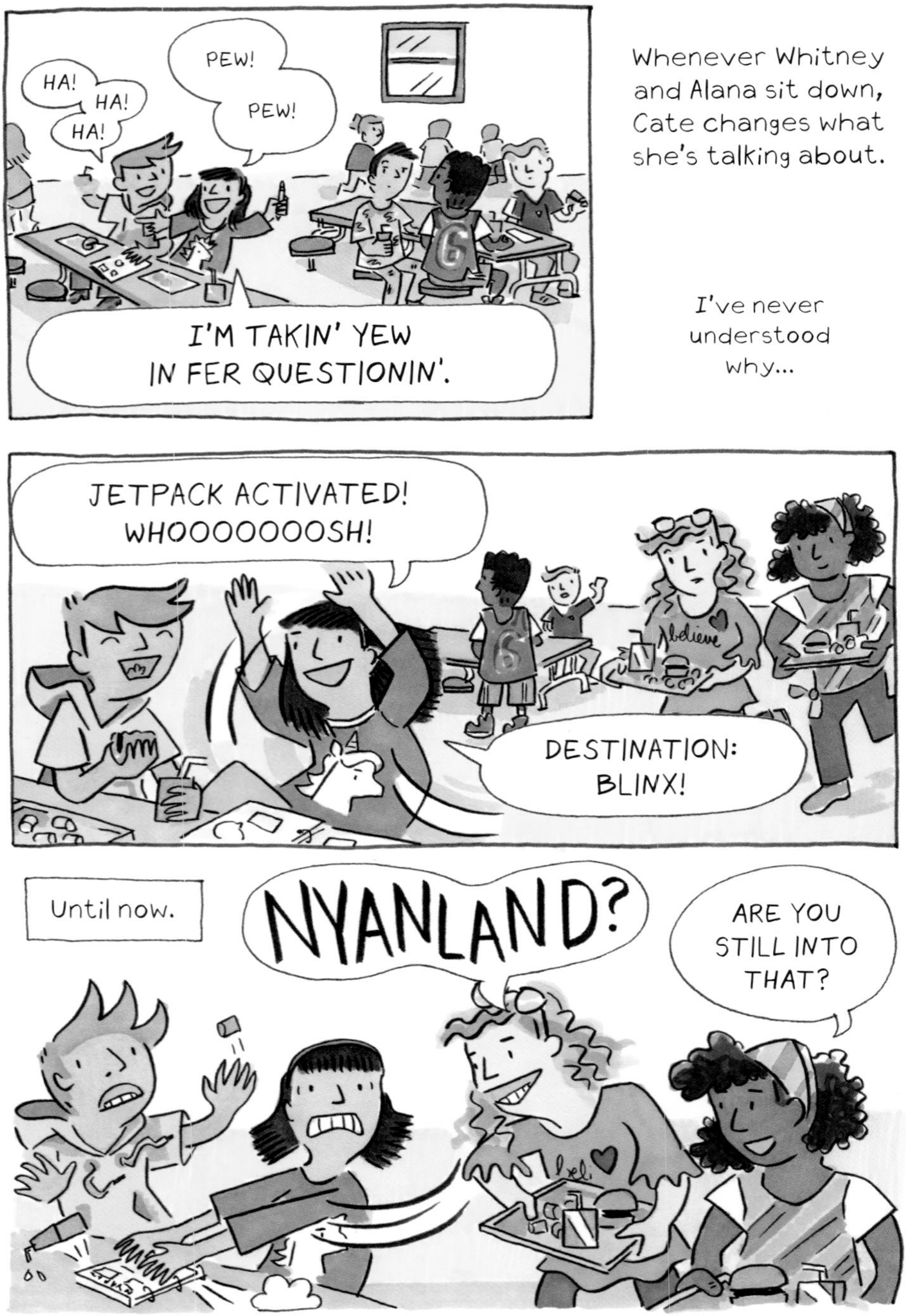
HA! HA! HA!
PEW! PEW!
I'M TAKIN' YEW IN FER QUESTIONIN'.
Whenever Whitney and Alana sit down, Cate changes what she's talking about.
I've never understood why...
JETPACK ACTIVATED! WHOOOOOOOSH!
DESTINATION: BLINX!
Until now.
NYANLAND?
ARE YOU STILL INTO THAT?

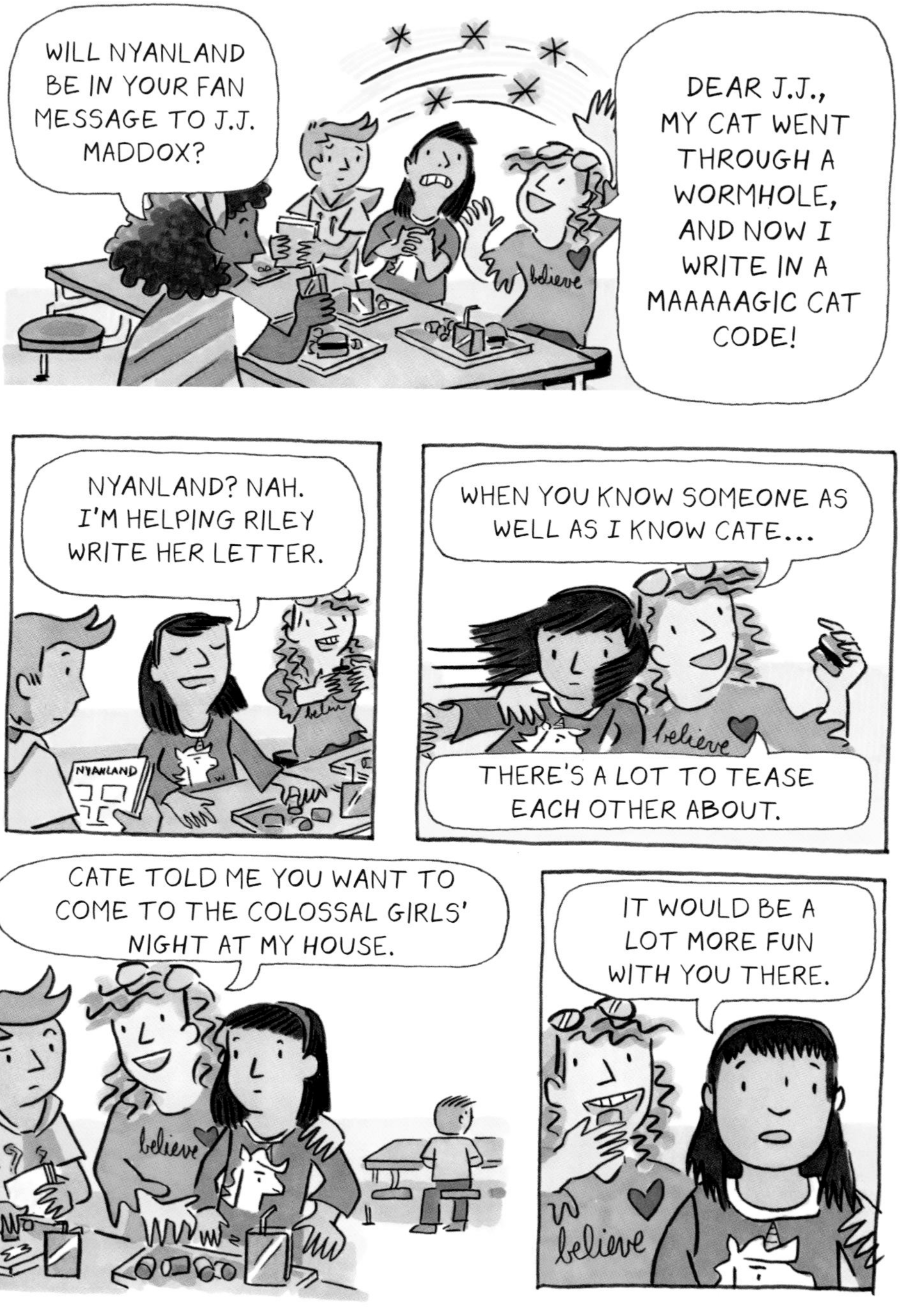
WILL NYANLAND BE IN YOUR FAN MESSAGE TO J.J. MADDOX?
DEAR J.J., MY CAT WENT THROUGH A WORMHOLE, AND NOW I WRITE IN A MAAAAAGIC CAT CODE!
NYANLAND? NAH. I'M HELPING RILEY WRITE HER LETTER.
NYANLAND
WHEN YOU KNOW SOMEONE AS WELL AS I KNOW CATE...
THERE'S A LOT TO TEASE EACH OTHER ABOUT.
CATE TOLD ME YOU WANT TO COME TO THE COLOSSAL GIRLS' NIGHT AT MY HOUSE.
IT WOULD BE A LOT MORE FUN WITH YOU THERE.

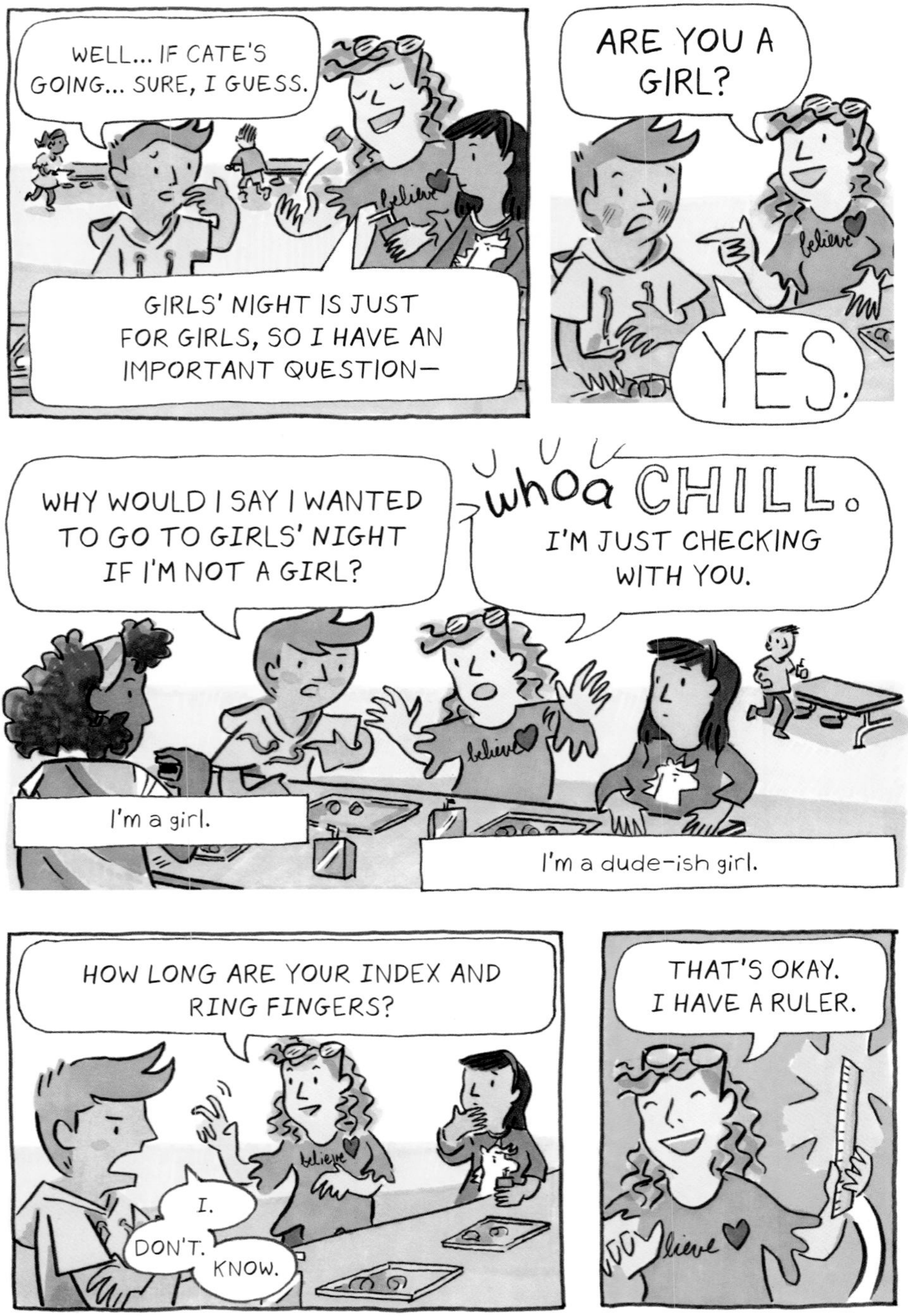
WELL... IF CATE'S GOING... SURE, I GUESS.
GIRLS' NIGHT IS JUST FOR GIRLS, SO I HAVE AN IMPORTANT QUESTION—
ARE YOU A GIRL?
YES.
WHY WOULD I SAY I WANTED TO GO TO GIRLS' NIGHT IF I'M NOT A GIRL?
whoa CHILL.
I'M JUST CHECKING WITH YOU.
I'm a girl.
I'm a dude-ish girl.
HOW LONG ARE YOUR INDEX AND RING FINGERS?
I.
DON'T.
KNOW.
THAT'S OKAY. I HAVE A RULER.

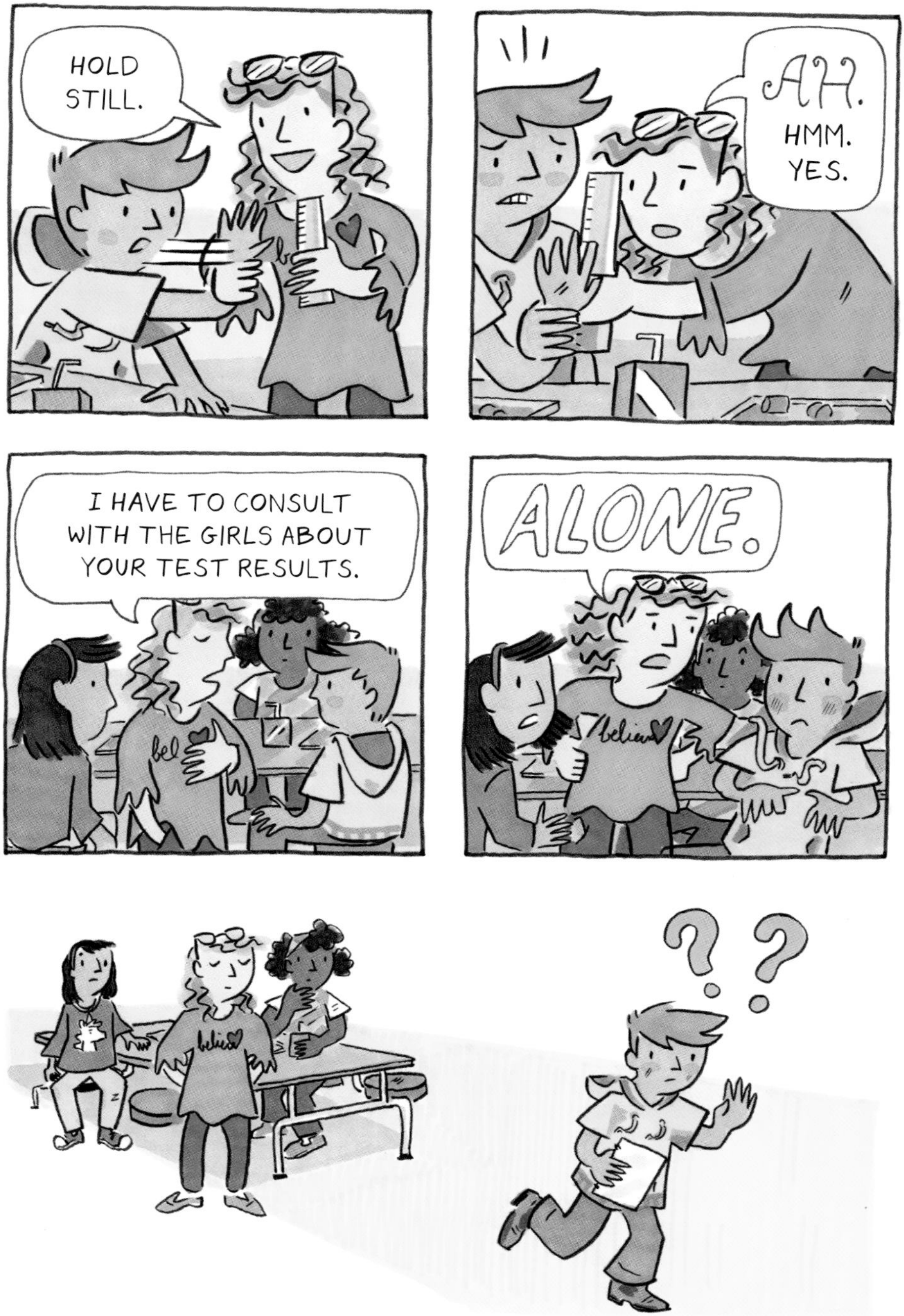

HOLD STILL.
AH.
HMM. YES.
I HAVE TO CONSULT WITH THE GIRLS ABOUT YOUR TEST RESULTS.
ALONE.
??

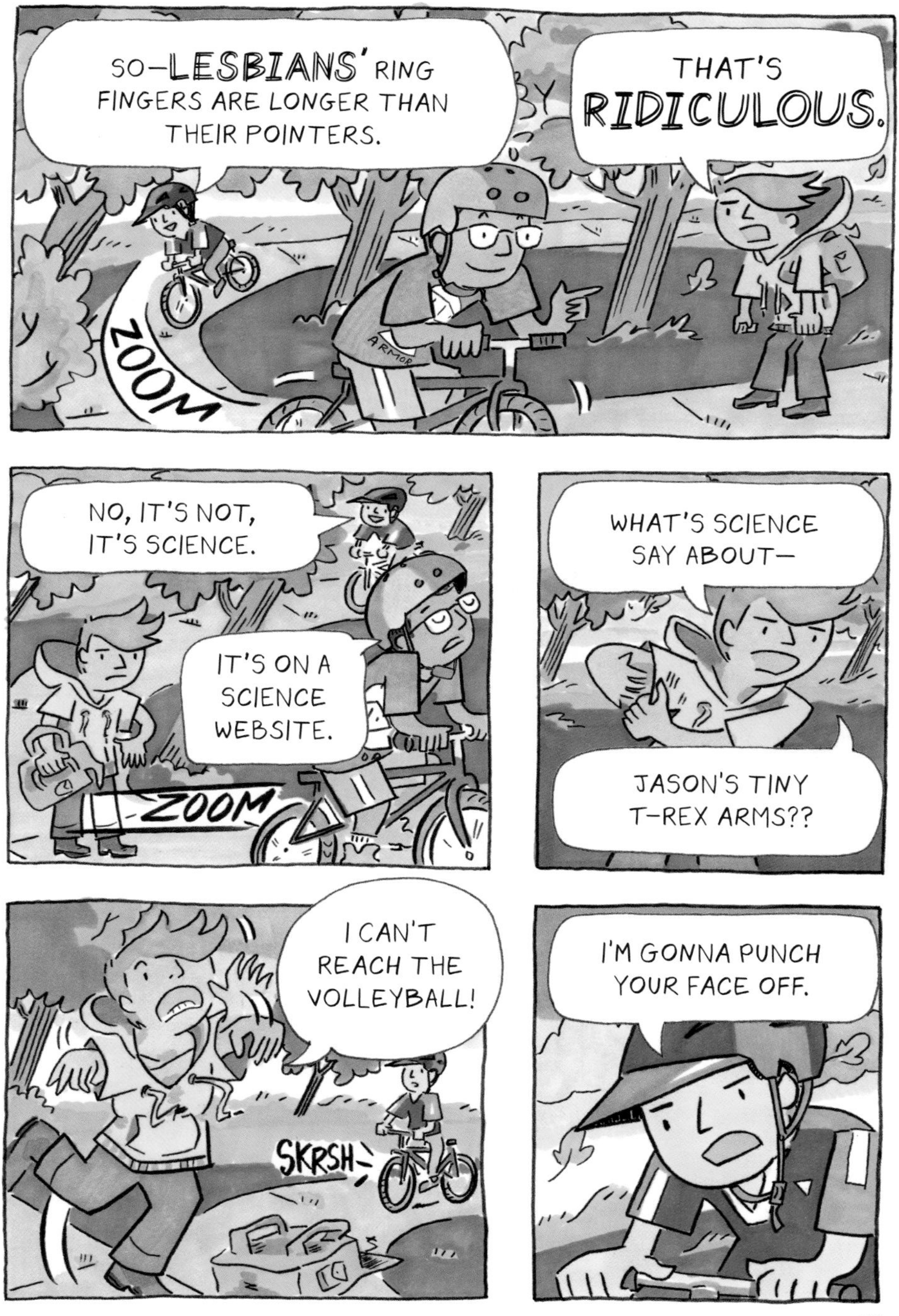
SO—**LESBIANS'** RING FINGERS ARE LONGER THAN THEIR POINTERS.
THAT'S **RIDICULOUS.**
ZOOM
ARMOR
NO, IT'S NOT, IT'S SCIENCE.
IT'S ON A SCIENCE WEBSITE.
ZOOM
WHAT'S SCIENCE SAY ABOUT—
JASON'S TINY T-REX ARMS??
I CAN'T REACH THE VOLLEYBALL!
SKRSH
I'M GONNA PUNCH YOUR FACE OFF.

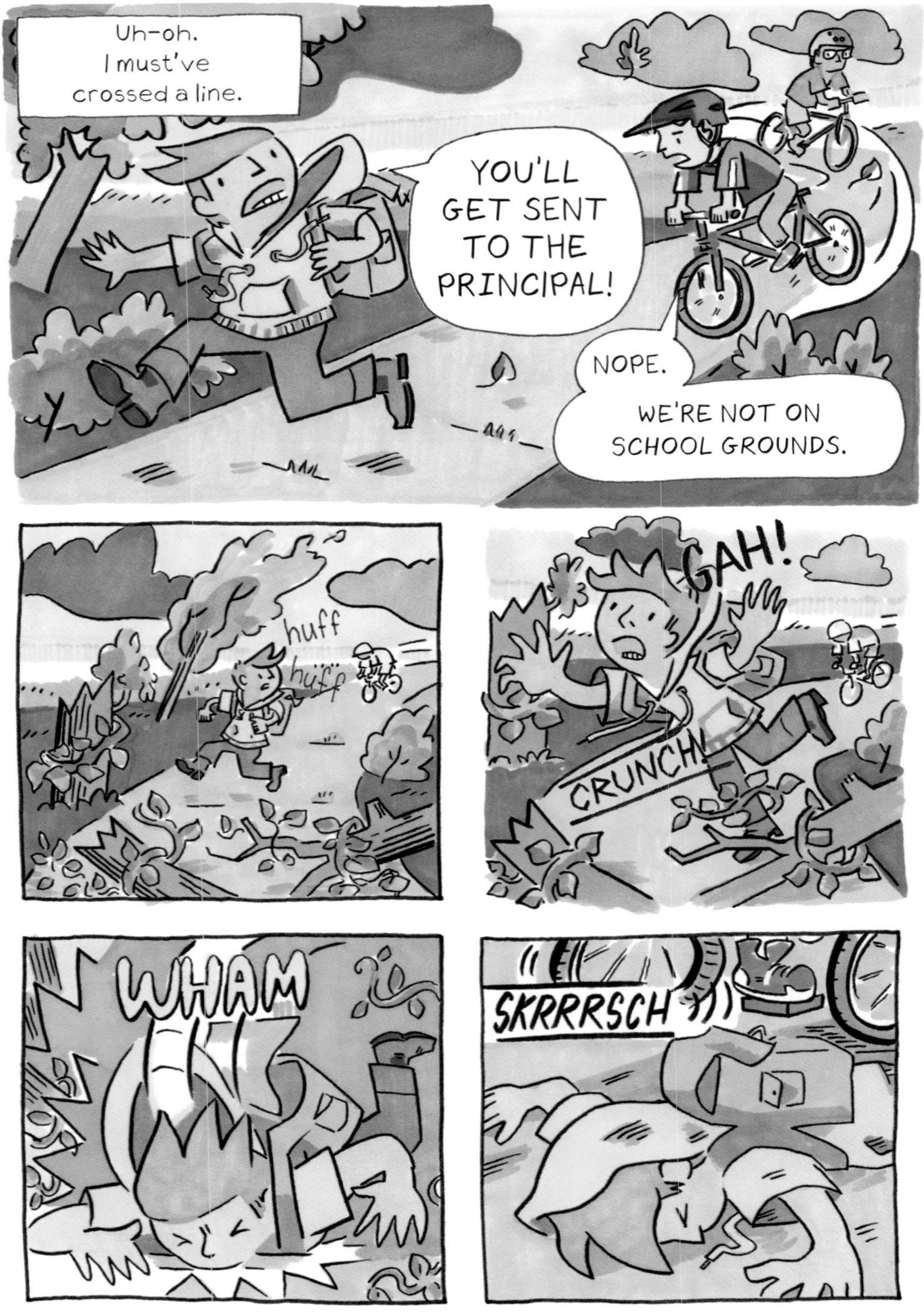
Uh-oh.
I must've crossed a line.
YOU'LL GET SENT TO THE PRINCIPAL!
NOPE.
WE'RE NOT ON SCHOOL GROUNDS.
huff
huff
GAH!
CRUNCH!
WHAM
SKRRRSCH

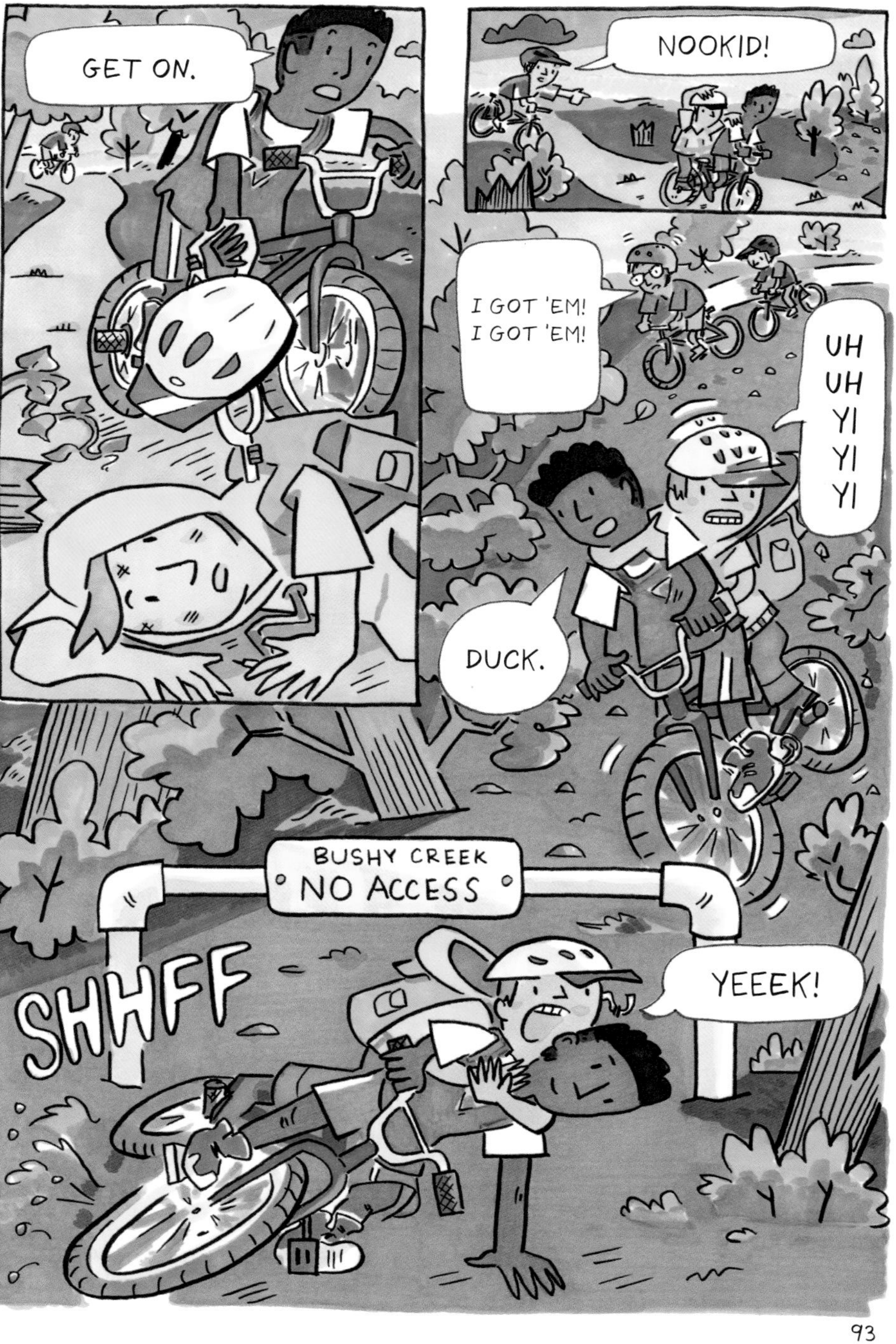
GET ON.
NOOKID!
I GOT 'EM! I GOT 'EM!
UH UH YI YI YI
DUCK.
BUSHY CREEK NO ACCESS
SHHFF
YEEEK!

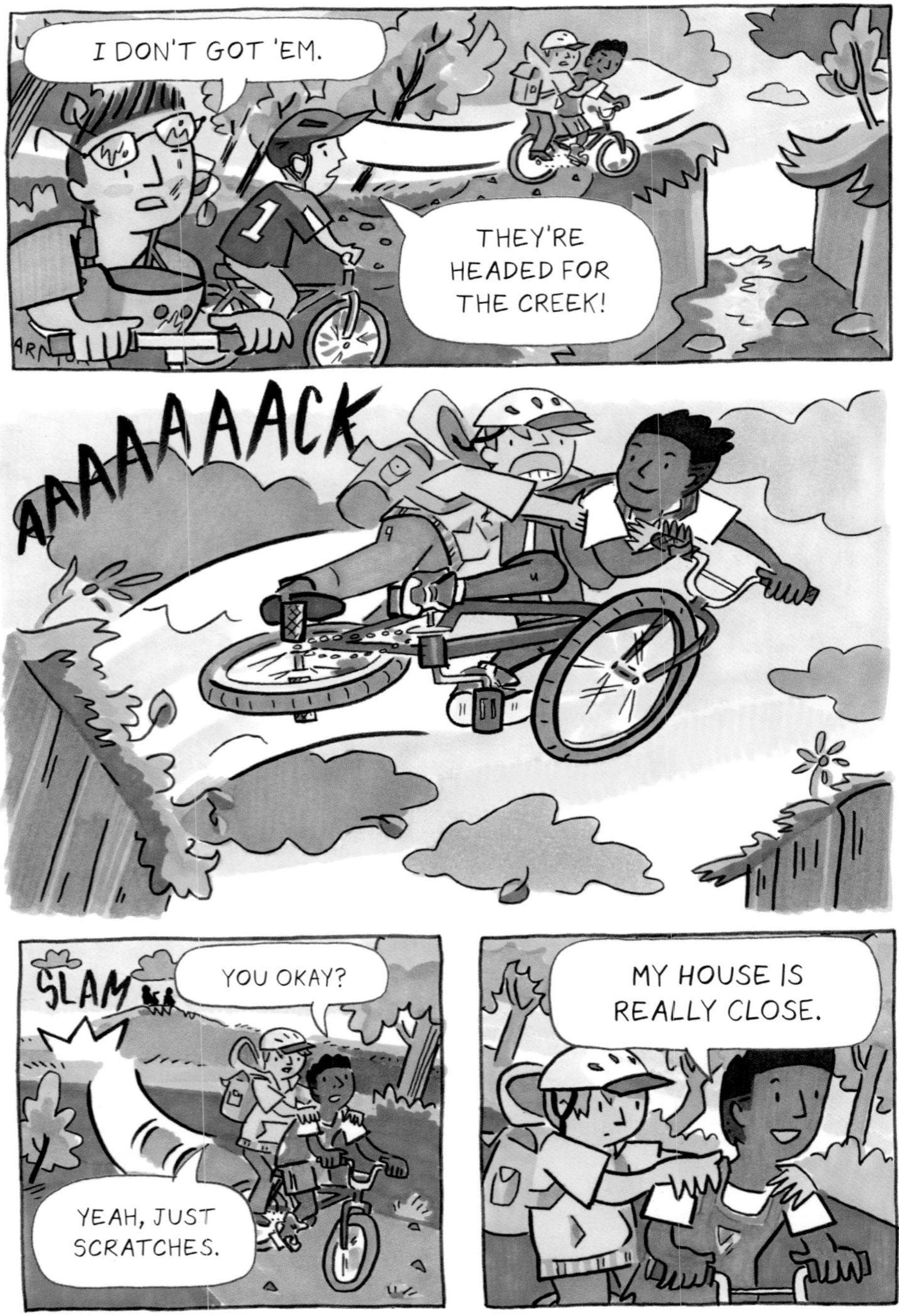
I DON'T GOT 'EM.
THEY'RE HEADED FOR THE CREEK!
AAAAAAACK
SLAM
YOU OKAY?
YEAH, JUST SCRATCHES.
MY HOUSE IS REALLY CLOSE.

CHAPTER 10

WHY ARE WADE AND JASON CHASING YOU?

SCIENCE FINGERS LE LESBIAN SCIENCE FINGERS SCIE NC VG

uh-

I MADE FUN OF JASON'S TINY ARMS.

RILEY!

SOMETIMES YOU GOTTA STOP AND THINK BEFORE CRACKING JOKES.

bump

bump

SOMETHING FUNNY TO YOU MIGHT SEEM MEAN TO SOMEONE ELSE.

YEAH. I KNOW.

CHAPTER 11

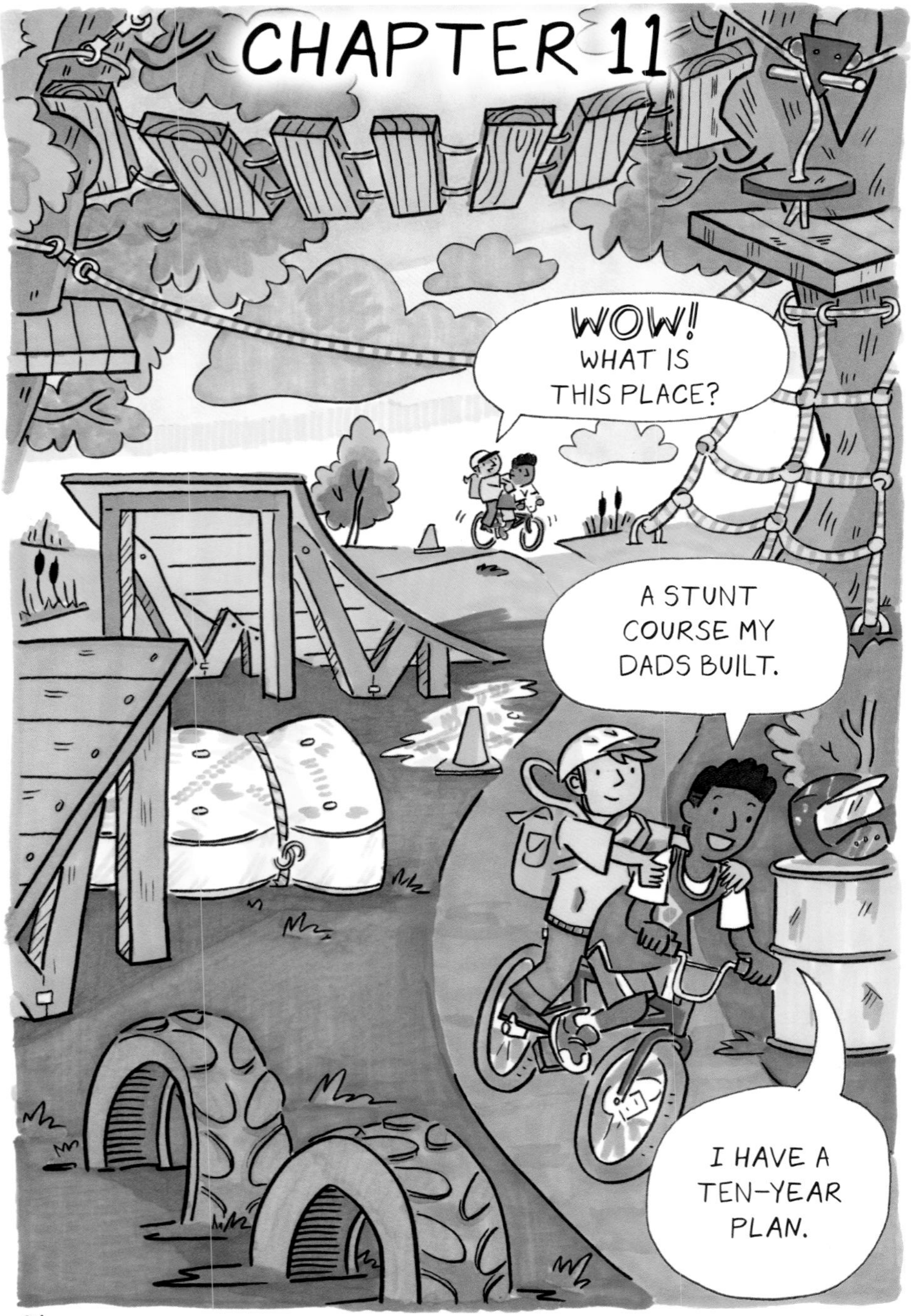
WOW! WHAT IS THIS PLACE?
A STUNT COURSE MY DADS BUILT.
I HAVE A TEN-YEAR PLAN.

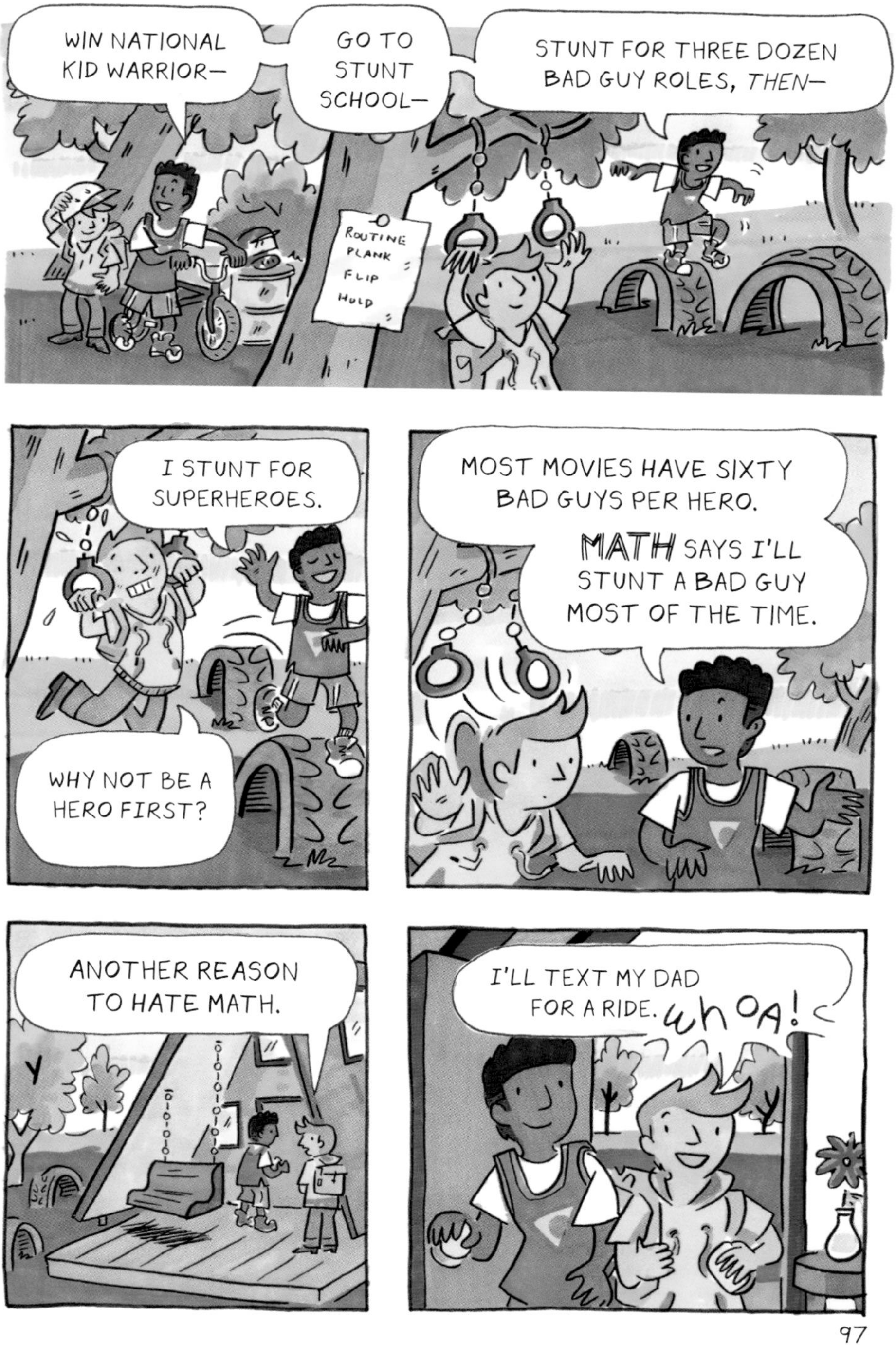
WIN NATIONAL KID WARRIOR—
GO TO STUNT SCHOOL—
STUNT FOR THREE DOZEN BAD GUY ROLES, *THEN*—
ROUTINE PLANK FLIP HOLD
I STUNT FOR SUPERHEROES.
WHY NOT BE A HERO FIRST?
MOST MOVIES HAVE SIXTY BAD GUYS PER HERO.
MATH SAYS I'LL STUNT A BAD GUY MOST OF THE TIME.
ANOTHER REASON TO HATE MATH.
I'LL TEXT MY DAD FOR A RIDE.
WHOA!

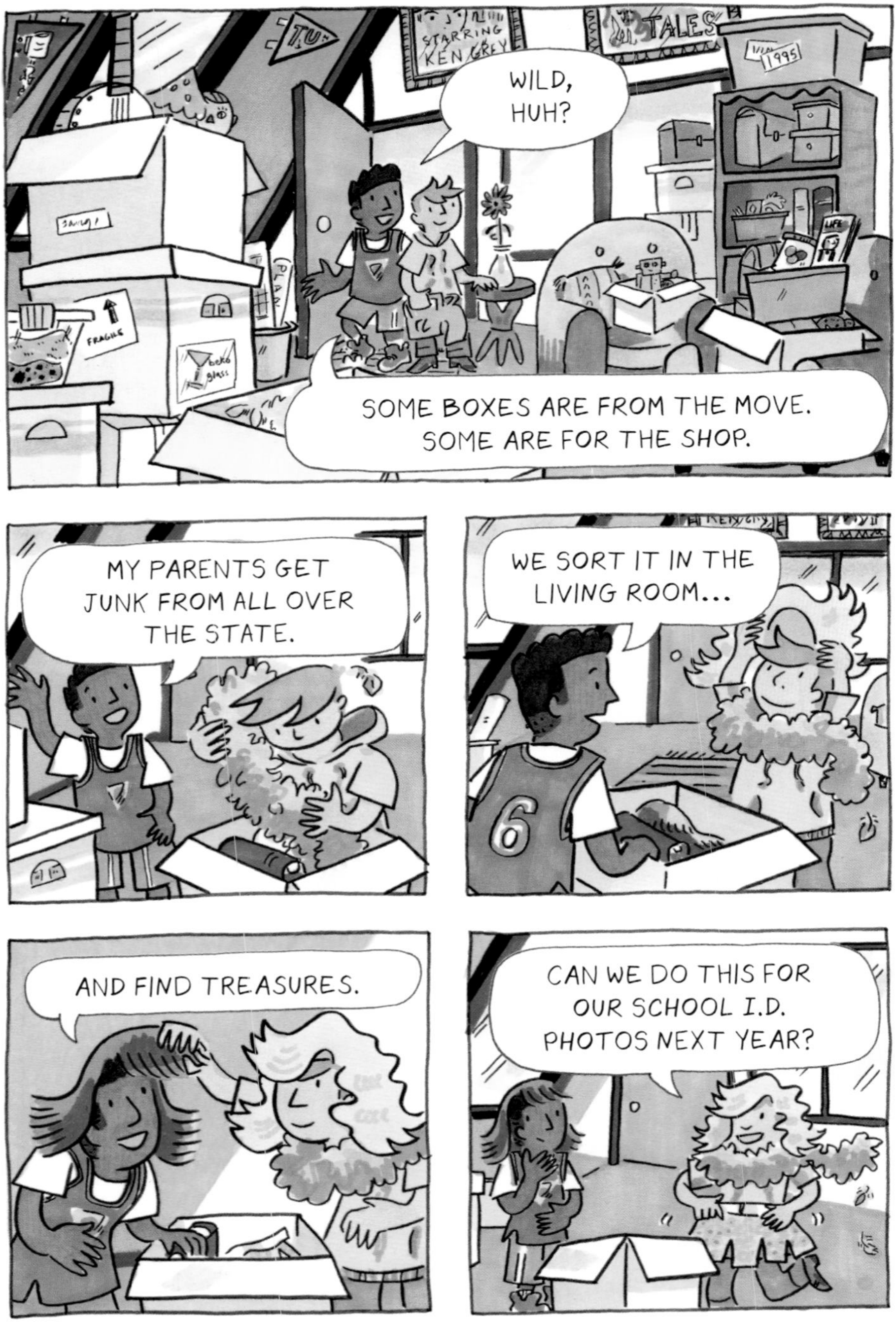

STARRING KEN GREY
TALES
1995
WILD, HUH?
FRAGILE
SOME BOXES ARE FROM THE MOVE. SOME ARE FOR THE SHOP.
MY PARENTS GET JUNK FROM ALL OVER THE STATE.
WE SORT IT IN THE LIVING ROOM...
AND FIND TREASURES.
CAN WE DO THIS FOR OUR SCHOOL I.D. PHOTOS NEXT YEAR?

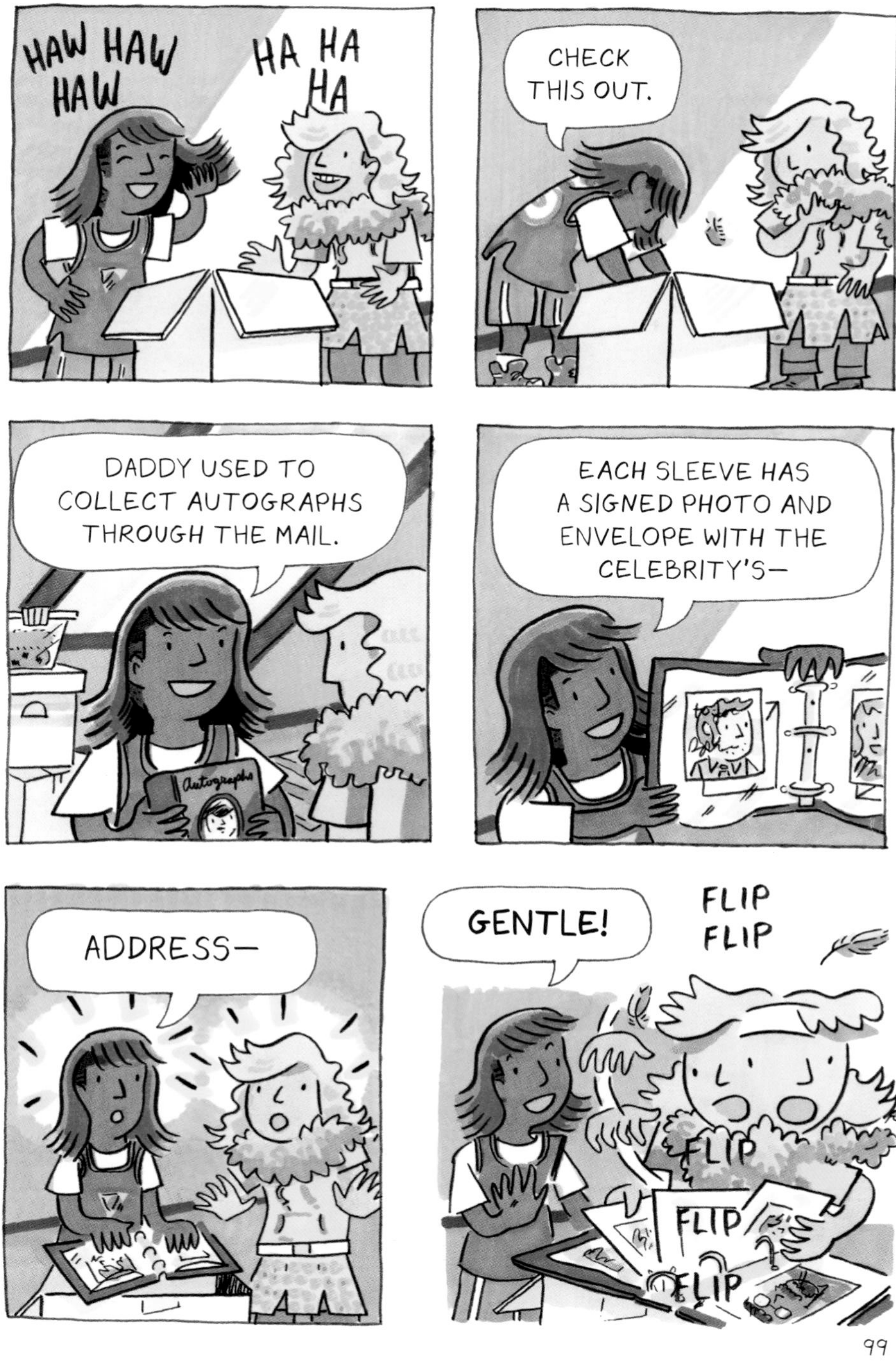
HAW HAW HAW
HA HA HA
CHECK THIS OUT.
DADDY USED TO COLLECT AUTOGRAPHS THROUGH THE MAIL.
Autographs
EACH SLEEVE HAS A SIGNED PHOTO AND ENVELOPE WITH THE CELEBRITY'S—
ADDRESS—
GENTLE!
FLIP FLIP
FLIP
FLIP
FLIP

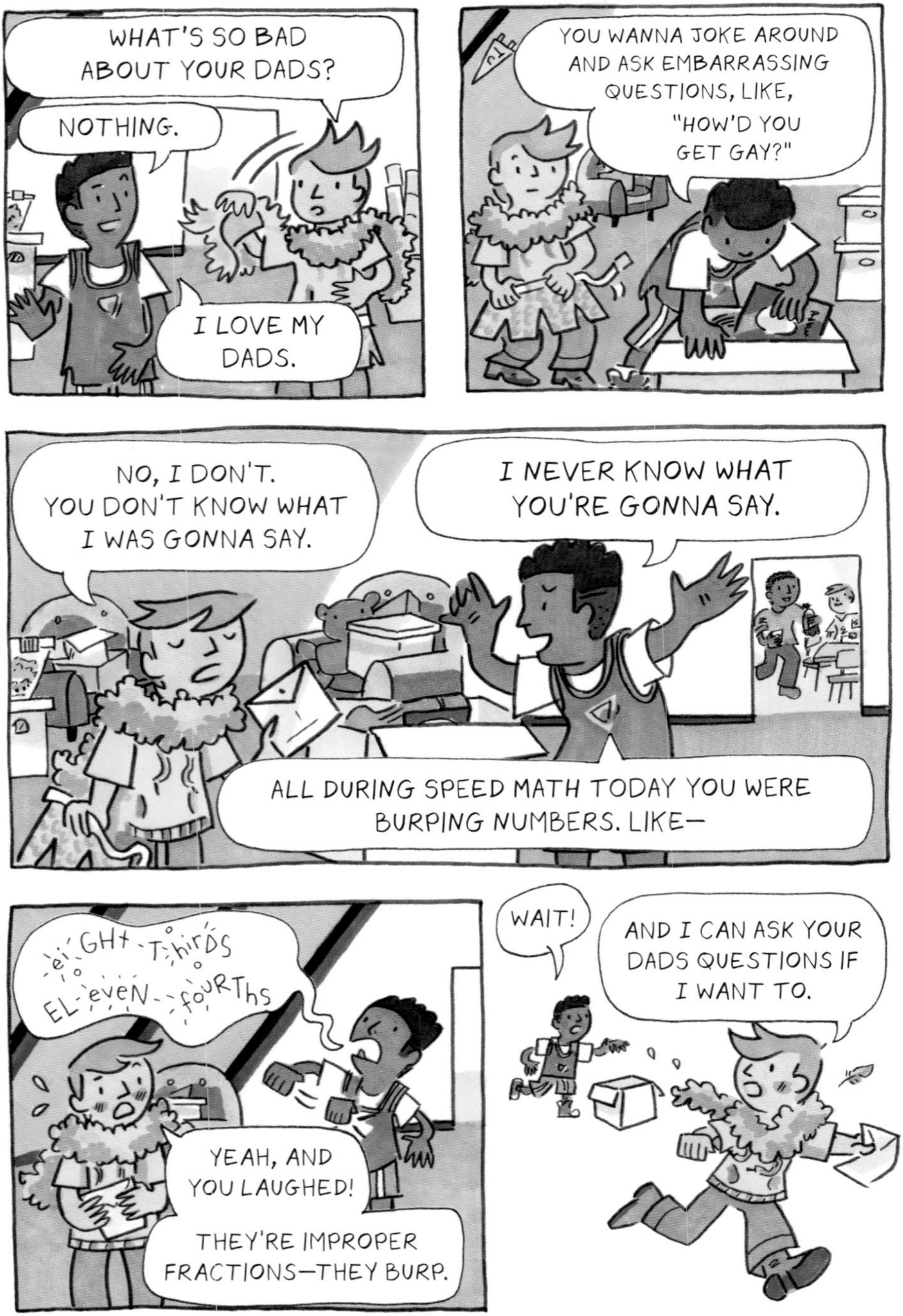
WHAT'S SO BAD ABOUT YOUR DADS?
NOTHING.
I LOVE MY DADS.
YOU WANNA JOKE AROUND AND ASK EMBARRASSING QUESTIONS, LIKE, "HOW'D YOU GET GAY?"
NO, I DON'T. YOU DON'T KNOW WHAT I WAS GONNA SAY.
I NEVER KNOW WHAT YOU'RE GONNA SAY.
ALL DURING SPEED MATH TODAY YOU WERE BURPING NUMBERS. LIKE—
eiGHt Thirds
ELeveN fouRThs
YEAH, AND YOU LAUGHED!
THEY'RE IMPROPER FRACTIONS—THEY BURP.
WAIT!
AND I CAN ASK YOUR DADS QUESTIONS IF I WANT TO.

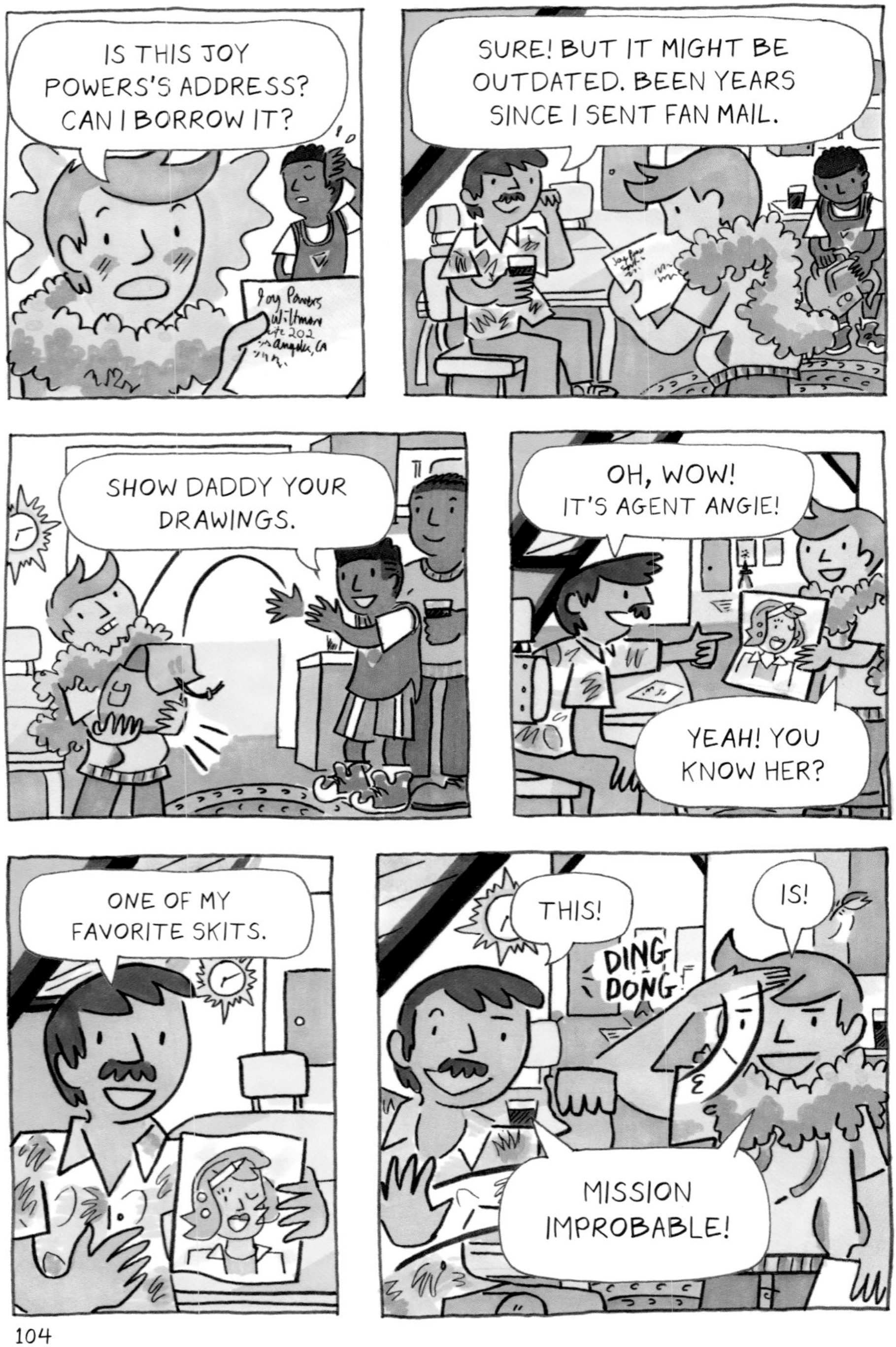
IS THIS JOY POWERS'S ADDRESS? CAN I BORROW IT?
SURE! BUT IT MIGHT BE OUTDATED. BEEN YEARS SINCE I SENT FAN MAIL.
SHOW DADDY YOUR DRAWINGS.
OH, WOW! IT'S AGENT ANGIE!
YEAH! YOU KNOW HER?
ONE OF MY FAVORITE SKITS.
THIS!
DING DONG
IS!
MISSION IMPROBABLE!

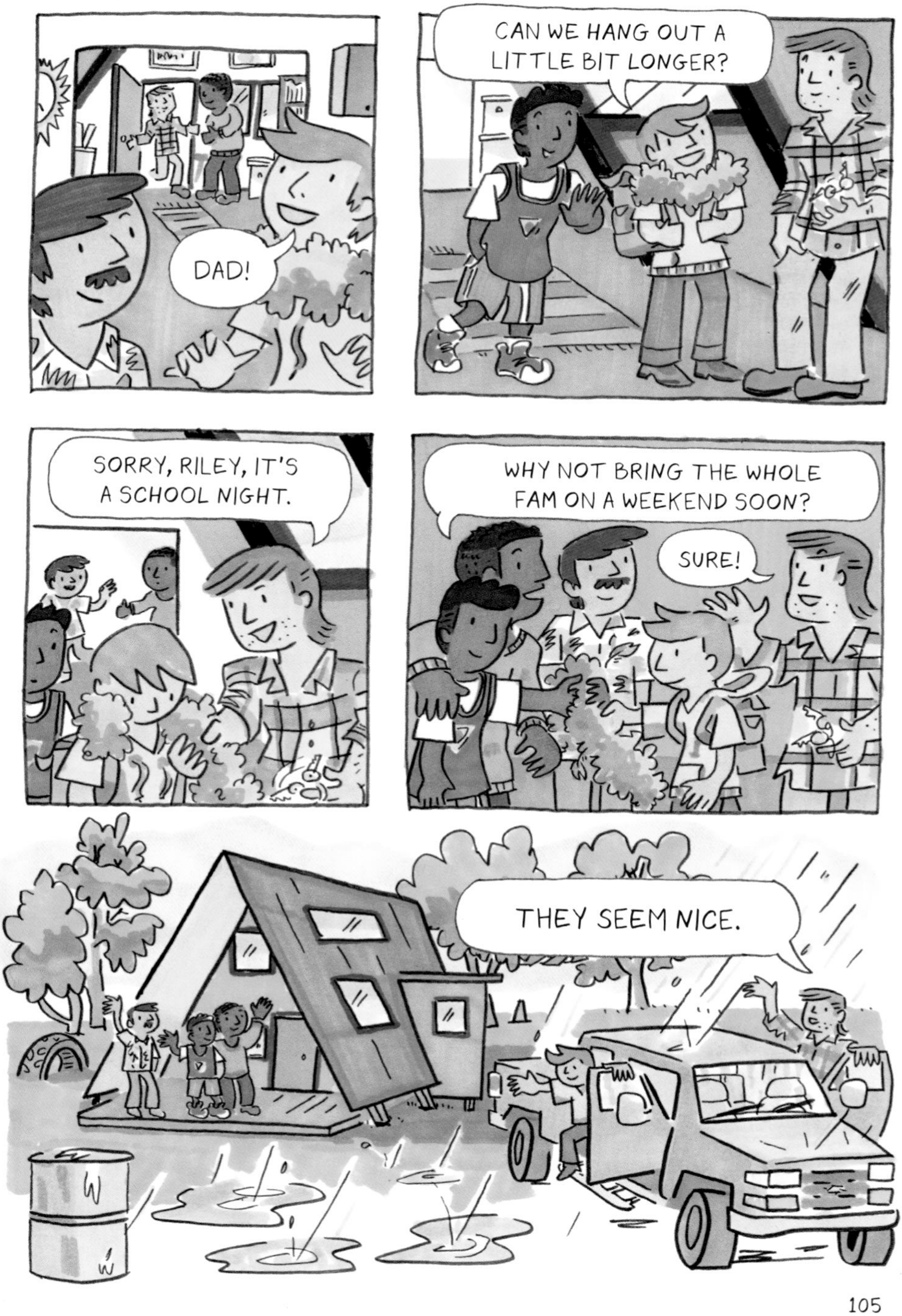
DAD!
CAN WE HANG OUT A LITTLE BIT LONGER?
SORRY, RILEY, IT'S A SCHOOL NIGHT.
WHY NOT BRING THE WHOLE FAM ON A WEEKEND SOON?
SURE!
THEY SEEM NICE.

CHAPTER 12

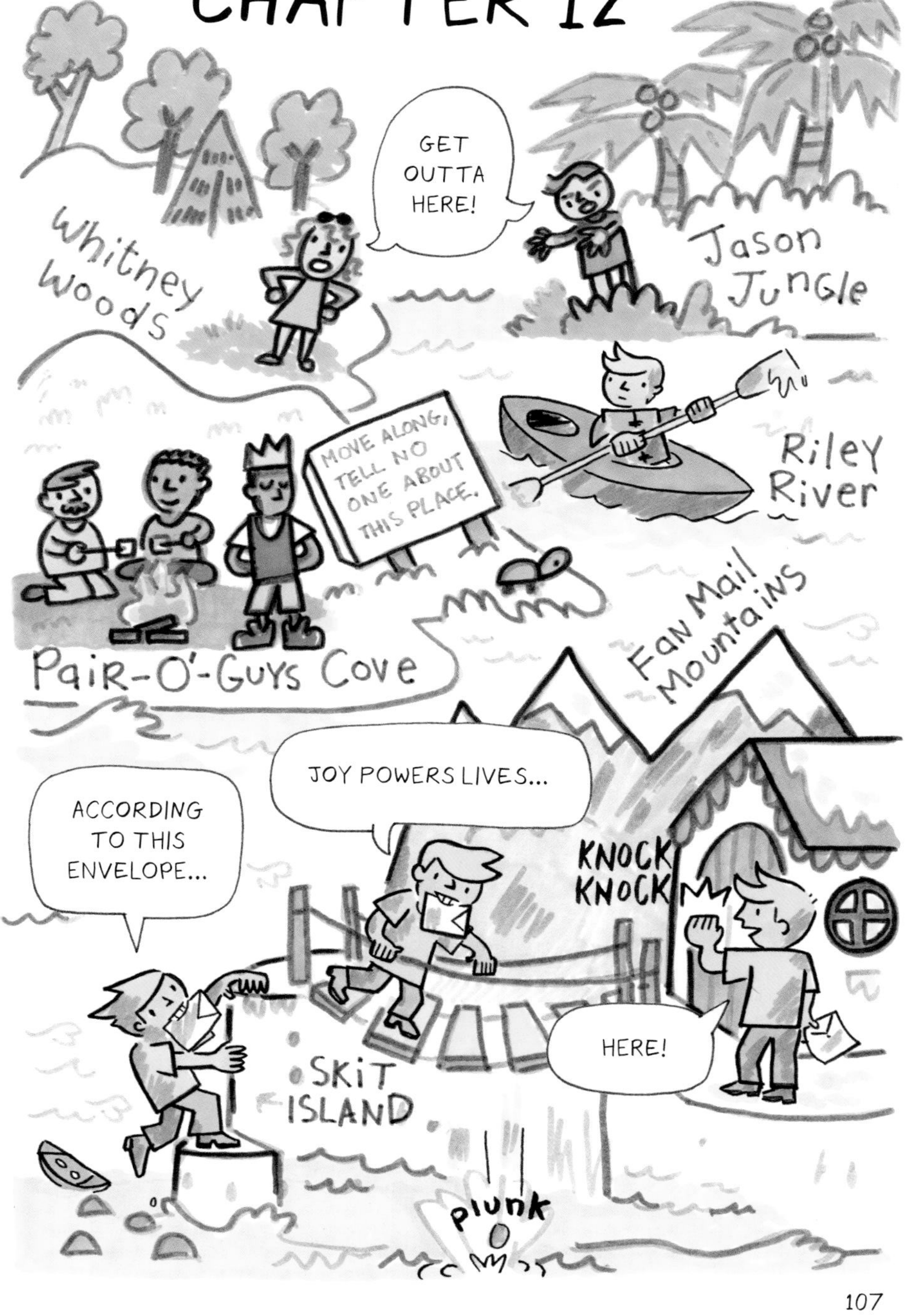
Whitney Woods
GET OUTTA HERE!
Jason Jungle
MOVE ALONG, TELL NO ONE ABOUT THIS PLACE.
Riley River
Pair-O'-Guys Cove
Fan Mail Mountains
ACCORDING TO THIS ENVELOPE...
JOY POWERS LIVES...
KNOCK KNOCK
HERE!
SKIT ISLAND
plunk

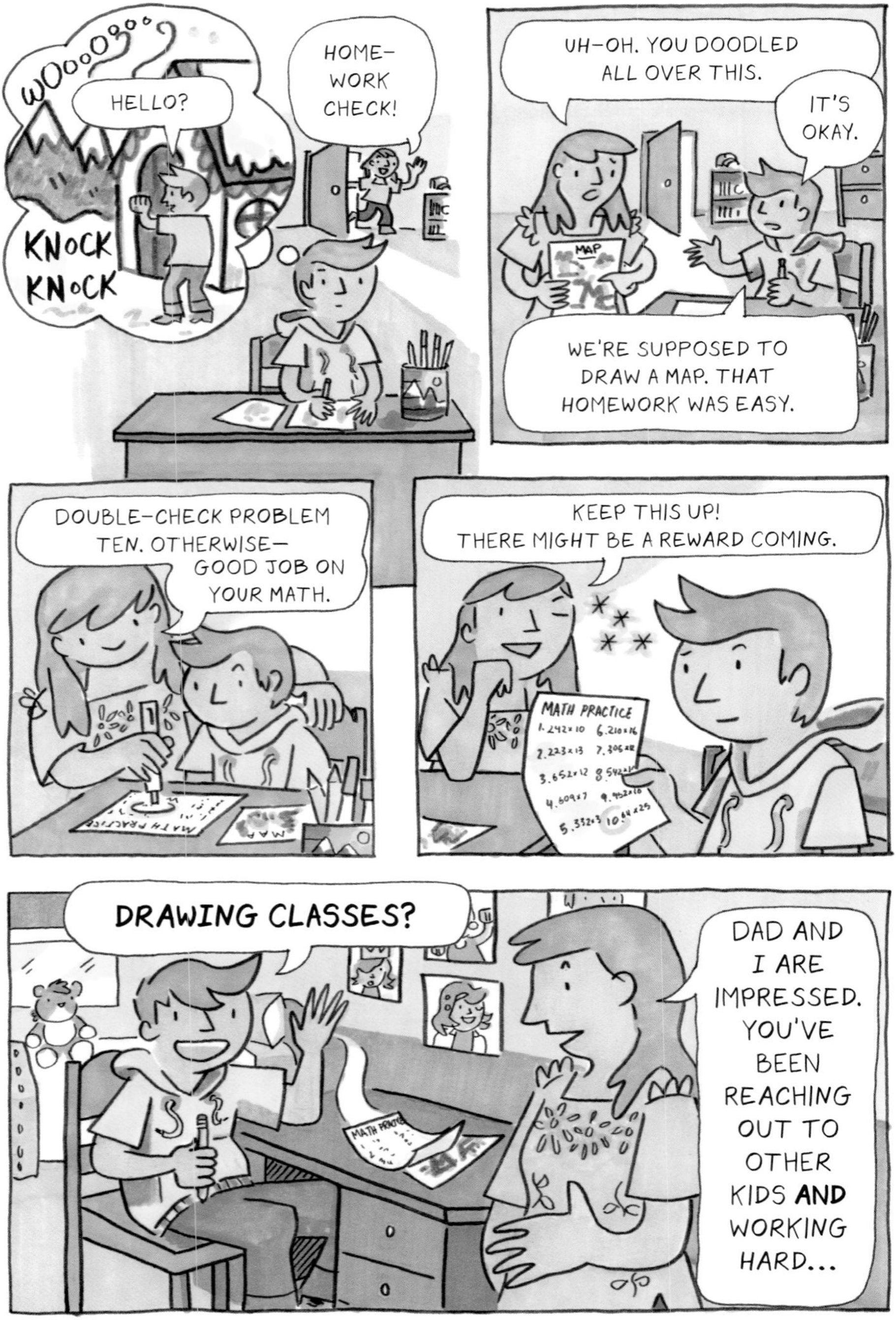
WOooOoooo
HELLO?
KNOCK KNOCK
HOME-WORK CHECK!
UH-OH. YOU DOODLED ALL OVER THIS.
IT'S OKAY.
MAP
WE'RE SUPPOSED TO DRAW A MAP. THAT HOMEWORK WAS EASY.
DOUBLE-CHECK PROBLEM TEN. OTHERWISE—
GOOD JOB ON YOUR MATH.
KEEP THIS UP! THERE MIGHT BE A REWARD COMING.
MATH PRACTICE
DRAWING CLASSES?
DAD AND I ARE IMPRESSED. YOU'VE BEEN REACHING OUT TO OTHER KIDS **AND** WORKING HARD...

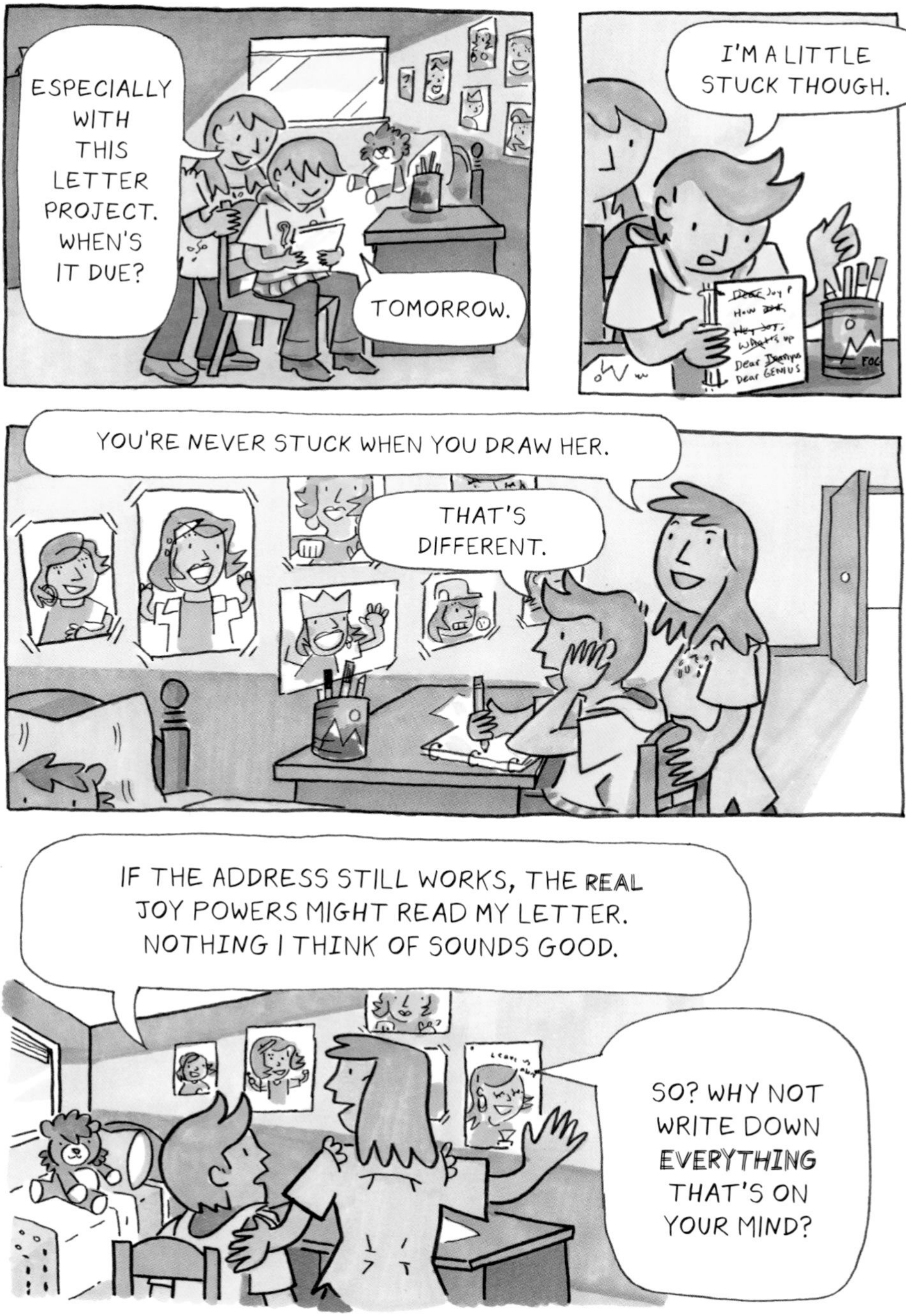
ESPECIALLY WITH THIS LETTER PROJECT. WHEN'S IT DUE?
TOMORROW.
I'M A LITTLE STUCK THOUGH.
YOU'RE NEVER STUCK WHEN YOU DRAW HER.
THAT'S DIFFERENT.
IF THE ADDRESS STILL WORKS, THE REAL JOY POWERS MIGHT READ MY LETTER. NOTHING I THINK OF SOUNDS GOOD.
SO? WHY NOT WRITE DOWN EVERYTHING THAT'S ON YOUR MIND?

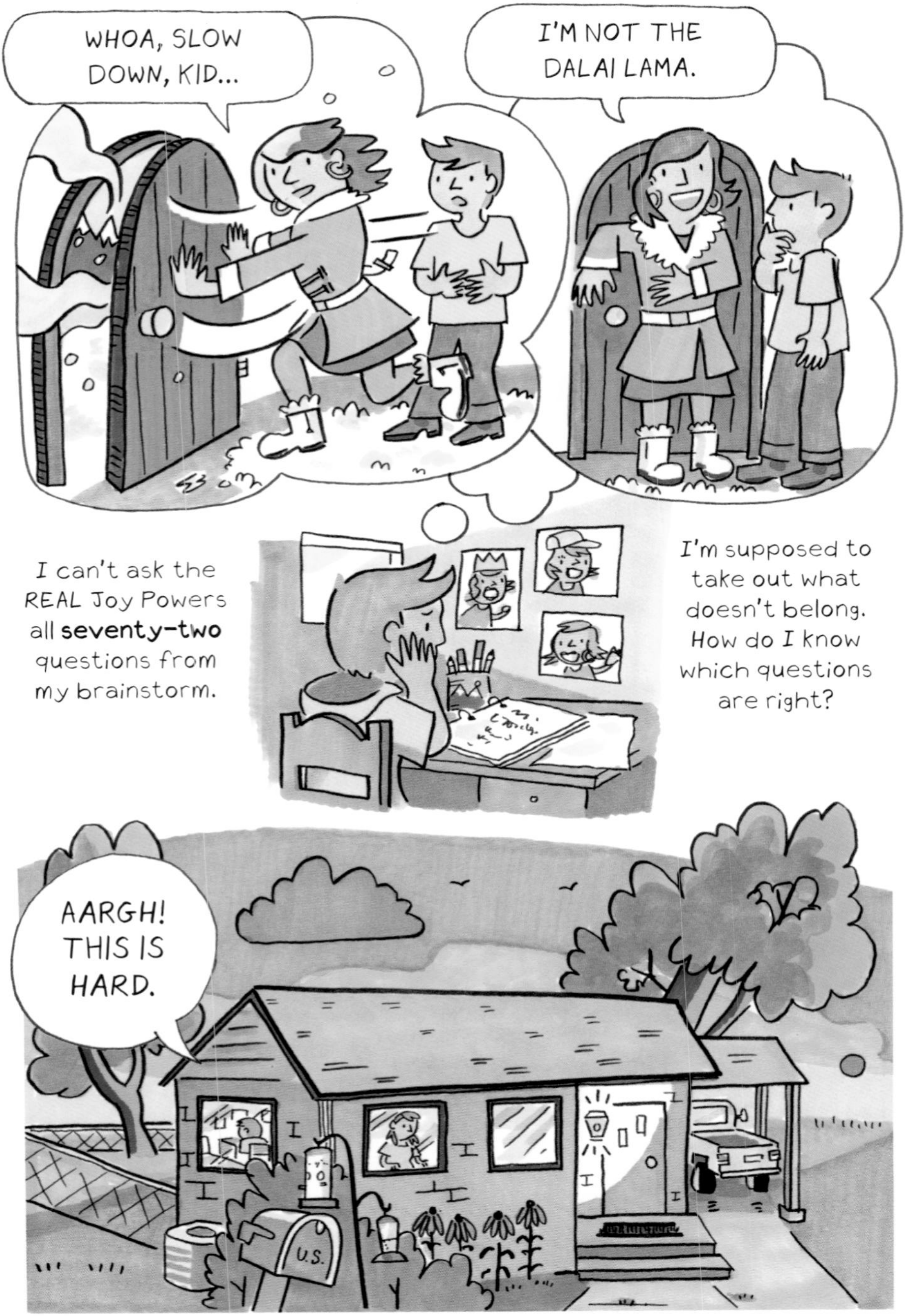
WHOA, SLOW DOWN, KID...
I'M NOT THE DALAI LAMA.
I can't ask the REAL Joy Powers all **seventy-two** questions from my brainstorm.
I'm supposed to take out what doesn't belong. How do I know which questions are right?
AARGH! THIS IS HARD.
U.S.

The next morning, I ask Danny about the Whitney situation.

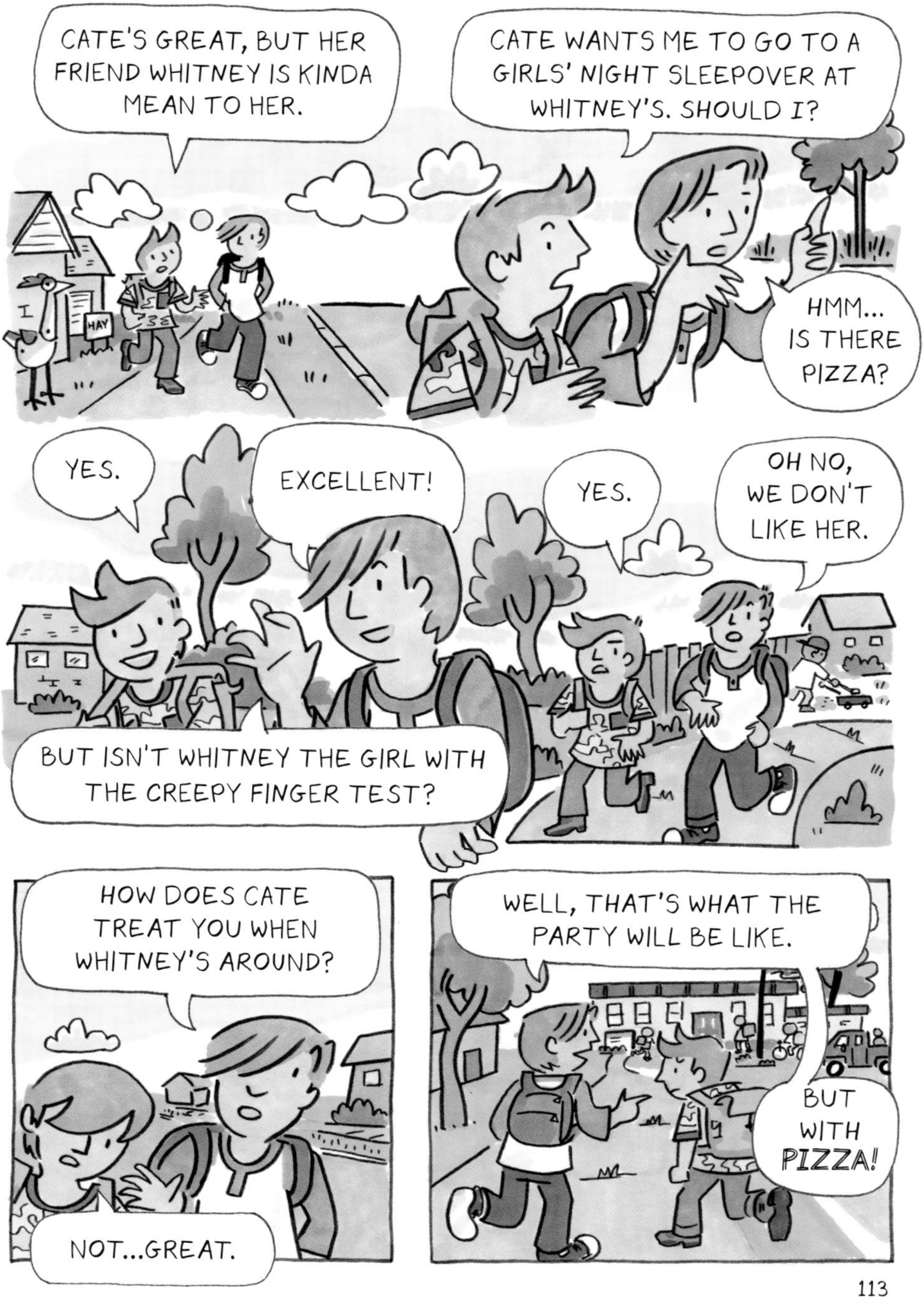
CATE'S GREAT, BUT HER FRIEND WHITNEY IS KINDA MEAN TO HER.
CATE WANTS ME TO GO TO A GIRLS' NIGHT SLEEPOVER AT WHITNEY'S. SHOULD I?
HAY
HMM... IS THERE PIZZA?
YES.
EXCELLENT!
YES.
OH NO, WE DON'T LIKE HER.
BUT ISN'T WHITNEY THE GIRL WITH THE CREEPY FINGER TEST?
HOW DOES CATE TREAT YOU WHEN WHITNEY'S AROUND?
NOT...GREAT.
WELL, THAT'S WHAT THE PARTY WILL BE LIKE.
BUT WITH PIZZA!

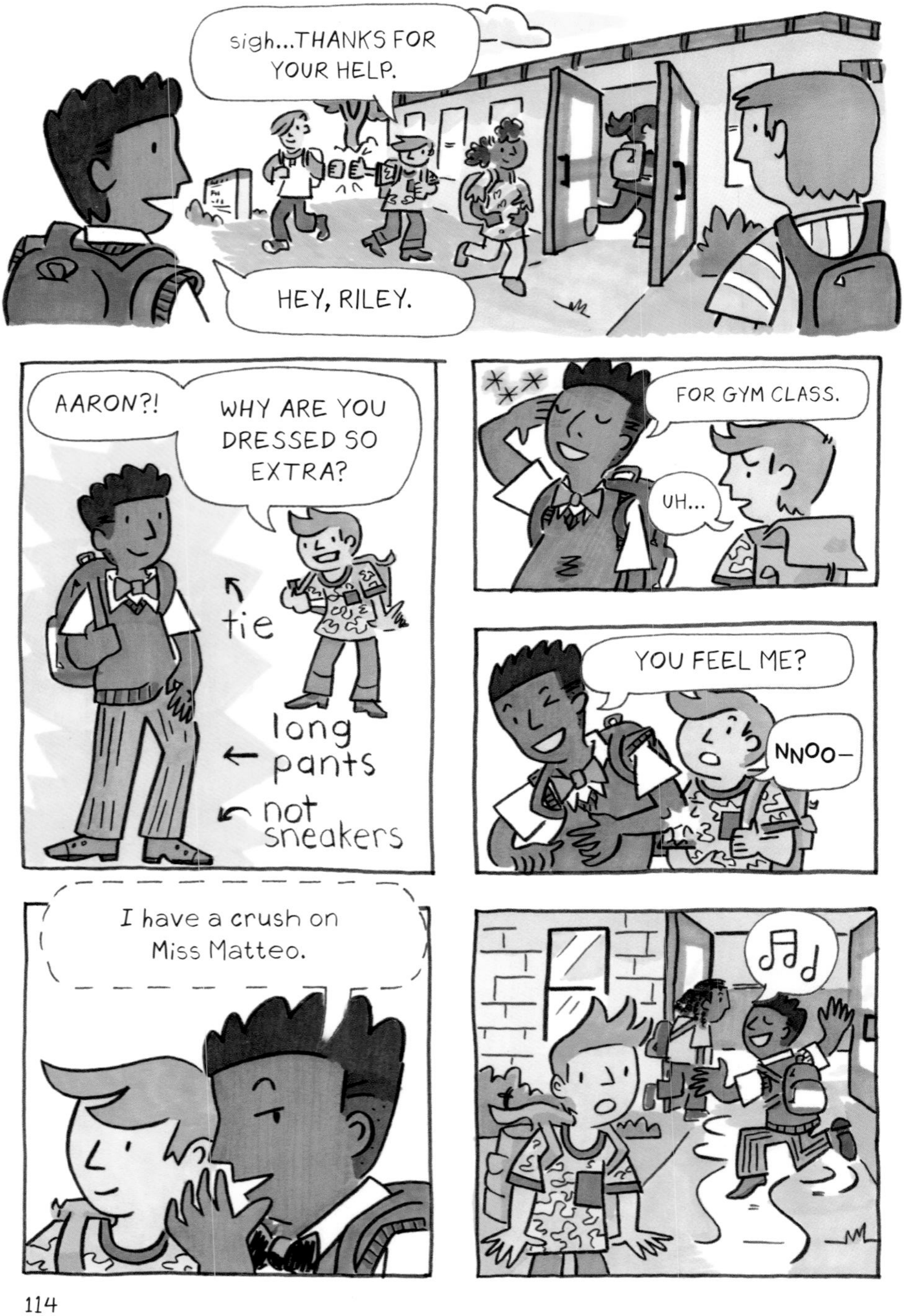
sigh...THANKS FOR YOUR HELP.
HEY, RILEY.
AARON?!
WHY ARE YOU DRESSED SO EXTRA?
tie
long pants
not sneakers
FOR GYM CLASS.
UH...
YOU FEEL ME?
NNOO–
I have a crush on Miss Matteo.

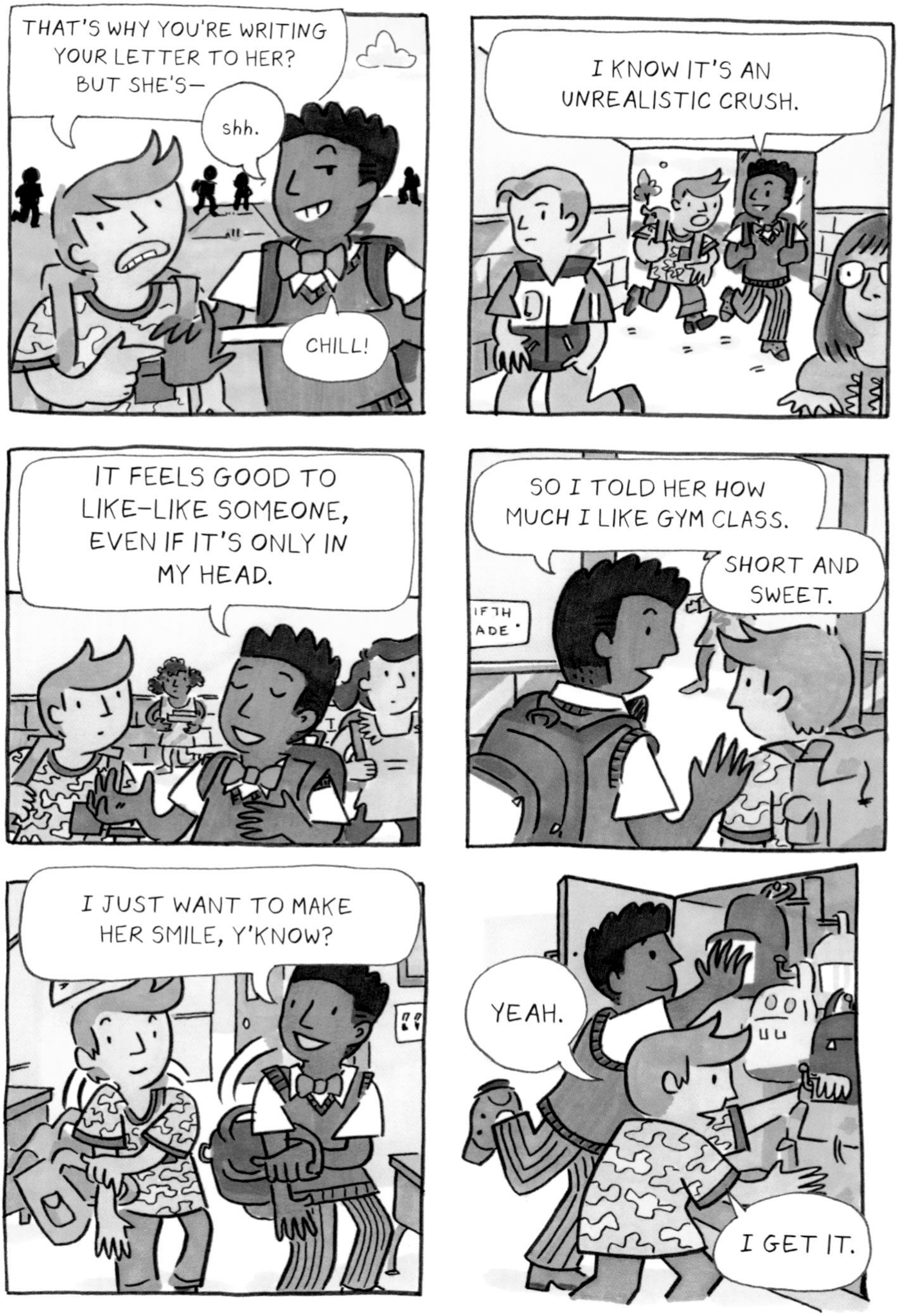
THAT'S WHY YOU'RE WRITING YOUR LETTER TO HER? BUT SHE'S—
shh.
CHILL!
I KNOW IT'S AN UNREALISTIC CRUSH.
IT FEELS GOOD TO LIKE-LIKE SOMEONE, EVEN IF IT'S ONLY IN MY HEAD.
SO I TOLD HER HOW MUCH I LIKE GYM CLASS.
SHORT AND SWEET.
I JUST WANT TO MAKE HER SMILE, Y'KNOW?
YEAH.
I GET IT.

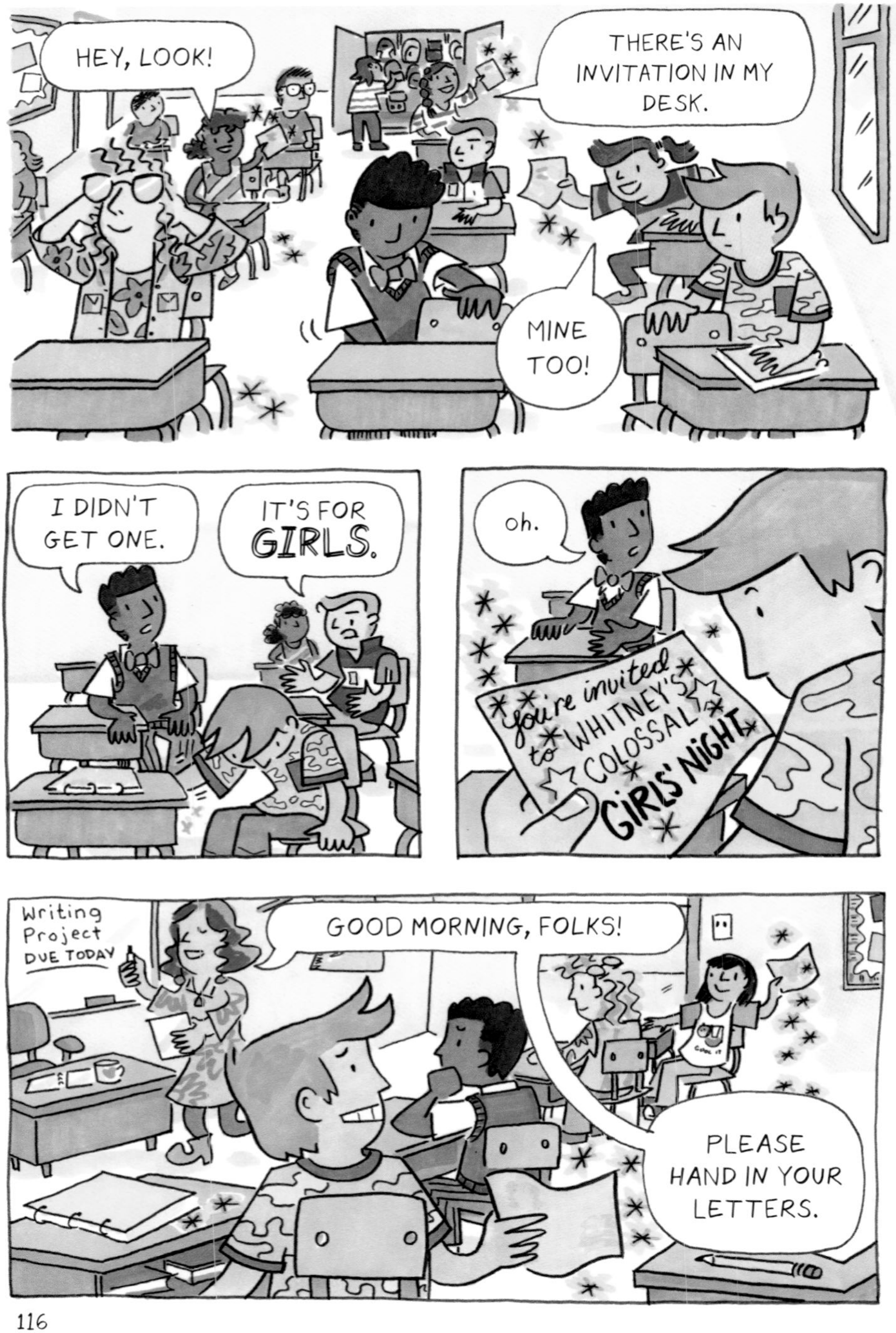
HEY, LOOK!
THERE'S AN INVITATION IN MY DESK.
MINE TOO!
I DIDN'T GET ONE.
IT'S FOR GIRLS.
oh.
You're invited to WHITNEY'S COLOSSAL GIRLS' NIGHT
Writing Project DUE TODAY
GOOD MORNING, FOLKS!
PLEASE HAND IN YOUR LETTERS.

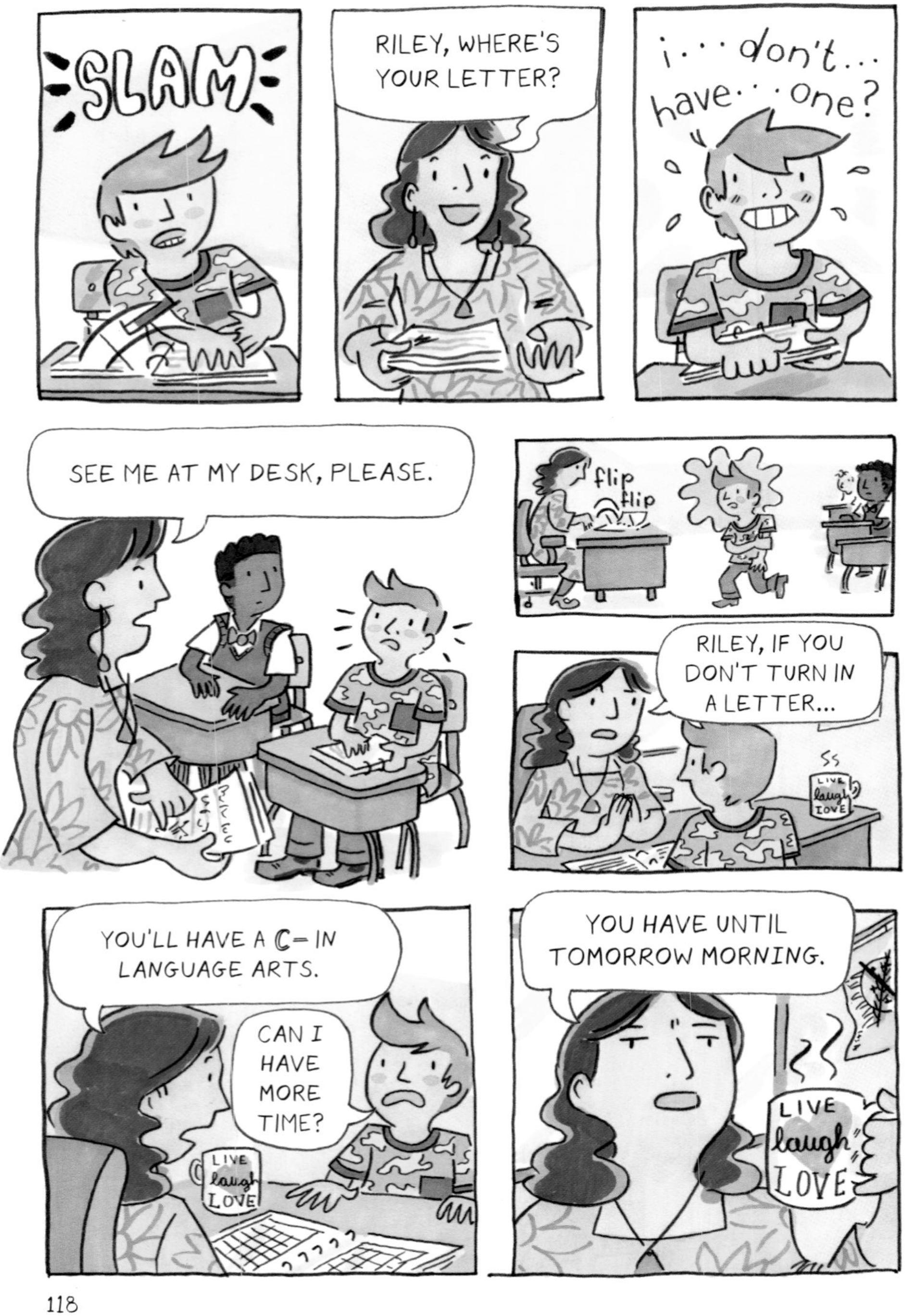
SLAM
RILEY, WHERE'S YOUR LETTER?
i... don't... have... one?
SEE ME AT MY DESK, PLEASE.
flip flip
RILEY, IF YOU DON'T TURN IN A LETTER...
LIVE laugh LOVE
YOU'LL HAVE A C- IN LANGUAGE ARTS.
CAN I HAVE MORE TIME?
LIVE laugh LOVE
YOU HAVE UNTIL TOMORROW MORNING.
LIVE laugh LOVE

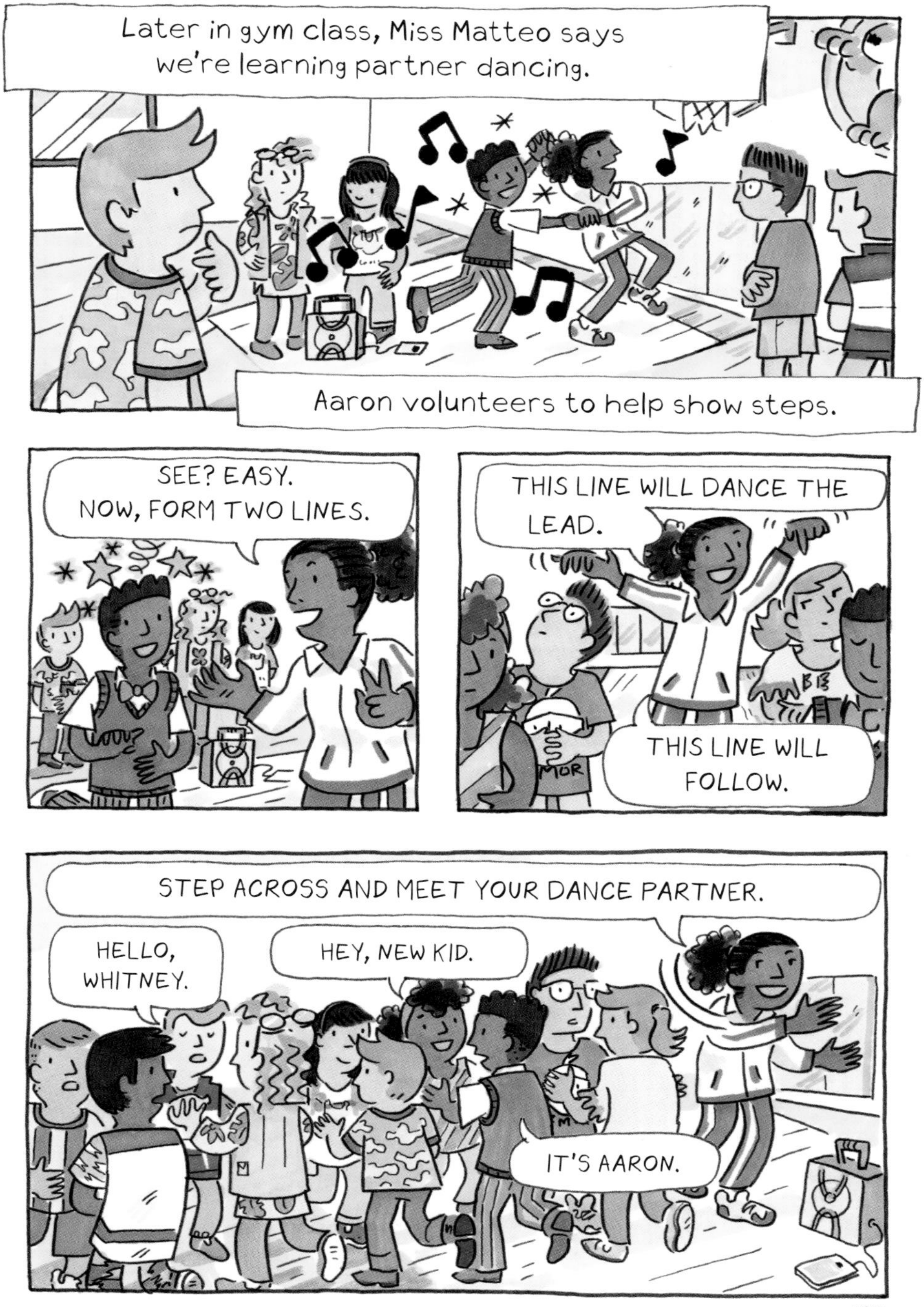

CHAPTER 13

Later in gym class, Miss Matteo says we're learning partner dancing.
Aaron volunteers to help show steps.
SEE? EASY. NOW, FORM TWO LINES.
THIS LINE WILL DANCE THE LEAD.
THIS LINE WILL FOLLOW.
STEP ACROSS AND MEET YOUR DANCE PARTNER.
HELLO, WHITNEY.
HEY, NEW KID.
IT'S AARON.

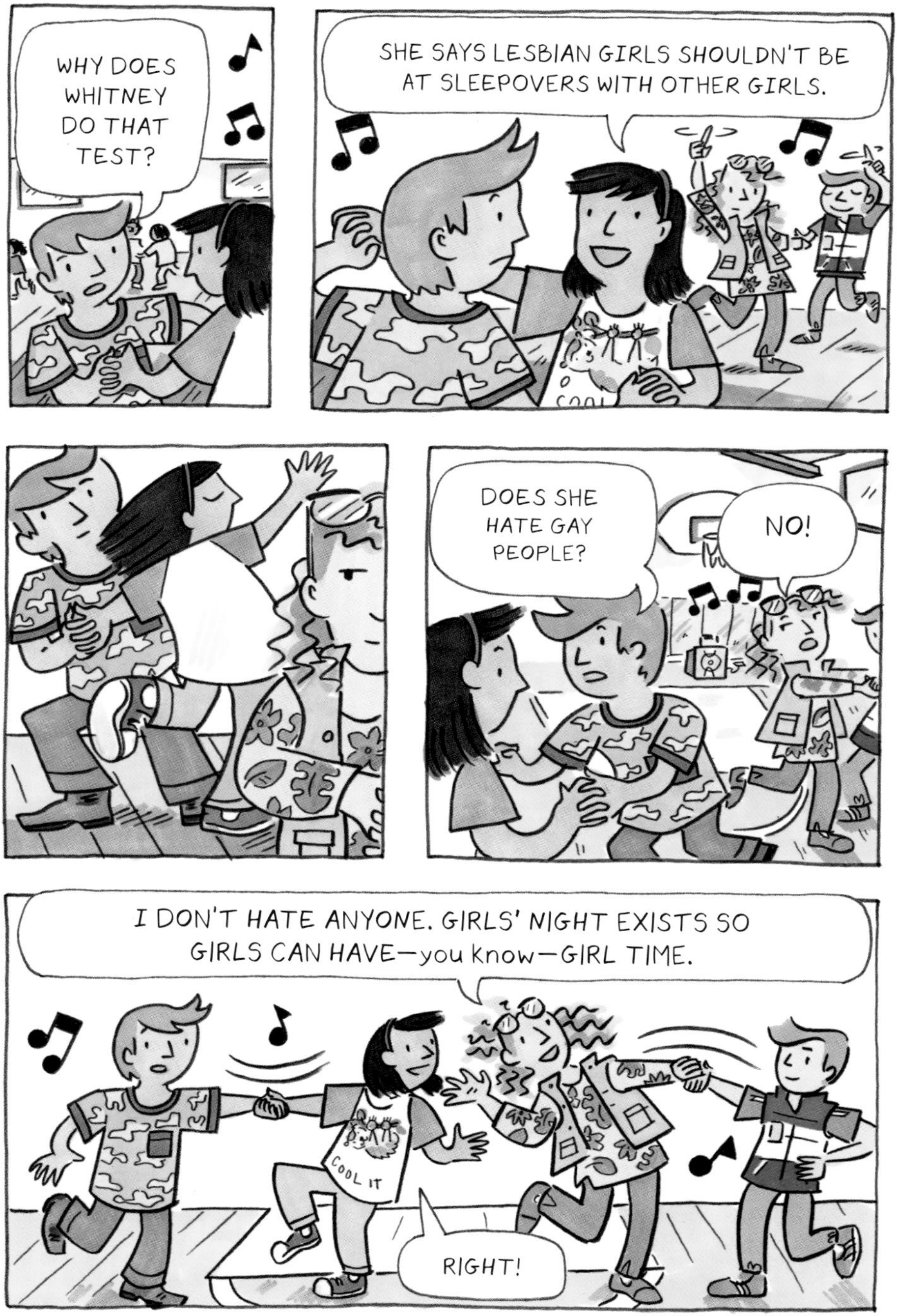
WHY DOES WHITNEY DO THAT TEST?
SHE SAYS LESBIAN GIRLS SHOULDN'T BE AT SLEEPOVERS WITH OTHER GIRLS.
COOL
DOES SHE HATE GAY PEOPLE?
NO!
I DON'T HATE ANYONE. GIRLS' NIGHT EXISTS SO GIRLS CAN HAVE—you know—GIRL TIME.
COOL IT
RIGHT!

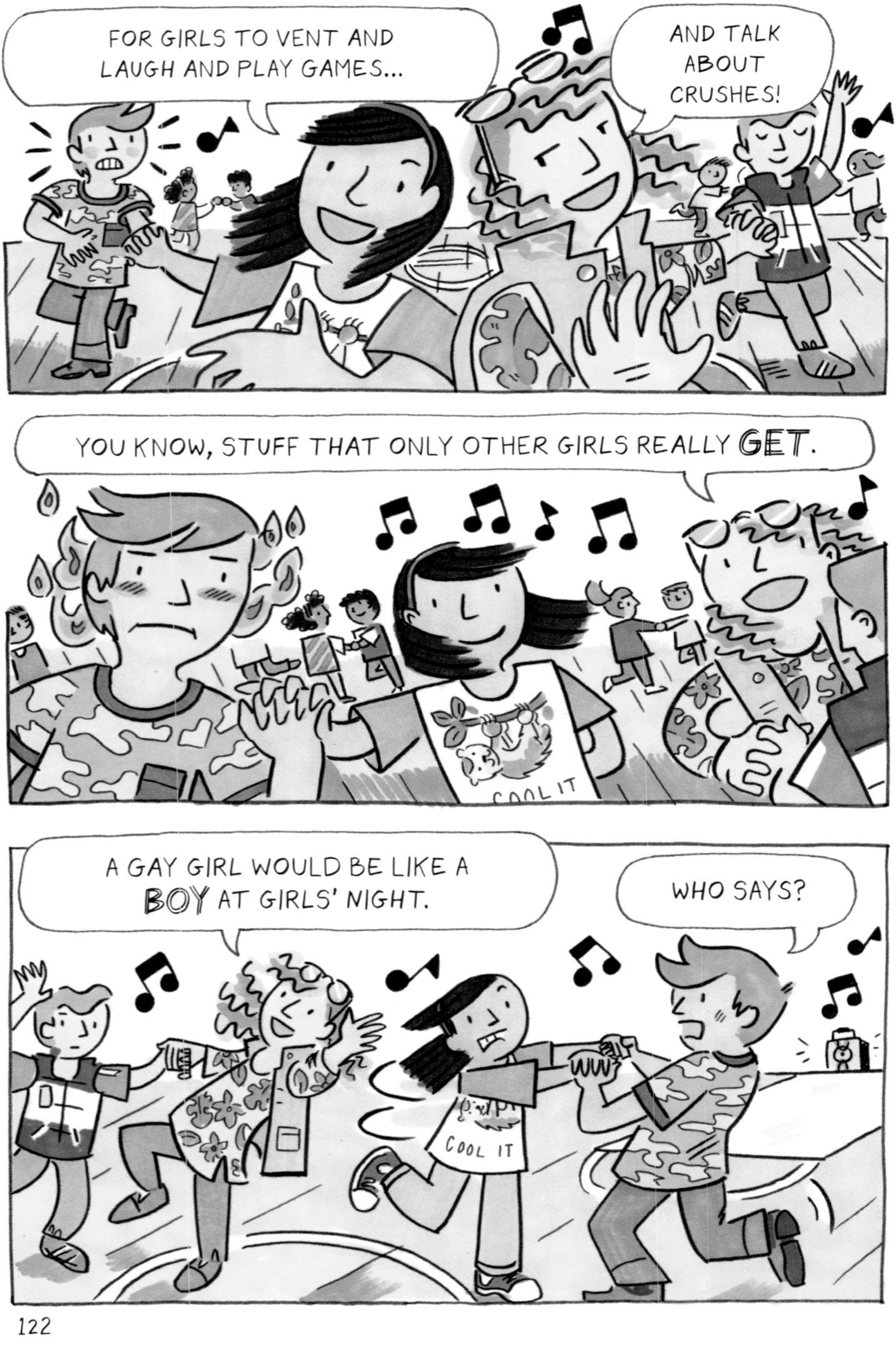
FOR GIRLS TO VENT AND LAUGH AND PLAY GAMES...
AND TALK ABOUT CRUSHES!
YOU KNOW, STUFF THAT ONLY OTHER GIRLS REALLY GET.
COOL IT
A GAY GIRL WOULD BE LIKE A BOY AT GIRLS' NIGHT.
WHO SAYS?
COOL IT

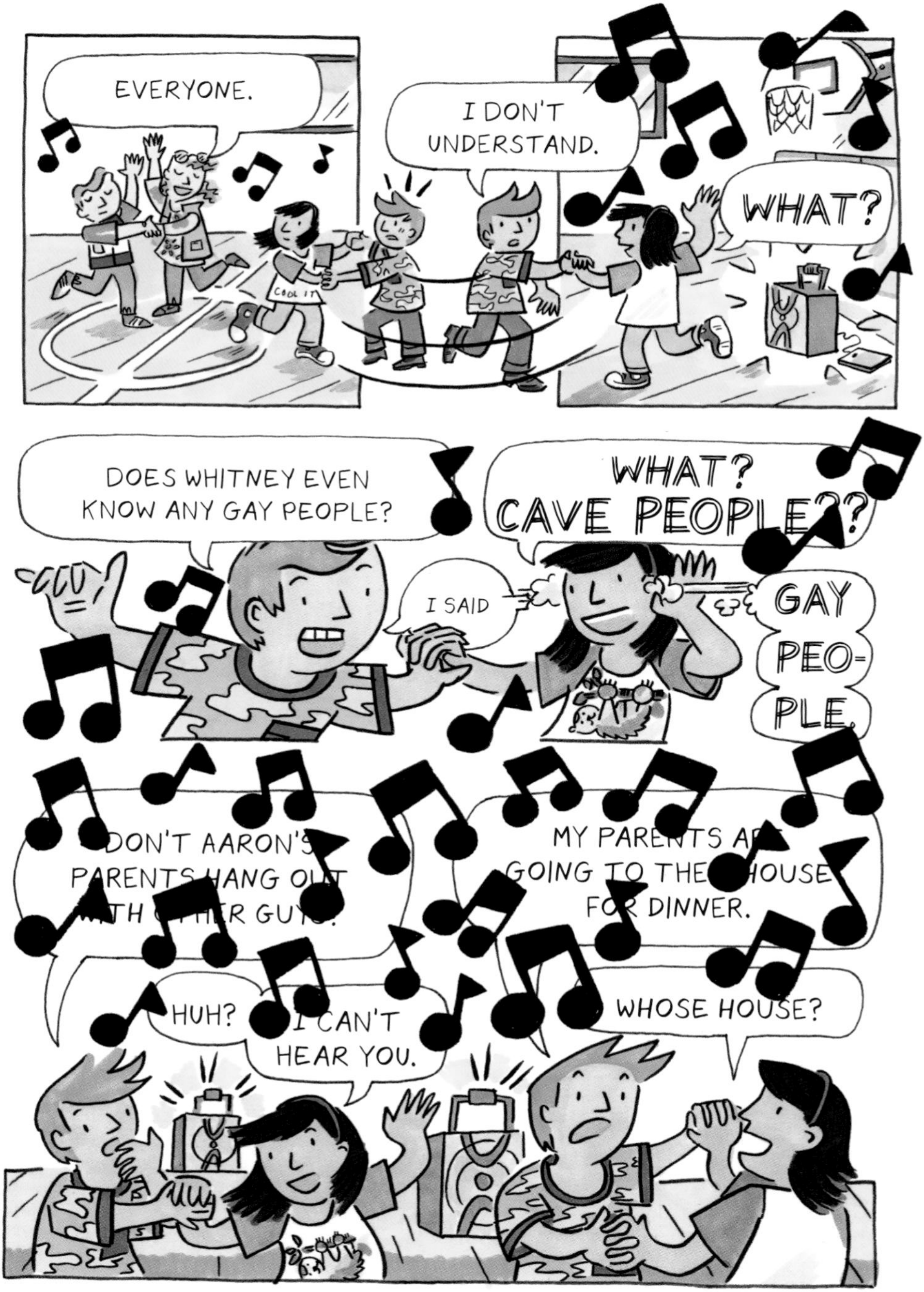
EVERYONE.
I DON'T UNDERSTAND.
WHAT?
DOES WHITNEY EVEN KNOW ANY GAY PEOPLE?
WHAT? CAVE PEOPLE??
I SAID
GAY PEO-PLE.
DON'T AARON'S PARENTS HANG OUT
MY PARENTS A
GOING TO THE HOUSE
FOR DINNER.
HUH?
I CAN'T HEAR YOU.
WHOSE HOUSE?

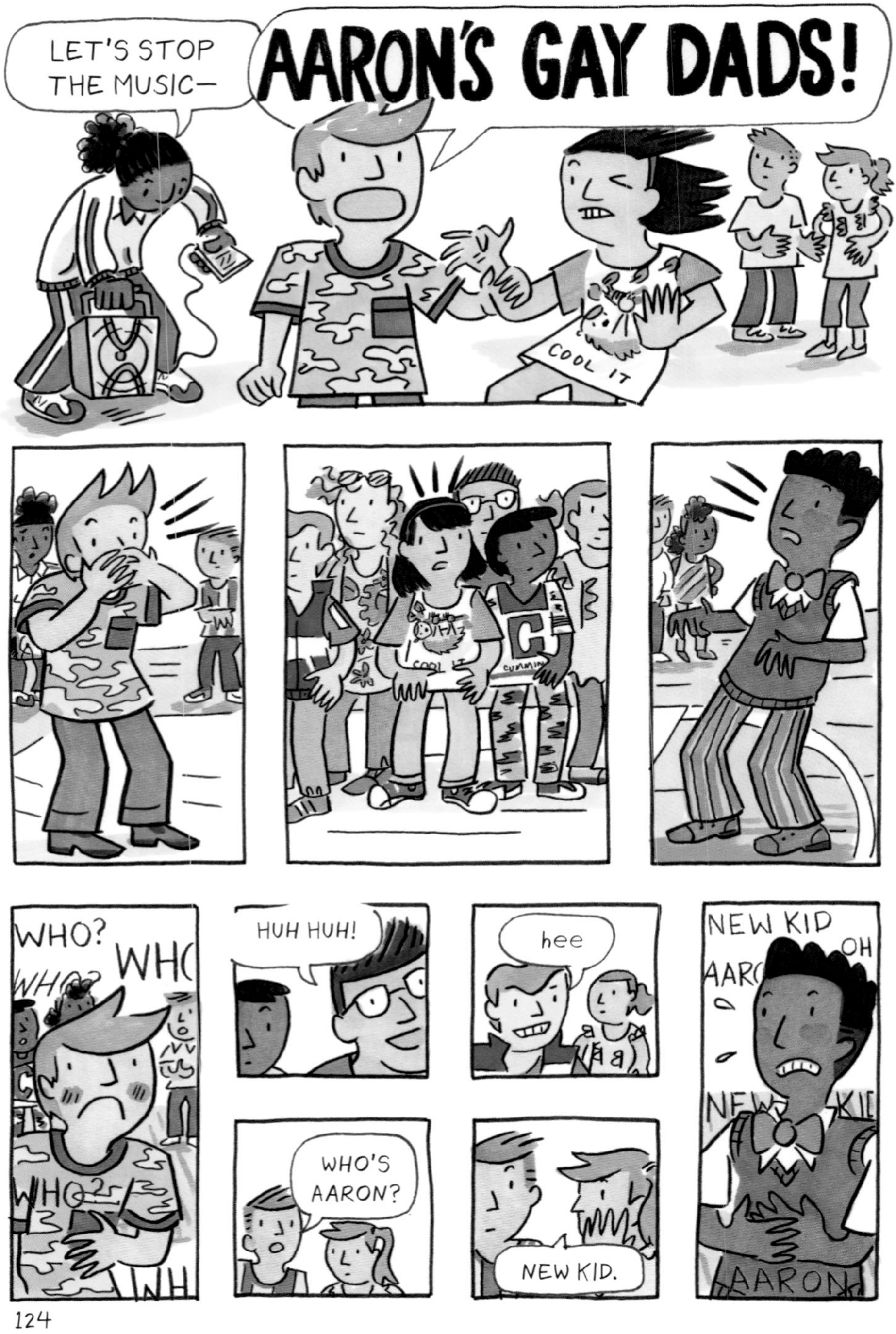
LET'S STOP THE MUSIC—
AARON'S GAY DADS!
COOL IT
WHO?
WHO
WHO?
WHO?
WH
HUH HUH!
hee
WHO'S AARON?
NEW KID.
NEW KID
OH
AARON

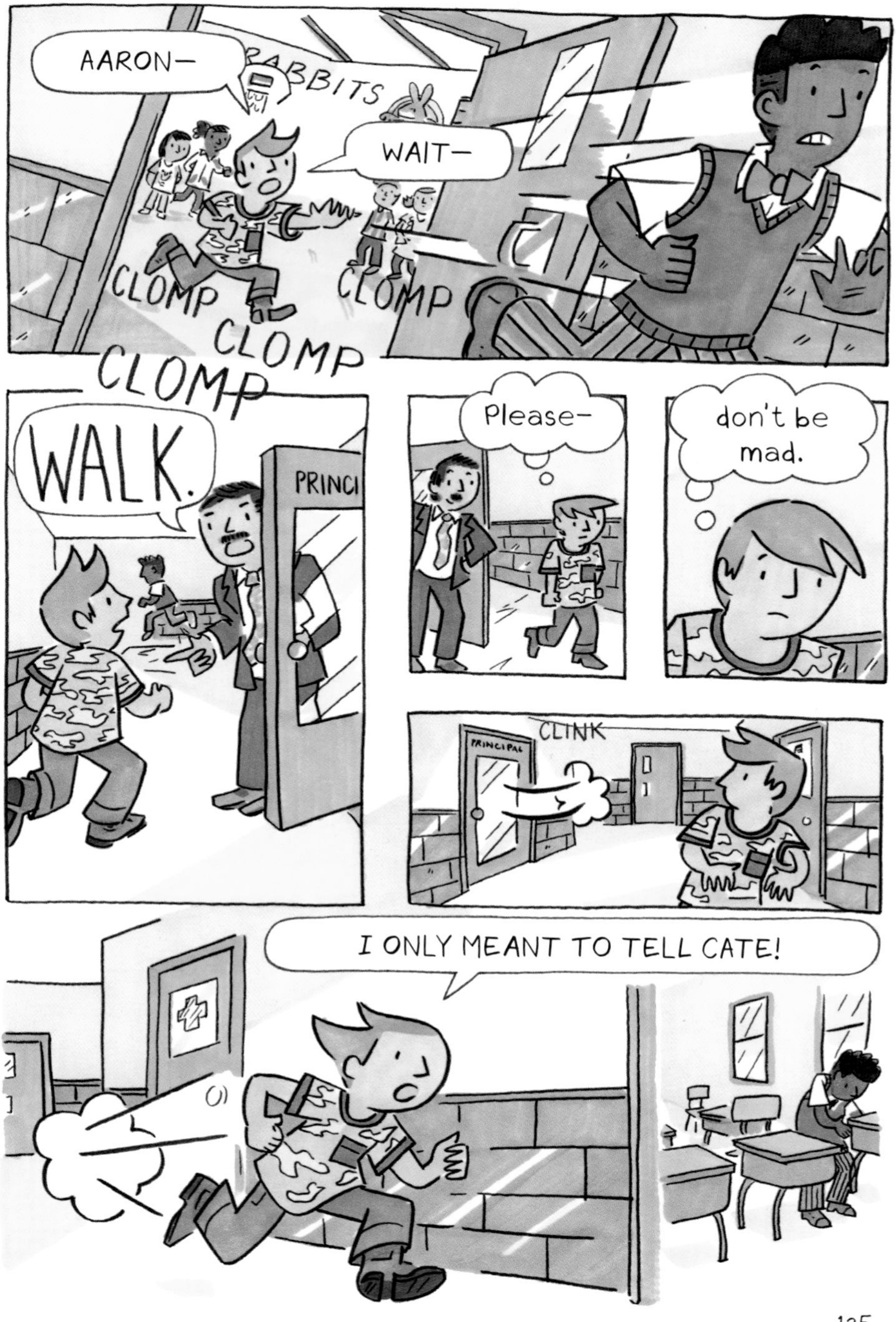
AARON—
RABBITS
WAIT—
CLOMP
CLOMP
CLOMP
CLOMP
WALK.
PRINCI
Please-
don't be mad.
PRINCIPAL
CLINK
I ONLY MEANT TO TELL CATE!

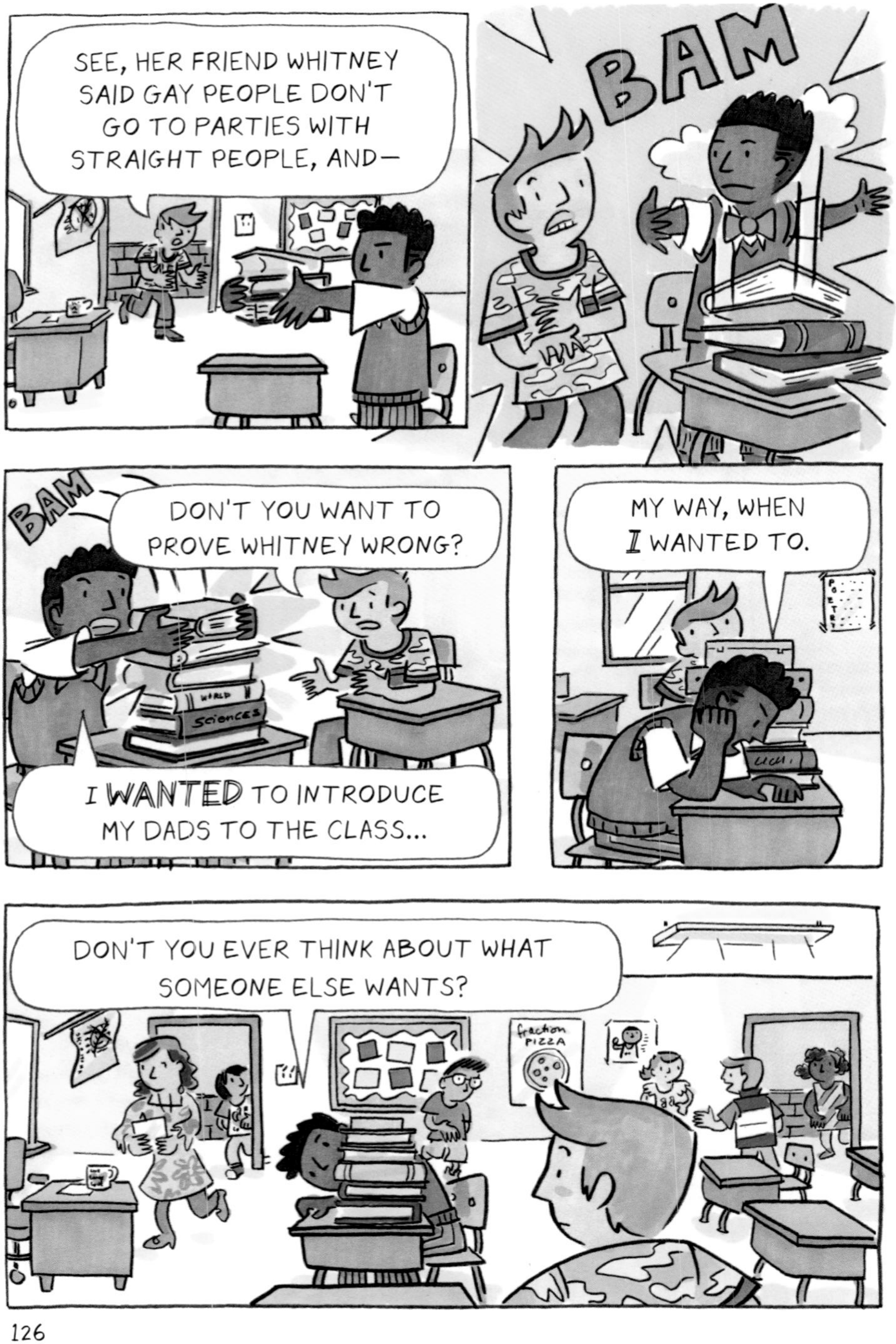
SEE, HER FRIEND WHITNEY SAID GAY PEOPLE DON'T GO TO PARTIES WITH STRAIGHT PEOPLE, AND—
BAM
BAM
DON'T YOU WANT TO PROVE WHITNEY WRONG?
I WANTED TO INTRODUCE MY DADS TO THE CLASS...
MY WAY, WHEN I WANTED TO.
DON'T YOU EVER THINK ABOUT WHAT SOMEONE ELSE WANTS?

CHAPTER 14

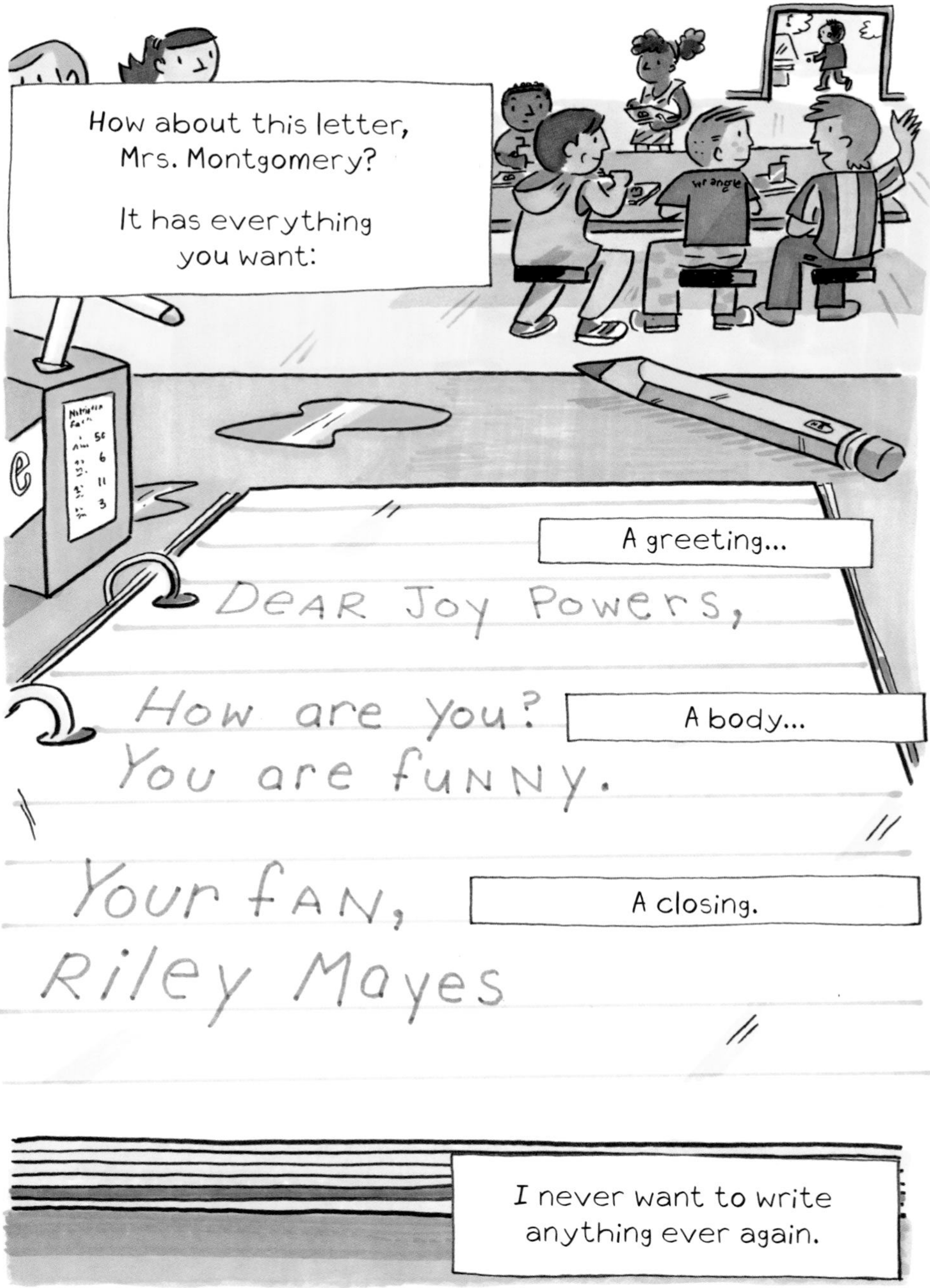

How about this letter, Mrs. Montgomery?
It has everything you want:
A greeting...
Dear Joy Powers,
How are you? You are funny.
A body...
Your fan, Riley Mayes
A closing.
I never want to write anything ever again.

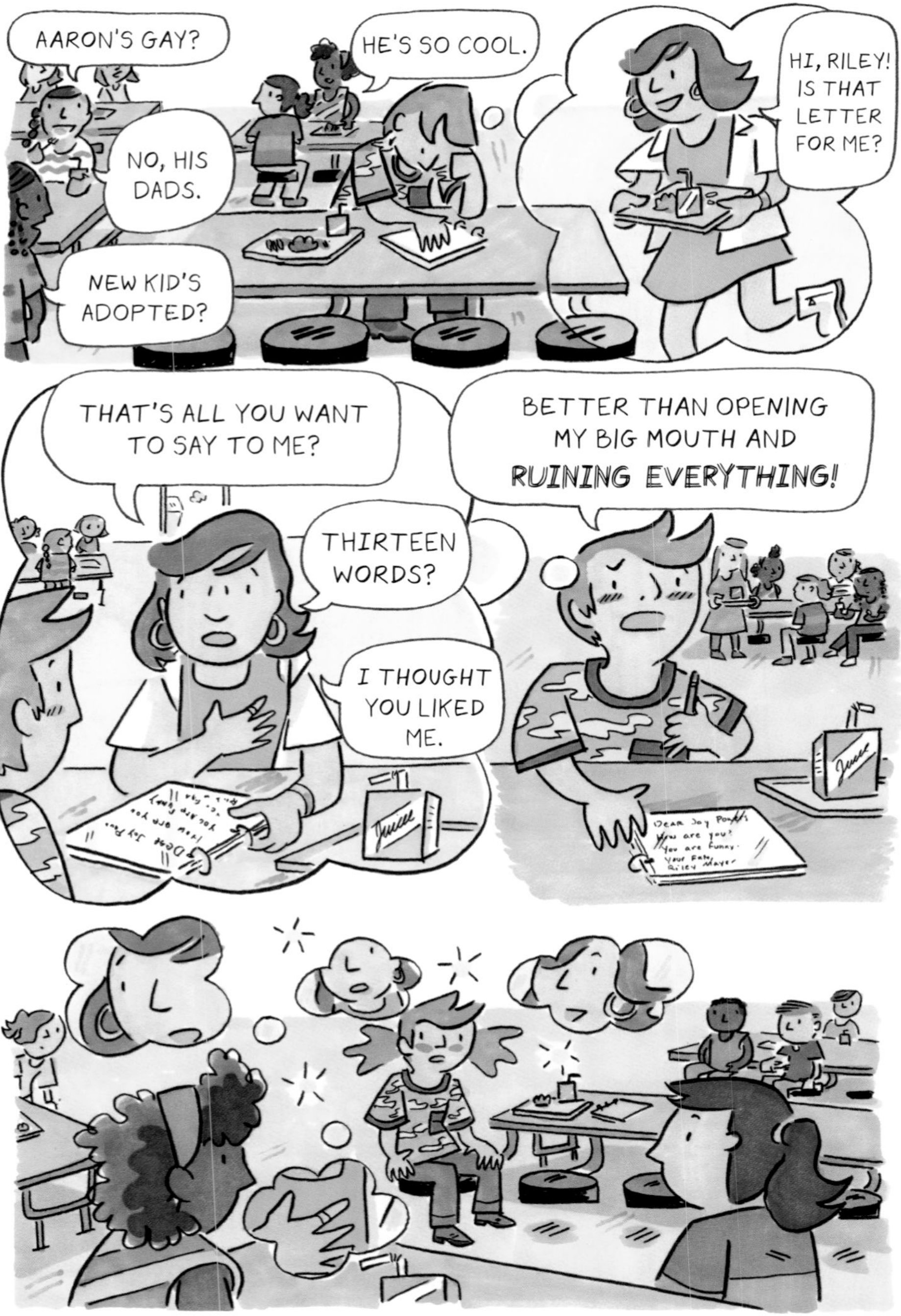
AARON'S GAY?
NO, HIS DADS.
NEW KID'S ADOPTED?
HE'S SO COOL.
HI, RILEY! IS THAT LETTER FOR ME?
THAT'S ALL YOU WANT TO SAY TO ME?
THIRTEEN WORDS?
I THOUGHT YOU LIKED ME.
BETTER THAN OPENING MY BIG MOUTH AND RUINING EVERYTHING!

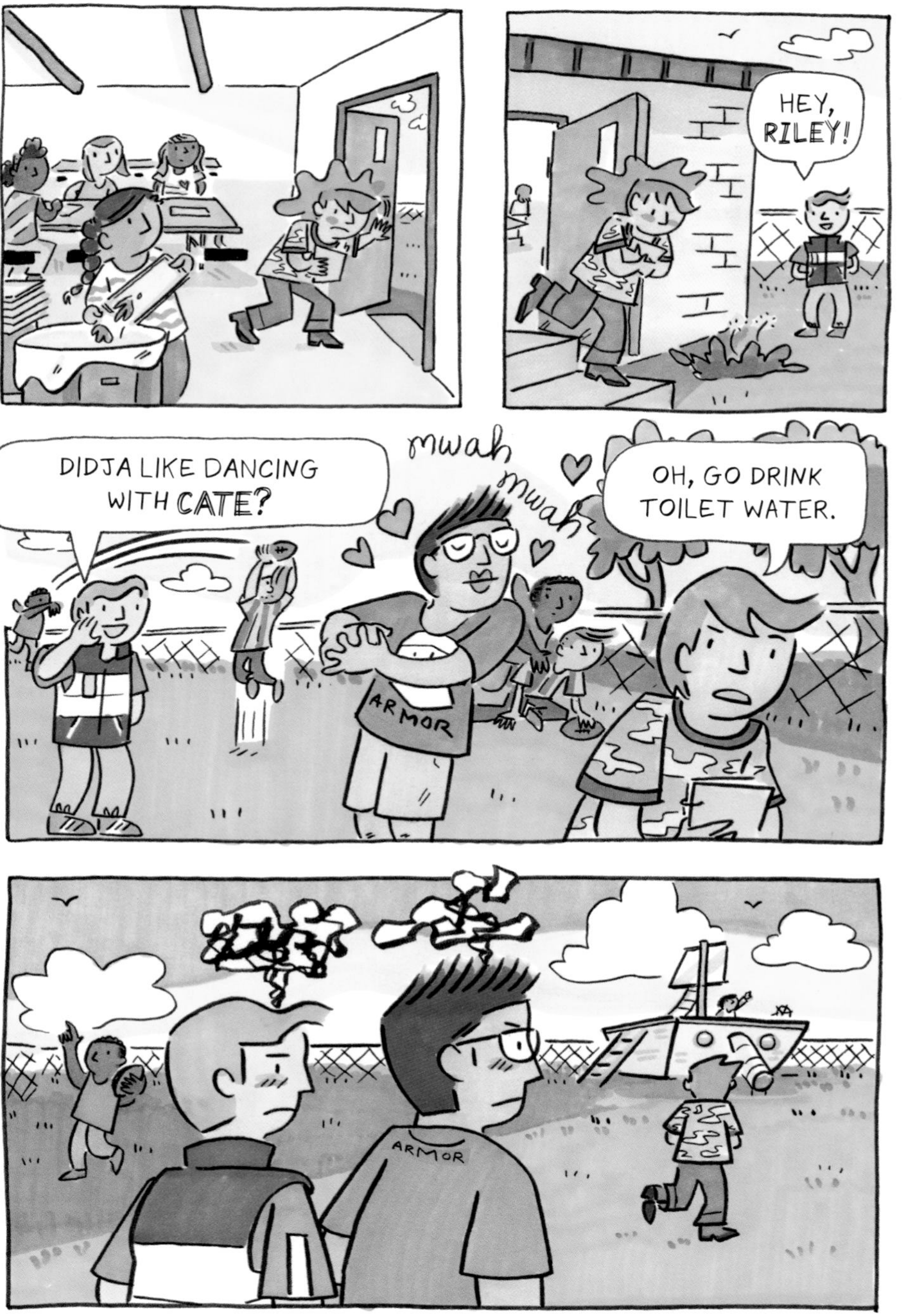
HEY, RILEY!
DIDJA LIKE DANCING WITH CATE?
mwah
mwah
OH, GO DRINK TOILET WATER.
ARMOR
ARMOR

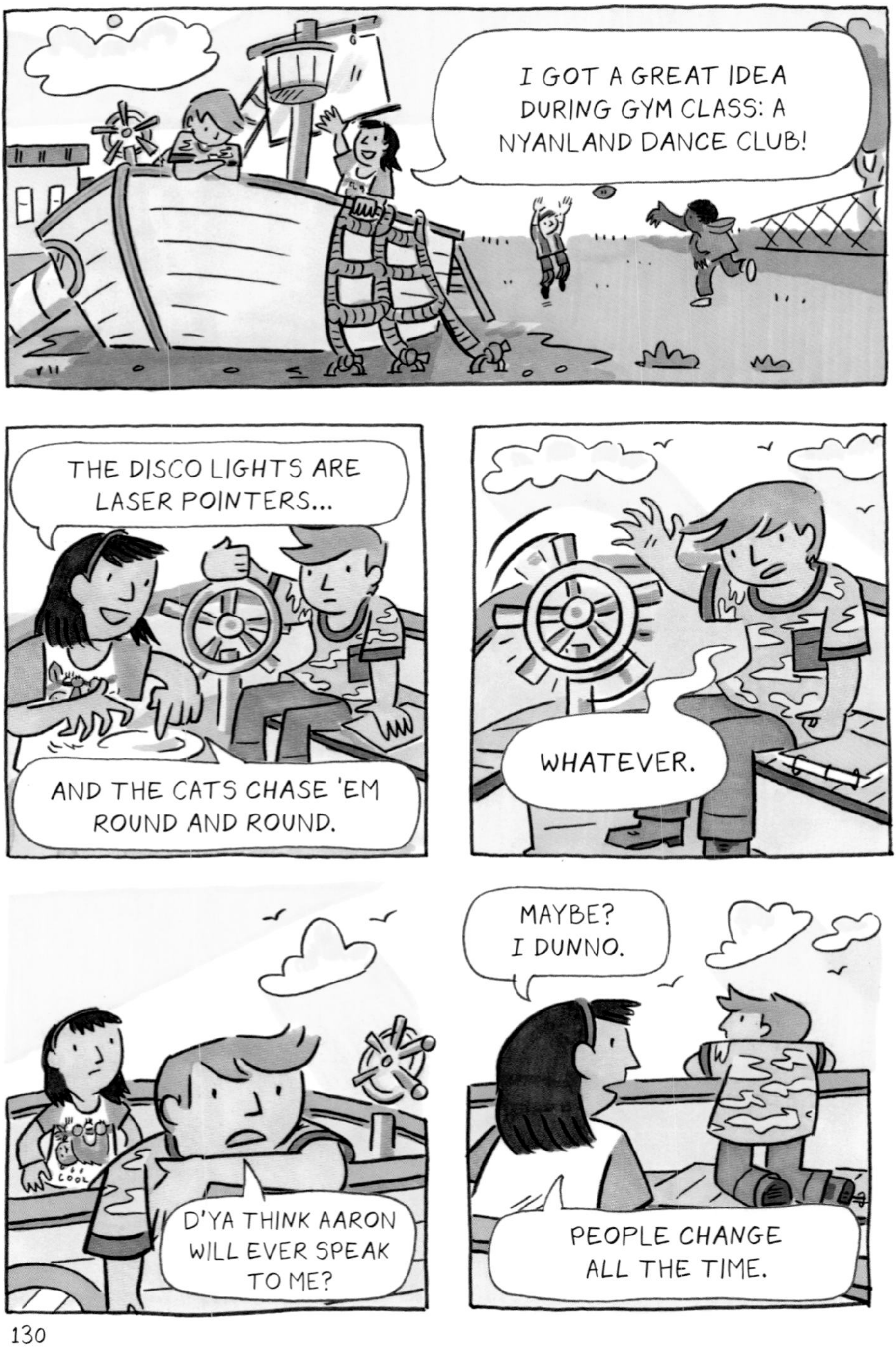
I GOT A GREAT IDEA DURING GYM CLASS: A NYANLAND DANCE CLUB!
THE DISCO LIGHTS ARE LASER POINTERS...
AND THE CATS CHASE 'EM ROUND AND ROUND.
WHATEVER.
D'YA THINK AARON WILL EVER SPEAK TO ME?
MAYBE? I DUNNO.
PEOPLE CHANGE ALL THE TIME.

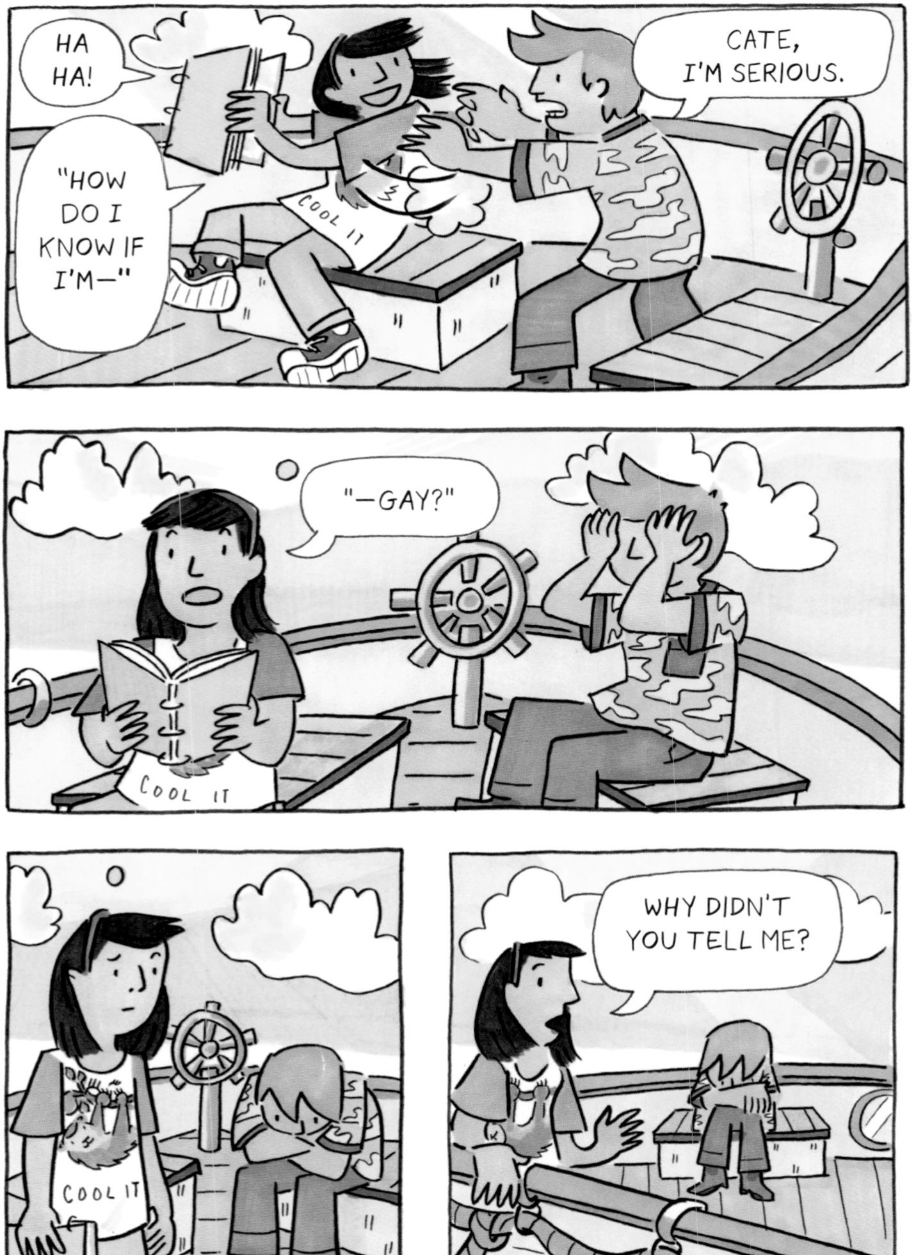
HA HA!
CATE, I'M SERIOUS.
"HOW DO I KNOW IF I'M—"
COOL IT
"—GAY?"
COOL IT
COOL IT
WHY DIDN'T YOU TELL ME?

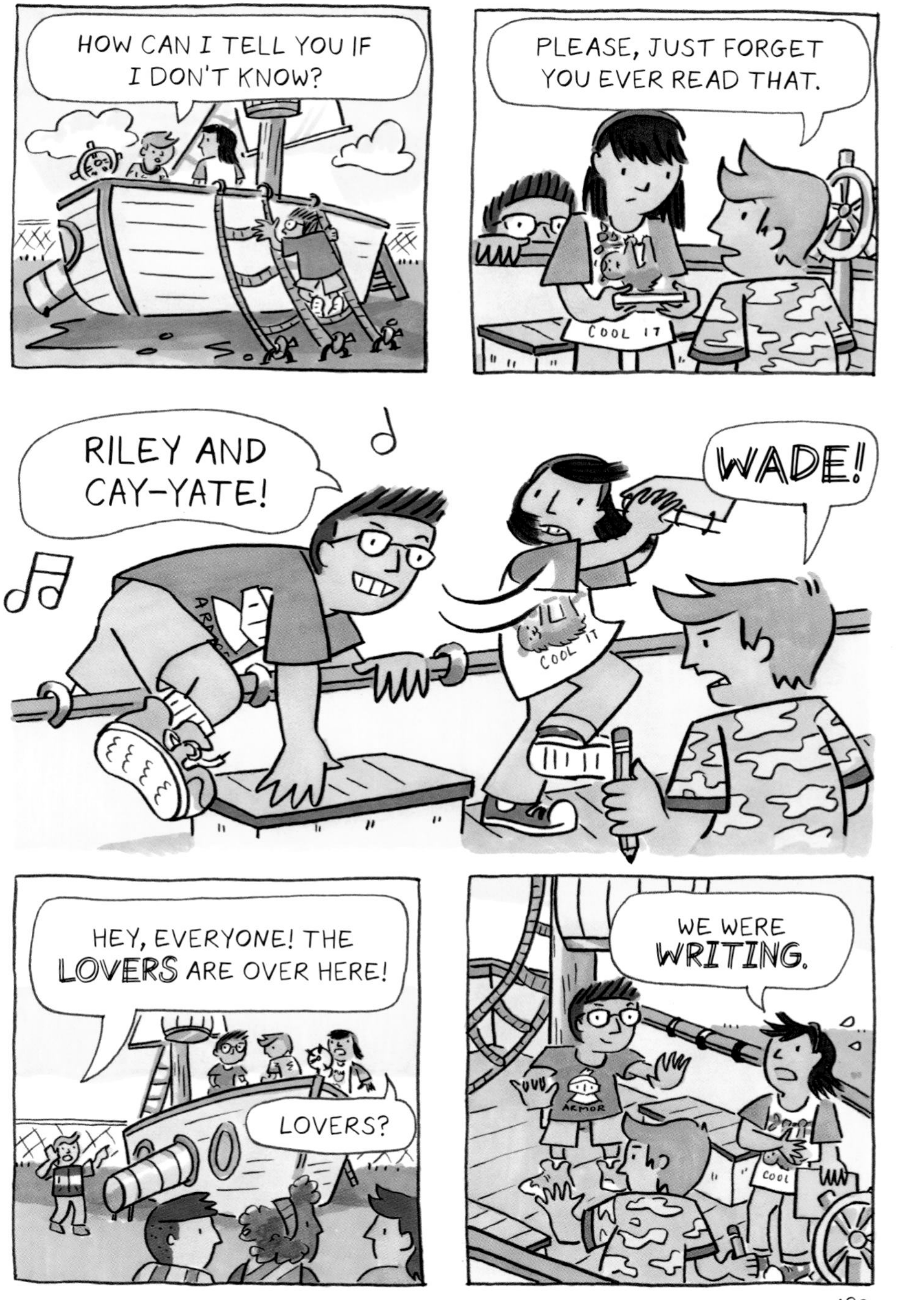
HOW CAN I TELL YOU IF I DON'T KNOW?
PLEASE, JUST FORGET YOU EVER READ THAT.
COOL IT
RILEY AND CAY-YATE!
WADE!
ARMOR
COOL IT
HEY, EVERYONE! THE LOVERS ARE OVER HERE!
LOVERS?
WE WERE WRITING.
ARMOR
COOL

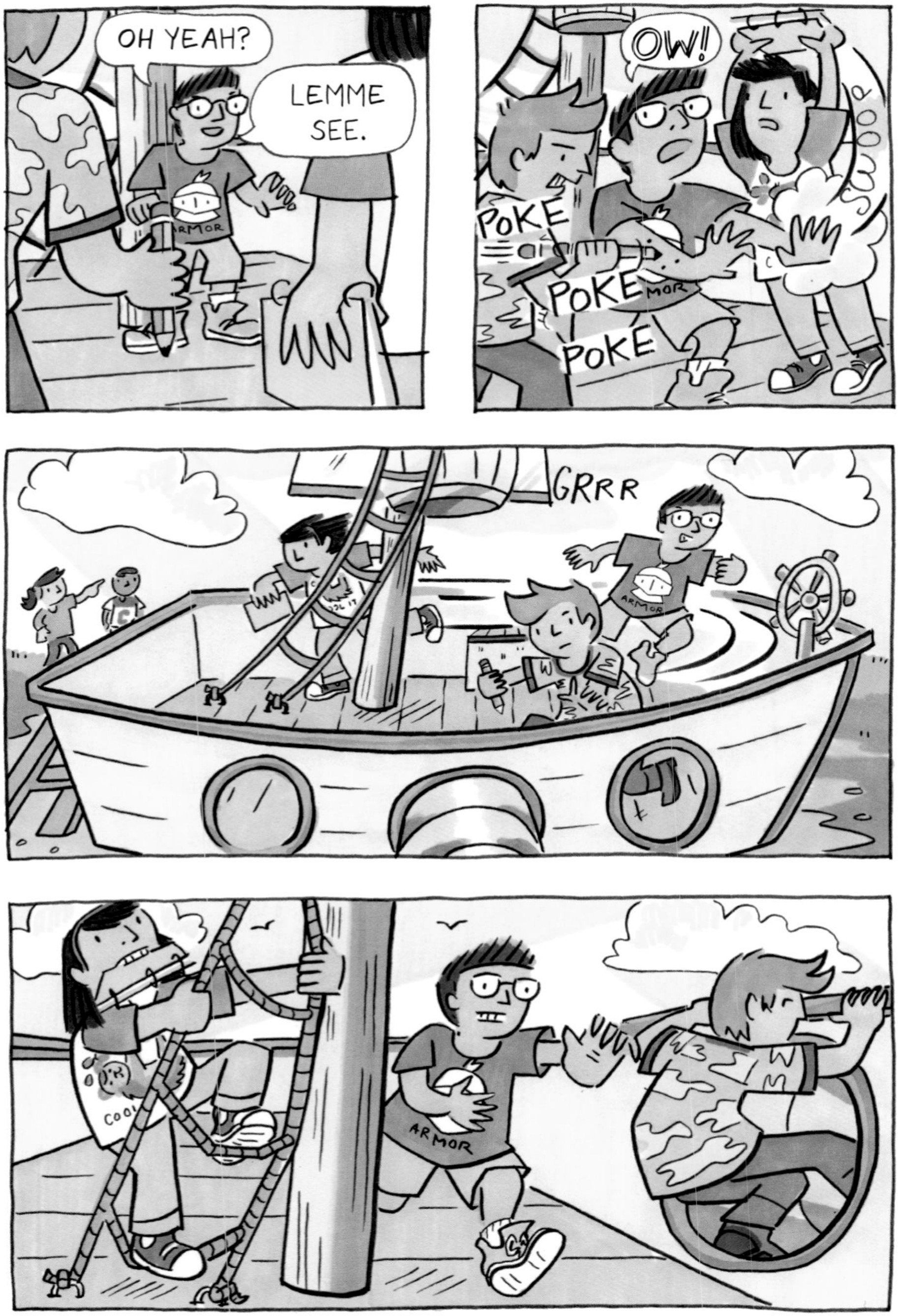
OH YEAH?
LEMME SEE.
ARMOR
OW!
SWOOP
POKE
POKE
POKE
GRRR
ARMOR
ARMOR
COOL

135

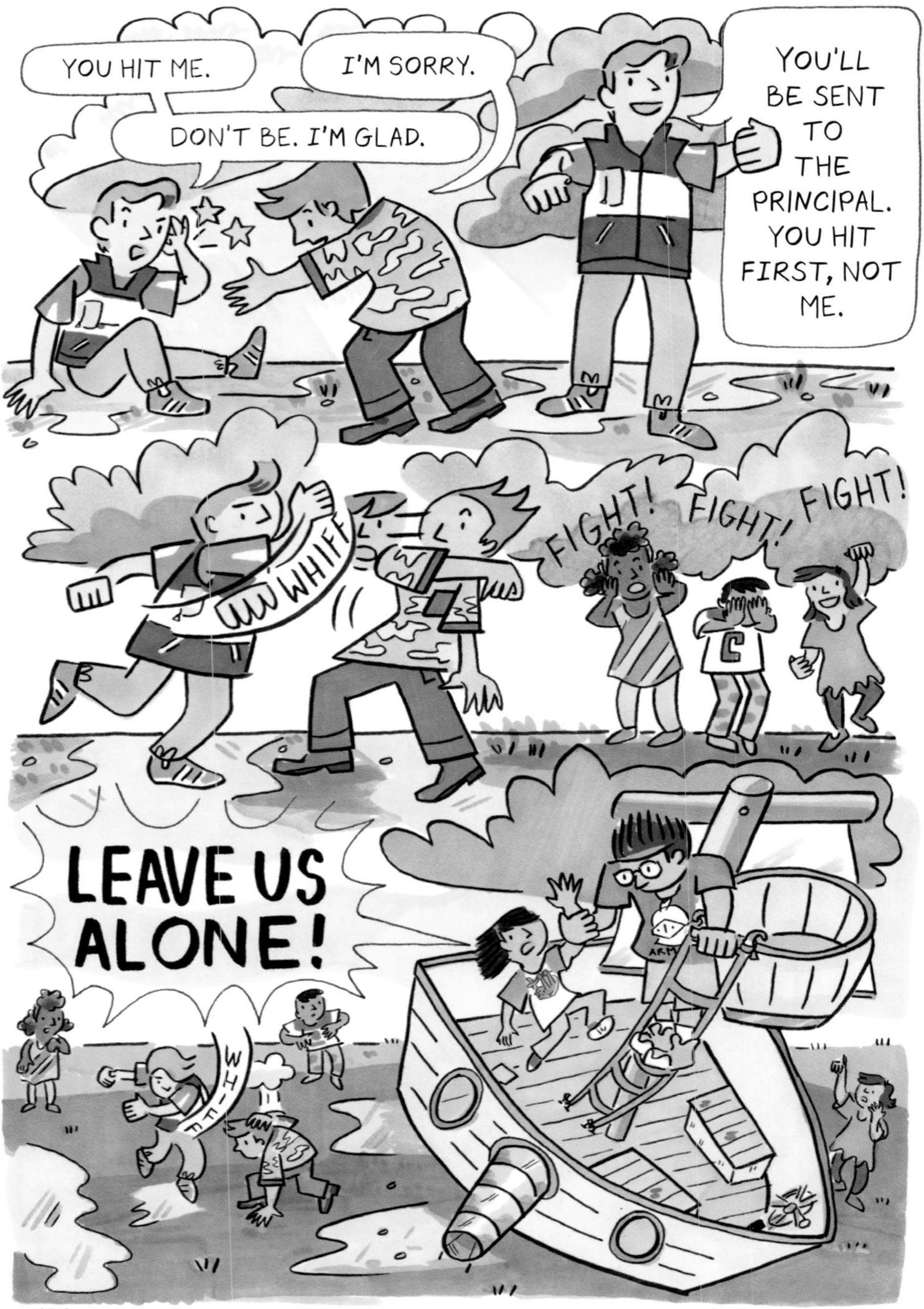
YOU HIT ME.
I'M SORRY.
DON'T BE. I'M GLAD.
YOU'LL BE SENT TO THE PRINCIPAL. YOU HIT FIRST, NOT ME.
WHIFF
FIGHT! FIGHT! FIGHT!
LEAVE US ALONE!
WHIFF

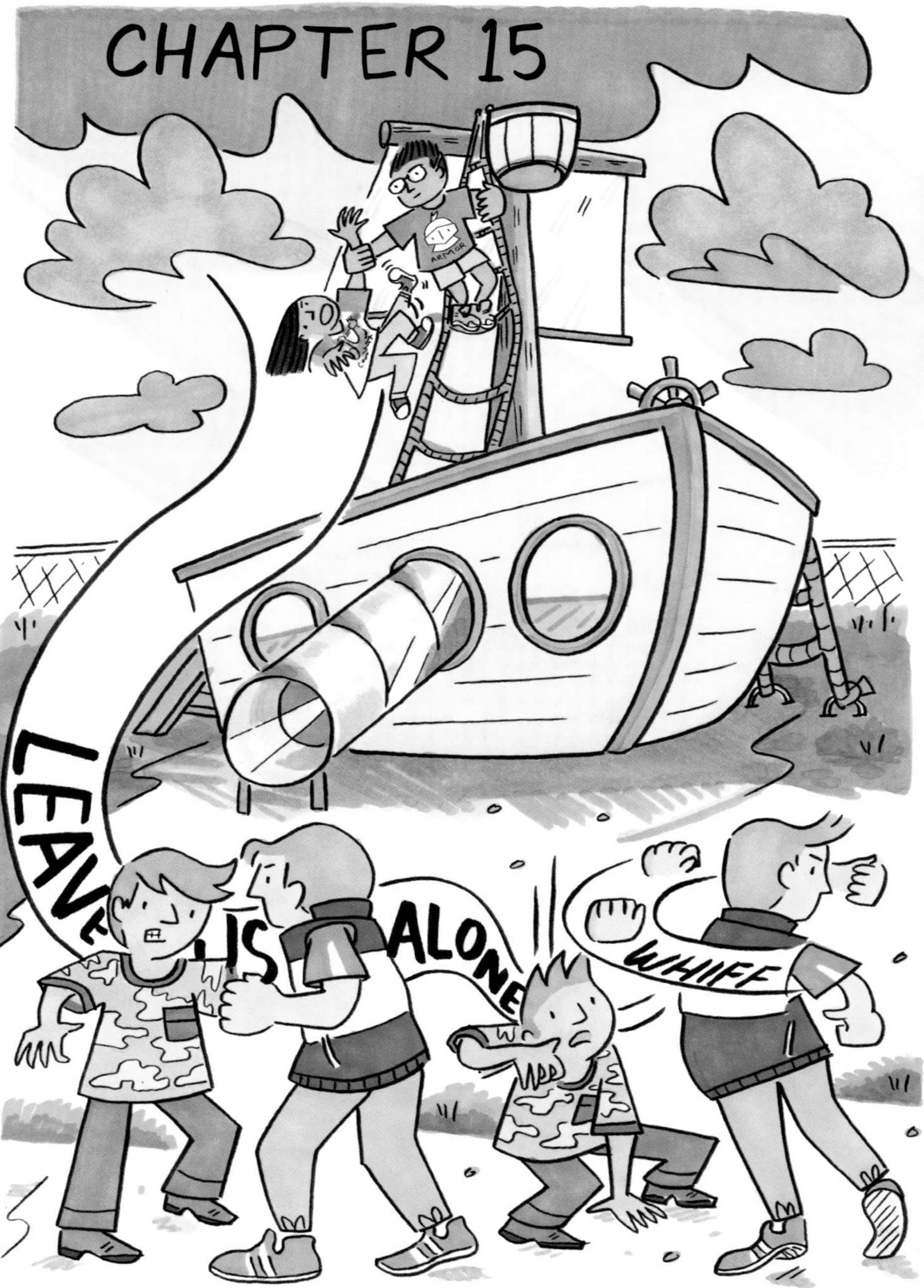
CHAPTER 15
ARMOR
LEAVE US ALONE
WHIFF

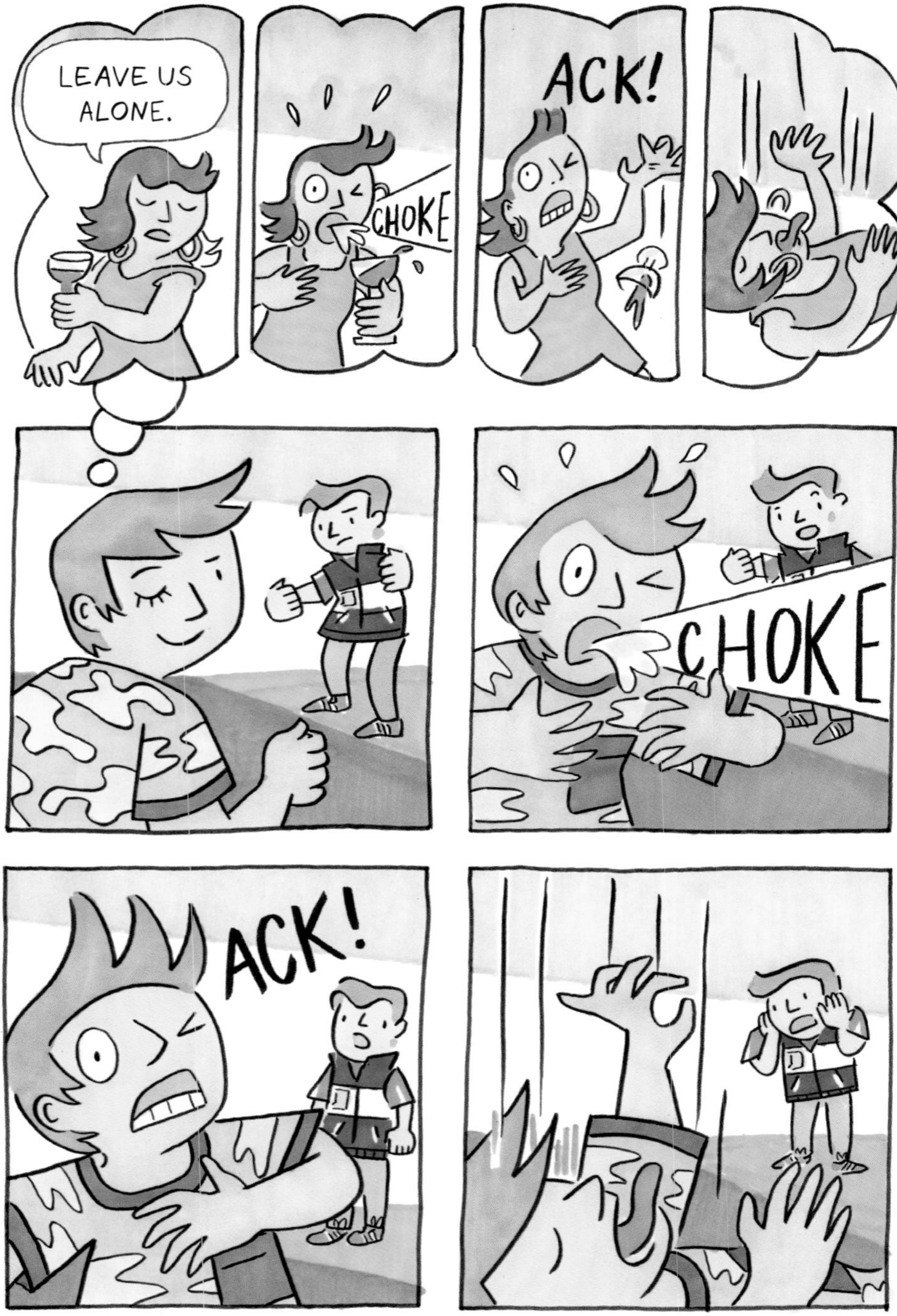
LEAVE US ALONE.
CHOKE
ACK!
CHOKE
ACK!

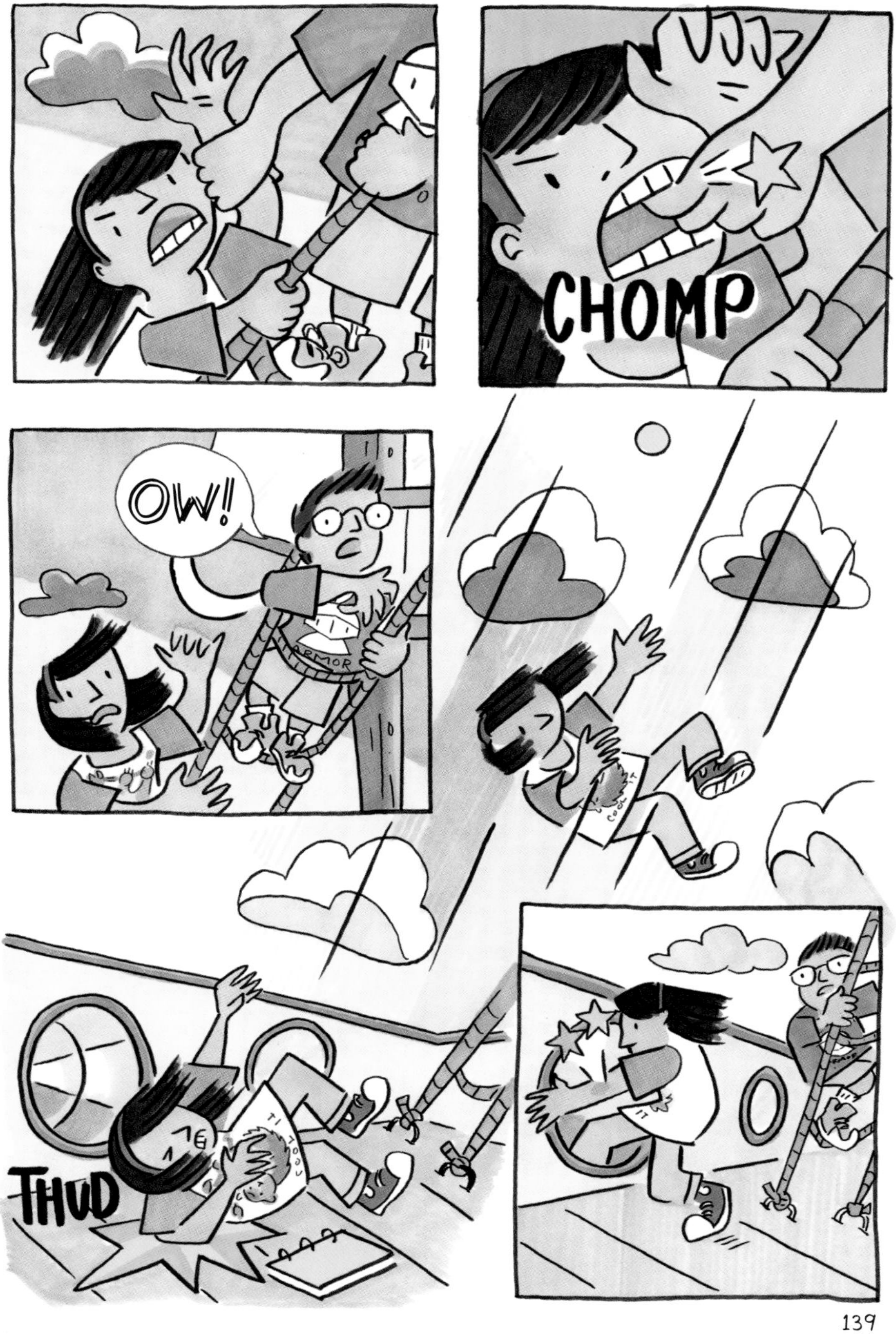
CHOMP
OW!
ARMOR
COOL IT
THUD

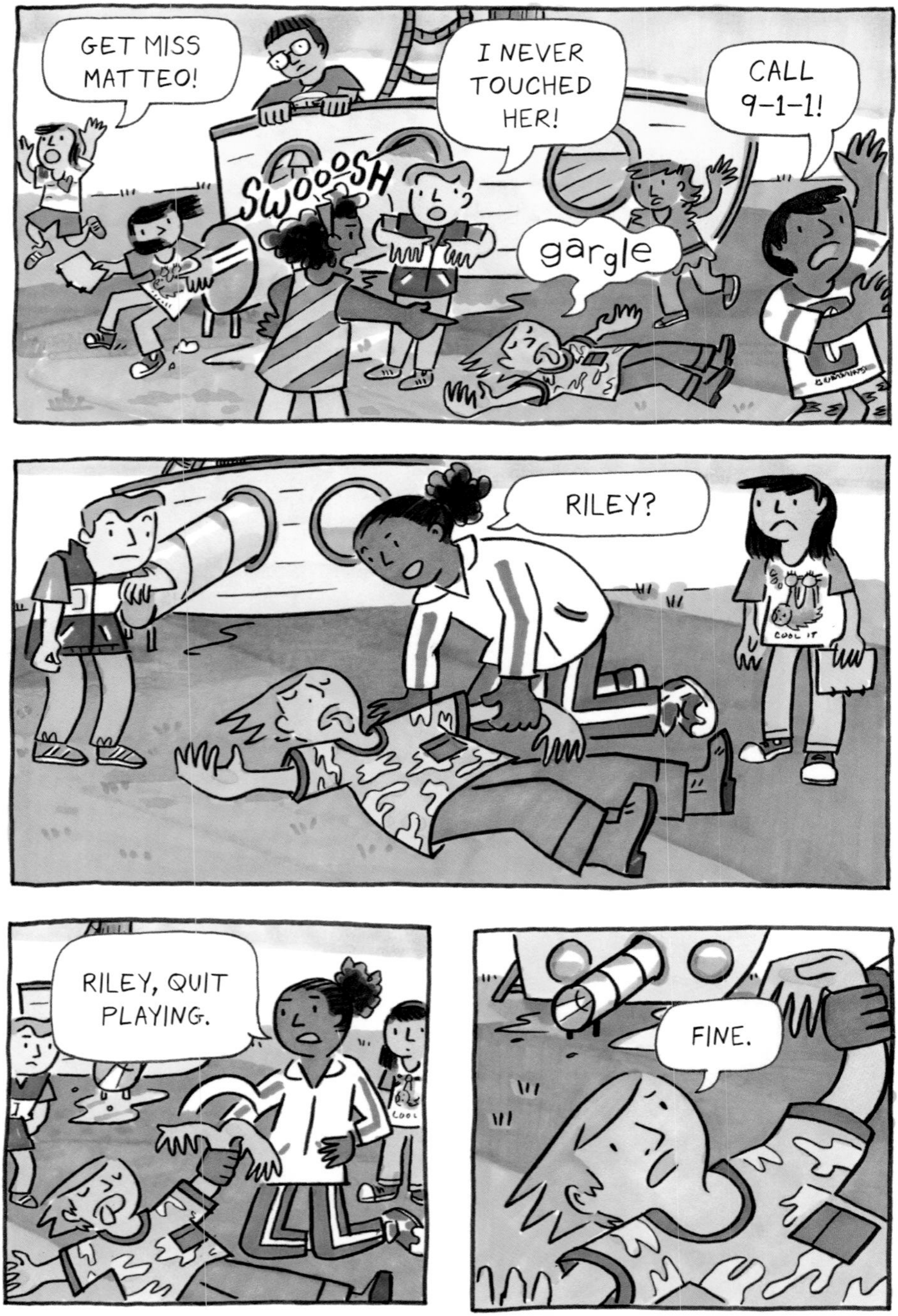
GET MISS MATTEO!
SWOOOSH
I NEVER TOUCHED HER!
gargle
CALL 9-1-1!
RILEY?
COOL IT
RILEY, QUIT PLAYING.
FINE.

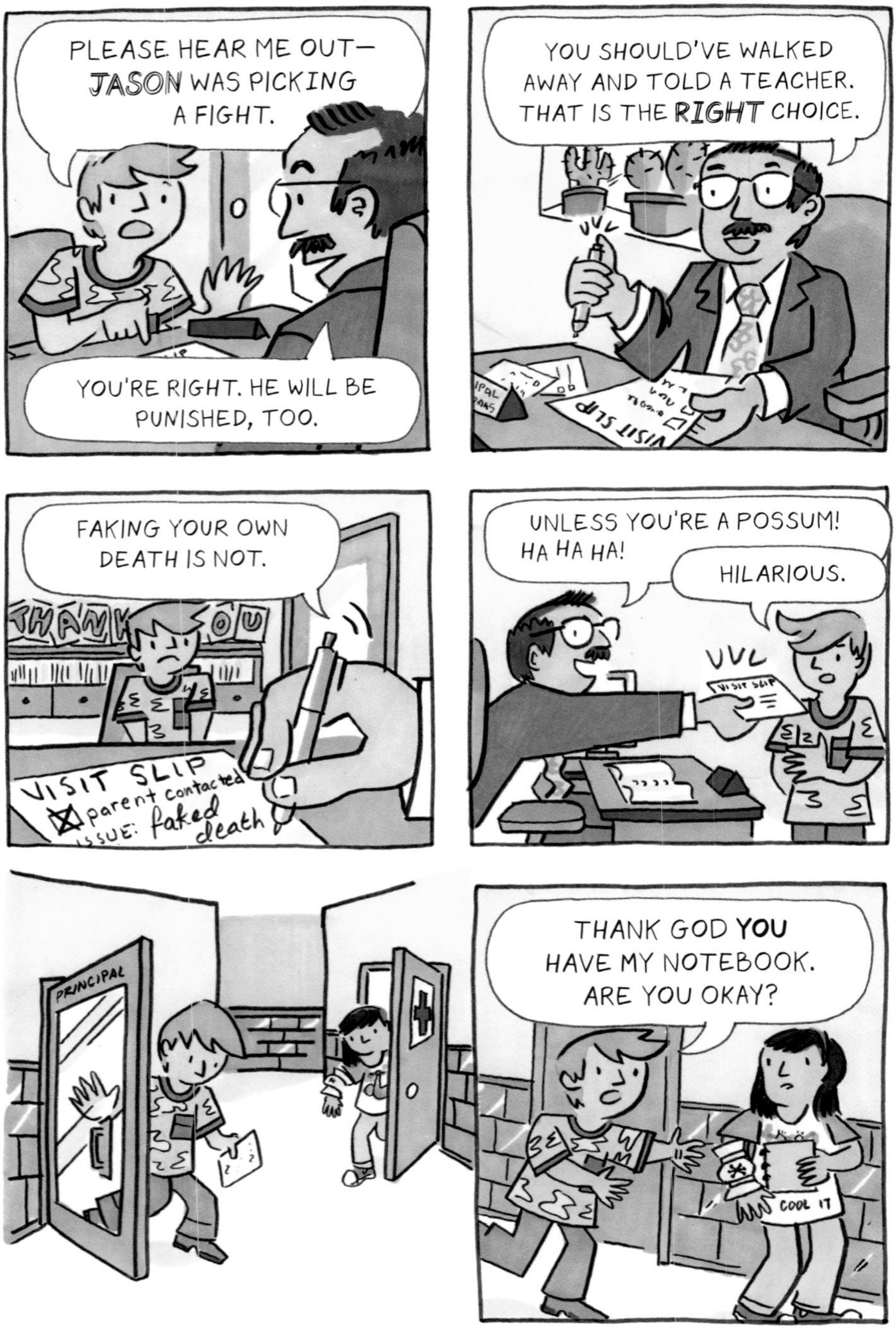
PLEASE HEAR ME OUT—JASON WAS PICKING A FIGHT.
YOU'RE RIGHT. HE WILL BE PUNISHED, TOO.
YOU SHOULD'VE WALKED AWAY AND TOLD A TEACHER. THAT IS THE RIGHT CHOICE.
VISIT SLIP
FAKING YOUR OWN DEATH IS NOT.
VISIT SLIP
parent contacted
ISSUE: faked death
UNLESS YOU'RE A POSSUM! HA HA HA!
HILARIOUS.
VISIT SLIP
PRINCIPAL
THANK GOD YOU HAVE MY NOTEBOOK. ARE YOU OKAY?
COOL IT

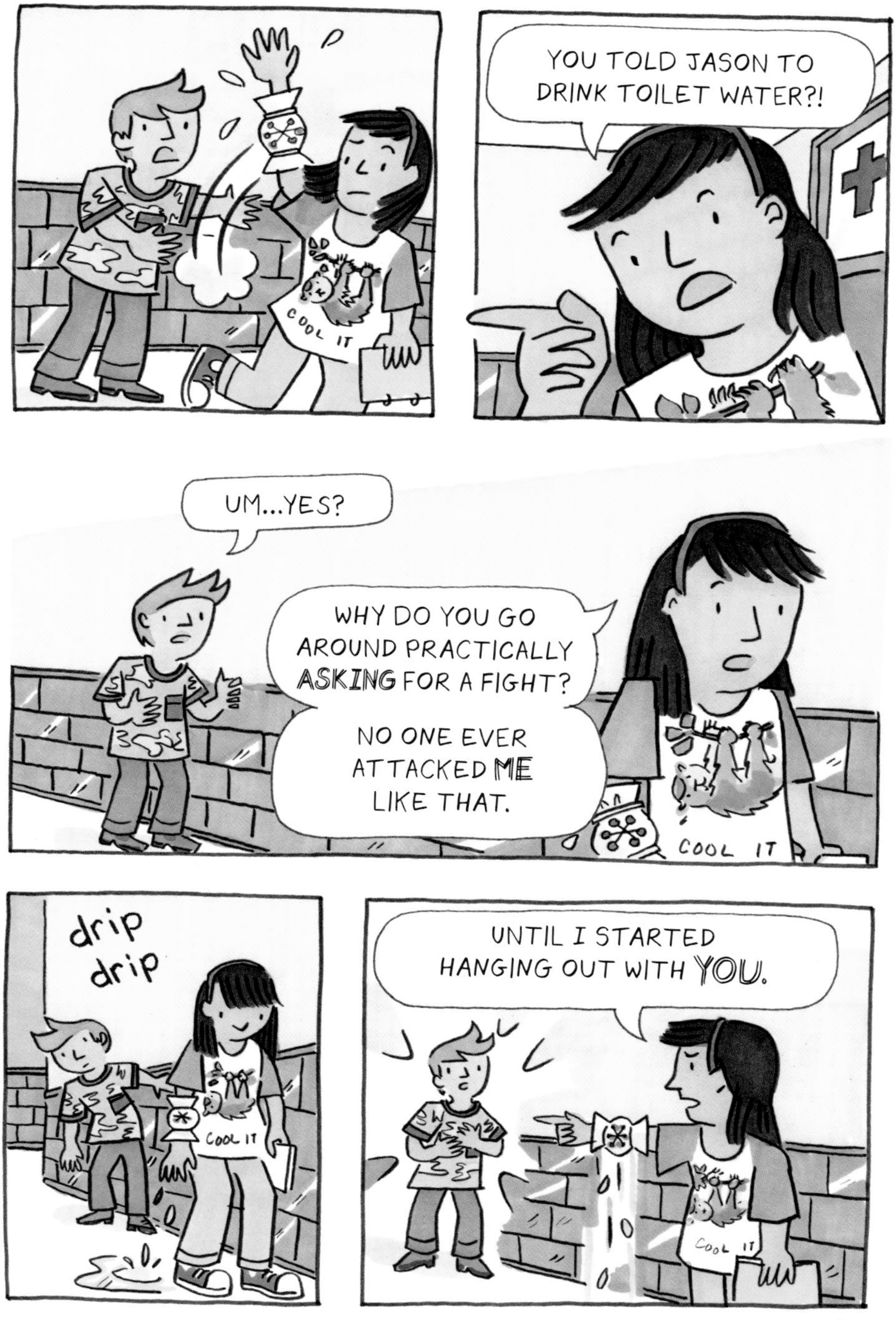
YOU TOLD JASON TO DRINK TOILET WATER?!
COOL IT
UM...YES?
WHY DO YOU GO AROUND PRACTICALLY ASKING FOR A FIGHT?
NO ONE EVER ATTACKED ME LIKE THAT.
COOL IT
drip drip
COOL IT
UNTIL I STARTED HANGING OUT WITH YOU.
COOL IT

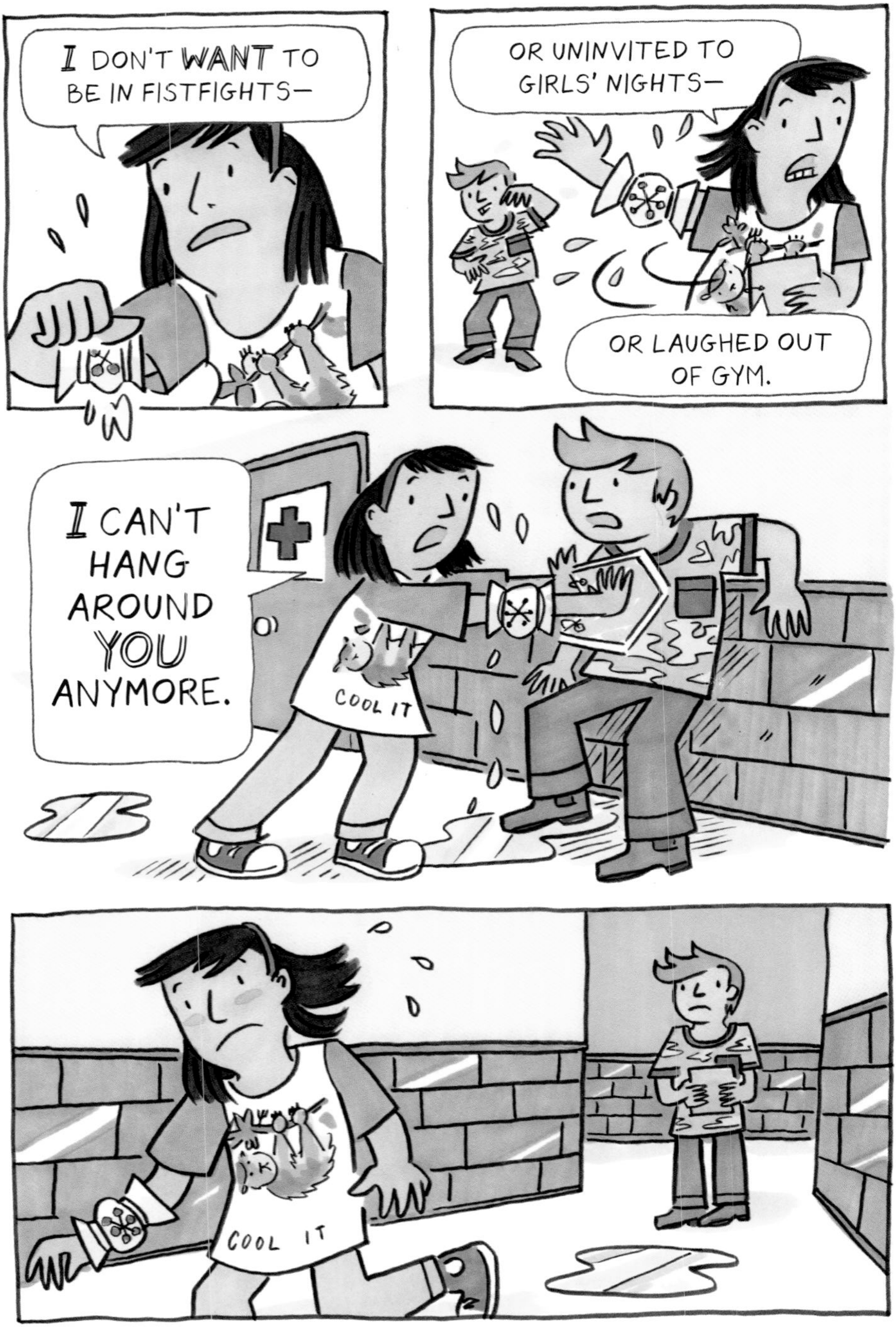
I DON'T WANT TO BE IN FISTFIGHTS—
OR UNINVITED TO GIRLS' NIGHTS—
OR LAUGHED OUT OF GYM.
I CAN'T HANG AROUND YOU ANYMORE.
COOL IT
COOL IT

CHAPTER 16

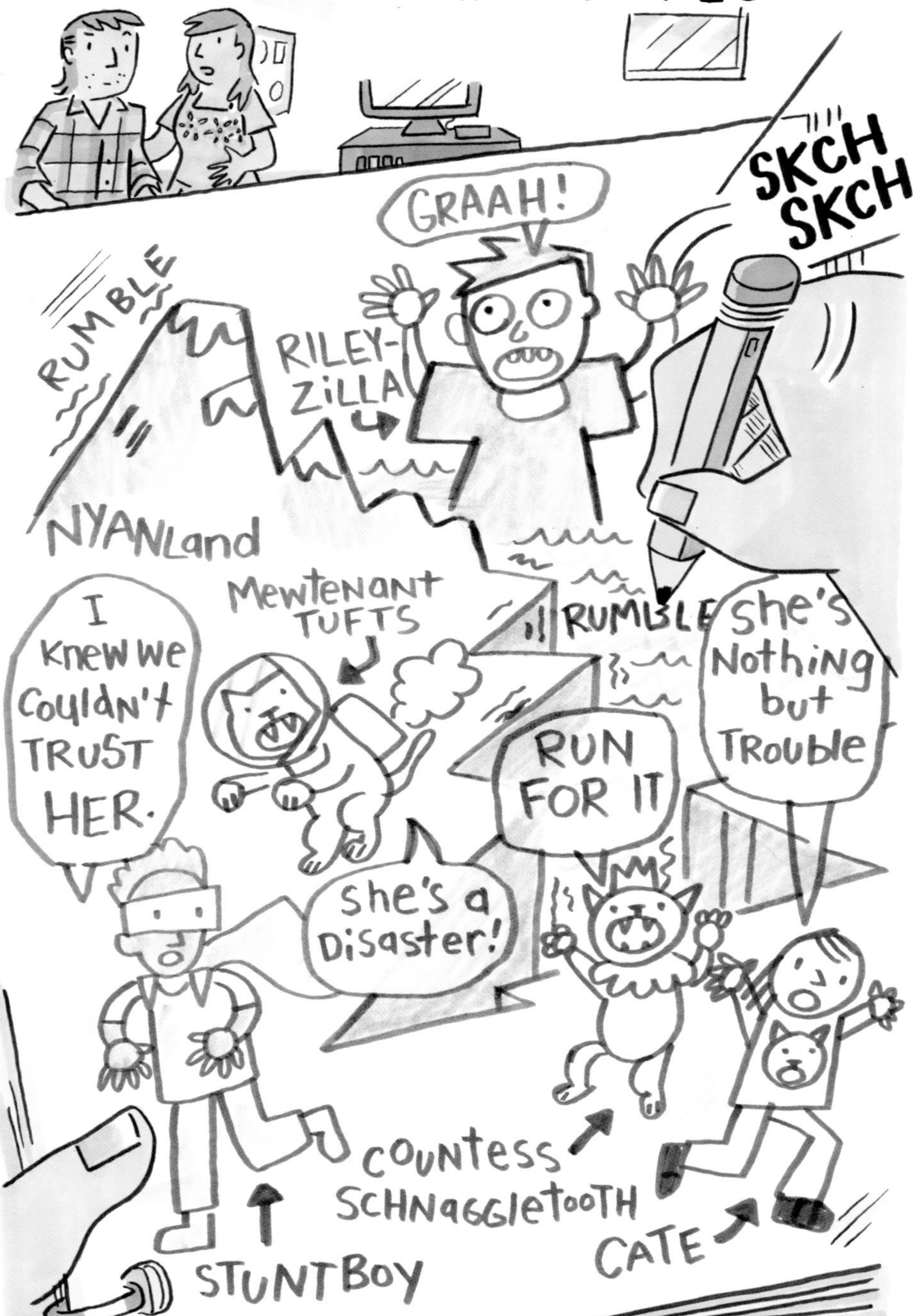
SKCH SKCH
GRAAH!
RUMBLE
RILEY-ZILLA
NYANLand
Mewtenant TUFTS
RUMBLE
I knew we couldn't TRUST HER.
RUN FOR IT
She's Nothing but Trouble
She's a Disaster!
COUNTESS SCHNAGGLETOOTH
CATE
STUNTBOY

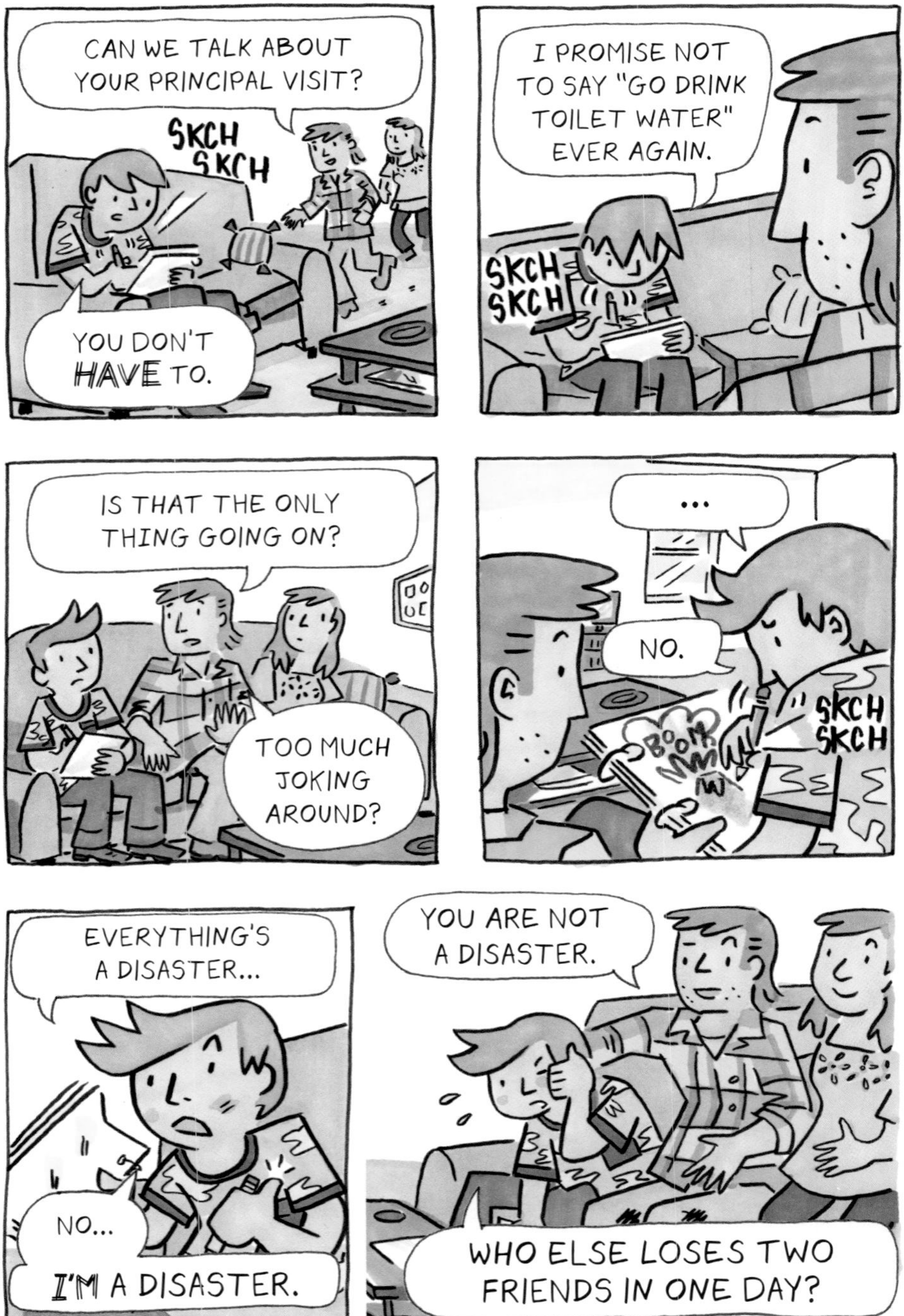
CAN WE TALK ABOUT YOUR PRINCIPAL VISIT?
SKCH SKCH
YOU DON'T HAVE TO.
I PROMISE NOT TO SAY "GO DRINK TOILET WATER" EVER AGAIN.
SKCH SKCH
IS THAT THE ONLY THING GOING ON?
TOO MUCH JOKING AROUND?
...
NO.
SKCH SKCH
BOOM
EVERYTHING'S A DISASTER...
NO...
I'M A DISASTER.
YOU ARE NOT A DISASTER.
WHO ELSE LOSES TWO FRIENDS IN ONE DAY?

147

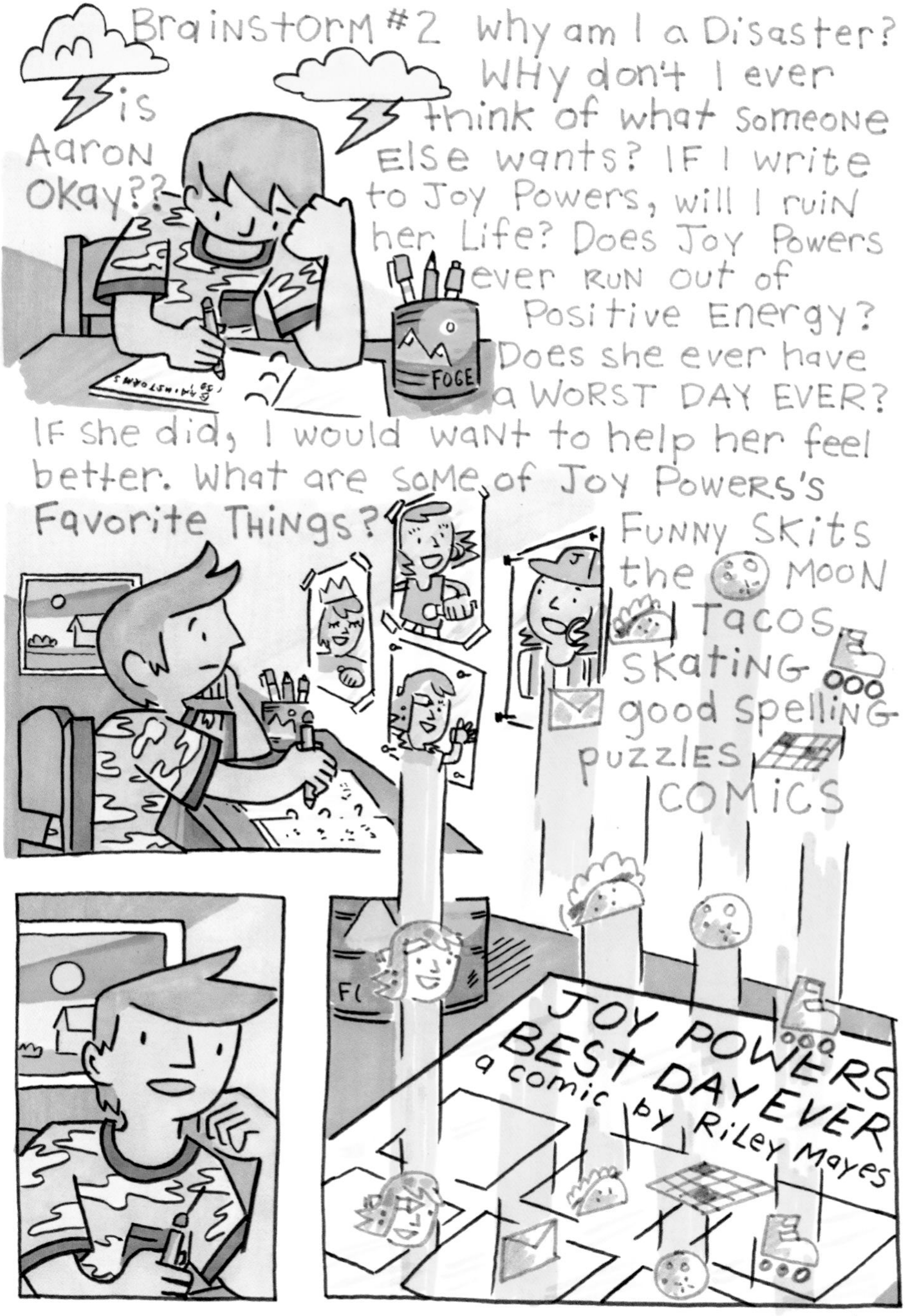

Brainstorm #2 Why am I a Disaster? WHy don't I ever think of what someone Else wants? IF I write to Joy Powers, will I ruin her Life? Does Joy Powers ever run out of Positive Energy? Does she ever have a WORST DAY EVER? IF she did, I would want to help her feel better. What are some of Joy Powers's Favorite Things?
is Aaron Okay??
FOGE
Funny Skits
the MOON
Tacos
Skating
good Spelling
puzzles
COMICS
JOY POWERS BEST DAY EVER
a comic by Riley Mayes

THE END (FOR NOW)

151

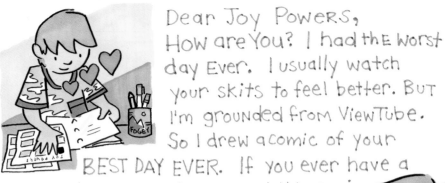

Dear Joy Powers,
How are You? I had thE worst
day Ever. I usually watch
your skits to feel better. BuT
I'm grounded from ViewTube.
So I drew a comic of your
BEST DAY EVER. If you ever have a
worst day ever, please reAd this Comic.
Hopefully you will FeeL better. I have
Questions for you. Actually I have
1,000 Questions, but I'll pick four
to ask you if you have time.
#1. Have you ever scared off
a FriEND By being too weird? #2. Are you

MAY I HAVE AN
ENVELOPE?

DON'T
SEAL IT.

MRS. MONTGOMERY
NEEDS TO READ IT FIRST.

I don't want Mrs. M to read it.
This letter is between Joy Powers and me.

So I write a second,
different letter to turn in.

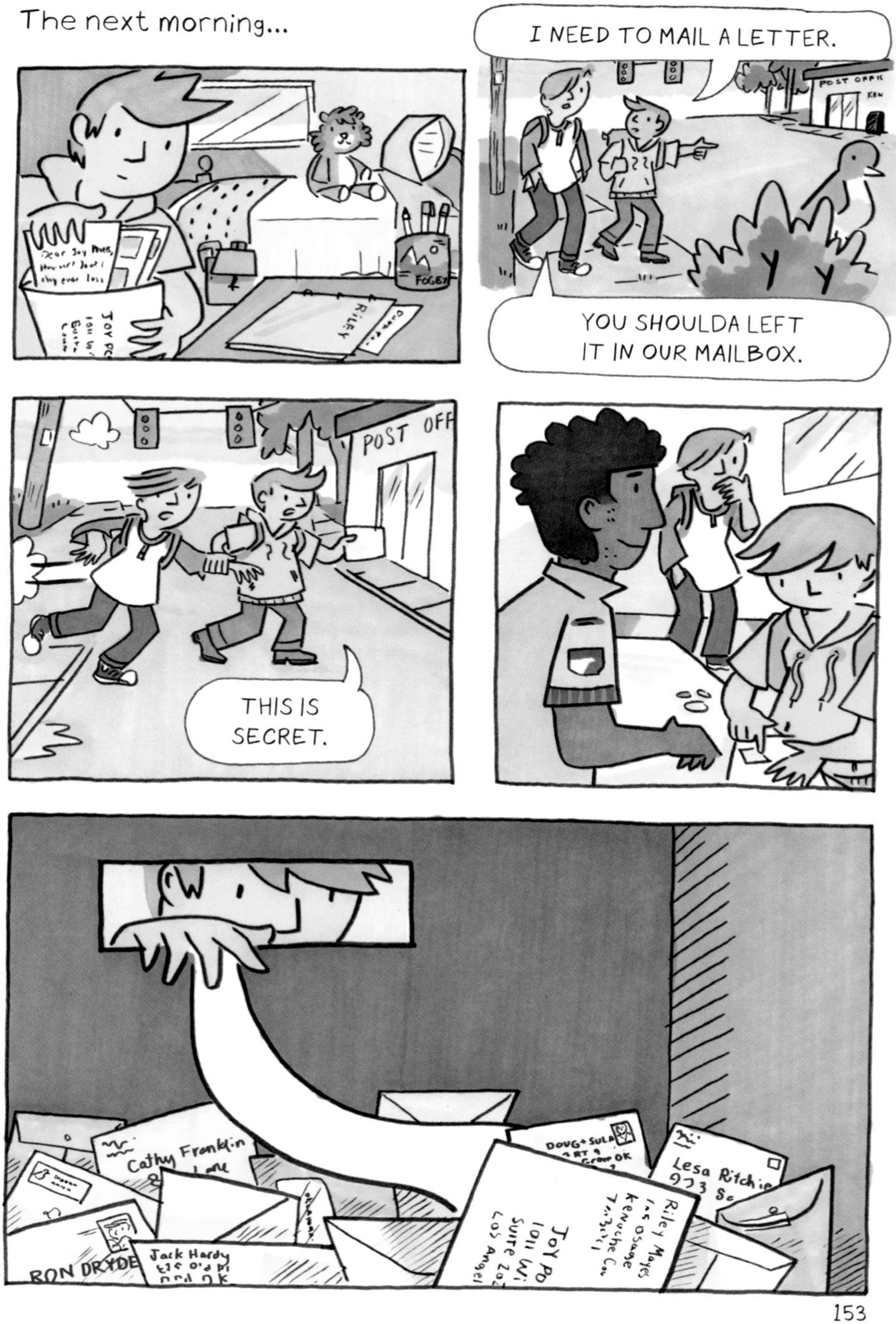
The next morning...
I NEED TO MAIL A LETTER.
YOU SHOULDA LEFT IT IN OUR MAILBOX.
POST OFF
THIS IS SECRET.
Cathy Franklin
Lesa Ritchie
Jack Hardy
RON DRYDE
Riley Mayes
JOY PD

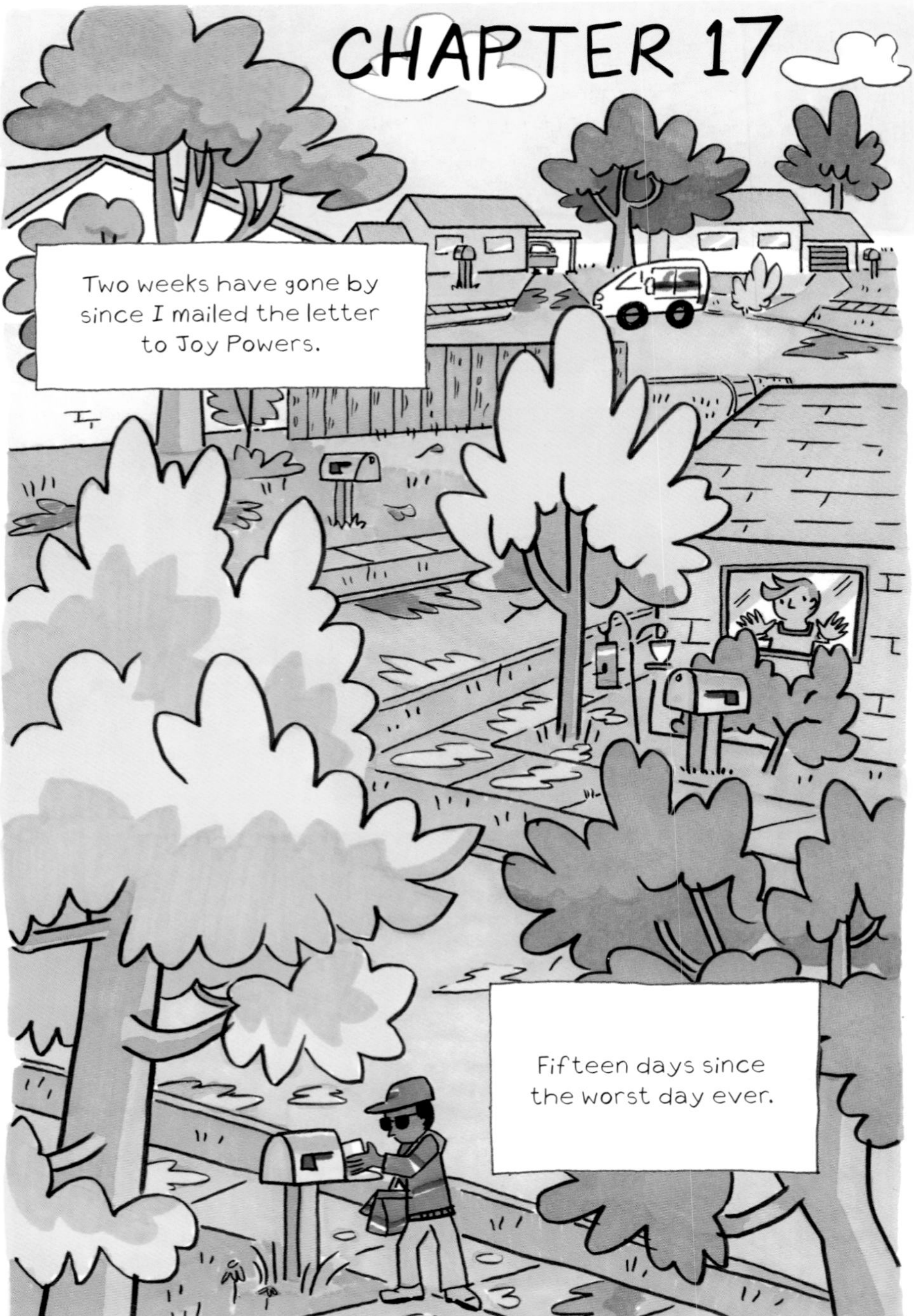
CHAPTER 17
Two weeks have gone by since I mailed the letter to Joy Powers.
Fifteen days since the worst day ever.

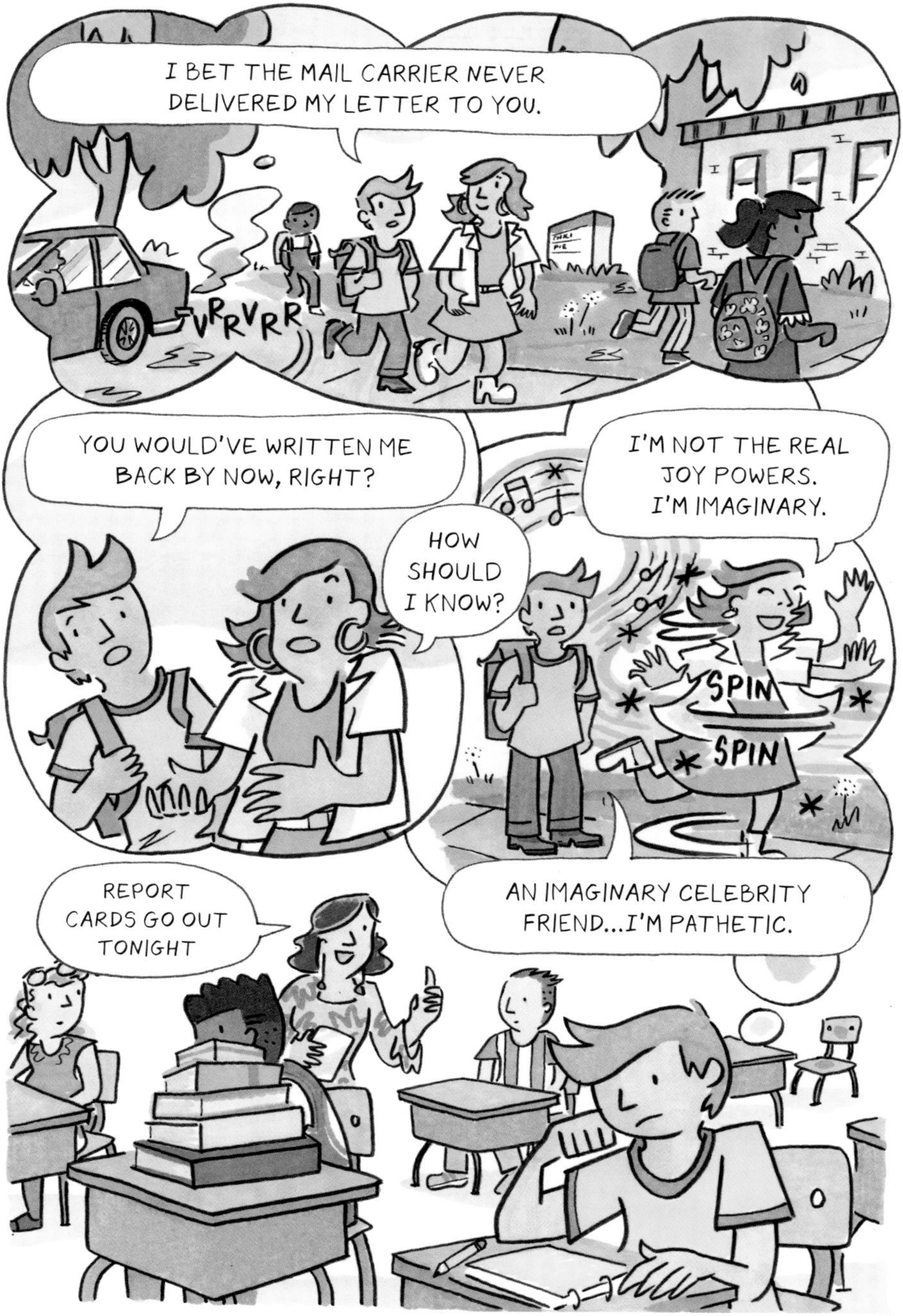
I BET THE MAIL CARRIER NEVER DELIVERED MY LETTER TO YOU.
VRRVRR
YOU WOULD'VE WRITTEN ME BACK BY NOW, RIGHT?
HOW SHOULD I KNOW?
I'M NOT THE REAL JOY POWERS. I'M IMAGINARY.
SPIN
SPIN
REPORT CARDS GO OUT TONIGHT
AN IMAGINARY CELEBRITY FRIEND...I'M PATHETIC.

The more Cate describes this drawing competition, the more I want to go to girls' night.

THERE'S TWO MODES OF DRAWING CHARADES.

THE USUAL TEAM MODE AND THE ONE-ON-ONE DUEL, THE **DRAW-DOWN.**

TEAM MODE

① Player takes a clue from JAR.

host writes clues before party

UNICORN

② Player draws clue.

③ Team Guesses clue.

④ Point given to team.

Ah, yes, a UNICORN

DRAW-DOWN DUEL

① Reigning Champ declares a CHallenge.

SNACKS   SO Be it

② Newcomer picks CLUE CATEGORY.

cookies   chips

amuse us!

③ Party guests write clues, put them in jar, then watch. (there's NO guessing.)

OH NO. I can't draw an EMPANADA, what IS IT?

④ First person who CAN'T draw a clue LOSES the DUEL.

CHAPTER 18

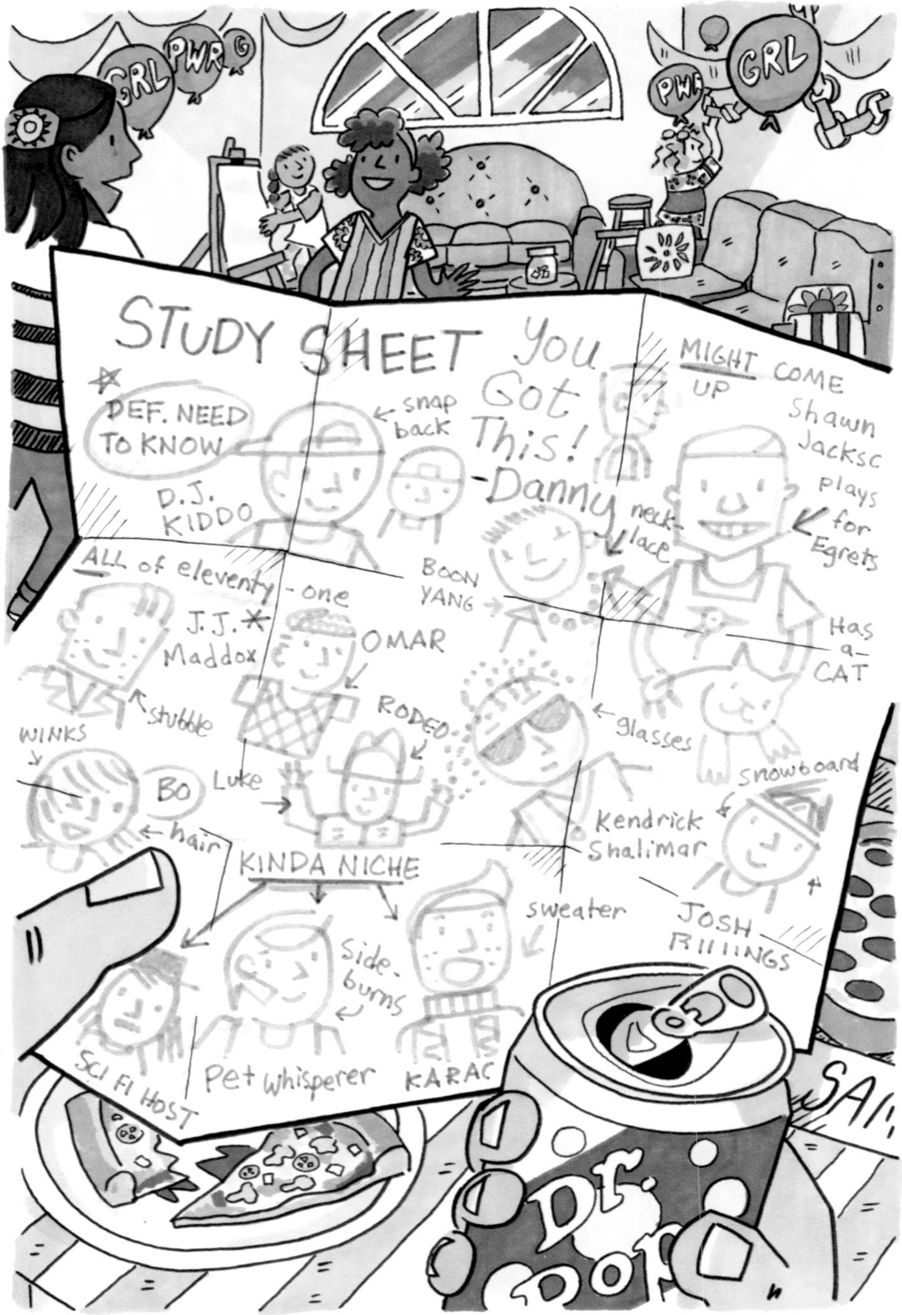
GRL PWR G
PWR GRL
STUDY SHEET
You Got This! -Danny
MIGHT COME UP
DEF. NEED TO KNOW
snap back
D.J. KIDDO
Shawn Jacksc
plays for Egrets
neck-lace
BOON YANG
ALL of eleventy-one
J.J. Maddox
OMAR
stubble
Has a CAT
RODEO
glasses
WINKS
BO
Luke
hair
snowboard
Kendrick Shalimar
KINDA NICHE
sweater
JOSH BILLINGS
Side-burns
SCI FI HOST
Pet whisperer
KARAC
Dr. Pop

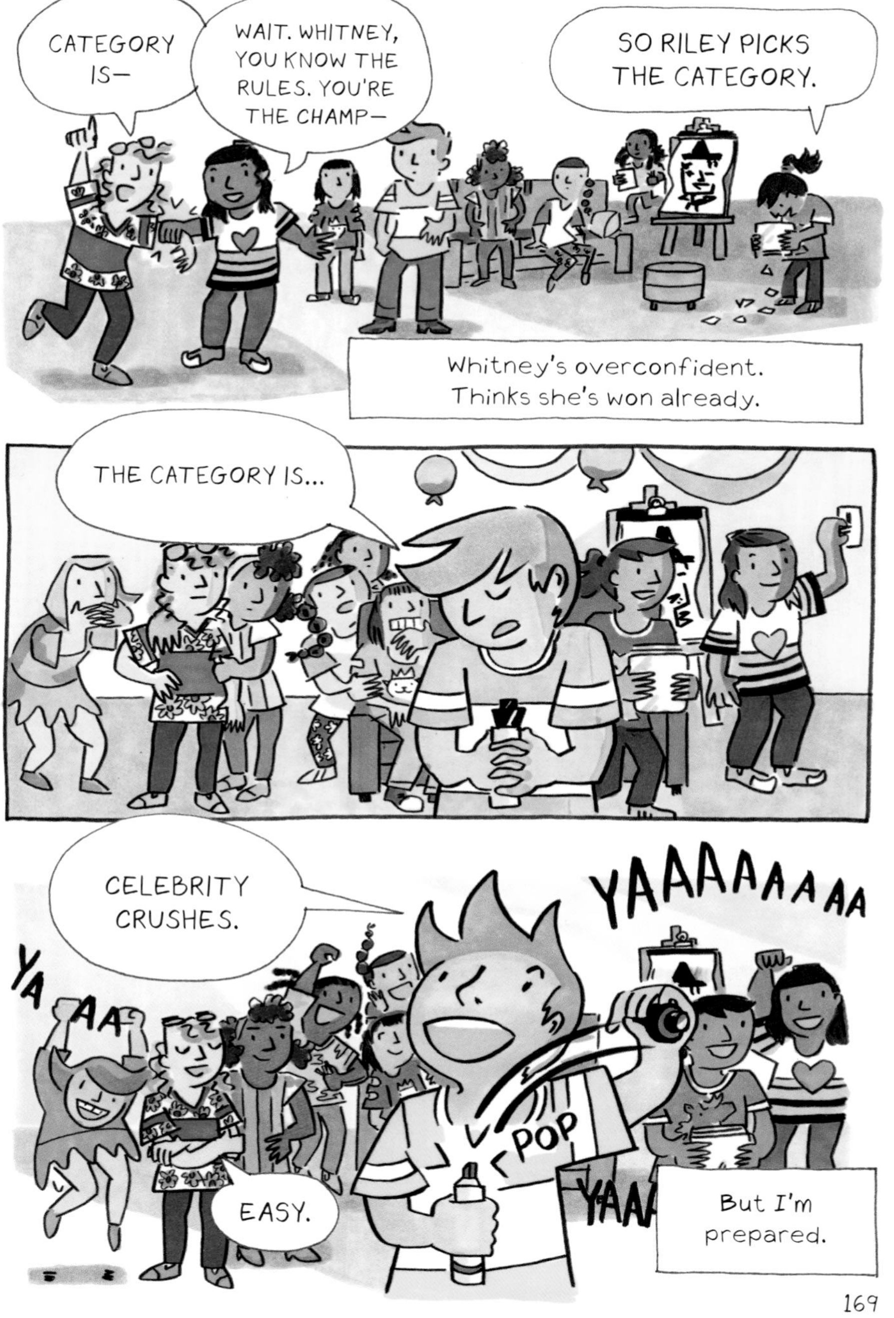
CATEGORY IS—
WAIT. WHITNEY, YOU KNOW THE RULES. YOU'RE THE CHAMP—
SO RILEY PICKS THE CATEGORY.
Whitney's overconfident. Thinks she's won already.
THE CATEGORY IS...
CELEBRITY CRUSHES.
YAAAAAAAA
YA AA
YAAA
POP
EASY.
But I'm prepared.

These crushes are wilder than *I'd* practiced!

CHAPTER 19

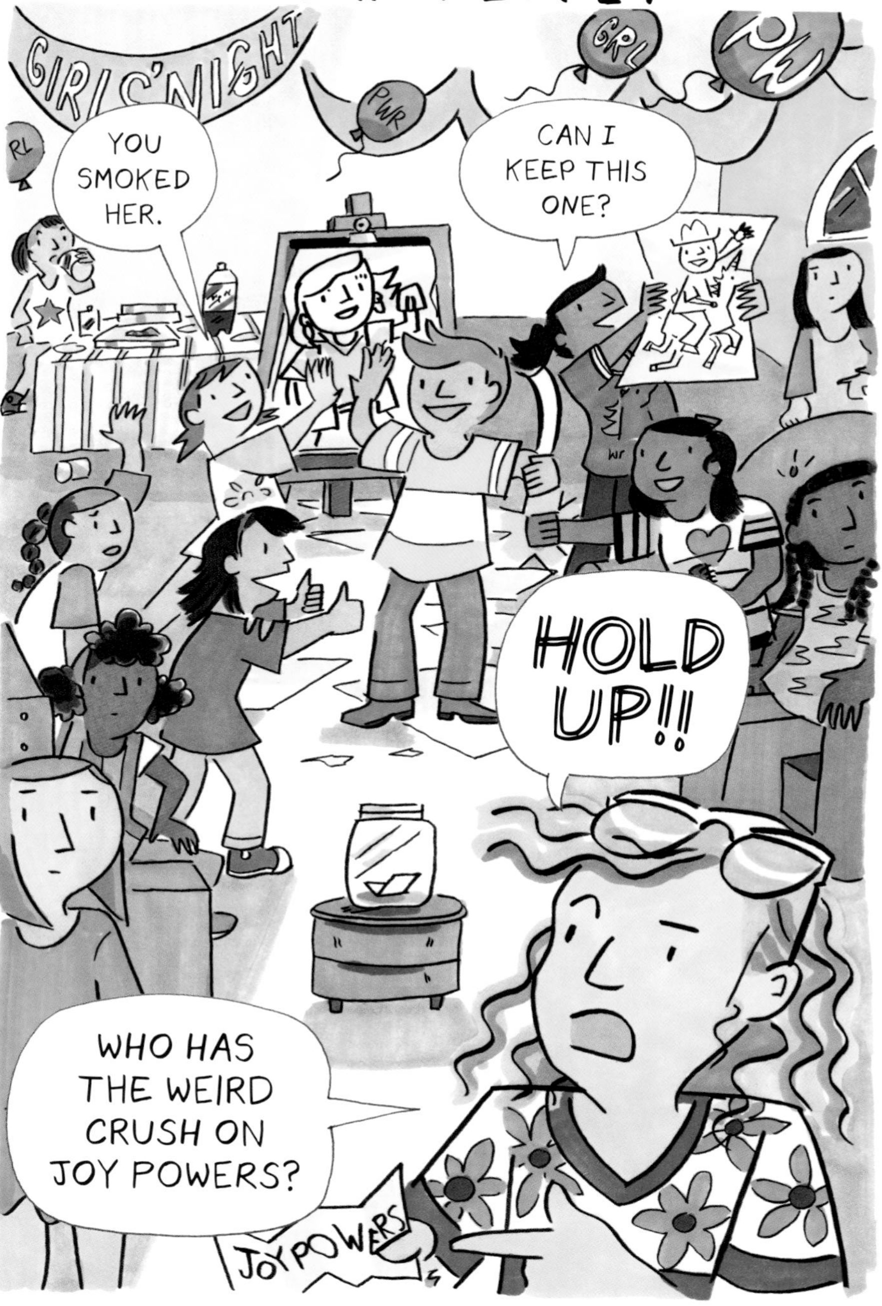
GIRLS' NIGHT
RL
PWR
GRL
YOU SMOKED HER.
CAN I KEEP THIS ONE?
HOLD UP!!
WHO HAS THE WEIRD CRUSH ON JOY POWERS?
JOY POWERS

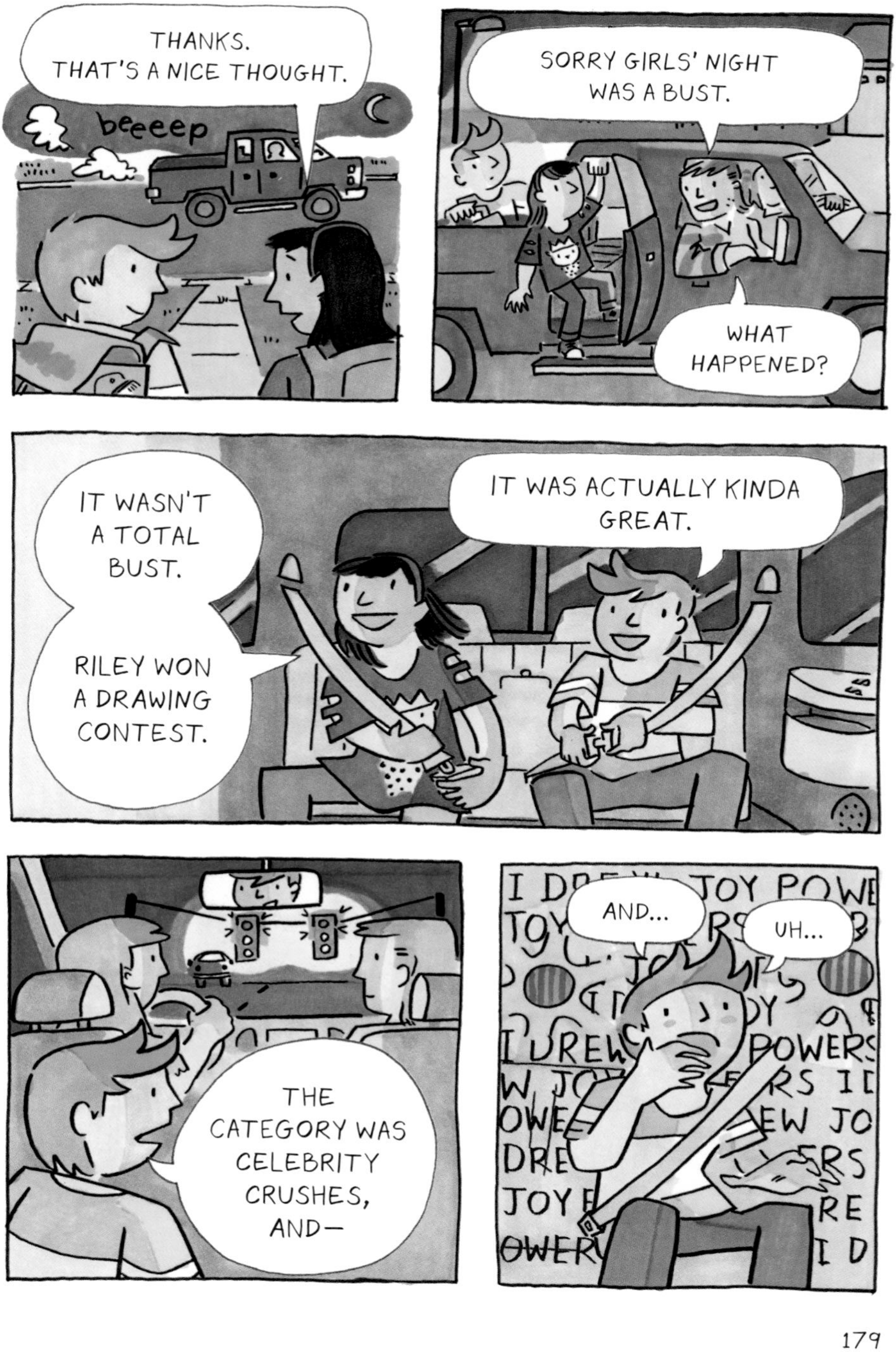
THANKS. THAT'S A NICE THOUGHT.
beeeep
SORRY GIRLS' NIGHT WAS A BUST.
WHAT HAPPENED?
IT WASN'T A TOTAL BUST.
RILEY WON A DRAWING CONTEST.
IT WAS ACTUALLY KINDA GREAT.
THE CATEGORY WAS CELEBRITY CRUSHES, AND—
AND...
UH...

181

CHAPTER 20

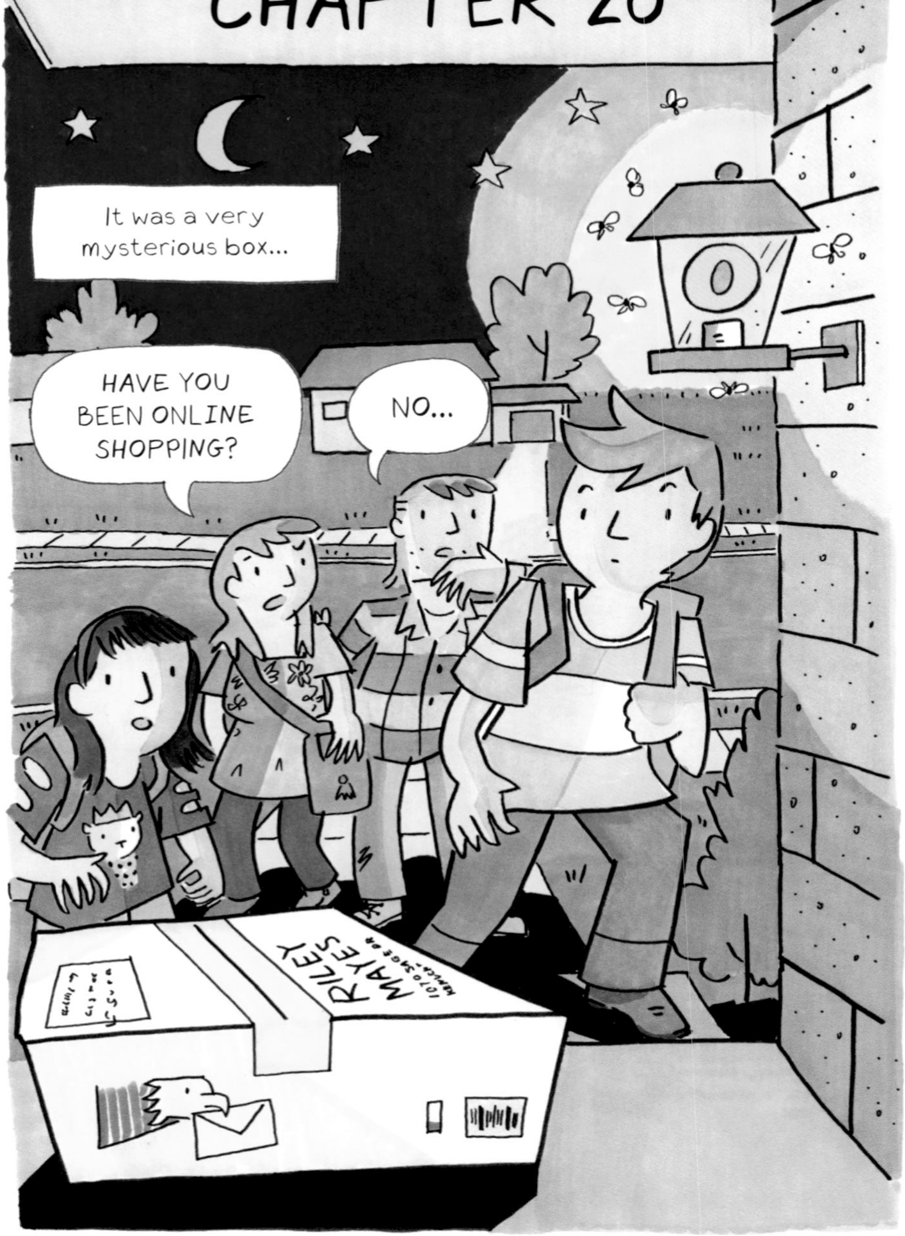
It was a very mysterious box...
HAVE YOU BEEN ONLINE SHOPPING?
NO...
RILEY MAYES

#2

JOY POWERS

Dear Riley,

When I got your comic, I'd truly had one of my WORST days ever. Thank you for sending me a BEST DAY EVER! I'm so sorry to hear about your worst day. Hopefully you'll get some positive energy from these DVDs, no View Tube required.

In answer to your questions:

① "WILL YOU DRAW SOMETHING SO I KNOW YOU ARE JOY POWERS AND NOT A ROBOT?"

Okay, here:

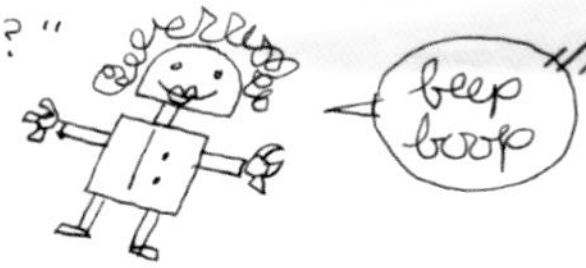
beep boop

② "DO YOU KNOW HOW AWESOME I THINK YOU ARE?" Stop.

You'll give me a big head and I'll need to buy new wigs.

③ "HAVE YOU EVER BEEN SO WEIRD YOU SCARED OFF A FRIEND?"

What do you mean by "weird"? If you mean absurd and silly, my friends all love that. Maybe you mean something else. Friends know me really well. People are scared of UNFAMILIAR things. So a friend wouldn't be scared of me. If I make a WEIRD MISTAKE I'll apologize. But if I'm being myself and someone thinks I'm "strange," they need time to get to know me better.

④ "WHAT DO YOU DO IF YOU RUN OUT OF POSITIVE ENERGY?" Well, I don't go to the MOON but I do talk to friends, write, sing songs, or do something nice for someone else. We have to get off our butts and MAKE more positive energy— Like you did for me by drawing a comic.

Riley, I can't wait to see the positive energy you make next!

Your Fan,

Joy Powers

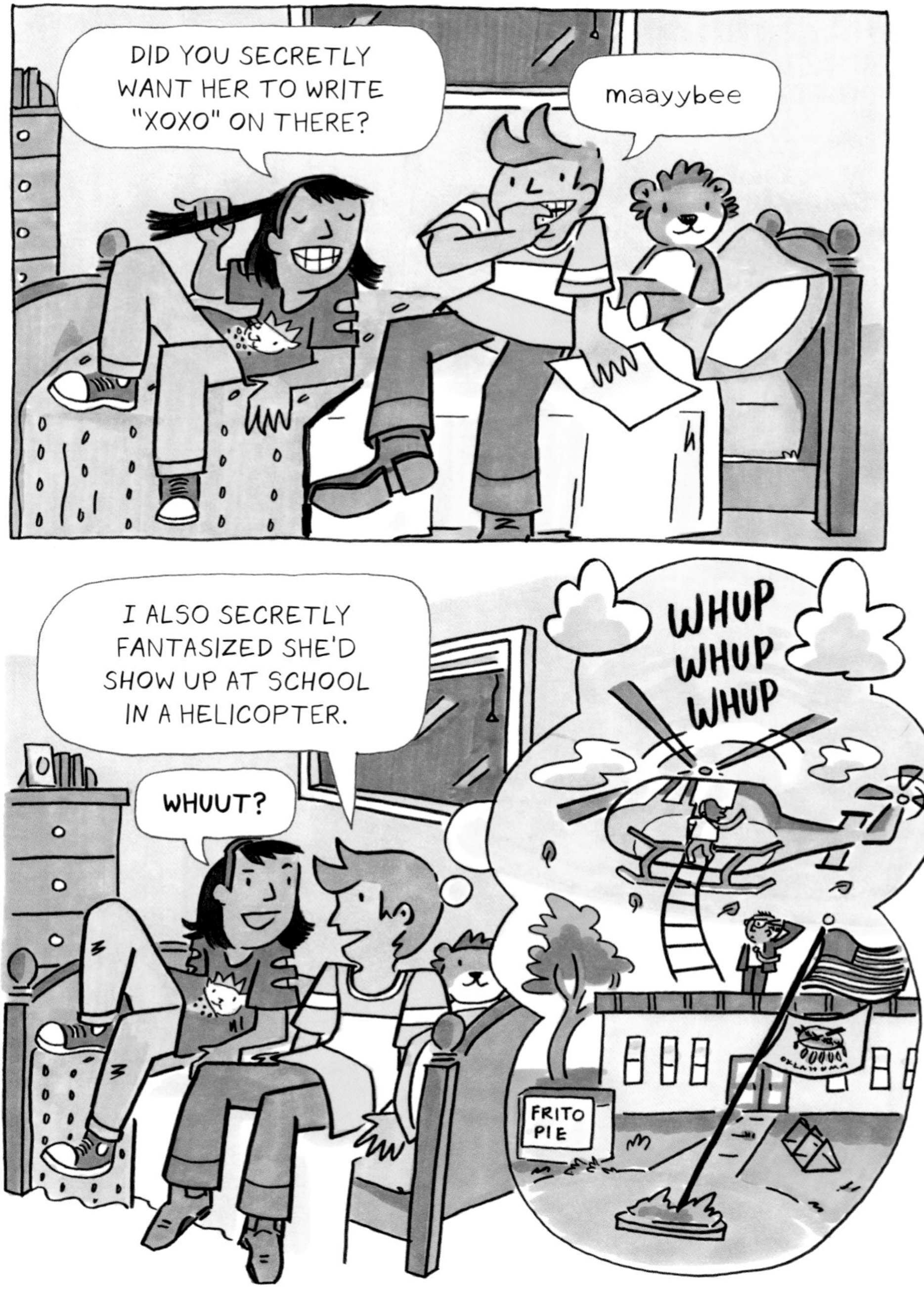
DID YOU SECRETLY WANT HER TO WRITE "XOXO" ON THERE?
maayybee
I ALSO SECRETLY FANTASIZED SHE'D SHOW UP AT SCHOOL IN A HELICOPTER.
WHUP WHUP WHUP
FRITO PIE
WHUUT?

CHAPTER 21

CHAPTER 22

They have classes in photography...

sculpture...

WR·K·R·K·R

pottery...

basketry...

finger weaving...

painting...

storytelling...

QUIET, PLEASE!

and video production...

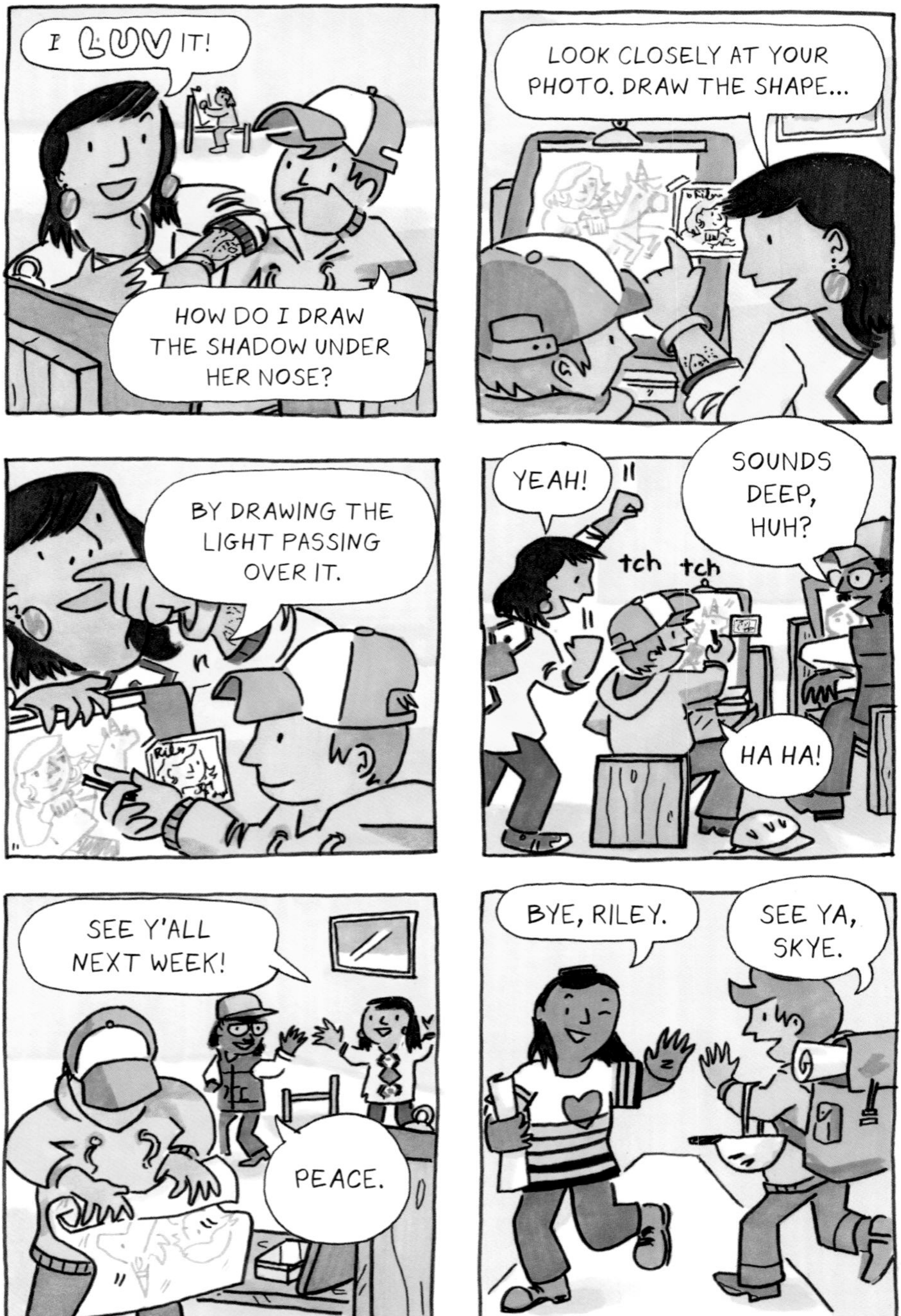
I LUV IT!
HOW DO I DRAW THE SHADOW UNDER HER NOSE?
LOOK CLOSELY AT YOUR PHOTO. DRAW THE SHAPE...
BY DRAWING THE LIGHT PASSING OVER IT.
YEAH!
tch tch
SOUNDS DEEP, HUH?
HA HA!
SEE Y'ALL NEXT WEEK!
PEACE.
BYE, RILEY.
SEE YA, SKYE.

Cate and Aaron and *I* make a new issue of our funny magazine every month.

I FINISHED THE CRUSH PORTRAITS!

GREAT! CATE INKED THE NYANLAND EPISODE.

CHAPTER 23

This is our zine!

NEXT ISSUE: A visit to BLINX!

STUPENDOUS STUNTBOY

212

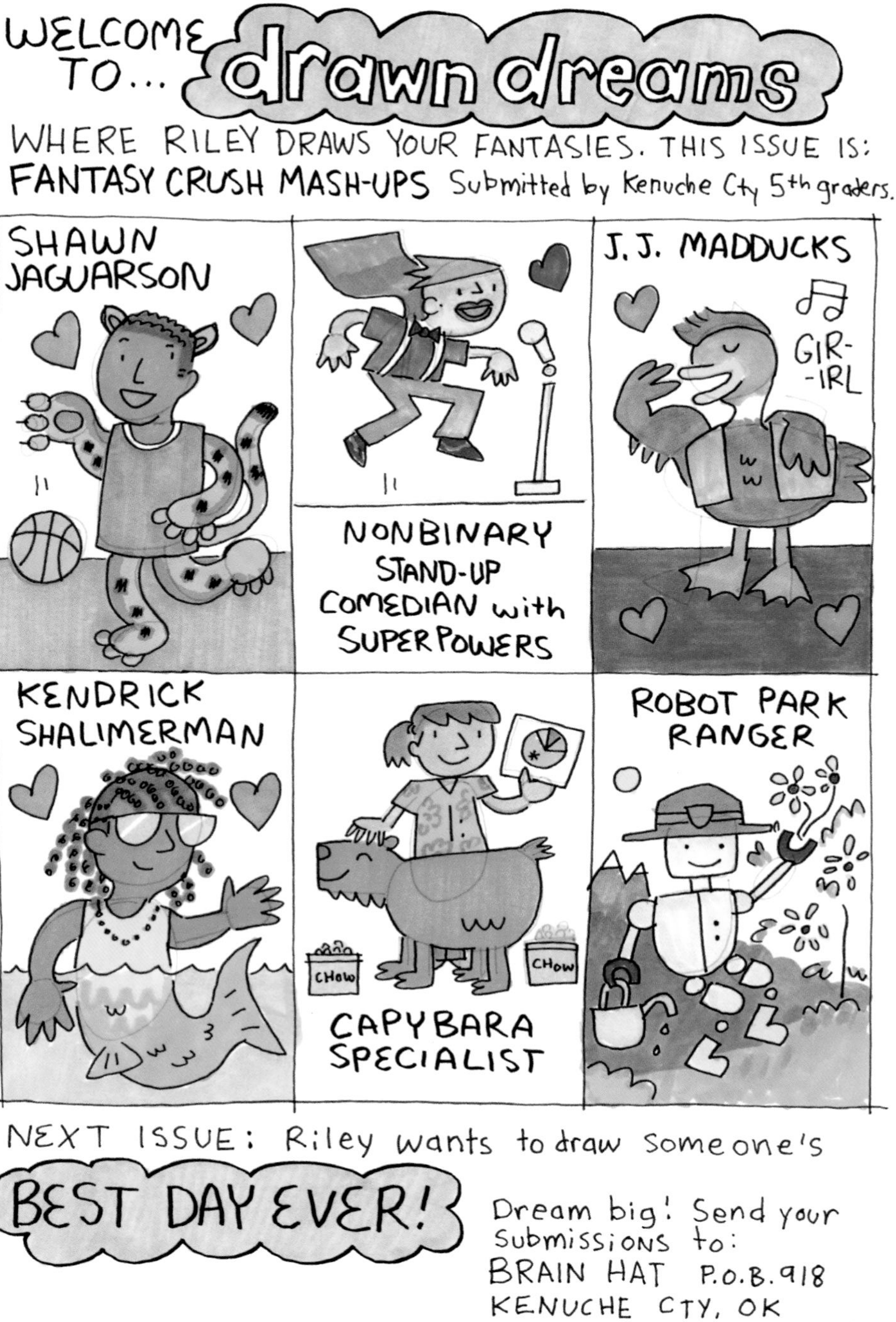
WELCOME TO... drawn dreams
WHERE RILEY DRAWS YOUR FANTASIES. THIS ISSUE IS:
FANTASY CRUSH MASH-UPS Submitted by Kenuche Cty 5th graders.
SHAWN JAGUARSON
NONBINARY STAND-UP COMEDIAN with SUPERPOWERS
J. J. MADDUCKS
GIR-IRL
KENDRICK SHALIMERMAN
CHOW
CHOW
CAPYBARA SPECIALIST
ROBOT PARK RANGER
NEXT ISSUE: Riley wants to draw someone's
BEST DAY EVER!
Dream big! Send your submissions to:
BRAIN HAT P.O.B. 918
KENUCHE CTY, OK

It's worth it to find the few people who truly get you.